An

FINAL KILL

Alicia's smile was tight, her eyes distraught. Her pale blond hair, ordinarily smooth and shiny, was tangled, as if she'd been nervously running her fingers through it.

As for Jancy? Abby remembered her as a cute kid with a brown ponytail, dressed in Catholic school plaids. Now Allie's child was dressed all in black, had a short, spiked hairdo with orange and purple streaks, and a strange, staring expression in her eyes—which were so heavily made up Abby wondered how she could hold them open.

Still, Helen's reference to Hades, whether god of the dead or hell, had been a bit strong. Little Jancy had simply become a teenager.

Alicia grabbed Abby's hands and held on as if they were her only lifeline. "You've got to help us," she said, her voice shaking. "*Please,* Abby. I couldn't think of anywhere else to go."

Looking into Alicia's familiar green eyes, Abby knew she should be happy to see her old friend. Not only that, but she owed her so much. If Alicia hadn't helped her, back when her own world was falling apart—

But something was very, very wrong. And some instinct—the kind that raises hairs on the back of one's neck—told Abby that Trouble with a capital T had just walked through her door.

> "Meg O'Brien is a highly skilled writer
> who keeps things interesting."
> —*The Romance Reader* on *Sacred Trust*

Also by MEG O'BRIEN

THE LAST CHEERLEADER
CRIMSON RAIN
GATHERING LIES
SACRED TRUST
CRASHING DOWN

THE
FINAL

MEG O'BRIEN

KILL

MIRA

ISBN 0-7783-2087-1

THE FINAL KILL

Copyright © 2006 by Meg O'Brien.

All rights reserved. Except for use in any review, the reproduction or utilization of this work in whole or in part in any form by any electronic, mechanical or other means, now known or hereafter invented, including xerography, photocopying and recording, or in any information storage or retrieval system, is forbidden without the written permission of the publisher, MIRA Books, 225 Duncan Mill Road, Don Mills, Ontario, Canada M3B 3K9.

All characters in this book have no existence outside the imagination of the author and have no relation whatsoever to anyone bearing the same name or names. They are not even distantly inspired by any individual known or unknown to the author, and all incidents are pure invention.

MIRA and the Star Colophon are trademarks used under license and registered in Australia, New Zealand, Philippines, United States Patent and Trademark Office and in other countries.

www.MIRABooks.com

Printed in U.S.A.

Dear Reader,

So many people wrote to me about *Sacred Trust*, saying it was their favorite book of mine, I decided to write a sequel. *The Final Kill* is that sequel, in that it involves many of the same people and places.

Sacred Trust came out in May 2000 from MIRA Books. It's not necessary to read *Sacred Trust* first, but if you'd like to know more about Abby's life before this story—what happened to her two years ago, her relationship with Ben and with the Prayer House—you can order Sacred Trust by going on my Web site, www.megobrien.com, and clicking on one of the many links to online bookstores on my "Books" page. You can also order any of my books from your local bookstore.

Please also leave a note for me on my Guest Book page. I love to hear from readers, and I answer all Guest Book notes, as well as all e-mail, the address of which is also on my Web site.

With best wishes,

Meg O'Brien

Prologue

It all began with the lilacs. The day he sprayed the poison and turned them all brown, I knew I would have to kill him.

It felt strange, getting so upset over lilacs. Even stranger was planning a murder over their loss. But what goes around comes around, and Frank Frett himself was a killer. Oh, he might have been a hardworking man, not a bad sort to his friends and coworkers. But I knew that, on his days off, he killed. He killed wildlife, fish, trees, whatever still had a breath to give. I should have known he would get to my lilacs one day.

Lilacs had been my favorite flower since childhood, and I had planted them around the perimeter of my garden shortly after moving here five years ago. There were twelve in all, having grown from two-foot stubs to six-feet high by five wide in no time. They cast a beautiful lavender haze over the daffodils and tulips in spring, and in the summer they lent a nice filtered shade to the hydrangeas and violets. I had put a comfortable wooden bench under one of the lilac bushes that I'd shaped into a tree. More than anything, I loved sitting out there in the shade on hot afternoons.

The lilac bushes also served the purpose of making the wild berry bushes along the fence behind them look more attractive. My little niece, Lolly, who is four, loved coming here in the summer to ride the horses and pick the blackberries. It was something she looked forward to every summer, and it had felt good to be able to provide this kind of fun for her. Toward the end of the summer I'd bake juicy, sweet pies from the berries and sit them on the windowsill to cool, the way my grandmother always had back home. I'd invite my sister and Lolly to come over and finish them off with me, and we'd play Scrabble amid the leftover piecrust crumbs.

But of course, when Frank Frett murdered the lilacs, he got the blackberries, too. The spray must have blown everywhere, even hitting the top of a beautiful old maple tree that used to turn a gorgeous gold and copper in the fall.

Let me be clear about this. It wasn't so much the loss of the lilacs themselves, although that was bad enough. It was the total disregard for living things, and the devastation. By the time Frank Frett had finished with his spraying, the entire perimeter of the garden looked as if an army had come through it with a flamethrower. I have no idea how many days after the spraying it was before I looked out one morning and saw it—the otherwise green, lush garden entirely circled now by pitiful brown shrubs and trees.

I had complained, of course. I told him that he might have warned me ahead of time. Even given me a chance to argue the point. After all, I paid him a hefty month's rent, and legally, as long as a tenant is current on the rent, the property belongs to the tenant—not the landlord.

He argued that only the house belonged to the tenant, not the land. And he hadn't had time to cut the lilacs and berry bushes back this year. To spray poison on them was the quickest and easiest way to go.

I wanted to say that if he'd spent less time camping, fishing and killing deer, he might have had enough time left over to cut the berries back.

Oh, I know. There are far more things to worry about in life than some dead lilac trees and crispy-crunch berry bushes. There's the war in the Middle East—whichever one is going on at any given time. And there's South Africa. There are people being slaughtered and starving over there, and young kids here buying engagement rings with conflict diamonds in them, blithely unaware of what they're doing, but saving a penny or two. Here in the United States, in fact, there are homeless people all over the streets of every major city.

So what's the big deal about lilacs?

It's only a big deal because it matters to me. It cuts me to the quick to know they've been poisoned, every bit as much as if he'd taken an ax to them and chopped them right down. They mattered to me. I'd waited all winter for them to bloom. Now they wouldn't bloom for years, if ever. And Frank Frett didn't give a damn that he'd killed these things that I'd loved.

There was, therefore, only one thing to do: I would have to kill the killer.

1

Abby Northrup wasn't, by nature, vengeful. In fact, it was more in her nature to be at peace, especially since she'd come to live in this private little apartment at the Prayer House. There were times, however, and situations…

She took the small sheaf of papers she'd been reading and set them down on the table next to her chair. Carrying her cup of lukewarm coffee, she went into her office and sat at her computer. Opening a new document, she began to write out a plan. There was no rage in her words, no heat. Just a hard, cold resolution.

She did it as a Q & A: Where is the lilac killer now? Out in the potting shed? Or has he gone into town? And what should she use? Poison? Ah, yes. The perfect karmic weapon.

Better yet, an ax. Or perhaps a knife from the kitchen. But Sister Edna would surely spot it missing. Would she turn her in? Or cover for her? Would anyone understand why she'd done what she'd done?

The abbey bells sounded a solemn tone over her head, announcing the midnight hour. The timing was perfect. She began to jot down her plan, and drew a map of the property alongside her keyboard. Here was the garden shed. And here the stables, then the well house. Or perhaps she'd find him in the little shack on the hill that hadn't been used in years, except for that one time when someone...

A shiver ran through her. Never mind that now.

She would go first to the stables. If he wasn't there, she would wend her way across the field to the well house. It was on the way to the shack on the hill, so if she hadn't found Frank Frett by then, she'd just keep going uphill.

Leaving her office, she went into the adjoining living room. There she took a gun and ammunition from the antique Spanish armoire. Quietly shutting the armoire doors, she crossed to her bedroom, where she removed her jeans and shirt and slipped on cargo pants and a plain black jersey with long sleeves. Next she strapped the ammo around her belt. She dragged her hiking boots out from under the bed, then pulled them on. Finally, she stood still for a moment with her eyes closed and her arms out, level with her chest. *I am strong,* she said silently to herself. *I will not fail.*

Opening her eyes for one quick look around, she didn't see it at first. Then it was there, on her pillow, as if it had appeared through some ancient magic spell while her eyes were closed.

Which was foolish, of course. It was only a piece of paper. A note, put there hours ago while she was still in her office.

She stooped down and picked it up. It read:

You won't win. Don't even try.

2

So her quarry knew she was after him. She ignored the note, crushing it in her fist and tossing it into a corner. Picking up her gun bag and equipment, she stepped out into the tiled hall, listening for any unusual sounds. There were three floors to the old Spanish abbey, each of them with someone living on them, but it didn't surprise her that she didn't hear a thing. No one here ever spoke after midnight.

Across the wide, semidark hallway from her apartment was a carved oak door. She opened it and went swiftly through a short, narrow corridor and then a door that opened into a rose garden near the front of the house.

It was a little before one a.m. now, and June gloom was upon the entire Carmel Valley, bringing damp, biting temperatures. As she stepped outside she cursed herself for forgetting a jacket. Too late to turn back for one, though.

Just above the rim of a nearby hill, a half moon veiled by clouds managed to look eerie rather than helpful. It cast no solid shadows, only pale glimmers of gray that turned every would-be shadow into formless, evanescent ghosts moving deep within it. She pulled a small flashlight out of her pants pocket, turning it on but shading it with her other hand and pointing it only toward the ground. It was important to watch for snares.

Newly blossoming roses assailed her nostrils with a rich scent that was far too powerful, overriding all other senses. She quickly moved away from the garden, keeping her back against the wall of the adobe convent. Along this side was an arched stone colonnade over a cobbled walk. She followed the colonnade to the field in back, where several small buildings stood. One was a women's center for learning, another the horse barn and another a greenhouse. A tiny adobe chapel had been built several yards behind the convent by a couple of runaway Carmelite friars in the 1600s. They put down stakes here when the rest of their party sailed off, and after they died, no one lived here until the early 1900s, when the nuns came. They found the humble little monastery the friars had built and expanded it for their use.

The gentle old friars, Abby thought, would never have been the type to murder living, growing things. If there were lilacs in their gardens back then, they would have brought them inside in huge, fragrant bunches to dress their kitchen table for breakfast, lunch and dinner.

As she paused there on the edge of the field, her mind played tricks. Several coastal live oaks dotted the ankle-high grass, their black branches dripping with moss that swayed and twisted like angry snakes in the dank wind. The perfect setting for the demise of one Frank Frett, she thought, shivering.

Or me.

She shook herself, feeling a tremor of anxiety. *Focus, Abby.*

It worried her that her mind had been wandering. Did her target know she would do that? Did he know she'd be an easy mark, once surrounded by her beloved gardens and the multitude of wonderful scents in the night air? That she'd go off on some historical reverie of days gone by and lose her concentration for the job at hand?

Possible. He knew too much about her, didn't he? So, then. She would have to go against her norm, act in some way he wouldn't expect.

Carefully steering away from the oak trees and the greenhouse beyond them, she picked her way along a rutted track to the horse barn. Thick old eucalyptus trees lined the track, but they were too far apart to provide absolute cover. Abby crouched and moved swiftly but silently between each one, standing only when she knew she couldn't be seen from the windows lining this side of the dilapidated barn.

Barely breathing, she listened for even the slightest sound. Certain rustlings, she knew, came from the four horses inside, softly snorting. Now and then a hoof thudded against the floor of a stall. The other sounds were night animals: raccoons, mice, coyotes. Of them, the raccoons worried her the most. She'd gone up against the fierce little buggers more than once, and they'd love nothing more than to chomp down on her foot and run off with it. At one point, when she'd tried to shoo one away outside the Prayer House kitchen, he'd grabbed the broom from her and carried it off in his paws.

A spotlight at the front of the barn shone bright as day on a corral and about fifty square feet of open ground. Both stood between her and the barn. The thought of being that exposed worried her, but she had no other choice. If Frank Frett was in there and she ran to the greenhouse and gardening shed without first checking out the barn, she would only be handing him her back.

Watching a few moments, she didn't catch any movement at the windows along this side of the old building. Still, she knew there were cracks here and there in the wooden siding where the boards had warped from the winter's hard rains. Frett could have stationed himself at one of those cracks, where he could easily see out, yet be invisible to her.

Abby took her gun from its bag and held it at the ready, then ran as silently as she could toward the barn. Her heart pounded under the too-bright spotlight, and the only thing in her mind was, *He can see me now. The man is evil, spawn of the devil, and if he's at one of those windows, he can see me now.* Her imagination, always in top form, was so strong she could almost feel him grabbing her from every side. He was before her, no, behind her, he had a finger on the trigger of his own gun—

Damn.

As she came within feet of the barn, she saw that one of the two big doors in front, usually locked up at night, stood half-open. An invitation.

How considerate. But sorry, Frank. I have other plans.

Veering off toward the far side of the building, she ran the way she'd been taught, barely touching the ground and with little sound. But as she reached that side, her heart jumped to her throat.

The usual porch light wasn't on over here.

The fixture was on the wall at the far end of the stable. It should have illuminated this side dimly—just enough to see if someone else had gotten here before her—but the bulb had apparently burned out. Or Frett had knocked it out. It was so black here, it felt like the dark side of the moon. And the air was thick. Thick with fear. She thought she heard another heart beating, and her legs turned to jelly.

Several moments later, she realized she was hearing the heartbeat of one of the horses on the other side of the barn wall. Only then did she know that her hearing had improved because her own heart had actually stopped a few beats. She'd been holding her breath so long, it was a wonder she hadn't passed out.

She sucked in air, steadied herself and listened a few more moments for any human sounds.

Nothing.

But that might not matter. Frank Frett would know better than to reveal himself that carelessly. He could be anywhere inside the stables—in the tack room, the feed room, in Sister Ellen's office—and no matter where he was, he wouldn't make a sound.

She was so sure of that, she made an on-the-spot decision and did what any impulsive, get-the-job-done person like her *wouldn't* do.

She sat down.

She didn't barge in screaming like a banshee, hoping to shock her target and take him by surprise, risking a shot in the back. Nor did she sneak around to the back door or through a window the way he'd expect her to.

No, he'd be covering the back door, the windows, all the routes she might take to outwit him. After all, she was the type to barrel right in, wasn't she? That was pretty much what he'd said the other day, mixing both clichés and awkward metaphors. "You're an open book, Abby, and anybody can hear you coming a mile away."

Much to her chagrin, she had to admit he was at least half-right.

So, instead of the expected, she just sat down.

It shouldn't take long, she thought, squatting and easing her back against a tree opposite the barn wall. Five or ten minutes of absolute silence, and if he was in there, he'd get impatient and wonder where she was. He'd come out—and that's when she'd get him. Frank Frett wasn't the type to sit around, and several minutes without any kind of movement from her would drive him nuts.

While she waited, she imagined the things she would

do to the lilac killer, once he was good and dead. She'd get something from the gardening shed…lye, perhaps. Yes, lye. That should do it. She'd dig a grave just deep enough to dump him in it. Then she'd pour the lye over his entire body. It would eat away at his skin and other mucous membranes in no time. His eyes would go first, but whether it would eat through his bones, she didn't know. It really didn't matter. The pain is what mattered. The same kind of pain her lilacs had felt when they were burned by poison at the hands of Frank Frett.

Lye, she recalled, was what they used when they buried people in the old days to prevent diseases from spreading. She remembered, too, a story about St. Margaret Mary, who claimed to have had visions of the Blessed Mother and was told by her to begin a devotion to the Immaculate Heart of Mary. She did, and it was said that when they dug her up years later, her heart was still red and fresh, that the lye hadn't touched it. It was God's grace that her heart was preserved, the Church said, because of her love for the Blessed Mother. It was one of the miracles, Abby thought she recalled, that was used to prove her a saint.

Well, Frank Frett's heart would never be touched by God's grace. If they ever dug him up, they'd find it was cold, black and hard as a rock. Even lye couldn't eat through a heart that hated lilacs.

A too-sweet smell of hay filtered through the wall of the stable, along with the sweaty odor of horses in their warmed stalls. Abby's nose began to itch, and she pressed a finger under it to keep herself from sneezing.

That did nothing for the smell of manure, which was faint but enough to make her empty stomach clutch. She hadn't eaten in twelve hours, and she was hungry suddenly, though not in a good, healthy way. Instead, she really thought she was about to vomit. Covering her mouth with both hands, she gulped back the bile that rose in her throat, telling herself over and over, It's okay, it's okay, it's okay. Just don't make a sound, not a sound.

It was Frett himself who saved her. Just when she thought she couldn't hold it back any longer, she heard movement at the rear of the barn. She forgot all about throwing up and crouched, moving that way, listening for a direction. Then she saw him. He was crouching, too, and then running from the barn toward the little chapel, his body nothing more than a black form about fifty feet ahead of her.

She brought her gun up and pointed it at his back. "Stop!"

He twisted around, his own weapon raised. But she'd taken him by surprise, and she shot first. He went down.

Abby ran over to him, touching his leg with her foot. He didn't move, and the splattered red blotch on his chest told her she'd hit her mark.

"Gotcha," she said softly. "Your days of poisoning lilacs are over, Frank Frett."

"You think so?" he taunted, grabbing her pant leg and yanking at it. She was so surprised, she lost her footing and fell, dropping her gun. Stumbling to her feet, she picked it up, but he was already running again.

Reaching a live oak tree, he stood behind it for cover, and she ran in a zigzag pattern until she was close enough to shoot again.

It didn't work, and she saw it coming before she felt it. He stepped out from behind the tree and aimed his Shocktech 2003 at her. The thrust went straight to her heart, and she went down with an enormous rush of breath and a moan.

She wasn't faking it the way he had. The pain was sharp and stinging, and for a few seconds everything went black. Then, her vision clearing, she saw "Frank Frett" kneeling over her in the person of Ben Schaeffer, her lover, his face twisted in anger.

"Dammit all to hell, Abby! Why aren't you wearing your protective gear? A face mask, at least! Paintballs can blind you, you know."

3

Considering Abby's "injury," Ben wasn't all that gentle as he dumped her from his shoulder onto her bed.

"If you'd worn the damned chest protector I bought for you, this never would have happened!"

"Don't swear," she said, laughing facedown into her pillow. "The nuns might hear."

"I don't give—" He checked himself and lowered his voice. "And why the hell didn't you wear your face mask?"

"It makes me sweat," she said.

"So you'd rather lose an eye? Turn over."

"No."

"Turn over!"

She pressed her belly into the sheets rather than give in.

He tugged at her shoulder. "C'mon, Abby. I want to see how bad you're hurt. If you don't turn over, I'll turn you myself."

She knew he could do it, so she rolled over, grinning. "You think that silly little paintball did me in? No way."

"It got you square on the chest," he argued. "For God's sake, it almost knocked you out."

"Don't be so dramatic! All it did was smart and knock the wind out of me. A little. Besides, I got you first."

"So you did. But I, at least, was wearing my chest protector," he pointed out.

Pulling her jersey up over her chest, he swore again. His fingers carefully wiped the crimson glop from the flesh over her heart—where, despite her brilliant plan to one-up his character of "Frank Frett, the evil lilac killer," he'd managed to get her with a big red splat of paint. The spot where the paintball had hit was badly inflamed. Ben stroked it gently. "Abby, this is final. If you don't start wearing protective gear, I'm not—" He sighed.

"Not what?"

"Playing anymore." The tone of his voice told her he knew the words sounded ridiculous, but his eyes were dead serious.

She pulled him down on the bed beside her and nuzzled his neck, while at the same time pressing herself seductively against him. "You're not *playing* anymore? You sure about that?"

"I'm serious," he said sternly. "This game is getting out of hand."

She planted her lips against his ear. "And whose idea was it in the first place?" she murmured. "Who left me that scenario about some crazy gardener named Frank Frett killing off somebody's lilacs? And where the hell did you get that scenario, anyway?"

He rubbed noses with her. "From watching you with your rose garden, of course. You almost leveled poor Sister Binny that day you caught her with a spray gun."

She touched his lips with hers. "Only because I didn't know she was using organic spray. And I made it up to her by letting her have all the lavender she wanted."

"How kind of you. To be nice to a *nun,* of all people."

"Not as kind as you, leaving that barn door open for me so I'd walk right into your snare, *Frank Frett.* I can't believe you thought I'd fall for that."

"Ah, but you did believe my fake death."

"Okay, so I'm easy to fool where you're concerned."

Ben turned serious. "Easy to fool? What exactly does that mean?"

The way he said it made her think there was something she was missing. But she already regretted her choice of words. If there was something she was being a fool about, and lately her instincts had been telling her there was, she honestly didn't want to know it. Not yet. Life was complicated enough, as her mother would say, without looking for dust balls under the bed.

"I didn't mean a thing," she said. "And by the way, don't forget you promised to help us finish the remodel on the old friar's chapel out back."

"Don't try to change the subject, Abby. Dammit, this is it. It's the second time you've been hurt during one of our paintball capers, and that wasn't what the game started out to be."

She grinned. "I know. But don't pretend you don't enjoy it. It's our best sexual fantasy. If you hadn't knocked me off my feet tonight, just imagine what might have happened."

"I don't even want to think about what could have happened to you." He frowned. "Abby, ever since— Never mind. The point is, you're way too reckless. What if you'd lost an eye?"

"Oh, for heaven's sake, Ben. People play paintball all the time."

"They get hurt all the time, too. There are thousands of cases every year of people being blinded by a paint-ball—and worse." He swore. "I never should have taken you to survivor camp with me last fall. You've got to let this go, Abby."

"But you agreed I needed to get my self-confidence back. And my experience there made a great article for *Action Pursuit Games*."

"An article that barely paid you anything, and you already have more money than you know what to do with."

"Not true. There's the little chapel, and the Women's Center for Learning needs expanding, and the old horse barn could use a ton of work—"

He groaned. "Look, I admire the fact that you decided to buy the Prayer House from Lydia and help the nuns out. But why do you have to live here?"

And now we're getting to the real meat of things, Abby thought. *What he means is, Why weren't you happy enough living with me?*

"I love your apartment in town," she said. "But, Ben, you were out most of the time chasing criminals around Carmel, and I was alone. I wanted to be around people more."

"You could walk around Carmel Village anytime and be up to your knees in tourists from every hemisphere."

"But I can think better out here. It's quiet. Besides, I can still drive to the village whenever I want to."

The truth was, she didn't want to all that often. Windhaven, the multimillion-dollar Ocean Drive house that she'd lived in with her husband, still held too many bad memories. Just driving by it gave her the willies.

"And as for chasing criminals around in quaint little old Carmel," Ben said, "it's not exactly the way I thought it would be when I moved down here from San Francisco. I thought having a chance to be chief one day would be the perfect job."

"It's not?" Abby was surprised. They had never talked about this before.

"It could be," he said, "for the right person. But don't you ever get the feeling that living in Carmel is like living in a bubble? We're so isolated here. A two-hour drive to San Francisco, no direct flights out of Monterey to most cities…"

"Sweetie," Abby murmured, leaning over to kiss his cheek, "you're not old enough to be having a midlife crisis."

"Ha. I'm over forty."

"No!" she said mockingly. "You're that old? Good

grief, what's a young thirty-eight-year-old like me doing with the likes of you?"

"Growing old," he said, grinning, "and way too fast, if you're not careful."

She punched him on the shoulder. "Okay, so how about this? You get a hobby."

He snorted. "Like what?"

"Painting, maybe. Or golf."

"Great. Then there would be three million and one painters in Monterey County. And four million and one golfers."

She sighed. "You won't let me make you feel any better, will you?"

"Depends on how *you're* feeling now," he said, pulling her close and nuzzling her ear. "Hey, ya know what? I just figured out my new hobby."

She was about to agree that his new hobby was a fine one when the intercom next to her bed buzzed softly. Sister Helen, who acted as keeper of the front door at night, would never interrupt her when Ben was there unless it was important.

She pressed the button for two-way conversation. "What's up, Helen?"

The nun's voice was so raspy from allergies, Abby could hardly make it out. Turning up the volume, she put a finger over her lips to quiet Ben, who was still trying to nuzzle.

"There are two women here," Helen said. "Rather, a woman and a teenage girl who looks old enough to be Hades."

"Hades?"

"God of the dead. For heaven's sake, girl, don't you remember anything I taught you in high school? Anyway, the older one says they're seeking sanctuary."

"I haven't had a call from anyone setting that up," Abby said, looking at the clock. It read 2:38 a.m.

"I didn't think so," Helen said. "Do you think it's safe to let them in?"

"Keep them in the reception room. I'll be right there."

Yet one more abused family, she thought wearily, sitting on the edge of the bed and rubbing her eyes. God, there were so many more than a year ago. And the little she did for them never felt like enough. Food, clothes, a bed for the night…then off they went in the morning to the next way station. It really wasn't much.

"Abby?" Sister Helen's voice came over the intercom at the same time that Ben nudged her, calling her back from a suddenly overwhelming depression.

"Sorry, Helen," she said. "Tell them I'll be there in a few minutes."

"Of course."

Abby pressed the off button. She knew Helen would also call Sister Benicia, who would be glad to get up and go to the kitchen to heat leftover soup from dinner for the two women.

Abby bent over to plant a quick kiss on Ben, but he'd have none of it. Rolling her under him, he covered her from head to toe and pressed himself hard against her. "Just remember, I won this time."

"Hell, you can win all the time," she said, wiggling beneath him until it was clear he was aroused. "But I really must go," she added, laughing. "Duty calls."

He groaned and let her up. "Vixen. Okay, I'll go back to town and check in at the station."

"I thought you weren't working tonight," she said, tugging on clean jeans and a sweatshirt.

"I'm not. I just feel antsy after all that exercise."

"It's not the *exercise* that got you antsy," she said, tossing a pillow at him.

Abby reached for her boots, and Ben swatted her on the backside on his way to the bathroom. "I didn't say what *kind* of exercise. See you in the morning, Annie Oakley."

Abby looked briefly into the little mirror on the door that led into the convent, and brushed her shoulder-length brown hair back behind her ears with her fingers. No time for makeup. A clean flannel shirt to cover the paint splatters on her tee would have to do.

Downstairs, she entered the large old reception room with its antique furnishings and expensive rugs that Lydia Greyson had brought here from her own Carmel home when she owned the Prayer House. It was cold in here and, shivering, Abby noted both women were standing, warming their backs at the fireplace. She drew closer, then stopped midway, surprised to see that she knew both the older woman and the teenager with her: Alicia Gerard, one of her oldest friends, and Jancy, her daughter.

"Allie!" she said, crossing over to her and holding out both hands. "What on earth? I haven't seen you in, geez, what is it—two years?"

Alicia's smile was tight, her eyes distraught. Her pale blond hair, ordinarily smooth and shiny, was tangled, as if she'd been nervously running her fingers through it.

As for Jancy? Abby remembered her as a cute kid with a brown ponytail, dressed in Catholic school plaids. Now Allie's child was dressed all in black, had a short, spiked hairdo with orange and purple streaks, and a strange, staring expression in her eyes, which were so heavily made up Abby wondered how she could hold them open.

Still, Helen's reference to Hades, whether god of the dead or hell, had been a bit strong. Little Jancy had simply become a teenager.

Alicia grabbed Abby's hands and held on as if they were her only lifeline. "You've got to help us," she said, her voice shaking. "*Please,* Abby. I couldn't think of anywhere else to go."

Looking into Alicia's familiar green eyes, Abby knew she should be happy to see her old friend. Not only that, but she owed her so much. If Alicia hadn't helped her, back when her own world was falling apart...

But something was very, very wrong. And some instinct—the kind that raises hairs on the back of one's neck—told Abby that Trouble with a capital *T* had just walked through her door.

4

Alicia Gerard was forty-one, yet close up Abby could see that there were new stress lines in her forehead and around her mouth that made her look closer to fifty. Allie had always been beautiful, and still was. But her face now was more like a photograph that had blurred because life had moved slightly and unexpectedly, causing a distortion.

Abby had known Alicia Gerard since she was a reporter in Los Angeles, years ago. At that time, Allie's husband was just beginning as a legal aid attorney. In a short amount of time he became a legislator, and finally progressed to what he was now—a mover and shaker in the business world. Abby had followed the growth of his career, from a real estate developer to a Donald Trump-like mogul whose face had been on the cover of every important magazine in the world. More recently, H. Palmer Gerard, better known to friends and family as Gerry, had spoken in Washington before a committee on illegal immigration. As one of the top developers in the world, he shocked the committee by taking the position that restrictions on immigration from Mexico were unrealistic and should be eased, and that pay for illegal Mexican laborers should be raised.

Paying illegal aliens a decent wage wasn't a popular position, especially when the economy was in trouble and jobs were hard to come by. In an attempt to dilute Gerry's argument, politicians came down on him in the media, calling him an "elitist who had so much money he no longer felt any loyalty to hardworking Americans who were struggling to make a living for themselves and their families."

In response, Gerry then challenged the administration to create more jobs for U.S. citizens by cutting back on outsourcing—the hiring by U.S. companies of cheap labor in other countries at much lower pay than American employees commanded.

After his appearances on Capitol Hill, a storm of controversy began. Thanks to Gerry Gerard, the administration now had its hands full. If Gerry had been a politician, his career would almost certainly have gone downhill from there. But because of his powerful business ties, no one had dared to take an open stand against H. P. Gerard. Alicia's husband was feared by senators and presidents alike—not because he played dirty, but because he refused to. Some said he could run for and win the next presidential election on the votes of the poor alone. There were impressive leaders of blacks and Hispanics who swore they could get out the vote if he ran.

Abby took Alicia's arm and led her over to the sofa,

at the same time taking in the state of Jancy, who, she thought, must be fourteen by now. Named Jan Christine, and called Jan C. to rhyme with H.P., the spirited little girl had changed the spelling of her name to "Jancy" herself, at the age of eight.

Abby urged Alicia and her daughter to sit on the large, comfortable sofa that was at a right angle to the fireplace; she sat across from them in a stiff antique chair with a cane seat. Jancy flopped down at the far end of the sofa from her mother and took up a slouching position, her arms crossed in front of her chest in a defensive manner.

For a moment, Alicia simply looked at Abby, a question in her eyes: *Will you help us? Can we trust you?* Abby had seen it so many times. Just about every time, in fact, that women came to her, pleading that she help them escape whatever abuse they were running from.

Paseo, the underground railroad that she'd operated out of the Prayer House for two years, was a secret organization. Ordinarily, women were sent here through the local women's shelters. No one came here without their visit having been set up by a trusted third party, and great care was taken to ensure that they weren't followed here, and that no one could know where they went when they left.

Alicia, however, had simply shown up. Might she have led someone here who could cause trouble for the Prayer House?

Before Abby could begin to ask questions, Sister Benicia came in with a polished wooden tray. It held three cups, three bowls and a plate of her homemade brown bread. Beside it was a small dish piled high with butter, three butter knives and three spoons.

"I've brought everyone a bowl of soup and some nice hot cocoa," she said softly to Abby, setting the tray on the coffee table between her and the women. Abby thanked her, and the shy nun tiptoed out with barely a whisper of her rosary beads.

Abby turned to Alicia and Jancy. "Please, help yourselves. A warm bowl of Binny's soup usually helps me to relax."

She picked up a cup and put it on the sturdy mission-style end table next to her chair, then slathered a piece of bread with the butter and took a bite, hoping to set them at ease. Alicia picked up her knife and buttered a piece of bread, handing it to Jancy, who shook her head and turned away. Alicia sighed and set the bread down.

"Abby," she began, taking a napkin and twisting it nervously in her hands. "I meant it when I said I didn't know where else to go. I had a little…problem…in Carmel, and I remembered that you were here in the Valley, and that the Prayer House was kind of hidden…" She paused. "Out of the way, I mean. I thought you might put us up for the night."

As she talked, Alicia kept looking around. Once, when a cupboard door in the kitchen closed a bit loudly, she jumped.

Abby leaned forward and kept her voice low. "What happened? What's going on?"

Alicia shook her head. "Please, just trust me. Jancy and I need a safe place to sleep tonight. If you help us, I swear I won't bother you after that."

"You're not a bother," Abby said. "But tell me this, at least. Is it about Gerry? Has he…" She looked at Jancy. "Has he done something?" It was the most obvious question to ask a mother on the run, and came out without her thinking about it.

Alicia looked blank for a moment, then her eyes widened. "Oh, God no! How could you ask that?"

"Well, we haven't talked on the phone or seen each other in a long time. People change."

Alicia's eyes filled with tears. "I'm sorry, Abby. It's just that I've been so damned busy. But you've always been the kind of friend I felt I could turn to if I ever needed help. You're the most solid and dependable person I know."

Clearly, my friend doesn't know me all that well anymore, Abby thought—at least, not the insecure me that had grown out of searching two years ago for my friend Marti's killer.

But as for Alicia's plight, Abby had learned through her work with *Paseo* to be cautious in these kinds of situations.

"I need to know what's going on before I can decide whether I can help you, Allie. One thing I can't do is put the nuns and other women living here in jeopardy."

Alicia stood and walked back to the fire, although the reception room was quite warm now. She paused there a few moments. When she turned to Abby, the expression in her eyes was that of strain, fatigue and a touch of something else. Fear?

"I'm sorry, I didn't think of it that way," she said, her voice trembling. "I had no business coming here and bringing trouble into your home. I'll leave, Abby. I'll leave right now. I just…I mean, could you just…" She crouched down beside Abby and put a shaky hand on her arm. "Could you just keep Jancy a few days?"

Abby stole a glance at Jancy and saw that, though her chin was up and her lips drawn tight in a defiant expression, tears had spilled onto her cheeks. She wiped them away with the sleeve of her black jacket, the gesture of a five-year-old.

"Go ahead, leave," she said sullenly to her mother. "You always do. And you know what? I don't even care anymore."

Alicia sighed. "Honey, I wouldn't leave you if I didn't have to. But you'll be safer here with Abby—alone, I mean. Without me."

"Oh, sure, that's the point, isn't it?" Jancy laughed shortly. "No, Mother, the real point is, if you foist me off on your friend here, you'll be free as a bird. You won't have me to bother with anymore."

Alicia frowned and stood, folding her arms as she addressed her daughter. "I don't know about free as a bird, young lady," she said with an edge, "but I will have less worry if I know you're safe."

She sighed, and her voice shook. "Honey, I need to be on my own a few days. There are things I need to do. Please try to understand."

The bowls of creamy soup had become cold and glutinous. Abby carried them over to a sideboard to remove herself a bit from the argument. She needed a few moments to figure out how to respond to all this. Two phrases rang in her ears *"Go ahead, leave…you always do…"* And, from Alicia, *"I will have less worry if I know you're safe."*

What on earth had been going on in this family since she'd seen them last?

"Allie," she said, turning back, "if this isn't about some problem with Gerry, I don't understand why you wouldn't rather have Jancy stay with him."

"No," Alicia answered quickly, shaking her head. "Trust me, that wouldn't work right now."

"The thing is, I just don't think I can help you with this."

"Abby, please! I—it's just that he's in New York, and he's up to his ears in major business negotiations."

"But surely he'd want to help."

"Absolutely not!" Alicia said even more vehemently. "I want Gerry kept out of this as long as possible. Believe me, Abby, it's for his own good."

"Oh, for heaven's sake," Jancy said angrily, "why don't I just stay at the house in Big Sur alone? I'm sixteen, after all. I'm not a kid."

Alicia said, *"Jancy,"* reprovingly, while Abby just looked at the girl until her gaze fell away.

"Okay, I'm fourteen," Jancy snapped. "But I'm more grown up than most kids my age. If you only knew…"

Alicia looked at her in desperation, as if to say, "See what I have to put up with?"

Jancy turned away, her angry gaze pretending to examine the air.

Abby studied the two of them and thought a minute, while Jancy fidgeted and Alicia looked over her shoulder, as if expecting someone to jump out from a corner at any moment.

Despite whatever other factors there might be, Abby's strongest urge was to help. Alicia and Gerry had supported her when her job at the *Los Angeles Times* was on the line, years ago. Abby had written a story about a brilliant fifteen-year-old boy who, after having been orphaned at the age of five, had lived alone in an abandoned tenement building. The little boy had taken care of himself by stealing food off the streets and living with homeless adults who took care of him as best they could. Still, the situation he'd lived in was undeniably perilous.

The kid had talked to her only on the condition that she promise never to tell anyone who he was. Abby made the promise but vowed to do everything she could to help him after the story broke. She'd get a promotion and have plenty of money then, she reasoned, to do whatever was needed for him: high school, college…who knew what heights a kid that bright and self-sufficient might reach?

Abby shook her head now at the memory of those youthful fantasies. Instead of being promoted, she was fired for not giving up the boy's name, and accused of making the story up. Stone-cold broke, she was on the verge of being homeless when Gerry, a young legal aid attorney at the time, represented her in court pro bono, while Allie took her into their house until her salary started coming in again. Abby won the case against wrongful firing, kept her job, and once the story hit the wires she won awards around the world. Not only was her career saved, but she was able to help the kid just as she'd hoped. He was now a resident MD at Swedish Hospital in Seattle.

None of that would have happened without Alicia and Gerry. She owed them a lot.

But her job now, first and foremost, was to protect *Paseo*. When Lydia Greyson, a good-hearted Carmel philanthropist, became ill and sold the Prayer House to her two years ago, she had trusted Abby to keep *Paseo* going. And Abby did, using the money that came out of her ill-fated marriage to Jeffrey, and the sale of the multimillion-dollar house on Ocean Drive. She had been still recovering from the monstrous act that killed her best friend, Marti Bright, though—and the attack that nearly killed her, as well. So at first, more or less sleepwalking through life, she just plowed money into *Paseo,* giving it little thought otherwise. It was her plan, indeed, to do that and no more.

It didn't take long, however, to become emotionally involved. Some of the stories of abuse she heard— stories the women who came to the Prayer House for help had told her—were horrendous.

So, protecting *Paseo* was her first priority. And to take Alicia and Jancy in without knowing what kind of trouble they were in might risk the secrecy and safety of the other volunteers, and the moms and kids as well.

While she was considering all this, Allie picked up her purse and motioned to Jancy. "C'mon, honey, we have to go."

"Al—"

"No, it's all right, Abby, I never should have come here. I'm sorry."

Her voice was shaking and her stride unbalanced, as if she were too tired to walk straight. She took Jancy's arm, though, and pointed her in the direction of the door. Abby hesitated a few seconds more, but Allie's condition and the sudden expression of fear on Jancy's face was what settled it.

For some reason, the girl was afraid to leave here. But why?

Abby could still hear Lydia Greyson's voice: *People don't listen to children. They pooh-pooh their fears, as if a child can't possibly have all that much to worry about. Don't do that, Abby. Don't ever, ever do that. You don't know how much harm you could be doing to that child.*

"Allie," she said quickly, "don't go. Of course you can stay. For tonight, at least. All right? You can sleep here, both of you."

Tears filled Alicia's eyes. "Oh, Abby, thank you so much! I promise, you won't regret—"

"Wait," Abby said, interrupting. "Don't make too much of this. You need to understand that I can't keep Jancy here alone, as much as I'd like to help you with that. The fact that she's a minor could be a problem. And since I don't know what's going on, I have no idea what might come up."

"Tonight, though?" Alicia said with the first glimmer of hope in her voice. "You said, both of us? And no one will know?"

"Absolutely no one," Abby said firmly. "I don't know what you're running from, Allie, but you'll be safe here."

And God help me if I do end up regretting this.

Allie let out a long breath, as if a huge burden had been lifted from her shoulders. Jancy didn't say a word, but sat biting her black-painted fingernails to the quick. Abby noted that otherwise they looked freshly done, and now that the first moments were over, she also recognized Jancy's black jeans jacket as being from a famous designer.

She looked at Alicia's shoes and recognized them, too, as having cost somewhere in the neighborhood of seven hundred dollars. Back in the days of her marriage to Jeffrey, Abby had learned to have an eye for fashion like that. At least one thing seemed certain: Allie and Jancy wouldn't suffer from a lack of funds, wherever they ended up.

There was a bellpull by the doorway into the reception room, a leftover from the days when the cloistered Carmelites lived there. Preserved for history's sake, it also had a functional use. Within a minute or two of Abby's gentle tug, Helen appeared from her room near the front door. Abby asked her to have someone take Alicia and Jancy to the second floor.

"There's a room prepared?" Abby asked.

Helen shot her a look as if to say, "Isn't there always?" To Alicia and Jancy, she said, "All right, then, come with me."

But Helen was limping, and Abby didn't want her to climb the stairs. "Sister Liddy is probably up already. Why don't I ask her—"

"I'm not that useless yet," Helen grumbled, lumbering to the door with a frown.

Abby knew when to fold 'em, so she contained her usual smile at Helen's crustiness and turned to Alicia. "Okay, then. You and Jancy go with Sister Helen. She'll take you to your room."

Alicia hugged her. "How can I ever thank you enough?"

"A donation would be nice," Abby said, with a laugh. "A *big* one, for the Women's Center for Learning."

"It's a promise," Alicia said, squeezing her hard.

Abby took her by the shoulders. "No, seriously, just take care of yourself and Jancy. Do you have a cell phone with you?"

She nodded.

"If you need anything in the night, then, don't hesitate to call me." Abby took a piece of notepaper and a pen from a desk and wrote her private cell phone number on it.

"I'll only be a floor away," she said. "Since the night's almost over, you might as well sleep in. Call me when you're up, and I'll let Sister Benicia know. She'll fix you something to eat."

Allie nodded again and squeezed her hand. As she and Helen headed for the door, Abby touched Jancy's arm and pulled her back a bit.

"Are you all right?" she asked in a low tone. "Is there anything special you want or need?"

Jancy gave a shrug, but tears filled her eyes again. Closer up, Abby could tell that what she had thought was heavy eye shadow was actually swollen lids that she'd apparently tried to cover up by reapplying her makeup several times. The shadow had creased and flaked, and some of it had fallen, leaving rivulets of black glitter on her cheeks.

Abby's ability to spot troubled kids was usually right on target, and this one was shouting "trouble" all over the place.

But Jancy shoved her hands in her pockets, sniffled and shrugged. "What good would it do?" she said tiredly.

"*Jancy,*" Alicia said in a firm tone. She gestured for her daughter to catch up. "We've bothered Abby enough for tonight."

"See what I mean?" Jancy murmured.

Abby followed Jancy and the two women into the hall. Instead of turning right toward her apartment, she paused and watched as they started up the curving mahogany stairs toward the second floor. Helen had to grasp the railings on both sides to pull herself up each stair, and Abby didn't know whether to feel bad for her or angry with her. *She could be so damned stubborn.*

Standing there, she felt a sudden chill. While she was glad she'd let Allie and Jancy stay, she would have felt better if she'd known what was wrong. Something to do with Gerry, after all? Alicia clearly didn't want him to know where they were or what had happened. For someone as afraid as she was, there had to be a good reason for keeping her husband out of it.

Add to that Jancy's attitude. The child exuded anger and pain out of every pore, which could either be normal teenage acting out—or a sign of abuse. But Gerry? Was he really capable of that?

Abby didn't know. She hated to think that way, but she hadn't been around him recently enough to spot signs of abuse.

Her questions, or some of them, were answered moments later. Before Jancy, Helen and Alicia even made it to the landing between the first and second floor, there was a loud, abrupt banging on the front door.

All four women stopped moving and stared at one another.

"It's them!" Alicia said in a low, frightened voice. She didn't say who, and there was no time to ask questions. Abby raised a finger to her lips, while with her other hand she motioned for them to keep going. Alicia turned and ran farther up the stairs, with Helen doing her best to keep up. But Jancy still stood as if frozen, staring down at the carved double doors. They were old and thick, of Spanish design and meant to protect the early Carmelites from intruders. They couldn't be broken down by anything less than a battering ram, but there were newer windows here on the first floor that were far more vulnerable.

Abby's automatic reaction was to protect the woman and child under her care and ask questions later. Running as silently as possible up the stairs, she whispered to Helen to go back down and give them a minute or two before she opened the door. Grabbing Jancy's arm, Abby pulled the girl after her. She followed numbly, as if in shock.

"It's okay, you'll be okay," Abby whispered, but by the time they had reached the second floor and the Sacred Heart statue, Jancy was sobbing. Abby grabbed her arm and forced Jancy to face her.

"Stop it! Stop it right now! They'll hear you!"

Jancy gulped and nodded, then rubbed her nose with the sleeve of her jacket. The heavy makeup was wearing off, and she looked more her age now, young, frightened and vulnerable. Abby saw that Allie was waiting for them, half-hidden behind the statue. Allie took Jancy's hand and pulled her down the corridor to the left, whispering for Allie to follow.

They ran to a room near the big, oval solarium that overlooked the front gardens. By this time, the noise at the front door had escalated. The banging continued, growing louder and louder. Then a male voice shouted. "Abby? Abby, open up!"

Confusion set in. *Ben?*

Another voice followed his. "FBI! Open the door!"

A quick look at Alicia and Jancy told Abby they

were terrified. She knew everyone in the Prayer House must be awake by now, and Helen would have to open the door, or someone else would.

Pulling on Alicia and Jancy's hands, she whispered to them to crouch down as she led them into the solarium. Although the room was pitch-dark, there were floor-to-ceiling windows on three sides. It was possible that anyone moving about in here could be seen by someone standing way out in the garden, by the rim of trees.

Abby, going ahead, dropped to her knees, then inched along the inner wall in a belly crawl. There, she felt along the edge of one oak panel. Finding the right spot, she pressed. The bottom third of the panel swung open, revealing a small, dark cubbyhole.

"Here!" she whispered to Alicia and Jancy, urging them to crawl across the floor the same way she had. They did, and when they got to her she said, "You'll have to squat down, and it'll be a tight fit, but I'll come for you as soon as it's safe."

"What is this?" Alicia asked, peering into the dark hole with a tremor in her voice.

"A modern-day version of a priest's hole," Abby said. "I remodeled the solarium, and I'm the only one who knows it's here. Get in! There's a lock on the inside so no one else can open it from out here."

She pushed them both harder than she meant to, but the male voices were louder now, as if coming from inside the downstairs foyer. Her own anxiety ran high, and she began to shake. *What the hell was going on?*

Making sure the two women were safely in the priest's hole and the inside lock was in place, she went quickly down the stairs. Entering the foyer, she slowed and rubbed her eyes as if she'd just woken up.

She didn't have to pretend much to look surprised; the scene in her foyer worked pretty well as a wake-up call.

Ben stood there with another man, talking to Helen. Abby studied the other man before walking up to them. He was dressed in a dark blue blazer and khaki pants, and he was tall, even taller than Ben, who was just over six feet. He had silver hair that complimented his tanned face and steel-gray eyes, and he held himself with an air of assurance. When he looked up and saw Abby, he nodded to Helen and said politely, "That'll be all. Thank you very much, Sister."

Helen shot a glance at Abby. She nodded and Helen left, walking toward the kitchen. Abby noted that the front doors were open behind Ben and this man. In the semicircular gravel drive, the bright motion lights revealed two police cars and at least three unmarked cars. There were several figures in dark suits, some of them on one knee behind the open car doors. They had guns drawn and pointed directly at the Prayer House, as if expecting an attack by insurgent nuns on the lam.

"What's going on?" Abby asked Ben, trying to steady her voice. "What is the FBI doing here?"

"We want the two women who came here earlier," the other man answered for him.

"I don't understand."

"Special Agent Robert Lessing," he said, holding out a hand. Abby shook it. His palm was dry and warm. No nerves, she thought, for this fellow. Too bad that couldn't be said for her.

"We know they're here," Lessing said. "And I'm sorry to disturb you, Ms. Northrup, but this is FBI business. We need to take those women in for questioning."

"I still don't understand. Who are you talking about, and what did they do?"

"Please, Ms. Northrup," he said irritably, "it's been a long night. Trying to hide these women can only make it worse for you. Do you really want to be charged as an accessory?"

"Accessory?" She looked at Ben. "To what?"

"Murder, Abby," Ben said.

"Murder!"

"Chief, I asked you not to—" Lessing began.

Ben ignored him. "I got a call on my cell phone, on my way back to the station. A man was murdered in a room at the Highlands Inn. There was an envelope of photos in the room, photos of two women—actually, a woman and a teenage girl."

Abby was shocked, but went for total innocence. "So you identified the woman and girl in the photo as the women who came here earlier? Without even having seen who was actually here?"

"Abby, I heard Sister Helen on the intercom. She said there was a woman and a teenage girl seeking sanctu- ary. This is a small town, and I don't believe in coincidence. Besides that, this sort of thing doesn't happen here every day."

"But you'd like it to, wouldn't you?" she said testily. "Shake things up a bit in this boring little bubble. Isn't that what you called Carmel? A bubble?"

"I didn't say it was boring," Ben snapped, his voice rising. "And please don't do this."

"Do what?"

"Act as if I'd tell the FBI about your work here for no other reason but a personal desire to stir up some action."

She stared at him as disbelief filled every pore. "You told them? Everything?"

Ben was one of the few people she'd told about *Paseo*. She had sworn him to secrecy—and tonight, he had told the FBI. Just like that, he had betrayed the trust that women were promised when they came here for sanctuary.

"I trusted you," she said softly. "You swore never to—" She broke off as her voice failed.

"This is different," Ben argued, looking decidedly awkward. Nevertheless, his voice was firm. "If these women are killers, you aren't safe, Abby. No one is safe while they're here."

She suddenly couldn't think straight. Was what he said true? Had Alicia, someone she'd known for years as one of the nicest people in the world, actually murdered someone? Was she in fact running from the FBI?

One thing she'd learned over the years was that people you think you know well can change. And given extenuating circumstances, they don't always change for the better.

The other thing she'd learned, though, was that the police and federal agencies—given their own extenuating circumstances—can't always be trusted to know what the hell they're doing.

"Well," she said to Agent Lessing, "I'm sorry I can't help you, but the women who were here are gone."

Ben stared at her. "C'mon, Abby. This is no time for games."

Agent Lessing's voice was even harsher. "If you're harboring criminals—"

"I could be arrested as an accessory to the crime," Abby said calmly. "I know. You made that quite clear."

"Or as a coconspirator," he said. "Either way, you'll go to jail."

"Abby—" Ben began.

"Ben," she interrupted, "if you had called me before rushing out here with your merry little band of Men in Black, I could have told you not to bother. The women you're looking for are most definitely not the ones who came here earlier. And they are not here now."

"I know you, Ab," he said irritably. "And I don't believe you. Dammit, I'm worried about you, and I'm getting tired of you hiding things when you know I'd worry even more!"

"And I'm getting tired of you worrying about me as if I were a child. I can take care of myself!"

"Yeah? Well, I can remember a time when you

couldn't," he said just as angrily. "You wouldn't even be alive now if—"

Before he could finish, footsteps sounded from the hallway stairs. Startled, Abby turned to see a blond woman of about thirty, dressed in a trim black pantsuit and white blouse, accompanied by three men.

"We've checked out every floor," she said to Agent Lessing. "No sign of them. Quite a few upset nuns, though."

"How did you get up there?" Abby said, furious now. "You had no right—"

"This says I do," the woman answered, producing a folded court paper from the inside pocket of her suit jacket. "Kris Kelley, special agent."

Abby opened and scanned it.

"It's a search warrant," Ben said.

"I can see that," she replied shortly.

There was a buzz, and Agent Lessing pulled a two-way radio out of his pocket. "Lessing," he said, and listened.

After a few moments he murmured, "Right," and hung up. Turning to Ben, he said, "They haven't found anyone on the grounds, either."

"You've actually been searching my property?" Abby said, feeling more than ever violated.

"The warrant covers that, too, Ms. Northrup," he said. "What you have in your hand there is a copy. You may keep it and check with your lawyer about it, if you like."

"You seem to have come prepared," she said, striving to sound calm again. "This must be a very big case—with a very important corpse. Mind telling me who it is?"

"Sorry," Agent Lessing said, shaking his head.

"Why not? It'll be all over the news by morning."

"So you'll find out then," he answered.

"Look," Ben said to Lessing, "we aren't getting anywhere here. I suggest we go back to the station."

"Just one more question," Lessing replied. He turned to Abby. "Where did those women go from here?"

"I have no idea. But as I told Ben, the women who were here aren't who you're looking for."

"Oh?" Lessing smiled. "And how would you know that?"

"Because they were old friends," she answered coolly. "One is a teacher, a woman in her fifties. She'd brought her niece with her, on a field trip. They were driving through town and stopped to say hello, and I gave them some hot soup and cocoa. We talked a bit, and they went on their way."

"Old friends, huh? And they just dropped by—all the way out here in Carmel Valley—to say hello in the middle of the night?"

Abby shrugged. "They were tired. They've been touring the old missions and needed a pit stop on the way to I-5. As you probably know, there's not much open in Carmel at night. Besides, everyone who knows me knows that I'm up half the night."

Ben stared at her for a long moment, as if by doing so she might break and give herself up. But then he said to Lessing, "That's true. Abby's a freelance writer. She does her best work at night."

The agent gave Ben a weary look. "We're getting nowhere here. Let's all go back to the station."

Ben turned to Abby, and for the first time his voice was soft. "Ab? You'll be all right?"

Too little, too late, she thought bitterly. He'd betrayed her, and he wasn't getting off that easily. "Of course I'll be all right," she said irritably, "once all of you people get out of here and I can get to bed."

"I…I'll see you in a little while," he said.

"No. It's almost three in the morning. I'll call you. Later."

He looked taken aback. Shaking his head, he led the way out of the foyer and onto the front drive. The female agent lagged behind. Just before she went through the doorway, she said to Abby, "I've heard about you. A couple of years ago, wasn't it? You must be pretty tough, to have gone through all that and come out unscathed."

Unscathed? Abby thought. *Hardly.*

But that was the point, she realized suddenly. *The woman somehow knows there are things about me that haven't healed, and that I don't always act wisely, but out of leftover emotions—good and bad.*

"What are you, some kind of shrink?" Abby said.

"No. Just someone who admires the work you're doing. There have been times—" She broke off and looked toward the front door, where the men were gathered around the cars.

"You were saying?" Abby prompted.

"Nothing. Gotta run," the woman said. "Looks like everyone's leaving."

5

Abby locked up and stood at a front window, watching till every car had gone down the twisting, oleander-lined driveway to Carmel Valley Road. There they turned right, heading back into town. Finally. The FBI woman's words kept repeating themselves in her mind. *To have gone through all that…come out unscathed…*

How does a woman end up unscathed, Abby thought, when she's so brutally raped she'll never be able to carry a child? How does she even end up close to being what other people call "normal"?

And the rape was only the beginning. What followed had nearly killed her, just as Ben had said. If he hadn't been there…

Which didn't excuse his betrayal tonight.

Glancing at her watch, she decided to wait ten minutes before going up and releasing Alicia and Jancy, just to be safe. In the meantime, she looked for Helen, wanting to thank her for her help. When she didn't answer the knock on her door, Abby quietly opened it to make sure her old friend was all right, but glancing around, she saw that Helen wasn't there.

The room was small, no more than a "cell," as the nuns in former times had called their ascetic cubicles. Most had held little more than a bed, a chest of drawers and a crucifix. Though Helen could have had the biggest, nicest bedroom in the house, this was what she'd asked for, and Abby had built this room to her specifications.

"I can't sleep if there's too much space around me," Helen had muttered. "Or too much clutter, for that matter. Those young sisters and the others can have their big, pretty rooms with their flowered curtains and sheets. To my mind, that's all nonsense."

Sister Helen had been Abby's teacher in high school, and though Abby had feared her at the time, she'd come to love her as an adult. The job of answering the bell that announced nighttime visitors was actually a perk. Because of the arthritis in both her hips and knees, it had been painful for Helen to climb the stairs every night. This way, she could remain on the first floor at all times.

The elderly nun would be aghast, of course, to think she had special privileges, or if she knew that Abby and the other women had come up with this solution to ease her discomfort. Helen was from the old school of Catholics. She believed in suffering and in "offering it up" in exchange for more stars in her crown in heaven.

Abby was no longer a practicing Catholic, despite the year she and her best friend, Marti, had spent in a convent at the age of eighteen. She didn't know if "offering it up" toward a better future in heaven was still a viable plan, but to each his own.

Come to think of it, she and Marti had both followed a different drummer. Going off to become nuns right out of high school seemed to be a wacky thing to have done later on. But they'd honestly had some idea that to do so would better the world. When they didn't turn out to be the greatest of nuns, they left, went to college and became journalists.

Marti, though, became a famous photojournalist, while Abby married a guy who turned out to be no Prince Charming. He had an affair with a woman who had boobs out to "there" and dressed like a Hooters waitress. *In fact,* Abby thought, *I called her "the bimbo" every chance I got—until I finally had to stop and forgive her, given that she was my sister.*

And where was Karen Dean now? Off on some new adventure in Africa, God love her, trying to save her poor tattered soul by working with children who had AIDS.

Abby looked at her watch. A good ten minutes had passed since everyone had left. It should be safe now to go up and get Alicia and Jancy. *Alicia had damn well better have some good explanation as to what she was doing earlier in the hotel room of a dead man.*

In the solarium, Abby knelt down and tapped on the panel to the hidden cubbyhole. She waited, but didn't hear the inside bolt slide open.

"Allie, open up," she said in a low voice. "It's me, Abby. They're gone."

She waited a few more seconds and tapped again. "Allie? Jancy? It's okay. You're safe. Open up."

Leaning her ear against the panel, she heard a rustle and what sounded like someone sniffling. Another few seconds and the bolt was thrown. Abby opened the panel and saw Jancy, her face swollen and red from crying. The girl shuffled backward on her behind and leaned against the back wall, drawing her knees up to her chin.

"Allie?" Abby squinted, looking around the small dark space. She'd worried about squeezing the two of them into it, as the priest's hole was never meant to hold two people comfortably.

Well, hell, she thought, both fear and anger vying for a place in her head. *That doesn't seem to matter much now.*

Allie was gone.

Abby couldn't get Jancy to come out, so she sat on the floor just outside the paneled door, talking in gentle tones. "Where did your mother go? Do you know where she is?"

Jancy wiped her eyes with the sleeve of her shirt and murmured something Abby couldn't hear.

"Jancy," she tried again, "where is your mother?"

"I don't know," Jancy mumbled, covering her face with her hands. "Gone. Like always."

Like always. Her tone of voice set alarm bells off in Abby's head. "You said that before, honey. Does your mom go away a lot?"

Jancy shrugged.

"How often?" Abby asked.

"I don't know. At least once a month."

"Didn't I hear somewhere that she gives speeches around the country? Something about voting for better health care?"

"Ha."

"You don't believe that's what she's doing?"

"Oh, sure, she does that sometimes. But a couple times when my school tried to reach her on one of those trips, they couldn't. Her cell was off the whole three days she was gone, and when they called the hotel she was supposed to be staying at in Chicago, she wasn't even registered."

"What about when she got home? Did you ask her where she'd been? Maybe they lost the reservation and she stayed somewhere else."

Jancy made a sound like a snort but didn't answer. Abby studied her a moment, then reached for her hand. "C'mon, let's get you out of there."

Jancy turned away. Abby touched her arm gently until she looked at her. "C'mon, honey. It's okay."

"Will grown-ups ever stop saying things like that?" Jancy said angrily. "It's not okay. Nothing's ever okay!"

But she ducked her head and crawled out into the solarium, still not taking Abby's hand. "Oh, God, I'm stiff!"

Standing, she stretched, bending from the waist and touching her toes. Letting out a long breath, she rose slowly, then raised her arms over her head, bending from side to side in an exercise position Abby recognized as hatha yoga. It seemed to come naturally to her, as if she'd done it out of habit, without thinking. Abby watched her curiously.

When it seemed Jancy was loosened up, Abby took her to the nearby bedroom that was always prepared for unexpected visitors. "It's so quiet here," Jancy whispered. "Doesn't anybody live on this floor?"

Abby smiled. "There are eleven other women on this floor, and fifteen on the one above. It's quiet because the sisters observe the Grand Silence, and the women who aren't nuns join them in it, out of respect."

"Grand Silence?"

"That means they don't talk between night and morning prayers, except in an emergency."

Jancy rolled her eyes. "Emergency? Here?"

"You'd be surprised," Abby said. Two years ago, she'd been pushed from the chapel balcony at the end of this very floor. Murder and mayhem were the order of the day back then, and she was the one who'd brought it inside these walls.

"What about Sister Helen?" Jancy asked. "And the one who brought us our soup?"

"They're exempted from keeping silence at night because their jobs sometimes require they talk."

"Oh."

Abby was glad she didn't ask any more questions. Instead, Jancy sat heavily on one of the sparse twin beds with its coarse white linens. As she looked up at Abby her chin trembled, despite her brave attempt to hide it with a smile.

"What's going to happen to me?" she asked. "Do I have to stay here till my mom comes back?"

"I don't know," Abby said honestly. "There are still a lot of questions to be answered. Like, first of all, why doesn't your mom want you to be with your dad?"

"She told you, he has some important deal coming up. He can't come home."

"But now that your mom has left, if I tell him you're alone here and what's happened—"

"Believe me, he won't come home," Jancy said.

So her mother goes off on private little jaunts whenever the mood hits her, Abby thought, and her father's too busy to hang around. Or at least he's left her with that impression.

"You mentioned Big Sur," she said. "Is that where you've been living? I thought you were still in L.A."

"We are. But we come up to Big Sur sometimes. Look, I'm not supposed to talk about it. It's not even ours."

"What isn't?" Abby asked.

"The house in Big Sur. My dad's friends, Mr. and Mrs. Randolph, loaned it to my dad so we'd have more privacy. From reporters and stuff, you know?"

She looked at Abby quickly, anxiety showing in her eyes. "You won't tell anyone, will you? I shouldn't have said anything."

"Don't worry," Abby assured her. "My lips are zipped. But what were you doing at the Highlands Inn, if you weren't staying there?"

"Having dinner in the restaurant," Jancy said, yawning. "Can I go to sleep now?"

Abby had hoped Jancy might give her some clue as to what had actually happened, but the question had closed her down.

She studied the girl a moment, wondering if she should press for more. But the kid genuinely looked tired, and it wouldn't have surprised Abby if she simply fell over with her clothes on and stayed like that all night.

"Of course. Get some sleep," she said. On the side of the antique night table there was a button. "If anything happens that worries you, or if you just feel troubled, push this. It rings through to my room, and I'll come right up."

Abby took clean, plain white pajamas out of a drawer in the dresser, and put them on the bed for her. "Restrooms are down the hall on the right," she said. "It's communal, so you may run into some of the other women who live here. Don't let that bother you, just don't talk to them until after morning prayers. That's at six. And here's a clock so you'll know what time it is when you wake up."

Abby turned the tiny travel clock so that it faced the bed. "I see it's almost five, so you'll probably sleep through breakfast. When you're ready, come down to the kitchen. It's along the hall, the opposite way from where you and your mom came in. I'll tell Sister Binny to expect you. But watch out. She'll probably try to bury you under pancakes."

For the first time, Abby thought she saw a genuine smile pass over Jancy's face. It didn't last long, but she was ready to take anything she could get.

"Thank you," Jancy said softly. "I'm really sorry, Abby."

"Sorry?" Abby said, surprised. "For what?"

"For all this trouble. For making you do so much stuff, and for being such a brat. You've been really nice."

Abby smiled. "You're pretty nice to do stuff for, Jancy. Now, sleep tight, and I'll see you when you get up."

Closing the door behind her, Abby was still smiling, but her expression quickly turned to a frown. She might not know a lot about teenagers, never having raised one, but one thing she had discovered from friends' kids was that when they made such a fast turnaround from bratty to sweet, they usually wanted something.

Or they were planning something.

Like running away.

Abby didn't even try to go back to bed. In her apartment, she changed clothes, then sat for a few minutes in her double-wide armchair before going to the kitchen. *Ben and I used to sit in this chair and cuddle,* she remembered. *Used to. After tonight, will that ever happen again?*

She deliberately tried not to think of Allie and where she had gone, why she had left her child here alone even after Abby had told her that was out of the question. It was all too much for one night—Allie and Jancy appearing without warning, then the FBI, Allie under suspicion for murder...

And Ben. His betrayal.

Back to Ben. Always back to Ben.

She squeezed her mind shut against that worry, but other memories crowded in. Her eyes took in this small, compact living room that she'd built for herself, and the few things she'd brought with her from Ocean Drive. She'd sold the multimillion-dollar house "as is" and fully furnished, except for the photos of her and Murphy—

Damn. At times like this, she missed Murphy more than ever. Her adventurous little dog had gotten loose one day and been struck by a car out on Carmel Valley Road. One of the carpenters, who helped build the very room she was sitting in, saw it happen and picked Murphy up off the road and carried him to her. The thing that had gotten to her most was that he looked just as he had when asleep, so she didn't realize at first that he was gone. Then she saw the blood on the side of his head that was next to the carpenter's arm. He had thoughtfully hidden it from her until the first shock was over.

Abby chose a spot on the edge of the forest to bury him. There were five other workmen on the property at the time, and they all stood around with the sisters and other women to offer prayers. By the time the little ceremony was over there were heaps of flowers on Murphy's grave. The workmen brought wildflowers from the surrounding meadows, and it touched her heart to see their big, rough hands carrying those fragile little stems and placing them so carefully over Murphy's grave. The Prayer House women brought early spring flowers from the gardens, and several of them wept along with her.

It took Abby a while to get past the stage where she was looking for her little companion around every corner and expecting him to be there to greet her when she walked through the door. She would never get over the feeling that it was her fault he ended up in the road in the first place. Murphy had an adventurous soul, and he'd gotten away once when he was younger. She should have been watching him better the day he died, but she'd trusted him not to run like that again.

Trust was a bitch. It could hurt the person who trusted, and the one trusted, as well. She would have to remember that when deciding what to do about Alicia and Jancy.

And Ben.

Impatiently, Abby shook her head as if shaking dust out of a rug, and went to the kitchen. Binny was already cooking hot cereal, and she returned Abby's "Good morning" as she reached into the fridge for eggs to boil. The room was filled with the scent of oats, blueberry muffins and coffee.

A half-finished platter of sliced fruit was on the worktable, and Abby poured herself a cup of coffee and took up a knife to finish the job.

"You don't have to do that, you know," Binny said in her soft voice.

"I know. I just like to."

Abby stole a look at Binny as she stood over the stove, her ordinarily pale face pink now from the steamy cereal. She was still in the black cotton robe that she always wore until after she'd cooked breakfast, and a white kerchief held back her wispy gray curls. For the second time this week, Abby thought she looked as if she was losing weight, and Binny of all people didn't need that. She made a mental note to talk her into getting a checkup.

"You already do too much around here," Binny said in the voice she saved for a quiet reprimand. "Didn't I see you mucking out the stalls the other day?"

Abby smiled. "Oh, and what? I'm supposed to be above that?"

"No, you're supposed to save your energy for your real work," she said.

"Binny—"

"That's all I'm sayin'. That and no more."

Abby rolled her eyes and sighed. No one at the Prayer House was supposed to talk about *Paseo* unless absolutely necessary—a firm rule that kept everyone from slipping and saying something in front of the wrong people. Binny, though, was past the age where she followed rules.

And speaking of breaking rules, where was Helen?

"Have you seen Sister Helen?" Abby asked, cutting into a juicy ripe strawberry and popping half into her mouth.

"Not since last night when your visitors came," Binny said.

This wasn't at all like Helen. Abby was beginning to get worried. She was debating whether to rouse the other women and start a search party when Helen appeared on the back porch, wiping her boots on the bristles of the mud scraper.

"Where have you been?" Abby demanded, her voice rising with anxiety. "I was worried!"

"Oh, you were, were you? I seem to remember saying the same thing to you a few hundred times at St. Joseph's High. I guess that makes us *almost* even now."

Helen sat on the wooden bench next to the kitchen door and tugged off her wellies, the knee-high boots that she always wore for mucking about in the stables. Abby couldn't fathom why she'd been out there at this early hour. She was about to ask when Helen's face creased with pain as she tried to get one of the heavy rubber boots off.

"Here, let me do that," Abby said. Helen flicked her a grateful smile and leaned back, sighing.

"I used to dream of a handsome young man pulling my skates off for me," she said dreamily as Abby tugged at the first boot. "Down at the pond on my parents' farm, that was. There would be a fire for us to warm our hands, and he'd be wearing a navy-blue sweater and a bright red scarf. We'd be sipping hot cider, and when he looked at me with those eyes—" She groaned. "Oh, Lordy, those eyes."

"Helen!" Abby couldn't help it; she giggled. "I never knew that. Were you in love with this guy?"

"Ha. More like in love with my dream of him. Sometimes our dreams are better than the real thing, you know."

"You think so?"

"Of course. In our dreams, a man can be anything. In real life, he's just another human being like the rest of us. Warts and all."

She gave Abby a pointed look.

"Are we talking about Ben now?" Abby asked, sighing. She knew Helen had reservations about Ben—or rather, Ben and her as a couple. She'd always thought he would let Abby down one day. And of course, he had. Today.

"He just wanted to make sure we were safe," Abby said, half in an attempt to convince herself.

"I doubt that. Following the rules, he was. Always following the rules."

Abby's hands were poised over the second boot, but she sat back on her heels.

"You've been a nun for almost fifty years, Helen. Since you were twenty-five. And you cracked a pretty strict whip when I was in school. Are you telling me now that it's a bad thing to follow rules?"

"I'm telling you he shouldn't have brought them here," she said, frowning. "Not those FBI people. He broke your trust."

Abby pulled the other boot off and Helen winced. "Ouch! Don't take it out on my poor feet, child! I'm just telling you what you already know."

Mornings in Carmel Valley could be cold, especially when there was fog, as there was today. Helen's foot, when Abby took off the mended black cotton sock, was icy. She took it in her hands to rub it. "I'm sorry. I didn't mean to tug so hard. But, Helen, when you were Marti's and my teacher, you never talked like this. You were so…" Abby searched for the right word. "Religious."

She thought it best not to tell her that Marti and she sometimes called her a "mealy moral mouth."

The truth was, though they'd feared Helen then for her strictness, she was the best teacher they'd ever had. Deep down, they loved the valuable things she'd taught them. When she moved from St. Joseph's High to the motherhouse, where Abby and Marti were training as nuns, they felt a healthy combination of anxiety and excitement.

Helen didn't let them down. Despite her brusque attitude, Abby and Marti had always suspected their teacher had a heart of gold. She would sneak peanut butter and jelly sandwiches out of the motherhouse kitchen for them in the late afternoons, when their stomachs were growling and dinner wasn't for another two hours.

And were they ever hungry. Aside from attending college classes all day to become teachers, they were still nuns, and had to follow all the rules demanded of the other sisters: up at 4:00 a.m. for prayers, Mass at six, scrubbing floors, taking turns in the community laundry…. The work of keeping up a large Gothic-style "mansion" that housed one hundred and fifty nuns, five stories and 1930s tile floors that needed polishing every week, never ended.

"My dear girl," Helen said irritably, interrupting Abby's thoughts, "religion doesn't make you blind and dumb. At least, it shouldn't. Do you think I got to be this old without knowing what people are all about?"

"Of course not," Abby said. "I guess I'm just surprised that you're—"

"What, jaded? Nuns don't have a right to get jaded? Lordy me, girl, it's been years since I've made the sign of the cross right—'in the name of the Father, the Son,' and all that—instead of just saying one, two, three, four. You get burned out! And you should know that better than most. It's not like we haven't been through this all before."

"But you're still a good person, Helen. And, in your own way, a good nun."

"Ha. In my own way, huh? Well, thank you—I think. My point is that you don't have to be religious to be good, girl. That's where some of those churches get it all wrong. God loves us all, and he's not about to let the people he loves go to hell just because they didn't say a certain set of words in front of a certain kind of preacher and get water dumped all over their heads."

Abby smiled. "Tsk-tsk, Sister Helen Marie. You sound more like a renegade every day."

"Well, maybe I've been hanging around you too long," she grumped.

Abby took a cup of green tea and went into her office, debating whether she should put aside her anger and hurt of the night before and call Ben. She could at least ask if they'd caught whoever had committed the Highland Inn murder.

In the end, she decided it wouldn't be wise to show too much interest. Ben wouldn't even have to wonder why she'd asked; he'd know right away that she'd lied through her teeth the night before, and that Alicia and Jancy had been here.

Rubbing the weariness lines in her forehead, Abby wondered if she should call social services to see what her options were with Jancy. But even that she waffled about. Instead, she called a private investigator she often used when relocating abused women. Bobby had helped her out many times when she'd had to have a violent husband tracked to make sure she and *Paseo* didn't relocate his battered wife anywhere near him.

She started out by asking him to look for Allie, and gave him certain information about her that she didn't think the police or FBI had. With any luck, that might help him—and her—to get to Allie first.

Jancy came down to the kitchen around ten, and Binny buzzed Abby over her office intercom to let her know. Since Binny was already busy getting lunch started, Abby put her phone calls aside and scrambled up some eggs for Jancy. She'd insisted she wasn't hungry, so Abby tossed some cheese, onions and roasted garlic cloves into the eggs, thinking the aromas might tempt her to eat. It worked. When Abby asked her if the eggs tasted okay, she shrugged and kept on eating—gargantuan praise from a teenager.

Abby sat across from Jancy at the wooden worktable and drank a fresh cup of green tea.

"Don't you eat?" Jancy asked.

"I did, at six o'clock this morning," Abby said.

"Do you ever sleep?"

"Sure. Not much last night, though. How about you?"

Again, Jancy shrugged. "I kept hearing noises, like real loud footsteps on the ground. I thought maybe it was bears."

Abby smiled. "We don't have bears around here. You probably heard the horses."

At this, Jancy's eyes lit up. It was easier to see that they were a brilliant green, now that most of the makeup had worn off.

"You have horses here?"

"Four of them. Do you like to ride?"

"I love it!" But her smile turned to a frown. "I guess I won't be here that long, though, huh? You've got to find somebody else to take me."

"One day at a time," Abby said. "Let's see how it goes."

She washed up their dishes, and Jancy surprised her by offering to dry. After that, Abby invited the girl to join her while she practiced for her black belt in Kenpo.

"What the heck is Kenpo?" Jancy asked.

"It's a form of martial arts. I need to work on it every morning, if I'm ever going to get that belt."

"You're not going to practice on me, are you?" Jancy said somewhat cautiously.

"Well, I hadn't planned on it, but since you're here…" From her expression, Abby wasn't sure if Jancy knew she was kidding.

They went down the hall to the gym Abby had installed, and found Davis Bowen, her Kenpo teacher, waiting patiently in a meditative state in front of the small rock fountain he'd urged her to include in her remodeling plans. His own house was high on a hill above Clint Eastwood's Mission Ranch Inn, and the view along the coastline was drop-dead gorgeous. Davis also had flowers and three different fountains in his courtyard.

"We need all the beauty we can get in this world," he'd told Abby long ago. "I think if everyone lived surrounded by nature and beauty, there would be no wars."

"Same thing if everyone got a massage every day," Abby had reminded him, smiling.

"Ah, yes…another one of my dreams for creating peace on earth."

She left Jancy with Davis and went to the locker room to change into her white *gi* and brown belt. She'd made her way to brown fast, pouring her angry energies into working up from blue after Marti was murdered and she herself had nearly fallen to the same fate. If anyone ever came after her again, she swore, they wouldn't stand a chance. "First black belt" had stumped her so far, though.

Jancy watched her work out with Davis awhile, but a few minutes later, when Abby turned toward where she'd been, she saw her in front of the fountain instead. She was in a lotus position, palms up and resting on her knees, eyes closed.

Abby shot a surprised look at Davis and caught him smiling just before she sent him a Twisting Vine—including the kick to the groin and fingertips to the eyes. Davis was perfectly capable of protecting himself, so she didn't do any damage. However, it gave her some small sense of satisfaction that she'd almost managed to catch him off guard. Not that she didn't love Davis, but when they practiced she went into a zone where he became just one more enemy needing to be struck down.

They continued like that for another half hour. When they'd finished, Jancy was looking around the walls at the black-and-white framed photos Sister Liddy had taken of Davis and Abby training. Usually, when people looked at those pictures, they had something nice to say about them. Even flattering.

Not Jancy, though.

"I can tell from these pictures, and just from watching you today," Jancy said matter-of-factly, "that you're trying way too hard. That's why you can't get your black belt."

"What do you mean?" Abby asked, only slightly offended that Jancy didn't comment on how wonderful she was to have made it this far at all.

"Well," Jancy said, shrugging, "it seems to me that you're learning all these moves so you can know how to hurt someone—not just to defend yourself. So you're going at it way too hard."

"You think so?" Abby said testily.

Jancy shrugged again. "It shows that you're insecure. Maybe you should practice meditation. Meditating could help build your self-confidence."

"Well, thank you so much for the advice," Abby said sweetly. "Do you think meditating could get you to stop shrugging so damned much?"

"Abby?" Davis said.

She bit her lip and turned to him.

"I'm afraid I have to agree with your young friend here," he said mildly. "Whatever those pictures are in your mind while we're working out, maybe they need to be a bit more…friendly. I nearly lost all hope of having children today."

Abby flushed. "Oh, God, Davis, I'm so sorry. I had no idea—"

He grinned. "Abby, the point is moot. I'm *gay,* remember?"

"Oh…right."

"So I won't be having progeny. I sure would like to know who you're thinking of, though, when you go off in that world of yours."

Abby could have told him. A three-hundred-and-sixty-degree, clockwise-twisting circle down the opponent's arm? *Jeffrey.*

Left foot to six o'clock, in a right cat stance facing twelve o'clock? *Jeffrey.*

Right kick to the groin, fingers stabbing the eyes? Who else but her former bastard husband…*Jeffrey?*

She sometimes thought of Marti, the horrors of her final hours, but that took her to places that made her truly afraid of what she might do.

"Sorry," Abby said again. "Really. I'll work on that."

When Davis left, she gave Jancy a pair of her own black jeans and a black jersey top to wear. Then she pinned the girl's multicolored hair up and covered it with a small veil borrowed from Narissa, one of the expostulants at the Prayer House. Giving her a once-over, Abby said, "Okay. That looks pretty good—you could pass for a nun in this getup."

They headed out to the stables. Now that it was daylight, she could see that there were no agents or cops nearby. If anyone happened to be watching from one of the surrounding hills or roads, they just might take Jancy for one of the young sisters.

When they got inside the stables, Jancy talked to the horses, asked their names and rubbed their noses. She clearly loved the animals, but no longer seemed interested in riding.

"I just don't feel like it right now," she said, sliding down into a sitting position and leaning her back against the outside of the stall.

She's depressed, Abby thought. Nearly all the young girls who came through here with moms on the run were depressed, to some extent.

"Maybe someday I'll take vows and all that," Jancy said, her fingers twisting in the veil as if it were hair. "It must be easier than living in this stupid world."

"Well, if that's what you want," Abby said, sitting beside her.

"All my life, I've wanted to be like Audrey Hepburn in *The Nun's Story,*" she said.

"Really? All your life?" Abby smiled. "You're fourteen, Jancy. When did you see that movie?"

Jancy blushed. "Last year, on video. But you know what I mean."

"Yeah. I became a nun at eighteen."

"You?"

"You don't have to sound so surprised. It was a temporary fling," Abby said.

"Wow. I never would have thought that you... I mean, my mom told me about you once, and I thought you were rich. You know...one of those society matrons."

Abby laughed. "A society matron? God forbid."

"Sorry."

"That's okay. Have you informed your parents of your plans to become a Bride of Christ?" Abby asked.

"Once. We were driving by a convent and I told my dad. But he pointed at bars on the windows. He said they lock the nuns up in there."

Attaboy, Gerry. Keep the kid off that *vocational track.*

"It does seem that way to some," Abby said. "But actually, in those convents where there are bars on the windows it's because the nuns want to lock the world out."

"Really? On purpose?"

"On purpose."

Jancy seemed to think about that. "Those people last night were looking for us, weren't they? Mom said if they catch us they'll lock her up."

Abby saw no point in telling her anything but the truth. "They said you and your mom had something to do with a man who was found dead at the Highlands Inn last night. They want to question her. And you, too, since you were with her."

She let that sink in a moment before she asked bluntly, "Did Alicia kill him, Jancy?"

The girl gave a small jump. "No way! We just found him like that!"

"Can you tell me how you and your mom 'just found him like that'?"

Jancy shook her head and didn't answer.

"You must know you can trust me by now," Abby said. "I won't repeat a word to anyone."

Jancy hesitated, but then it began to pour out. "He…the guy…he was some sort of reporter. I don't remember his name, but that's what Mom said. Some old guy."

"Old?"

"Fifty, at least."

Abby tried hard not to smile. "So did your mom know this guy well?"

"I guess. He was eating in the restaurant, and so were we. Mom went over and talked to him. I don't know what they talked about, but he seemed pretty mad. He got up and walked out, and when she got back to our table she was mad, too. I wanted to go into Carmel and walk around the shops after dinner, but she said no, she had business to take care of. So I sat in the lobby while she made a phone call, and when she got done she said we were going to visit somebody."

She wiped her eyes, as if to clear them of unpleasant images. "It was awful. We went outside and up the driveway to some room that looked like a private condo from the outside. You know, not in a hallway like a hotel. Mom knocked on the door. Nobody answered, but the door was open a little, so Mom pushed it open more and we went inside. She called out a couple of times—"

"What name did she call?" Abby asked.

Jancy shook her head. "I can't remember. I wasn't really listening, because I felt like somebody could walk in any minute and shoot us for trespassing. All I wanted to do was get out of there." She took a breath, and her voice began to shake. "Then we saw him. This guy, the same one in the restaurant, that reporter. There was one of those big square tubs with jets right in the middle of the bedroom, and he was there—"

She gave a shudder. "There—there was blood in the water all around him. It looked like somebody had—had cut his throat."

"My God, Jancy! What a horrible thing to see."

She began to cry, covering her face with her hands.

"I'm sorry, honey," Abby said, putting an arm around her shoulders. "Look, I just have one more question, then we'll table all this and do whatever you want. Okay?"

Jancy nodded and wiped her face on her sleeves.

"Did your mom call the police?" Abby asked. "Or did someone else?"

"I think it was the maid. She came in with towels or something, and when she saw us and this dead guy, she started screaming. She ran out, and Mom said she'd tell the police about us and we had to get away as fast as we could."

"And that's when you came here?" Abby asked.

"Yeah. Mom said this was the one place in the world she knew I'd be safe."

Abby started. "She said it just that way? That *you'd* be safe?"

"Yeah, just like that. At the time I didn't think it was odd, but now… I guess we're thinking the same thing, huh?"

"I guess we are," Abby said. *And kudos to this bright little girl for figuring out that Alicia had planned to leave her daughter with me all along.*

Now the question was: Why?

6

Eleven men and one woman—Kris Kelley—sat around an interview table in the Carmel police station. It was just before dawn.

"Pass these along, please," said a twelfth man, who was clearly in charge. He stood at the end of the table, passing slender blue folders to the man on his right.

The lead agent was over six feet tall, with a ruddy tan and eyes like polished nickel. His taut physique was that of a man in his twenties, belying his actual age of fifty-six. The deep lines in his face and the untouched gray hair were the only telltale signs that Robert James Lessing had lived a difficult life. Those who didn't know him might assume he belonged to a country club and played tennis every day—an incorrect assumption that served him well in his work.

He took a seat at the long table next to Ben Schaeffer. "You've all met Carmel's chief of police?" he asked the assemblage.

They nodded. Every eye scanned Ben, but no one

smiled. Lessing turned to Ben. "I understood the sheriff would be here, as well."

"He will be," Ben said. "Soon as he can. MacElroy's putting together a tactical team."

"All the more reason he should be here," Lessing said with an edge.

"This is the way it's done in Monterey County," Ben replied coolly. He didn't much like being here, either. "Granted, we don't have many murders in Carmel, but this one at the Highlands seemed routine—at least, until you folks showed up. The sheriff is following standard practice in bringing together a tactical team from the various law enforcement agencies in the county."

Lessing spoke dryly. "The murder at the Highlands Inn was anything but routine, Chief."

"Yeah, I've pretty much figured that out." Ben looked at the other agents, who were busily writing in pocket-size notebooks. "And since I'm already on the tactical team," he continued, "maybe you'd like to tell me what the hell is going on. You've got agents swarming all over the place, knocking on doors in the middle of the night—"

"One specific door," Lessing corrected sharply. "Which, aside from the fact that you've been kind enough to lend us your facilities, is the only reason you are privy to this conversation."

Ben stifled his anger. This was his ground they were stomping all over, and he hadn't loaned them his facilities willingly. The fact of the matter was, they'd commandeered them.

It only made matters worse that they had come down on Abby and the Prayer House that way.

"My hospitality—*and* my facilities—" he said, his brown eyes fixed on the agent with an unmistakable warning, "won't last long if you don't tell me what you're *really* here for and what the hell you want."

"I thought I'd made that clear," Lessing replied. "We're here because of the murder at the Highlands Inn. And, of course, we'd like your cooperation."

"That still doesn't tell me a damned thing," Ben said. "To begin with, you've admitted that the murder at the Highlands was far from routine. I already knew that. If it wasn't, you wouldn't be here. As I understand it, the victim was a journalist for a Washington, D.C., newspaper. A Woodward-and-Bernstein type, probably digging into some sort of government secrets. My guess is he got too close to the truth about someone or something, and got his throat cut before he could write a book about it. As I hear it, that's not exactly something new."

Lessing sighed and glanced at Kris Kelley. "There are a few people here other than Chief Schaeffer who haven't been filled in yet. Would you like to do the honors? I really don't think we can wait any longer for the sheriff."

Kris nodded and stood, smoothing her skirt. Ben knew she couldn't have slept much all night, any more than anyone else. Yet she looked crisp and fresh in a beige suit she'd somehow managed to change into. He couldn't help noticing it was almost the same color as her collar-length hair. He supposed she was nice looking, especially with that great tan. Abby's dark hair and creamy complexion were just the opposite—

He shook himself mentally. *What the hell am I doing?*

"As some of you know," Kris said, "the woman we're looking for is Alicia Gerard, the wife of multimillionaire H. Palmer Gerard. So far, we've discovered that the victim was attempting to blackmail Ms. Gerard, and that she was seen having an angry conversation last night with him at the Pacific's Edge restaurant in the Highlands Inn. A short time later, she was observed knocking on the door of the victim's room, a room he'd reserved for three nights. Last night was his second night there."

She cleared her throat and took a sip of water, then began again. "At ten-twenty or so last night, the hotel maid walked into the room and found Alicia Gerard and her fourteen-year-old daughter, Jancy, standing over the victim. He was lying in a whirlpool tub and his throat had been slashed. In fact, he was nearly beheaded. It was a brutal crime."

She paused and swallowed hard, as if the scene she'd witnessed the night before was too dreadful to return to, even in her mind. "The minute Alicia and her daughter saw the maid they ran, but the maid later identified them from photos we found in the victim's room—"

"Hang on," Ben said. "Since when do maids deliver clean towels at ten-thirty at night?"

"Way ahead of you," Lessing said. "The victim called and asked for them. Said housekeeping hadn't cleaned the bathroom that morning. Kris?"

The agent began again. "The photos were of Alicia Gerard and her daughter, Jancy—candid shots taken on the street, at a mall, one of Jancy outside her school. Obviously taken by someone who'd been observing them over a period of time. The husband, H. P. Gerard, wasn't in them."

"Hold on," Ben said. "H. P. Gerard's wife is who you were looking for at the Prayer House? So this reporter guy is viciously murdered at the Highlands Inn, presumably by the wife and/or child of one of the biggest movers and shakers in this country, and all of a sudden a lightbulb goes on and you say, 'Oh, that's where the killers are! At a convent out in Carmel Valley.'" He laughed shortly. "Yeah, that makes a whole hell of a lot of sense."

Agent Kelley answered him in a scathing tone. "It does if your girlfriend is one of Alicia Gerard's oldest friends—*and* if your girlfriend takes in women and children on the run."

"Which you wouldn't even have known if I hadn't—"

"*Confirmed* it for us," she said firmly. "We knew about Abby Northrup's work long before you decided to enlighten us, Chief Schaeffer. We hardly had to rely on you to inform us—"

"Like hell," Ben said, interrupting angrily.

"Easy," Lessing said quietly. "Let's keep personalities out of this."

"This is not about personalities," Kris said sharply. "It's about not having an outsider at our meetings."

"Chief Schaeffer is hardly an outsider," Lessing reminded her, "any more than you are. And so far he's been cooperating fully."

"Fully? You may think so, but—"

"I cooperated because you told me that Abby and the Prayer House were in danger," Ben said, interrupting again. "There wasn't even time to find out who you were after."

It was the fear that Abby might be hurt that had made him screw up, dammit. What a fool he was, confirming their suspicions about Abby's work with *Paseo* when he'd made a promise a year ago never to tell a soul. And now, because he'd thought it was his duty to do so— and that the suspect might be a danger to Abby and the Prayer House—he'd blabbed to the damned FBI.

Abby would never forgive him.

"I've had enough," he said, standing. "You're welcome to stay here until you're done, but I've got work to do."

"Chief—" Lessing raised a delaying hand.

"No. From everything you've said so far, this is nothing but a plain and simple homicide. If that's the case, I sure don't need you to help solve it. In fact, it looks to me like you're wasting taxpayers' money with all this hoopla, but hey, don't let me stop you."

He stormed out, slamming the door. Papers on the table scattered from the breeze it created.

Lessing looked at Kris Kelley. "We've got to tell him," he said heavily. "Everything."

"Oh, hell," she sighed. "I'll go get him."

7

Ben didn't have to wonder long if his bluff had worked. He had barely leaned back in his chair, boots on his desk, when Kris Kelley sailed into his office.

"Look," she said tightly, as if saying the words might choke her, "I'm sorry. I didn't mean to offend you. We need you back in there."

"*You* look," he said, swinging his feet off the desk and planting them firmly on the ground. "This is my town. If anything bad happens to it or the people in it—"

"I know, I know," she said irritably. "I'm trying to apologize, Chief!"

"And I appreciate that. But if you and the gang in there want any further cooperation from me, you'll have to damn well tell me what's really going on. You can't expect me to sit there and listen to bunk about it being only a homicide when there's a gaggle of government agents sitting around my conference table."

Kris half smiled. "A gaggle?"

He didn't smile back.

"Okay," she said, shrugging. "You've got it. We'll tell you everything. But you'll have to swear not to repeat anything you hear in that room. Not to anyone you work with, your friends, Abby Northrup…no one."

Ben almost told her to forget it. For a few minutes in there his pride had been hurt, and he'd wanted to force them to take him into their confidence. Now that he'd won the point, though, he'd probably be better off to walk away and wash his hands of the FBI. Tell them to get the hell out of here, and let the chips fall where they may.

The only thing that kept him from doing that was the thought that being on the inside might be the only way he could protect Abby.

Hoisting his six-foot-two frame out of the chair, he rested his hands on his hips. "Okay," he said. "I'm in."

Ben took the same chair he'd had before, next to Lessing, who gave him a nod as if Ben had merely excused himself a few minutes to use the restroom. Kris Kelley's expression was noncommittal as she took her own seat.

Lessing looked at a man halfway down the table. "Agent Bollam?"

"Sir." The agent walked over to the light switch, flicking off the overheads. Pulling a cart that held a slide projector from a corner, he positioned it behind and to the right of Agent Lessing. Pointing it toward the far wall so that everyone could see, he said, "I'd like to begin with some background."

He brought up a photograph of two people who looked to be in their twenties or early thirties. The woman had long, curly, strawberry-blond hair that looked windblown and covered half her face. It didn't hide her smile, though, nor her beautiful large hazel eyes. The man had black hair, and his arms were around the woman from behind, holding her tightly and smiling, his cheek against hers.

"These are Alicia Gerard's parents," Bollam said, "Pat and Bridget Devlin." Behind them was a sign that read Dublin Automotive Services, and in one of the open bays was a dark blue car that Ben, a classic-car nut, recognized as an Irish-built MG Midget, circa 1960s.

"That photo was taken about forty years ago," Bollam said. "Pat and Bridget Devlin would be in their sixties now."

He changed the slide to one that depicted the scene of an accident. There were police cars, ambulances and a crowd gathered along a highway with a steep cliff on one side. At the bottom of a ravine was wreckage.

"Some of you might recall hearing about a school bus being blown off the road in Ireland in the seventies. Twenty-eight out of the twenty-nine children aboard were killed."

A few of the agents nodded.

"Pat Devlin was—*is*," he corrected himself, "a brilliant man, a scientist with ties to the IRA. His specialty, in those days, was building explosive devices. After the school bus attack, fragments of the bomb were found, as were certain 'fingerprints,' as they say—details in its construction that led straight to Pat Devlin."

"My God," Ben said. "H. P. Gerard's father-in-law? He blew up that bus?"

"Long before Alicia ever met H. P., of course. She would have been around five at the time. And while Pat Devlin did build the bomb the IRA used, he may not have known precisely what it was about to be used for. Reportedly, he was so sickened by the deaths of those children, he tried to get out of the IRA. As the country's top expert in explosives, however, Devlin was too useful to them. They threatened his family if he tried to leave."

"But he did leave," one of the agents pointed out.

Lessing nodded. "He somehow got false papers for his family and fled Ireland overnight with Bridget and Alicia, leaving their home just as it was—food on the table, mail in the box, cat in the yard."

"Incredible," Ben said. "How do you know all this?"

"I can't reveal our sources," Lessing answered. "Sorry. But let me get to the point. We have solid information—not just chatter—that a splinter group of the IRA calling themselves The Candlelights are using Pat Devlin again. This time, he's in America, and he's building the most devastating explosive device this country has ever seen. The Candlelights plan to use it on the fourteenth of this month—exactly one week from today."

He paused, and his mouth twisted slightly. "Unfortunately, we've had no luck finding The Candlelights, and we don't know where they plan to attack. Our mission, therefore, is to find Pat Devlin. That bomb must never be completed."

Good God, Ben thought, *be careful what you ask for. All I wanted was a little more action, and now...*

Lessing's cell phone rang, and he left the table for a few minutes to take the call. When he returned, Bollam began again.

"As I was saying, Pat, Bridget and Alicia Devlin left Ireland rather abruptly when Alicia was five, using false papers to enter the United States. That would be thirty-five years ago. We know they lived under different assumed names in Philadelphia for a while, then Miami and Los Angeles. We also know the Irish police spent three years looking for them without success, before moving on to what they called 'more important' matters. Meantime, this splinter group of the IRA, The Candlelights, was also looking for the Devlins. Every time anyone thought they'd caught up with them, however, they'd find an empty apartment or house. The Devlins apparently knew, somehow, when they were about to be caught."

Ben spoke up. "So you think someone was helping them out."

"We have to assume that was the case," Bollam said.

One of the agents at the table asked, "Do we know where this group, The Candlelights, came from? What's their agenda?"

"As I understand it," Bollam said, "in the early days of the Troubles, as they call it, women in Ireland used to leave a candle burning in a window every night, to welcome the men home after their 'activities.' We don't know why, but the name seems to have been picked up by this new splinter group. As to their agenda, it's the same as all terrorist groups—to throw people into fear and create chaos."

He flipped the slides to show two plain, inexpensive-looking cottages and an apartment house. "The Devlins' cottages were in Philadelphia and Miami. The apartment house is on Crenshaw in L.A. This is all we have on them. Over the years, the Irish police and the IRA apparently gave up hunting for them. There's been little interest, until recently, in finding Pat Devlin."

He stopped to take a sip from his glass of water, then pulled out a handkerchief to wipe his chin and tie where the water had dribbled.

"Ah, geez, Joe," a pink-faced agent with bright red hair said. "You were looking so professional up there till now."

There was mild laughter from the other agents, and a smile from Bollam. "Just don't forget I'm your senior," he said.

"In age, maybe," the first agent came back with.

"We don't have much time," Lessing reminded them.

Everyone quieted down and Bollam continued. "As I was saying, no agency with an interest was ever able to find Pat and Bridget Devlin. There's no record of them having become naturalized citizens, so if they're still in this country, they're here illegally. Unfortunately, it seems they've changed their names and identity papers every time they've moved, so they're living as much underground as if they were in a witness protection program."

"Is that a possibility?" Ben asked.

"Not that we know of—and presumably, we would. To hide out the way they have, there must have been someone helping them. Especially recently, given the new technologies we have for finding terrorists—" he paused and looked around the table "—it must be someone with experience at hiding people, someone who can provide false identities and money."

There was a small silence, then Ben said testily, "You'd better not be suggesting that Abby Northrup is involved in some way. If so, that's crazy—"

"I hadn't really thought of that until just now," Lessing broke in, raising a steel-gray brow. "But thank you for your input, Chief Schaeffer. I'll keep it in mind."

Ben began to retort but decided against it.

"Bolly?" Lessing said.

Agent Bollam put the photo of a man on the screen. "We now come to last night's murder. This is the victim, John Duff. We know he was working on an article about splinter groups of the IRA and their connection to other terrorist organizations. Further, we know that while writing this article he stumbled on the whereabouts of Pat Devlin. We also know that Duff, an alcoholic, had been on a downward slide. We believe he dumped the original article and turned his attention to

Alicia Gerard, the Devlins' daughter. He must have seen the wife of H. P. Gerard as being a golden goose that could ease the pain of his financial woes."

"Blackmail?" Ben said.

Bollam nodded. "A large deposit to his bank account was made yesterday, just hours before he was murdered. We traced the deposit back to Alicia Gerard, and we have to assume that Duff was demanding money from her to keep silent about her parents' whereabouts. It could even be that he threatened Alicia herself with exposure. She was born in Ireland and her papers of entry were as fraudulent as those of her parents. Of course, in ordinary times, marrying an American citizen would have made her legal. But since 9/11…well, there are no guarantees that her marriage to H. P. Gerard would be taken into consideration. She could well be declared illegal and deported, if her status came to the attention of certain authorities."

"Are we talking about the Patriot Act here?" Ben asked.

"Initially. But there are other laws that have sprung up, as well, since 9/11—laws that might cause someone innocent to be deported simply because they appear to be guilty, an enemy of the state, so to speak."

"I'm surprised to hear you admit that," Ben said. "I thought there were more controls over that sort of thing now."

"Yes, well, that and other fairy tales…" Lessing said. "We also have to assume, and we're ninety percent sure of this, that Alicia Gerard knows where her parents are, and has been helping to cover their tracks for years."

Ben studied the face on the screen. This man, Duff, looked familiar. In his sixties or so, he had thinning gray hair and a somber, ascetic look. Thinking back, Ben was sure that when he'd had a subscription to the *Washington Post,* he'd read articles in it by John Duff. He thought he recalled that Duff had won a Pulitzer years ago for a series of articles. Searching his memory, though, all he came up with was something about illegal immigrants educating their kids here in the U.S.

He shook his head. "I can't see Alicia Gerard—a woman who makes speeches around the country about the need for better health care for everyone, a woman most of the country knows and loves for her kindness and charity work— I just can't see her cold-bloodedly slitting someone's throat."

"Did you ever have to do something desperate to protect someone you loved?" Lessing argued. "A mother or father? Any family member?"

"No," Ben had to admit. "My parents own a grocery store in Gilroy. Thankfully, they've lived pretty quiet lives."

There *was* that time two years ago when he'd had to kill someone to save Abby, but he wasn't about to talk to these people about that.

Lessing turned back to Bollam and nodded. The agent cleared his throat. "Now we come to the real reason we're searching for Alicia Gerard. Everything we've said up to now about Duff blackmailing her, and that she *may* have killed him to silence him, is true according to our information. It is also true, however, that we've been having Alicia Gerard followed for the past three months. Our interest in her did not begin with this murder."

"Oh?"

"She was already being followed by the FBI," Lessing said. "One of our agents was only minutes behind Alicia when John Duff was murdered at the Highlands Inn last night. We can't know for certain that she didn't murder Duff, but according to our agent's report, it would seem she wasn't in the room long enough for that."

"Just how long do you think it takes to slit a man's throat?" Ben said. "A minute—half a minute? You can't rule her out."

"True. The point is, and I can't go into detail, our agent has reason to believe she didn't do it."

"So you raised all this ruckus about Alicia Gerard being wanted for murder," Ben said irritably, "when you pretty much knew she didn't do it? Why, in the name of God—"

"Isn't it obvious?" Lessing said. "We need Alicia Gerard to lead us to her father. Without him, The Candlelights are incapable of waging this attack. Thus, we're using the murder at the Highlands as a reason to get as many law enforcement agencies as possible looking for Ms. Gerard—without having to tell them the reason why."

"But you must have some idea of what their target is," Ben said impatiently. "I can't believe that's all your informant could tell you."

"Believe whatever you wish," Lessing said shortly. "Nevertheless, the target isn't our main concern. Or, to put it another way, the entire country is their target. Unfortunately, we can't protect the entire country. Bolly?"

The agent put up a slide that listed various chemical agents. "It's all about bioweapons now," he said. "The latest research has resulted in chemicals that, unlike a conventional destructive bomb, can travel through the air. This is similar to the 'dirty bombs' that use conventional explosives to fling radioactive isotopes out into the air in a cloud of dust. Now, with the right kind of explosives, they can do that with bioweapons. Within hours, millions of deadly particles could reach as far north as Maine and as far west as Los Angeles, killing every living being in their path."

"Not everyone," Lessing said, "would be in their path, of course, depending on how the winds carry the particles. Also, the chemicals' effects might only last as long as a half hour. People who were in their basements, for instance, or rooms without windows, while the particles were passing through, might have a slim chance of surviving. But can you imagine what it would be like to survive such a thing? Millions of funerals for weeks on end, tiny little caskets and beside them weeping mothers…" He shuddered. "Mothers who will undoubtedly wish they, too, were dead."

"My God," Ben said. "This is the kind of device Pat Devlin is building? Is this man crazy, or just plain evil?"

Lessing didn't answer, but the strained expression on

his pale face and that of the other agents told him they were not only in agreement, but afraid. Everyone here undoubtedly had a family—wives, children, mothers, fathers. Many of them probably lived in various parts of the country, and no one could count on being safe.

The red-haired agent spoke up. "Aside from being evil, this whole thing is stupid. Don't these people know they're going to start a chain reaction that will only come back and bite them?"

"I doubt they care," Lessing said. "At least, not about their individual lives. Think of the al-Qaeda suicide bombers. These small splinter groups like The Candlelights are willing to do almost anything to prove themselves to al-Qaeda, because if they can succeed in that, al-Qaeda will back them with money. That's why The Candlelights are targeting the U.S.—to get their hands on al-Qaeda's funds. Not that they're linked by any common philosophy, but their goals are the same—to create chaos and keep people in fear." Lessing shook his head. "Goddamn idiots! Once these chemicals are released, they could be distributed over hundreds of miles by the force of the blast. From there, the jet stream could disperse them thousands of miles in any direction."

"Thousands of miles…" one agent said softly.

"A modest estimate," Lessing said. "One needs only to think of Chernobyl."

"We must have defensive bioweapons," Ben said. "Why can't we use them to counteract this attack?"

"For one thing," Lessing said, "since we don't know

for certain what kinds of chemicals will be used, we don't know what we would need to combat them. And even if we did, imagine if the White House was hit. The closest research labs we could turn to for help are at the Aberdeen Proving Ground and Fort Detrick. Presumably, they would both be decimated as soon as the toxins reached them through the air. There could be no one left there to implement defensive weapons—no one at all."

"Christ," one of the agents muttered.

"What about antidotes, then?" Ben asked.

"Unfortunately, there are so many new and more virulent strains being found, it's a race to keep up. And due to budget cuts—" he swore under his breath "—well, I won't get into that."

"Are there other agencies helping?" Ben asked. "The CIA?"

"We've had no luck finding Pat Devlin, either," Kris Kelley said. "We've been working on this since the chatter first began, three months ago."

He looked at her curiously. "You're CIA?"

"You must have heard we have to work hand in glove with other agencies now," she said with a shrug and a slight hint of irony. "I was sent here to share."

"How about sharing this, then?" Ben said. "It's not exactly a secret that there are labs in the U.S. still researching *offensive* bioweapons, despite the ban against that kind of research in 1969. So how come we can't use whatever they've come up with to fight this attack?"

Kris looked surprised at his knowledge. But she nodded and stood again. "It's true that there are, shall we say…*rumors*…that such banned research is still going on. Trying to prove it is something else."

"But surely," Ben said, "armed with this information of an impending attack, you can go to the top—to the president, if necessary—and get all the help you need to prevent it."

"Because we're CIA?" Kris's smile was grim. "Who at the top is going to admit, even to us, that they know anything about covert labs in our country producing banned biowarfare weapons?"

"And even if they were to admit it," Lessing said, "how could we possibly use such weapons? They would have the same effect of obliterating half the world, if not more. Do we really want that? It would be Hiroshima a thousand times over."

He shook his head. "No. Our *only* move is to find Pat Devlin. Without the kind of Armageddon bomb he's building for them, The Candlelights would have to scrap this attack."

He shrugged and looked tired. "At least for now. As far as the future is concerned? Well, we must assume there are younger, newer, perhaps even smarter Pat Devlins coming up in the world…and that our enemies will eventually find them."

8

A heavy silence fell in the Carmel police station conference room as some of the agents stared into space or sipped from their water glasses. One had his chin on tented fingers, eyes closed and lips moving silently. Another shook his head back and forth slowly, as if to displace the scene his imagination had conjured up with something better…standing on a dock on a summer day with a fishing rod, perhaps.

"Okay," Lessing said crisply, corralling their thoughts. "Everyone please get on with the assignments we talked about earlier. Chief Schaeffer? May I see you in your office, please?"

"Of course." Ben led the way, and noted that Kris Kelley was coming, too.

When they were all sitting, Ben behind his desk and the two agents in visitors' chairs, Lessing said, "We need to talk about your friend, Abby Northrup, and her connection with Alicia Gerard."

"What about it?" Ben said.

"Well, as you've just heard, we need to catch up to

Alicia Gerard, and quickly. We may not have found her at the Prayer House earlier, but I think we all know that she was there. She may have left before we got there, but she was there."

"I don't see why you think—"

"Abby Northrup knows more than she was willing to tell us," Kris Kelley interposed.

"Maybe, maybe not," Ben answered. "But get to the point. What do you want to do?"

"Bring her in, question her officially," Lessing said.

Ben shook his head. "Won't do any good. Her guard'll be up and she won't tell us a thing."

"Aiding and abetting a terrorist—" Lessing began.

"Even if she did help Alicia Gerard," Ben said evenly, "nothing you've said proves that Alicia herself is a terrorist."

"We don't know for certain, though, do we?"

"I know Abby," Ben said. "She would never help someone accused of murder, let alone of terrorism."

"Oh, for heaven's sake, what's your problem?" Kris said, clearly exasperated. "Aside from the fact that you're sleeping with her."

"Kris," Lessing said warningly.

She shot him a cold glance. "I just meant that if he's going to work with us, he needs to keep an open mind."

"My mind is wide open," Ben said angrily, "and whether or not I'm sleeping with Abby Northrup has nothing to do with this case."

"Then what *is* the problem?" Lessing asked. "Are

you saying you've changed your mind about cooperating with us?"

Ben sighed. "No. But it's complicated. When I met Abby a few years ago, she was going through a bad time. Her husband—" He broke off. "Never mind that. Abby swore never to divulge anything about the women and children that come to her for help, and I'm sure that includes Alicia Gerard. For Abby, it's a vow as sacred as any those nuns take. In fact, sometimes I think…"

"You think what?"

He sighed again and rubbed his face wearily. "I don't know."

Lessing looked at Kris. "I'd like you to see what Gerry Gerard's up to these days. You've met him, haven't you?"

Kris hesitated a moment. "Yes. Once."

"Seems like that was before you were CIA. You did some bodyguard work, right?"

"For a year or so," Kris said. "I only worked for Gerard once. I doubt he'd remember me."

"Still, you must have done a workup on him—his habits, personality, local haunts, friends, all that."

"I did, but I don't have access to it anymore. I worked for a private company then. My files are their property now."

"A & S Investigations, if I remember from your profile," Lessing said. "I'm sure once they know your position now, they'll hand over anything you need."

"But—"

"Let me know if you have any problems," Lessing said, ending the conversation. He yawned and glanced at his watch. "Hard to believe, but it's nearly eight in the morning, and none of us had dinner last night. I think we should break and go eat."

"You and the others go," Kris said, not meeting his eyes. "I'll stay here in case anything comes in. I'll call you on your cell if I get any news."

"Okay. Can we bring you something?"

"No," she said flatly.

Lessing went back into the meeting room. When he was gone, Kris put her head in her hands and groaned. "I'm so hungry I could eat my foot."

"Why didn't you let him bring you something?" Ben asked.

She scowled. "Have you ever had a meal with a bunch of FBI agents? They can talk for hours about the case they're on, and anything they brought me would be cold and revolting by the time they got back."

Ben smiled. "Well, there are some frozen breakfasts in our dining room. Ham-and-cheese pockets, and there should be fresh coffee in there by now."

"Sounds fantastic." Kris stood, then hesitated. "Are you coming?"

"Sure," Ben said, though the last thing he thought he should do was spend any more time with this woman.

After a quick meal and several cups of coffee, the tension between Ben and Kris had abated somewhat. She sat across from him at the utilitarian metal table. "You guys call this a dining room?" she said, looking around at the small, simple quarters.

"Anything that's got food and coffee rates as a dining room for a cop," he countered. "By the way, what was all that about Gerard? It sounded like the last thing you wanted was to be assigned to him."

"Gerry Gerard's an asshole," she said. "Plain and simple."

"That's not what I've heard about him," Ben said. "If you believe the media, he's a saint—and he's about to be crowned president of the greatest country on earth."

"Yeah, well, he's not campaigning yet, is he? You know what happens during campaigns."

"You mean all the dirty little secrets come out?"

"And the next thing you hear is that they've decided not to run because they want to spend more time with their families." Kris's laugh was short.

"Wow. Is this bitterness all personal, or do you think he could be involved in this upcoming attack?"

"Oh, I doubt he'd be in on it. It wouldn't benefit him to destroy half the country. Look, what do you say we talk about you for a while?"

Ben sighed. "Okay, but I warn you, it won't be all that interesting."

"I don't know about that. You like your job here?"

He shrugged. "It's okay. Not as much to do as in the city."

"You worked in San Francisco before this, right?"

"So you've done your homework," he said with a flicker of irritation. "What about it?"

"Well, you seem overqualified to be a police chief in a small town like this."

His eyes narrowed. "Are you flattering me, or is that a criticism?"

"Neither. Just making a statement that should be obvious to anyone who's met you."

"Right." He stared tiredly at the cold dregs in his coffee cup. Funny how weary he'd been lately. Other than the moments he spent with Abby, his life seemed dull and gray. Boring. He felt as if he could sleep a whole week and not even wake up for food.

"You were talking before," Kris said, "about Abby Northrup taking a vow to help abused women and children. Did you mean that? A vow?"

"I talk too much," he said.

"No, really. I'd just like to know more about her. There's no hidden agenda."

He thought a moment then said, "I don't suppose Abby ever thought of it as taking a vow. But in her heart?" He smiled. "Sometimes I wonder if maybe in her heart Abby's as much of a nun as the sisters are."

Kris hooted. "That must make for tons of fun in bed."

Ben flushed. "That's not what I meant," he snapped. "Besides, I shouldn't have told you what I did. In fact, I don't want to talk to you about Abby at all. So drop it."

Kris studied him, her light blue eyes barely visible under blond bangs that kept falling over her face. Ben watched as she pushed them back, and wondered if she was flirting with him. A lot of women toyed with their hair as a sign of flirtation, he'd noticed. And a lot of the time it worked. Even he couldn't help the tiny little squiggle he felt in his belly.

"Okay," Kris said. "We won't talk about your lady love. But I'm sure as hell going to talk *to* her. And she'd better have answers."

"I said it before and I'm saying it now, Kris. That's not the way to handle Abby. It's all wrong."

"So, what would you suggest?" she asked, arching a brow. "How would you handle her?"

Ben thought for a moment. "I'll go out there and talk to her. She'll be curious. She'll want to know what's going on, what we're doing and why we want Alicia Gerard."

"And you can't tell her a thing, remember? Lessing as much as swore you to secrecy, so you can't tell her the truth—not a word of what you've learned here. What's left to say?"

"I'll decide that when the time comes," Ben said firmly. "And by the way, I don't have to answer to you. Don't forget that."

Kris opened her mouth for a sharp retort, but seemed to think better of it. "Cooperation, Chief Schaeffer," she said softly. "That's what it's all about these days. You think I like being here? I've got a seven-year-old son at home, and I've hardly seen him in three months. Ever since the 9/11 hearings, you know, they throw us out here to do any number of things we never had to do before. Holding the hand of a small-town cop is just one more humiliation."

Ben stared, his face burning with anger at the insult.

"If the FBI and the CIA hadn't let Alicia Gerard's parents slip through their net in the first place, this is one small-town cop who could be living a much more peaceful life right now. So thanks a lot for bringing trouble to my town. My *small* town," he amended.

Instead of responding, Kris looked at her watch. "Nine o'clock. I'm expecting—"

Her cell phone rang. Looking at the caller ID, she answered it informally. "Hi. How's it going? You did? McGuire, you're a champ! What time? Okay, I'll be there."

Hanging up, she turned to Ben. "There's something I have to do."

"No problem. I'll go out to the Prayer House," he said, sweeping the crumbs from his breakfast into his hand, then dumping them into a trash bin.

"No, wait," Kris said. "I may need some help with this. Can you stay? We can go out to the Prayer House together. Later."

He hesitated, but curiosity got the better of him. If this woman was going to be doing *anything* in his town, he'd better know what it was.

9

The Monterey airport was less than fifteen minutes from Carmel, and traffic was light. Alicia Gerard glanced at her watch and saw that it was barely eleven o'clock. She had plenty of time. Stepping out of the cab in front of the airport entrance, she strolled inside as if she hadn't a care in the world. It wasn't the first time she'd worn the black wig and dark red lipstick, and she was finally becoming used to it. In fact, she almost enjoyed it. In this disguise she could pretend to be anything. Anyone.

For the first few minutes she simply walked around the waiting area, seemingly looking at the boards with arrival and departure times. In reality, she was looking for someone—or several someones—unknown to her, but special.

After a while, she went into the women's restroom and stood at a sink, blotting her face with a damp paper towel and combing her hair.

A woman's voice issued from one of the cubicles, quietly reprimanding children who were in there with her. *Two children,* Alicia thought. *I can see their feet.* She smiled at her reflection in the mirror. No problem, then. There almost never was.

When the woman came out, each hand was holding on to a small child. One, a girl, looked to be about six. The other, a boy, was probably closer to seven.

Walking over to the sink, she said, "Billy, wash your hands. You, too, Lizzy. Here, let me get the soap for you."

She stole a glance at herself in the mirror but only shook her disheveled hair off her forehead and sighed as she dried the little girl's hands with a towel.

Alicia met the young woman's eyes in the mirror and smiled. "It's so hard to travel with little ones," she said sympathetically.

The woman rolled her eyes. "Tell me about it. Billy! Get back here!"

Quick as a flash, the little boy began turning on water faucets along the row of sinks.

"Oh, for heaven's sake, Billy, stop that! Stop it right now!"

She went after him, pulling the little girl along by the hand. When she caught up with Billy, she said in an angry undertone, "Do you want to be spanked? *Do you?*"

The boy grinned and looked as if he didn't much care. "You're not the boss of me," he said rebelliously.

How many times did I hear that from Jancy? Alicia asked herself, half smiling.

"Stay right here," his mother said. "Don't move an inch. I mean it! And hang on to your little sister."

When it looked as if he might actually mind her, she started at the first sink, turning off the faucets.

"Let me do that for you," Alicia said.

"Thanks, but—"

"You've got your hands full," Alicia insisted as she began to move down the line of sinks. "It won't take me a moment."

The woman sighed, smiled and took Billy's hand in a firm grip again. "Okay. Thanks. He's not always like this. Honest."

"He's probably excited about flying," Alicia said. "My kids were always a handful in airports. You get used to it after a while."

"Oh, they're not mine," the woman said. "I'm their aunt. And I don't think I'll ever get used to it! How many kids do you have?"

"Five," Alicia lied. "At last count, anyway."

She laughed and the woman did, too.

"I'm Jennifer Barber," the woman said. "And I'd shake your hand, but I'd have to let go of this human cyclone."

"God, no, don't do that!" Alicia said.

Both women laughed again.

"I'm sure glad we ran into each other," Jennifer said. "It's like…fate or something, you showing up just now." Suddenly, her eyes welled with tears.

"Oh, please, don't cry," Alicia said kindly. "Billy's not so bad. You should have seen my Kenny at that age."

"It's not that," the young woman said. "It's my dad.

He died yesterday, and I'm flying up to San Francisco for the funeral. My mom and sister completely fell apart, and I've had to take care of everything, including the kids. I've been so strung out, I guess I haven't been handling things very well. So I really appreciate you helping me out."

"It's nothing, really," Alicia said. "And I'm so sorry about your father."

She genuinely *was* sorry—sorry for this poor woman on the way to bury her father, and with all these burdens to bear.

But to be honest, Alicia was relieved, as well, knowing this could only help her own cause. Jennifer Barber needed a friend—and the minute she'd seen the woman, that was precisely what Alicia had counted on.

Sometimes it was an elderly lady, weighed down by too many packages, and sometimes it was a teenager with too many electronic gadgets, or a young mother carrying a baby—anyone, really, that she could attach herself to so that no one who might be watching for a woman alone would suspect her.

This was the way she'd been traveling for years, at least on these missions, and so far there had always been someone needing help or simply a companion. People were so isolated from other people these days, and airports seemed to bring out instant connections between strangers—connections that were over the minute the plane hit the tarmac.

"Tell you what," she said. "Let's see if we can get seats together, and I'll help you with the kids. I know it's only a forty-five-minute hop to San Francisco, but it'll give you a little bit of a breather. You'll feel so much better when you get there."

Jennifer gave her a shaky smile and said, "That is so good of you. I can't thank you enough."

"Not at all," Alicia said, taking Lizzy and Billy's hands as all four of them walked to the gate. "It'll be just like when my own kids were little. Believe it or not, you'll be missing all this some day."

While they waited for the plane to take off, Alicia held Billy on her lap so he could watch the baggage handlers out the window. Lizzy was nearly asleep on her aunt's lap. She held a little brown stuffed dog named Cody close to her cheek.

"Do you travel a lot?" Jennifer asked Alicia.

"Occasionally," Alicia said. "Not as much as I used to."

"You know, I don't think I even know your name," the young woman said.

"Oh, sorry! It's Faith. Faith N. Moore, believe it or not."

Jennifer smiled. "It sounds like 'faith in more.' Is that what your parents had in mind when they named you?"

"I'm not really sure. Come to think of it, I never asked."

"Oh. Sorry. They're gone?"

Alicia smiled but gave her a questioning look.

"I just meant," Jennifer explained, "that you said you never asked…as if maybe they had died."

"Oh! Where in the world is my mind these days?" Alicia said. "No, they're alive. They travel a lot, so I don't see them much, that's all." She smiled again. "Maybe I should get them to help me with a genealogy chart next time they're home."

"My sister does that," Jennifer said. "It's really a great thing to do for a family. Are you all from around here?"

"No," Alicia said. "I grew up in Kansas."

"Kansas! Wow! How on earth did you ever end up out here?"

Now that she'd had a moment to relax and settle in, Alicia realized that it might be best to turn the conversation around.

"Believe me, it's a very boring story," she said. "Tell me about you. Do you live in Monterey County?"

"Lord, no, but I sure wish I did. We're from Fresno, and my husband and I brought my sister's kids here to give her some time off. He's at a medical convention at the Doubletree, and we thought we could roam around the marina, drive into Carmel and go to the beach…things like that."

She sighed. "I guess vacations aren't in the cards this year. David had already committed himself to being a speaker, so he had to stay behind when I heard about my dad. And of course, I couldn't leave the kids with him."

"That's too bad," Alicia said. The plane was revving for takeoff, and the flight attendant came by to tell them the children would have to take their seats. Alicia lifted

Billy over the back of the seat in front of her and buckled him in.

"Hey, Billy," she groaned as her arms strained, "you're a big boy!"

Jennifer laughed and stepped out into the aisle to put Lizzy into the seat next to him. "He's grown a full three inches this year, and I don't know how many pounds!"

The two women talked between themselves during the short flight, and when they were over San Francisco, Alicia nudged Billy from behind and said, "Look! That's the city, the one where you're going."

"It's all foggy," Billy complained.

She laughed. "You're right, it is. But, look there—see the Golden Gate Bridge? It's just peeking up over the fog."

"Why do they call it golden when it's orange?" he asked.

Alicia looked across to Jennifer and rolled her eyes. "I'd like a dime for every time someone's asked that question." But to Billy, she said, "Maybe they thought people would think of it as the doorway to a golden life."

"Yeah, that'll happen," Jennifer said in a tired voice.

Alicia touched her hand. "Just hang in. You never know what the future might bring."

10

"It's me," Agent Kris Kelley said into her cell phone at the San Francisco airport. "She's gone. It's safe to come out now."

Arnie Pinnero, Ben's partner before he'd become chief of police, came out of the airport men's room and crossed over to them quickly. The short, skinny man was dressed in scruffy jeans, a leather jacket over a rumpled white T-shirt, and had an Oakland A's baseball cap pulled down over his eyes. Kris remembered that he'd been called to come to the station immediately on his day off, and this was the way he'd shown up—as if he'd just crawled out of bed. She couldn't possibly fault him for that, though. He, and Ben, too, had been an enormous help with this sting.

"Daddy!" Billy cried, jumping into his father's arms. Arnie hugged him and swooped up Lizzy at the same time.

"Hey, you guys! How 'zit goin'? Were you good for Aunt Kris?" His tone became comically pleading. "*Please* tell me you were good."

Billy giggled. "We were. We had fun on the plane, too, and there was this lady that played with us, so Kris—"

"*Aunt* Kris," Arnie admonished. "Remember, you call grown-ups *aunt* and *uncle,* even when they're not related. It's more polite."

He exchanged glances with Kris.

"They were great," she said. "When did you get here from Carmel?"

"Twenty minutes ago. I caught a break with the traffic." He grinned. "Well, the flashing red lights on the roof may have helped a little. How did it go with the target?"

"Pretty good. I'm sure she didn't suspect me at all, not with your kids in tow. Best cover I've ever had."

"Great. You can babysit, you know—anytime. But back to Alicia. Did you get anything out of her on the plane?"

"I think I picked up a thing or two of value, but I need to brief Agent Lessing on it first. Oh, and I did see which flight she got on from here."

"She didn't see you watching her board? Even with Billy and Lizzy?"

"Let me tell you something, Arnie. Your kids are the best little detectives I know. They spotted Alicia boarding that plane to Phoenix even before I did."

"Geez. It's that Harry Potter kid, and those movies," Arnie said, shaking his head. "Ever since their mom passed, they do that sort of thing."

"What sort of thing?" Kris asked.

"Oh, you know…follow people around, sneak up on them, lie about who they are. Next thing I know they'll be whipping up potions in the basement."

"Maybe they're just trying to be more like their dad," Kris suggested, smiling.

"You think?"

"That would be my guess."

"Hey, you're not a shrink, are you?"

"No, Arnie, I'm just CIA. It's our job to figure out people."

They began walking down the concourse toward the parking garage, Kris with Billy firmly in hand and Arnie carrying Lizzy.

"I know you told us that Gerard usually tries to blend in with a family, or some needy person," Arnie said. "But what did she use for a driver's license? She'd need that to get through the gate."

"She always carries fake ID, and some sort of disguise to match it. Lucky for me—and Agent McGuire, of course, who first spotted her at the airport in Monteray—we've seen her in this particular disguise before."

They stepped into the elevator to the parking garage, and Kris said, "It's funny, but in the last three months that I've been watching her, I never actually approached her the way I did today. I get the feeling she's a nice person."

"With a father who blows up schoolkids?" Arnie scoffed. "She'd have to have grown up in a cabbage patch."

"All I know is, she had a thirty-minute wait for the plane to Phoenix, and she offered to walk me to my car to help with the kids."

"I didn't need any help, though," Billy said, puffing out his chest.

"I'll bet you didn't, scout," Arnie said, rubbing his son's head. His expression changed to worry. "Were they really all right?"

"Angels," Kris said. "I've got a seven-year-old son at home here in San Francisco, so kids that age don't scare me. Teenagers, now—" She laughed, but then sobered. "I sure do miss Danny, though. I haven't seen him more than three times in the past month."

"Yeah, Ben told me something about that. It must be hard."

She nodded. "You're lucky to have a job that doesn't take you traveling all over."

"Don't think I don't know it," Arnie said. "But, these two rug rats? I wasn't too sure about lending them out when Ben suggested it, but I've got to admit I'm impressed. Don't know if I'd want them to do this all the time, though. They might end up being James and Janey Bond."

"Actually, I kind of see Billy as a plumber," Kris said.

"Yeah?"

She didn't elaborate. They walked through the mechanical doors to the outside, and Ben was standing there at the curb by a black limousine.

Kris walked over to it and said, "Something I don't

know? You were elected mayor of San Francisco in the past few hours?"

He laughed. "Not mayor, but yes, there is something you don't know."

He opened the door and waved her into the back seat. She paused, looking back at Arnie and the kids.

"Go ahead," Arnie said. "We'll be right behind you."

"Bye, Auntie Kris," Billy said, waving.

"Bye, I guess…" Kris said hesitantly. She stepped into the limo.

"Mommy!" A jumble of arms, legs and kisses smothered her in the seat.

"Danny! How on earth?" She hugged her son till he yelped and said, "Too hard!" Holding him back a few inches, she looked into his eyes. They were bright blue and dancing, the way his eyes always did. She'd almost never seen her son without a smile. And the day he was born, she had vowed that she never would.

"I can't believe you're here! Ben?"

He was still standing at the open door. "We all thought you guys needed a little reunion," he said.

"All?"

"Lessing, some of the other agents, me, Arnie… you've been on this case a long time."

Tears filled her eyes as she held Danny close to her. Then worry settled in. "How did you get him to come with you? I've left strict orders with the nanny—"

"Let's just say Lessing worked it out," Ben said. "And his nanny's right here." He pointed to the front passenger's seat. "Sara, right?"

The young woman turned her head and smiled nervously. "I hope it's all right, Ms. Kelley. I mean, they really were the FBI, I checked every single one of their IDs with the San Francisco office, and they said I could come along—"

Kris still wasn't sure. Danny's safety was one thing she'd always had to worry about. Finally she said, "It's okay, I guess. *This* time. But, Sara—"

"Mommy, aren't you glad to see me?" Danny piped up.

Kris broke off and hugged her son again, instead of threatening Sara with boiling oil. The nanny had never let her down yet, and Kris saw no reason to question Sara's decision this time.

"You bet I'm glad, little bug." She looked at Ben. "Now what?"

"I have to drive the limo back to my friend in Monterey," Ben said. "You and Danny can have a couple hours to visit, and Sara will be right up front here with me. When we get to Monterey, she and Danny will take a plane back here to San Francisco. Okay?"

"More than okay," Kris said, sighing and relaxing at last.

The next two hours were the best she'd had in months. Kris wondered if she should ask for a transfer to the San Francisco office when all this was over. Some sort of desk job, maybe, nine to five. That way she could be with Danny every night and on weekends, too. The years were slipping by too quickly, and she didn't even know how or when he'd gotten to be seven. It seemed as if it were just yesterday when she'd held him in her arms, a newborn, and thought how much his father was missing. Not that he could ever—

"Mommy, are you listening? I drew this picture for you. See, it's you up in an airplane, and I'm standing down here waving at you!"

It was all Kris could do to keep from crying. "It's a beautiful picture," she said. "Maybe you'll be an artist when you grow up."

Please, God, let him grow up. Let him grow up happy and strong…with me.

"Hey," she said, "do you remember that game we used to play with our fingers?"

They were in Monterey all too soon, and she found herself waving goodbye to Sara and Danny at the airport. An hour later she was back in the Carmel police station at the conference table, surrounded by the other agents, Lessing and Ben. There was some good-natured teasing about her "little vacation," not to mention the limo, which she took in stride before giving her report about the meeting with Alicia Gerard at the airport and on the plane.

"I'm sure she didn't know who I was, but even so, she wasn't very forthcoming. I'm assuming she's had to play her cards close to the vest all her life, and she either can't break the habit or doesn't dare, even now. I did figure out a few things from talking with her, though."

Kris went on to detail them. "For one thing, she genuinely likes kids. I think she would do anything she had to to protect her daughter. Which makes it all the more meaningful that she's taken off without Jancy and left her at the Prayer House—if, in fact, that's where she is. I don't think Alicia Gerard would do that just to run from a murder rap. Also, the woman has guts and smarts to go through with such an elaborate disguise and act, just to get out of town. We know she's done it many times over. As for her visit to Carmel, I suspect she was spending a few much-needed days with Jancy, and was taken by surprise by the murder of the reporter at the Highlands Inn. I'd say she didn't kill him, but she does have information that she has to get to someone, and quickly. I'm betting that someone is her father, Pat Devlin."

"Which at least confirms that we're on the right track," Lessing said.

"Right. And the most important thing is that we know now where Alicia's going—Phoenix, Arizona. Our agent down there will pick up Alicia's trail from the airport when she deplanes, and we'll probably find that she's meeting Pat and Bridget Devlin there."

Kris looked around the table, and then at Lessing. "So…if we're all in agreement on this, I'll just have to get myself a little ticket to Arizona. It's time we turned up the heat."

Alicia Gerard left the plane in Phoenix at three that afternoon. By three-fifteen, she had boarded a privately owned Piper Cherokee. Within minutes the small plane took off, flying north to Las Vegas. At the airport there, an exhausted Alicia Gerard met with a woman and borrowed a car to drive to Utah. In Utah, she boarded another private plane for Houston, Texas. By midnight she was in her parents' home in Galveston, as certain as she could be that no one had followed her.

It was the way she'd been taught, growing up. She never knew why, back then, just that someone was after them. She was told that she would always have to be both fast and wise.

It was wise, she thought, to have realized that the woman on the plane with her fake kids was the one who'd been following her the past few months. She didn't know how she knew, but somehow she was sure of it.

"I'm here, Daddy," she said as she sat with her father and mother at the Devlin house in Galveston. "Tell me what you need me to do."

11

Abby spent that morning on the phone calling mutual friends of hers and Alicia's, asking as casually as possible if anyone knew where she could reach Alicia. Some were immediately concerned, as if they knew something Abby didn't know. One, Polly Greenway, asked if she'd disappeared off the face of the earth.

"No, I just need to reach her," Abby said. "Why do you ask?"

"No real reason," Polly said. "It's just that she hasn't returned my calls in the past few weeks. That was my feeble attempt at being funny."

"Well, I hear she's been traveling a lot. I thought you might know if she's giving a speech somewhere."

"No, sorry. If I hear from her, I'll ask her to call you," Polly said.

Abby set the phone down, hot and discouraged. When the doorbell rang she ignored it, thinking Helen would get it. The ring became insistent, though. Irritated, she went to the door herself.

"Okay if we come in?" Ben asked.

Next to him stood the FBI woman—Grace? Abby couldn't remember. She stepped aside, though not happily. "Sure."

In the reception room, Ben sat on the sofa's edge, looking awkward and embarrassed, while the FBI agent continued to stand, declining a seat in the large armchair. Her arms were crossed in an aggressive posture.

Ben, wishing he hadn't had to bring Kris Kelley along, said, "We need to talk to you about Alicia Gerard."

"Alicia?" Abby said carefully. Allie's name was never mentioned the night before. Was she supposed to admit, now, that Alicia and Jancy had been here?

Come to think of it, where was Jancy? She'd been helping Sister Benicia make pies. *Don't let her come in here, please.*

"We know she's here, Abby," Ben said. "Look, I'm sorry, but Alicia Gerard is wanted for murder. You've got to turn her in."

Abby widened her eyes. "You think Alicia Gerard is here? And that she's a murderer?" Abby laughed softly. "That must mean you think I'm harboring a criminal."

"I didn't say that."

"It's exactly what you said. That Alicia Gerard is here and she's wanted for murder."

"Look, Abby. It's pretty obvious it was Alicia and her daughter arriving here last night when I was leaving. Please don't try to deny it."

"I don't know what else to do," Abby said, meeting his eyes. "She really isn't here."

Ben studied her.

"Lessing was right," Kris said irritably. "She's not going to tell us anything. We need to take her—"

Ben shook his head. "I've known Abby a long time, and I'm not so sure now. I think she's telling the truth."

"And I think you're being led by your pr—"

"That's enough," Ben said angrily.

Kris sighed and turned to Abby. "Let's say she really isn't here. You must know where we can find her, at least."

"Abby," Ben said, "there's more to this than murder." He looked at the FBI woman.

"It's true," she confirmed, sighing. "This is a matter of national security now. It's also a matter of the utmost urgency."

"National security?" Abby said. "What's going on?" *What has Alicia gotten herself into? In fact, what has she gotten* me *into?*

"I'm sorry," Ben said. He flicked a look at Kris. "We…well, we aren't at liberty to discuss it further."

"*We?* You and Grace are working together now?"

"My name's Kris," the agent said in a neutral tone. "Kris with a *K*. Last name's Kelley."

Abby folded her arms. "Well, Kris with a *K*, I don't remember inviting you here."

She knew that sounded churlish, but she couldn't help it. Ben had never come here before to grill her, in his job as a cop. He'd never sat in this reception room like this before, on the edge of the sofa, and not even smiling, as if he were a stranger.

More important, until last night he'd never had an FBI agent tagging along with him on any cases. Things were changing too swiftly, and she didn't like the way they were heading.

It might have been her instinct to protect Alicia, no matter what, that made her dig in her heels. Or it might have been the sudden, swift feeling of betrayal. In either case, she couldn't hold back her anger.

"I told you last night that Alicia wasn't here," she snapped. "Take it or leave it. I have business to attend to."

She rose.

"Abby, you've got to cooperate," Ben said, rising, too. His whole demeanor was one of frustration and anger. "It won't go well for you if you don't."

"And what the hell does that mean?" Abby said, looking from one to the other.

"There are laws now," Kris said carefully, "that would support us if we were to take you into custody and hold you indefinitely. We wouldn't even need a warrant. As for this place—" she looked around "—we can search it again, you know, and when we're through with it, I guarantee it won't look quite so nice. Or peaceful."

Abby was outraged. They were talking about laws that had sprung up since 9/11, many of which she considered unconstitutional. Anyone—the mothers she worked with, or even the woman or man next door—could be held without benefit of counsel, and without anyone even knowing where they were. Mention the word *terrorist* one too many times in an e-mail, and you never knew when the Men in Black might show up at your door.

Which, she knew, was probably an exaggeration, but not far enough from the truth for her liking.

She faced Ben angrily. "You would do this to me?"

"I wouldn't want to, Abby, you know that. But it's urgent that we find Alicia. We think she—"

"We think she can tell us something more," Kris interrupted, cutting him off, "about the murder at the Highlands. Let's say she didn't do it, for instance. She might have seen something that can lead us to the killer."

"So now there may be a *different* killer," Abby said disdainfully. "And all you want to do is bring Alicia in and talk to her, so she can help you out with that. Right?"

"Yes—" Kris began.

"No—" Ben said at the same time.

The agent gave him a withering look.

"Kris is right," he amended. "That's all we want from Alicia. You can tell her it's safe to come to the station and turn herself in. She doesn't have to hide out here."

"I told you, *she isn't here*," Abby said angrily. "And *I*, at least, am not *lying*."

"So, you're going to make this hard on yourself," Kris Kelley said. "Damn, Abby, I thought you were smarter than that."

"Just smart enough, *Grace*, to know when I'm being

threatened by a government agent—who, since I'm a taxpayer, is on my payroll."

Kris smiled, but her blue eyes were hard as glass. "I just think you should know the situation."

"But I *don't* actually know the situation, do I? All I know is that you're trying to trick me into turning in a friend for a murder I don't believe she committed, so that you can arrest her. Oh, and I do know one other thing—that she damned well *isn't here.*"

Abby turned toward the door. "Now, either arrest me or get the hell out."

"Kris," Ben said abruptly, "tell her."

"I don't have the authority—" she said with a warning look.

"Then I will."

"You can't do that, Ben! Let's go."

He ignored her. "Abby, please sit down."

"I'm fine standing," she said.

"Dammit, Abby!" He threw up his hands in irritation. "All right, then, stand."

She sat.

He groaned.

"I wash my hands of this, Chief Schaeffer," Kris Kelley said. "If this whole thing goes sour because of her—"

"It won't. Abby, listen. This has to be kept absolutely confidential. I know you can do that. But will you?"

"Go on," she said noncommittally.

Ben sighed. "Okay, here's the way it is. Kris isn't FBI, she's CIA. The agency and the bureau are working together, along with Homeland Security, to try to stop a major terrorist attack on the U.S."

"A terrorist attack," Abby said skeptically. "When? Where?"

"The when is a week from now. They don't know the where, and that's where Alicia Gerard comes in. They have good reason to believe that Alicia is connected to the people who are planning the attack. They need to question her—and fast."

Abby almost laughed, and would have, had the situation he put forth not been so serious.

"That's crazy," she said. "I've known Alicia for years, and I'd have known if she were involved in something like that."

Kris took an even more aggressive stance, her hands on her hips and her feet apart. "Did you know her parents came into this country illegally? Did you know that Alicia is illegal, as well?"

Abby felt a cold chill. "That's impossible," she said. "Allie's been married to H. P. Gerard for years. If that were true, every news agency in the world would have dug it up long ago."

"What Kris said is true," Ben told her. "Alicia's father has ties to the IRA, Abby. I'm not saying that Alicia's involved directly, but you know those little jaunts her press releases talk about—the ones where she's supposed to be talking to a group of librarians, say, in Winsocki? Half of them are canceled at the last minute. Do you know where Alicia goes instead?"

"There is no Winsocki," Abby said, thinking fast and

playing for time the way she often had when conducting a sticky interview as a journalist. "'Buckle down, Winsocki,' was a song in an old movie…with Lucille Ball, I think—"

"Abby, stop it! I know what you're doing. Just answer the question, please. Do you know were Alicia goes during those times?"

"I have no idea," she said after a moment. "But I suppose you're going to tell me."

"That's enough, Ben," Kris interrupted. "She obviously doesn't have any information, and the less she knows, the better."

"You mean the show is over?" Abby said. "And just when the plot was getting good."

But Ben went on. "People who have tried to reach Alicia Gerard during those times can't get through on her cell phone. And when they call her hotel, she isn't registered there. When she comes home she uses the excuse that she changed hotels and forgot to tell anyone."

Red flags went up. That was almost exactly what Jancy had told her. But how could Ben—or more accurately, the FBI and CIA—know about this? Hadn't they just begun to search for Alicia last night? After the Highlands Inn murder?

No. That was just their cover. The terrorism was the real story. How long had they actually been after Alicia?

She tried for more information. "I take it you got all this about Alicia's trips from her maid? Or someone else in the Gerard house?"

"Why would you say that?" Kris asked sharply.

"Because who else would know all that? And if that's the case, why haven't you had her followed long before this? Why wait until you have to go looking for her?"

Kris didn't answer, but her face turned a bright pink.

"Aah…" Abby said. "You have followed her. And I'll bet my next life that you've lost her every time. How impressive, *Grace*. Our Homeland Security millions at work."

"All right, that's it," Kris said sharply, turning to Ben. "Let's go."

Ben turned to Abby. "I wish you wouldn't do this, Ab."

"But I told you, I know nothing. Is this the part where you arrest me?"

"Let's *go*," Kris said again.

"I'll show you to the door," Abby said, feeling childish, but actually not all that bad. There was something about this woman that rubbed her the wrong way, and had from the first.

"Don't bother," Kris said angrily. "We wouldn't want to trouble you any further."

Ben followed her out of the room, and Abby watched through a window as they stepped off the adobe porch and walked down the drive to Ben's jeep.

Seeing the two of them working together like that caused a gulf in her heart that she couldn't explain. It was as if she were on one side of a wall now, with Ben on the other.

At least she still had her integrity. She hadn't betrayed Alicia the way Ben had betrayed her.

* * *

An hour later, Ben, Lessing and Kris sat huddled over a table at the Red Lion Tavern in Carmel, discussing the interview with Abby Northrup and whether they should go back to the Prayer House and threaten her with arrest again. If the three of them went, Lessing reasoned, and if they told her the rest—in particular, that Pat Devlin, who was making a doomsday bomb for the planned attack, was Alicia's father—she might listen more seriously and stop holding back what she knew.

They could, of course, search the Prayer House and grounds again, and more thoroughly, but with a building and property of that size, it would take a lot of people and time. Better if they could break Abby down instead.

What Ben, Lessing, and Kris didn't know was that even as they schemed and chowed down on thick, juicy hamburgers, Abby was well on her way to Las Vegas, Nevada.

She knew that the FBI and CIA, and maybe even Ben, would be hot on Alicia's heels—and that when they found her, Allie might disappear into the system for an unknown length of time. Abby couldn't let that happen. She didn't believe for a moment that her friend was connected to terrorists—or even that she'd killed that man at the Highlands. But there was certainly something odd about Allie's movements lately. And for Jancy's sake, if not for Allie's own, she had to find her.

If only there had been any word at all from Alicia—but there hadn't. All that she knew was what her P.I., Bobby, had told her—that Alicia had been spotted at the airport in San Francisco, boarding a plane to Phoenix. After that, he said, she had disappeared.

Abby had promised Jancy that everything would be all right, and she'd made a vow when she began her work with *Paseo* that she'd never break a promise to a child. The children who came to her were on the run as much as their moms. They had left their homes, their friends and everything they owned—toys, books, mementos…all the things that gave a child a sense of security. Even more, they'd been betrayed in the worst way, most of them by abusive fathers.

It was different with Jancy and Alicia, but in a way it was far more dreadful. What Jancy had seen in that hotel room would be with her all her life, and having her mother leave her afterward, the way Alicia had, would have totaled most girls her age. Jancy had taken it so bravely, it was all Abby could do not to gather her up in her arms and never let go.

But that instinct came largely out of her own grief, she knew, over never being able to have a child of her own. Because of this, she had learned to restrain herself with the children who came to her. Too much emotion coming from a stranger could be a scary thing for a kid in those circumstances.

That didn't mean she could just sit by and do nothing, however. And in this case, she knew something the authorities apparently did not—that Alicia had a close friend from childhood in Las Vegas, and that the two had been meeting three or four times a year for a long time.

Abby had never met the woman, but she knew her name—Tracy Marcetti—and her whimsical stage name—Willow Tree. The topless dancer had been dubbed Willow Tree by the men she entertained at the Roaring Buck Casino, men who swore she could bend better than any willow, given a pole to twist her lithe, nearly naked body around.

Alicia had told Abby about Willow a few years ago when they were drinking wine on the bayside deck of a Monterey restaurant, the hot sun and alcohol loosening their tongues. Afterward, a sober Alicia told Abby that she'd never mentioned Willow to anyone else at all, even her husband, Gerry. She swore Abby to secrecy, saying if the media ever got wind of her hanging out in Vegas with a topless dancer several times a year, they'd have a field day, and that could rub off on Gerry. But Willow had done her a very big favor once, and because of that the two women had bonded and become friends.

Abby never did find out what the favor was, but if anyone knew where Alicia was now, it just might be Willow Tree. And so, just hours after Ben and Kris Kelley's visit, leaving Jancy in Sister Helen's capable care, Abby was well on her way to Las Vegas.

The Roaring Buck Casino was on a side street, several blocks away from the Vegas strip. A molded horse's rear in bucking mode stuck out through the front window. The window glass was jagged, purposely designed to look as if the horse had bucked and crashed through it from the sidewalk. Upon entering, Abby saw that the horse's front end was low and in bucking position inside the window. The fake animal was old, dusty, and patrons had tossed their jackets over its head, as if they'd seen enough of the tattered steed.

The air was thick with smoke and the heavy odor of sweat. People were packed in shoulder to shoulder, blocking her view of the stage. But between the purple and pink lights and the patrons' cheers and hollers, it wasn't that difficult to know there was a show going on. Abby took a seat at the bar along the back wall and ordered a glass of Merlot. As the bartender slid it over to her, she said, "Thanks. Is that Willow up there on the stage? It's hard to see."

"Nah, Willow's on at ten."

Abby glanced at her watch, squinting to see the number in the dim light. "A half hour? Where is she now?"

The bartender looked her up and down. "That depends. What do you want with her?"

"We're old friends," Abby said, smiling and taking a sip of the wine. "I'm in town and I thought it might be nice to see her."

The bartender smoothed his jet-black curly hair and leaned on the bar. "Oh, yeah? Well, Willow doesn't see anybody before she goes on. How about you stay right here and wait. Have another glass of wine."

"Look—" Abby peered at the name tag on his white shirt. "Gary? I don't have much time. I just want to see Willow and say hi, that's all."

He looked her over again and said finally, "I'll ask her. What's your name?"

"Alicia," Abby said.

"Last name?"

She smiled. "Willow will know. I told you, we're old friends."

"We'll see about that. Wait here."

"Okay."

Abby watched him weave in and out of the crowded tables to a door at the side of the stage. She waited a few seconds, then followed him.

The door opened into a dark hallway filled with smoke and the smell of alcohol. At the far end, light fell across the floor from an open door. Voices were raised—a man's and a woman's. Abby walked toward them. Just as she reached the door, a woman with long, curly red hair, dressed in a gold thong and skimpy costume bra, ran out of the room and almost bumped into her.

"Sorry," she said automatically, pushing past Abby.

Abby grabbed her arm. "Hey, Willow. Going somewhere?" The woman was carrying a large tote bag and a jacket.

"What the—"

"That's her," Gary said from the doorway. "That's the one who wanted to see you."

"Who are you?" the woman asked in a low, frightened voice. She began to back away.

"I'm Abby. Sorry for the pretense, but Alicia's my friend. I was hoping you could tell me where she is."

"I don't know any Alicia—" She broke off and squinted, as if trying to see better in the dim light. "Abby? What's your last name?"

"Northrup. I live in Carmel, California, and I've known Alicia for years. She told me you were friends."

Willow turned to Gary, looking undecided. Finally she said, "It's okay, Gary. You can go."

She took Abby's arm and said, "Get inside." She half pushed her through the door.

Abby glanced around and saw that there were posters of Willow on three different walls. Letters and postcards addressed to her were Scotch-taped to a large mirror over a dressing table. Along one side of the room was a rack of costumes, some with feather boas, and some with men's ties around the same hangar. It didn't take much imagination to realize how they were used in Willow Tree's act.

"I'm curious," Abby said. "How did you know I wasn't Alicia?"

"What do you mean?"

"You were running. I think if you believed I was Alicia, you wouldn't run from her."

"I…" Willow turned to the mirror and began to check her makeup. "I guess I didn't think she'd come here."

"Then who did you think I was?"

Willow turned to Abby. "Look, I believe you're a friend of Alicia's, because she's mentioned you. But I've only got a few minutes. What do you want?"

"I need to find Alicia, and I'm pretty sure you know where she is."

The woman didn't answer.

Abby looked around the room. "According to Allie, you've been here a long time."

"Ten years," Willow said. "Ten very long years."

"Not as long as you and Allie have been friends, though."

Willow seemed to make a decision. Pulling out a straight, wooden chair, she said, "Here. We can talk while I finish getting ready."

Abby took a seat while Willow sat at her dressing table, touching up her makeup and hair.

"I have to go on in about ten minutes," Willow said, shooting a glance at Abby in the mirror, "so this will have to be quick. I don't know what I can tell you, anyway. I haven't seen Allie in ages."

"That's too bad," Abby said. "I was hoping to warn her."

"Warn her?" Willow said far too casually. She put her powder puff down, but not before Abby saw that her hand was shaking.

"She's in danger," Abby said. "But if you don't know where she is—" She stood.

Willow turned sharply. "Wait. Danger?"

"Of arrest," Abby said. "The FBI is looking for her."

"I...I didn't know. What did she do?"

"They say she committed a murder in Carmel. They came to me looking for her last night, and you're probably next."

Willow paled. "I don't see why they'd want *me*."

"If they discover your connection to Allie, they'll

want to question you about her whereabouts. In case they manage to force it out of you, I was hoping I could get to her first."

"But if I don't know anything…"

"I have a feeling that won't matter."

"What do you mean?"

"They could arrest you, try to make you talk."

"No way," Willow said firmly. "They can't just arrest people without some sort of evidence."

"The FBI," Abby said, "can arrest anybody these days. They can say you're involved in terrorist activities, for instance, and put you away without anyone even knowing. No lawyer, no bail, nothing."

"That's crazy!" Willow muttered.

"Tell it to the American Civil Liberties Union."

From Willow's expression, that threat, at least, had gotten to her.

"Look," Abby said. "You obviously know where Alicia is, and if I can see that, I'm sure the FBI will be able to. Why don't you just tell me, so I can get to her and warn her."

"But if we don't tell what we know, won't that make us accessories or something?"

"Not if they never find out," Abby said, shrugging.

Willow's mouth tightened. "I can't go to jail, Abby. You just don't know—"

She stopped abruptly as someone knocked on the door. "Three minutes, Willow!"

"I have to go," she said, pushing her vanity chair back and standing.

"Every minute counts, Willow. Tell me now, and when the FBI shows up, if you feel you need to tell them, fine. I'll at least get a head start on them."

The knock on the door came again. "Willow!"

She looked at Abby, then away, as if panicked and unsure. Finally she opened the middle drawer of her vanity and pulled a taped piece of paper off the bottom of the drawer.

"Allie gave me this phone number a couple years ago, just in case anything happened to Jancy and no one knew how to reach her. I was never to give this number to anyone, just call it myself in an emergency. I don't even know if it's still good."

She closed her eyes as if sending up a prayer. "Here, take it. That way, at least, nobody can find it if they do come here."

She grabbed a boa and ran out, a blur of copper hair and gold stiletto heels clattering across the wooden floor. There was nothing much between the hair and heels but a wisp of gold satin and sequins, a matter that obviously pleased the crowd as she reached the stage. Bluesy music began to play, a bass thumped in the age-old stripper rhythm and the shouts heated up.

Abby sat there a moment, staring at the piece of paper Willow had given her. Then she went to an old black pay phone in the hall and dialed "0" for an operator.

"I have an area code here." She read it aloud. "Can you tell me where it is?"

"Six-oh-one? That's Phoenix, Arizona," the operator said.

"Thank you." Abby hung up and dialed 411 for information. They gave her the number of an all-night car rental office in Vegas. She called it and confirmed that a car was available. Then she did something she almost never did. From her purse, she removed one of three sets of identification she always had on hand at the Prayer House—a fake driver's license and credit card, part of a stash she kept for women who were on the run. The money behind the credit cards came from a special fund she'd set up with her own money.

At the car rental office, she introduced herself as Katherine Gavney, handing over the driver's license and credit card in that name. Within minutes she had started on the drive south to Phoenix. Although Willow might be forced to tell the FBI that Alicia was in Phoenix, Abby had to try to get there first and make sure they never found her there.

Her mind was so intent on finding Alicia, she saw it too late—the coyote that crossed a few feet ahead of her in the road, causing her to swerve quickly to the side. The car went into sand, and the tires spun.

Oh, God, no. Not out here in the desert. Anything could happen to a woman here alone.

She pressed the accelerator again. When it didn't work, she stopped, knowing that if she did that much more, she'd just be digging a deeper hole.

Was that what she was doing? Digging a hole for herself that she'd never get out of?

Abby closed her eyes and breathed deeply until she was calm. *I know what to do for this. I've seen it in movies, if nothing else. All I need is a couple of boards....*

She reached into the glove compartment for the flashlight she'd made sure was in there before leaving the rental office, but when she flicked it on, the light was weak. Damn. She turned it off to save the batteries and slid out of the car, looking around. The night air was cold, and the stars in a pitch-black sky looked so close, she imagined she could almost reach up and grab one.

The reality, however, was that the only light down here was the narrow swath ahead of the car, where its headlights illuminated an empty expanse of sand. Everything else around her was black, and for a moment her head went all funny, the way it had on the hill in Carmel two years ago, where she'd almost died. Her bedroom in the Ocean Drive house slammed back into her mind, too— the body pounding into her, grinding, the naked hatred on the face above her, the terrible, terrible pain of the instrument that left her womb forever an empty void—

She grabbed hold of the car to steady herself. A noise sounded nearby, a crackle as of feet on hard rock. Her heart rose in her throat. She swung around toward the back of the car.

"Who's there?"

Nothing.

"Who is it?" she whispered, her voice failing her.

Something brushed across her feet, and she screamed. She spun around to the car door, ready to jump back in. Then, in the headlights, she saw the small desert animal skittering away.

My God, she thought, shaking and sitting back down on the car seat. I've been living in the Prayer House too long. All this while I've been thinking of myself as a relatively brave person, able to take care of myself no matter what. But the truth is, I've become a ninny. I've been hiding away in the Prayer House, afraid to face the real world. It's become my hideaway, my escape.

Think, Abby. You're in the middle of the desert and your car is stuck in the sand. Now, just what the hell are you going to do about that?

She got out again and turned the flashlight on, looking at the front tires as best she could in the weak beam of light. They weren't in too deep. And the tires were new, with good traction. There had to be something—

That was it. The rental car *was* new, and the rugs on the floorboards must be new, as well. The rubber that lined them hadn't been broken in yet, which would mean they were stiff.

She turned the flashlight off and set it on the front seat. Grabbing up all four carpets, she placed each one in front of a wheel. Climbing back into the car, she turned it on and pressed the accelerator again, holding her breath. After a couple of false starts, the car went rolling back onto the road.

Relief poured through her like a wave, leaving her limp now that the fear-induced adrenaline was gone. Abby whispered a prayer and thanked God, Goddess, her angels and even her old, abandoned saints for the news magazine show that had described the way auto carpets could be used for getting cars out of mud, ice and sand. *Thank you for keeping me safe.*

But then she remembered something Davis, her Kenpo instructor, had told her ages ago: that coyotes are known as tricksters, that they can take on different shapes, and are known to cause much trouble.

You need to be on constant guard, he had warned her, *after a coyote crosses your path.*

12

It was after nine o'clock and dark when Abby drove into Phoenix. She hadn't eaten since that morning at the Prayer House, except for a small snack of apples and cheese she'd bought at a service station along the road. Stopping at a retro diner connected to a motel, she slid into a booth and ordered a cheese and tomato sandwich, grilled.

"Anything to drink?" the waitress asked.

"Just water. Is there a pay phone here?"

"Down the other end by the restrooms," the waitress answered, nodding her head in that direction.

"Thanks."

While she waited for the food, Abby placed a call to Bobby.

"I'm here," she said. "Do you have an address for that phone number I called you about from Vegas?"

"Piece of cake," he said. "It's 13259 El Caballo. It's listed under a Eugene L. Davenport."

"Great. Thanks, Bobby. Call you later."

"Wait. You need anything else?"

"I'm not sure. I'll be in touch."

When the sandwich came she wolfed it down, left enough money on the table for it and the tip and gestured to the busy waitress that it was there. The woman nodded and smiled.

Back in her car, Abby stopped for gas again and bought a street map for Phoenix. Sitting behind the wheel with the map and overhead lights on, she didn't see the man watching her from a black car two parking spots away.

Less than a minute after she pulled out onto the highway, he was there behind her, leaving another car between them, sometimes two. When she turned onto El Caballo, he did, too, and parked even before she did— as if he already knew where she was going.

On El Caballo, Abby strained to see numbers on the houses. Some were set too far back from the road, but then in the next block numbers had been painted in white on the curbs. As her headlights struck each one in turn she could see that the one on her right was 13247, the next 13249. At 13259 she pulled to the curb and cut her engine and lights. For a moment, she sat there, looking around.

The property was entirely dark, but a pale reflection from a streetlight half a block down was enough to show her the outline of an older-style ranch home, with a swamp cooler on the roof. The other houses in the neighborhood looked new, and were all about a quarter acre apart. As Abby had passed them, she'd noted that most had cars in the drive and lights at the windows. This house was just the opposite. No sign of life at all.

She stepped out of the car and shut the door quietly. The scent of rotting cacti hit her like a club, making her stomach turn. The short, rancid cacti dotted the gravel lawn like so many forgotten dead bodies on a battlefield. Abby stood on the sidewalk and shivered.

She wondered if Bobby, who always got things right, had been given the wrong address. Or, more likely, Willow had deliberately given her the wrong phone number.

But Willow had said that she wasn't sure this number would still work. Had Alicia decided at some point not to trust Willow anymore? Had she changed the number, or moved and had this one disconnected?

That was, assuming the phone number was for a place Alicia owned, and not that of someone she'd known years before and no longer had any contact with.

Sighing, Abby walked up the concrete path to the front door. There was no porch, nothing but a concrete block for a step, and no doorbell. She knocked, and waited.

There were sounds inside that could have been someone tiptoeing across a room. Or rats. Large, noisy rats. Were they running for cover—or charging the door?

Oh, God, what am I doing here?

Just as she was about to leave, a floodlight came on above the door. It lit up the entire front yard, all the way to Abby's car.

"Who is it?" a woman's voice asked softly.

"I…it's Abby Northrup. I'm looking for a friend. Alicia? Is she here?"

There was a pause, then the door opened. The woman standing before Abby was dressed in denim shorts and a sleeveless white T. She had short dark hair, and no smile.

"What's this about?" she said crisply.

"I need to reach Alicia," Abby said, deliberately leaving out Alicia's last name again. No point, if this wasn't even the right place. "Someone said she might be here."

"I don't know anyone by that name. Alice?"

"Alicia," Abby corrected.

The woman shook her head. "Sorry, you've got the wrong house."

"Is this your phone number?" Abby asked, holding up the piece of paper Willow had given her.

The woman squinted at it and frowned. "No, it's not. Maybe it belonged to whoever lived here before."

The way she stood partially blocked Abby's sight into the room behind her. All she could see was that the room was dark, except for a flickering light that probably came from a television. She was almost certain she'd heard someone stifle a cough, though.

"Do you mind telling me how long you've been here?" Abby asked.

The woman began to shut the door. "Seven, eight years," she said. "Sorry, I've got to go."

"Just one more thing," Abby said quickly. She longed to stick her foot in the door like an old-time vacuum cleaner salesman.

"I've been traveling," she said with a slightly embarrassed laugh. "And you know how bad some gas station restrooms are. Could I possibly use your bathroom? I know it's an imposition, but—"

The woman shook her head and closed the door farther. "I'm sorry, but when I'm here alone I never let anyone in that I don't know."

"But—" Abby began.

"Sorry," the woman repeated. "There's a nice gas station just a few blocks away if you turn right from here. I have to go now."

She closed the door firmly, and Abby heard a lock slip into place, then another. The floodlights stayed on while she got into the rental car and turned right along the road. When she was just out of sight of the house, she pulled over to the curb.

There were no homes here, only palms that clattered and sighed in the dry breeze, and the everpresent cacti. When the glow from the floodlights at the house disappeared, Abby looked around quickly to make sure she was alone. No dogs, no people walking them....

Reaching onto the passenger's seat for the flashlight, she turned the switch on, but the batteries were now dead. She left her purse and stepped out of the car, locking it and heading back toward the house on foot. When she reached the driveway, she followed it to the rear. There could be a motion light back there, she knew, but it was a chance she had to take. There was someone else in that house, and it could be Alicia.

Or it could have been the woman's husband, watching television half-naked.

Abby's chuckle was soft and self-derogatory. There were any number of reasons the woman wouldn't want to let her in. Especially at this time of night. Still, Abby was certain she'd lied when she'd said she was alone.

Halfway to the back of the house, she stepped off the paved driveway and into gravel. Almost immediately, she stumbled over something in the dark. It was hard, and large enough to land her on her hands and knees. Swearing to herself, she stayed like that for several seconds, letting her eyes adjust more to the night.

Finally, she saw what she'd tripped over—a knee-high rock about three feet wide. The entire yard was strewn with rocks of all shapes and sizes, as if they'd been scooped off a mountain by a giant hand and thrown down here helter-skelter.

Now that she could see where she was going, she picked her way carefully to a window halfway up the outside wall. It was too high to see through, but there was a dim light on inside. Abby went back to a rock about two feet high and carried it over to the window, her back straining and arms shaking from the weight of it. The worst part was setting it down carefully, without a thud.

She had just stepped up onto the rock when the blow came. Her legs went weak and she sank to the ground. Something sticky covered her mouth and kept her from screaming. Then her head and face were covered with something rough that smelled like burlap. Her next thought was, *I can't see. I can't see.*

"Damned fool," she heard. "It's about time you learned your lesson."

Hands snaked around her ankles, pulling her across the rough terrain. Her back screamed in silent, excruciating pain as rocks and stones pulled her shirt up and scraped over her flesh.

I know that voice, Abby thought. *Who is it? I know that voice.*

Then she was gone.

13

Boiling sun scorched her left arm. The air was so hot and thick she could barely breathe. A heavy weight pressed down on her chest and lungs.

A fly buzzed. *A fly buzzed, and then I died.*

Was that right? she wondered numbly. *Didn't Emily Dickinson write that, or something like it?*

It might have been Millay. She was so morose at times. But no—

"Stop it, dammit, stop it!" she cursed at the fly. "My head hurts!"

Oh, God, it really hurts.

She tried to raise a hand to stop the incessant buzzing, but her hands were paralyzed. Opening her eyes, she saw blood on her shirt. Blood on the wheel.

Steering wheel.

Lifting her head, she saw that her hands were cuffed to the wheel of her rental car. The cuffs were silver metal, like police issue.

It all flooded back.

Someone had struck her with something. She wasn't

out long, because she remembered her mouth being taped, and a hood being placed over her head. She remembered being dragged across the backyard of that house. They must have dragged her all the way down the street to her car. Her back felt as if she'd been tossed into a fire. But the hood and the tape were gone. As consciousness returned full force, the intense pain brought a scream to her lips.

The fly stopped buzzing. Everything became still, then the noise began again.

But it wasn't a fly. Now that she was fully conscious, the noise was much louder than that.

What, then?

Machinery. A bulldozer or something, working nearby. It had stopped for a second or two. Did someone hear her scream?

Hope changed to horror as she saw what was coming directly at her. Not a bulldozer, but one of those machines with a giant scoop. The scoop was filled with junk—pieces of rusted metal, like parts from something. Before she could scream again the scoop rose up, then dumped its load. Tons of scrap metal rained down on the car's roof, making a hellish noise. Some of it poured through the half-open driver's window, scraping and covering Abby's legs and feet. The scoop backed up, lifted another load and moved toward her again. Another two scoops and she'd be covered, buried. She'd suffocate. No one would ever find her.

A sudden, horrific thought: What did they do with

scrap metal, or with something as large as a car? Did they set them on fire, like they did in garbage dumps?

No. They crushed them. Crushed them into blocks of metal that were a thousand times smaller than the original waste. Like a giant trash compactor.

This time she let loose with a scream born of deep-down, mortal fear. With every ounce of strength she could summon, Abby thrashed about, yanking at the handcuffs in sheer panic, then beating her head against the horn, trying to make it work. The scoop came closer and closer, rose up and—

Stopped.

Abby was still screaming and her wrists were bloody. Fresh blood from her head dripped into her eyes and down her face.

But there was a man at her window, peering in.

"Goddamn!" he yelled. "What the hell are you doing in there?"

Her door was yanked open, the pieces of scrap metal pulled aside. The man swore again as he saw the handcuffs. "My God, who did this to you?"

She couldn't answer.

"Never mind. I'll be right back."

Moments passed when her mind went dead, but then she heard a loud metallic snap, and another. Her hands came free from the wheel, and she felt herself being pulled from the car. The man lifted her gently, but her back still seared with pain. She couldn't help crying out.

He was speaking to someone else. "Call 911. This woman needs a hospital. Who are you?" he asked.

She looked into his eyes. "Angel," she answered before bursting into tears. But she didn't mean herself. She meant him.

At first, Abby thought she was dreaming. She lay on a cloud, and the only sound from the spheres was the beating of her heart. She began to count the heartbeats— *one-one thousand, two-one thousand, three-one thousand*—as if they were seconds ticking away her life. When a woman's voice sounded above her and Abby saw she was dressed in white, she thought it must be God. It was reassuring to know at last that God was indeed a woman. Reassuring, yet in some ways surprising.

"I've been wanting to talk to you for a long time," she said without words, understanding that God was good at telepathy. "You know, about why childbirth has to be painful, and why women have to have periods for forty years even when they don't plan to have children. Oh, and about people, and why we eat your cows—"

A nasty prick in her butt brought her out of delirium, assuring her that this couldn't be heaven, after all. It must still be her life on earth.

In other words, hell.

She didn't have time to wonder why that thought had come to her. A familiar voice sounded close to her ear. "Abby? Abby, wake up. It's me, Ben."

Her lips felt stuck together. She tried to moisten them with her tongue, but it felt like sand. "Ben?"

"You're at St. Joseph's Hospital, Abby. In Phoenix. You're going to be all right."

"How...?"

"The hospital found my number in your purse and they called me," he said.

She tried to ask him a question, but her mind kept closing down. Drifting off. When she finally said something, it made no sense. "The chickens...they're out of the coop."

She knew it made no sense because of the way Ben half smiled. "They've got you pretty well doped up," he said. "You had to have stitches in your forehead, but you'll be all right."

She tried to lift a hand to touch his, but couldn't. Moving her head to the side, she winced. Memories of being shackled in the car came back as she saw the restraints at her elbows. Panic rose in her throat. "Get these off me!" she tried to yell, though her voice was dry and rasping. "Get them off!"

Ben put a calming hand on her arm. "It's okay. They're to protect your back. They put them on you so you couldn't move around too much. I'm sure they'll take them off now that you're awake."

"My wrists," she said, taking a deep breath. "They hurt."

Ben nodded. "It looks like you really fought those handcuffs, Ab. The nurse put some kind of ointment on them. That's why the restraints are at your elbows instead of your wrists."

"Handcuffs," she said. Something important about the handcuffs. But she seemed to be drifting in and out.

"You learn anything?" a different voice said.

Abby forced her eyes open.

Lessing. The FBI agent, at the doorway.

Of course, she thought with sudden clarity. That's why Ben was here, too. They wanted to find out what she'd learned about Alicia—if she'd found her, or knew where she was.

Abby closed her eyes again and feigned sleep. But the mere fact of doing that made her really drift off. She struggled against it. *Help me not to say anything while I'm out,* she prayed at the last minute. *Help me...*

14

The morning sun blazing on her face woke her up, and for a moment she thought she was back in the car again. Panic rose in her throat, but then a young woman in a striped nurse's aide uniform came to her bedside.

"Hey, how we doin' today, Ms. Northrup?" the aide said.

"I don't know about you, but I feel like shit," Abby answered, with so much lucidity and force it surprised her.

"Sorry." The girl smiled. "You must be gettin' better. That's what they say when a patient gets grumpy."

Abby tried to smile back, but it hurt her forehead to do so. She looked at the girl's name tag. *Noreen.* "Can you help me sit up, Noreen? And get me a mirror?"

"Yes to the first. Not so sure you really want a mirror."

"It's that bad?"

"Pretty awful," Noreen said as she raised the head of the bed. "I could get you one of those black veils like in the old horror movies, if you want. You could walk around like that and nobody'd ever know."

Abby stared. "Is this what passes for a bedside manner these days?"

Even, white teeth flashed in the young aide's dark face. "Just tryin' to get a smile out of you, Ms. Northrup. You're not gonna be smilin' when you look in that mirror."

Abby couldn't help herself. She laughed. "You are the meanest, most sadistic nurse's aide I've ever seen. How old are you, anyway?"

"Thirty-two goin' on fifty," Noreen said.

"No, really."

"That's the truth. I've been doin' this work goin' on fourteen years now."

"But, you…" The woman looked like a high school student.

"It's the genes," Noreen said. "You got 'em, too, I can tell. What are you, a Pisces? Pisces get younger every year, you know."

Abby sighed. "*Mirror.* Please."

Noreen shrugged and took one from the bedside stand. "Don't say I didn't warn you," she said gently.

Abby took the mirror and studied the stitches on her forehead. Part of her hair had been shaved to accommodate them.

"They told me," the aide said, "that you got those hitting the steering wheel of a car to get somebody's attention. Tryin' to blow the horn, they said. That must've taken a lot of guts, Ms. Northrup."

"More like desperation. Did they tell you what happened to me?"

"Those two men who were here? They didn't even look my way." She folded her arms. "I sure did notice them, though."

"What do you mean?"

"Well, I may be speakin' out of turn—"

"Hey, why stop now?" Abby said.

"I just don't think they're very good friends," Noreen said.

"To each other?"

"No, to you. I may be wrong, but I sure wouldn't trust 'em."

"Really? Why do you say that?" Abby asked.

"I don't know…instinct, I guess."

Abby never discounted instinct. It was instinct that had made her distrust the woman at the house last night, and instinct that made her go back there.

It might not have been a smart move to return there without help, given the circumstances, but her instinct had been right. Something was wrong about that house, and she still couldn't be sure Allie wasn't there.

"Did I say anything to those men when I was unconscious?" Abby asked.

"Well, I wasn't in here all the time, of course," Noreen said, straightening up the sheets. "But I did hear you say a couple of things. Something about Las Vegas, I think. And some kind of tree."

"A tree? What kind of tree?"

"Hmm." The aide looked off into space and seemed to be thinking back. "Sorry, I just can't quite remember."

"Was it a willow tree?" Abby prompted.

"Yeah, that's it!" Noreen smiled widely. "I wouldn't worry about it, though, 'cause that's when you were still pretty out of it and didn't make much sense."

"In what way?"

She grinned. "You said you spoke to the tree."

Abby didn't smile. "And how did the men react to that?" she asked.

"Not the way I would've thought," Noreen said. "You know, like it was funny or weird or something. They just looked at each other, then hightailed it out of here like bunnies with their tails on fire. Haven't been back since."

Noreen folded her arms again and frowned. "Friends don't do that to a friend in the hospital. Do they?"

"No. You're right, Noreen. Friends don't do that to a friend. Whether they're in the hospital or not."

According to Noreen, paramedics had brought her in, and a man came along right after them. From her description, Abby was sure it had to be the man who'd found her in the car. Noreen confirmed that.

"Jenny, down in ER, is a friend of mine. She told me this guy told the police he'd been hired by a company in Prescott to clean up this junkyard and get rid of everything in it. He said he didn't know you or anything about you, and when he saw you there it was a real shock."

"Did the police believe him?"

"Jenny said they let him go, so I suppose they figured if he was nice enough to call 911 and get you here, he must have been all right."

Noreen, who turned out to be a wealth of information, also told her that a Dr. Blake had examined her the night before, and wasn't due to see her again till late afternoon.

"I know I teased you about the stitches, but that was just to get your juices going." Noreen patted her hand. "Dr. Blake had Dr. Morrissey—he's a plastic surgeon—come in and do your stitches. Dr. Morrissey said you'd be fine in a few weeks. He left orders for injections for the pain last night, and pills for after you woke up. He'll be back this afternoon to see you, too."

"I think I remember the plastic surgeon. Nice brown eyes and a soft voice? It's all kind of hazy."

"That's Doc Morrissey, all right," Noreen said. "Look, I'm getting off my shift now, but the day shift should be in soon with your meds. Now, if they don't take care of you right today, you yell out loud and clear. Don't take nothin' from nobody. Hear?"

Abby heard. She just wasn't going to be here long enough to worry about it.

She stuffed her empty stomach with Jell-O and saltines from her lunch tray, pulled on her blood-stained clothes and took her purse out of the closet. Checking, she found that there were still cards and money in there.

So she hadn't been robbed, thank God. Still, she thought it odd that her attacker wouldn't have taken all he could, to at least make it look like a robbery.

She looked up and down the hall. The nurses were all busy with charts or on the phones, and the aides must have been busy with patients. The hall was relatively empty. She walked in the opposite direction of the nurses' station to an exit door and took the stairs all the way down to the parking lot. As she stepped outside, the heat hit her like a blast from a furnace.

It was a small hospital, on a medium-size lot, but she was too exhausted after all those stairs to walk around it in the heat looking for her rental car. Belatedly, she realized there was no point in doing that, anyway. Lessing or Ben would have had it towed somewhere so that Forensics could go over it.

Out on the scorching pavement, she watched three cabs pass her by and reminded herself never again to fall for the old saw, "It's not that hot because it's dry heat," when applied to a hundred-and-seven-degree Arizona day. She was about to give up and go look for a used-car lot when a cab finally stopped.

"Take me to a good real estate office, please," she said, sliding into the cool, air-conditioned haven.

The driver, a woman with long black hair who looked of Mexican descent, said, "Okay, but you're not gonna rent a house with that face."

Geez. Was everybody an insult comic around here?

Then she realized why the other cabs had passed her by.

"How come you stopped for me, if I look that scary?" Abby asked.

"I used to have a husband who beat me up, too," the driver said.

"But I don't—" Abby began, then shut up.

The cab pulled up to a curb about five minutes later, and she saw the sign, Delgado Realty. It was a storefront office on a street with pawn shops, check-cashing companies, forty-nine-dollar mattress sales and greasy-spoon cafés.

"This can't be the best Phoenix has to offer," she said to the driver.

"It may not be as fancy as some," the driver said, "but my cousins own it." She smiled. "They'll treat you right, even with that face. Just tell them I brought you here."

Abby felt half cautious and half grateful. "What's your name?" she asked.

"Angelita," the woman said. "That means angel, but my ex used to call me the Devil's Spawn."

"You were lucky to get away from him, then," Abby said, thinking of the women who came to the Prayer House for sanctuary from similar partners.

"Get away?" Angelita scoffed. "Hell, I killed the bastard."

Abby didn't know quite what to say.

"You never get away from them, you know," Angelita said. "Not as long as they're alive. They track you down and they kill you for leaving them. I just got to mine first."

"And you got away with it?" Abby asked, shocked.

"You might say that. I got three years because it was self-defense, and I've done my time. It was worth it to be free of the bastard."

Abby handed her a twenty-dollar bill. "Here. Keep the change."

She pushed it away. "Nah, it looks like you're having a bad time. You keep it."

Abby didn't want to insult her by refusing. "Thank you," she said, and began to step out of the car.

"They have to learn that, you know," Angelita said.

Abby paused. "What?"

"That they can't treat us like that and not get killed for it. Then maybe they'll stop. If the law doesn't do it—and they *don't*, most of the time—we've got to do it ourselves."

Again, she didn't know what to say. Either Angelita was the smartest woman she'd ever known—or just plain crazy.

"Angelita," she said, searching for words and not finding any profound ones, "you are something else."

"Remember that," the driver said, grinning. "You send that sucker who roughed you up my way, and I'll kill him, too."

15

The desks and old wooden file cabinets in the real estate office were scarred and piled high with thick manila folders. The room seemed clean, though, and smelled like the library in the Prayer House, with bookcases along one wall filled with old and new volumes. As Abby entered, the only person in the room looked up and smiled.

"Help you?"

"I'm not sure. Angelita sent me. My name's Abby," she said.

The man stood, towering over her, and stuck out his hand. "I'm Jimmy Delgado, Angelita's cousin. Have a seat."

She shook his hand and glanced around for an empty chair. Every single one, it seemed, held files and law books. Angelita's cousin made a rueful grimace. "Sorry." He cleaned files off a chair with one swoop of his arm, then he took a few tissues from a box on his desk and dusted the seat of the chair, gesturing for her to sit.

Abby raised a brow at the mess on the floor, and he grinned. "Just old stuff I've been going through. It'll still be there later."

He was nice, she thought, and reassuring in clean khakis, a white shirt with the sleeves rolled up to his elbows and no tie. He had an angular face, dark Hispanic complexion and vaguely resembled the actor Jimmy Smits. Or maybe it was just the name, Abby thought. Either way, he was the kind of man you meet and know right away you'll like.

"What did you think of my cousin?" he asked, sitting in his own chair.

"I think she's a gutsy lady," Abby said.

"She tell you anything about herself?"

"As a matter of fact..."

Jimmy nodded.

"She's kind of a walking soapbox." He smiled. "She likes other women to know what she's been through, so maybe they'll get the message that they don't have to put up with it themselves. Not that I necessarily approve of the way she handled her own problem."

"She said she got three years. That doesn't seem very long for killing someone."

"You might say Angelita was lucky. The police caught him in the act three times, beating her to a bloody pulp. When she killed him and claimed self-defense, the police reports left no doubt that it was. Not to mention that she had the world's best lawyer."

"You?" Abby guessed. "I see you have plenty of law books on the shelves."

He smiled. "The real estate is a sideline. Kind of a hobby during the summer when everything slows down here."

He rested his arms on the desk. "But to get back to you, Abby. Angelita must have tagged you as an abused woman, too. Still, I don't think you came to a real estate office for help with that. Am I right?"

"You are. That's not to say I couldn't have used some help along those lines a couple of years ago."

"Ah…so Angelita was on the mark. Just off about the time?"

"A bit," she said, ending that part of the conversation. "I actually came here to ask for some information about a property here in Phoenix. I figured a Realtor might have access to that sort of thing."

"There are a lot of things we can access online," Jimmy said. "But you could have gone to the county offices for the same thing."

"I'm not too familiar with the area, and you were nearby," she said. "Besides, a Realtor might have more information about a specific property and its neighborhood than a busy clerk in a county office."

"Well, let me see what I can do." Jimmy straightened in his chair and turned to the computer on the desk. "What's the address?"

"It's 13259 El Caballo," Abby said.

He connected to the Internet. "Are you interested in buying this property?"

"Not at all," she replied. "It's badly run-down. I'd like to know who owns it now, and who's living there."

He turned back to her. "May I ask if this has anything to do with what happened to you?"

For a few minutes, Abby had forgotten about the stitches and the bloodstained clothes, despite the constant headache she'd had since leaving the hospital. But of course, it was obvious that something bad had happened.

"Are you asking if this happened there?" she said.

"Well, El Caballo Street and some of the areas around it have had a reputation for being high in crime. The city's trying to reclaim the area and there are developers building new houses out there. The project hasn't completely taken hold yet, though."

"I'll say," Abby murmured.

"If you don't want to tell me, it's okay," Jimmy said. "I'm just wondering…were you jumped?"

"Something like that. I was looking for someone I thought lived there, and the current residents weren't real happy to see me."

He sighed. "I'm sorry. Do you live in Phoenix?"

"No. This is my first time here in about twenty years."

"We can't be leaving you with much of an impression, then."

"On the contrary," Abby said. "It's left me with quite an impression—on the top of my head."

Jimmy stared a moment, then laughed. "At least they didn't rob you of your sense of humor."

He turned to the computer again. "Let's see now…."

He began a search, and Abby closed her eyes to rest them. The throbbing in her head wasn't helped by the clacking of the computer keys, but at least they were rhythmic, and it was cool in there. An old air conditioner rattled in a back window of the small one-room office, and between the different white noises as background, and the fact that she felt safe here, she began to relax.

"Abby?" A hand on her shoulder startled her.

"No!" she shouted, hitting out instinctively. "Get away!"

Jimmy stood at her side, his hands splayed outward to show that he wasn't going to touch her. "It's all right," he said quietly. "You fell asleep, that's all."

She forced her breathing to slow, and realized where she was. "Oh, God," she said, shocked at her outburst. "I'm so sorry."

"It's okay. I just brought you some water," he said. She followed his eyes to the desk where he'd placed a glass filled with water and ice cubes.

"Thank you," she said, grabbing the glass of water and gulping it down. "They gave me medication in the hospital. I guess it made me sleepy, and when I sat down…" She smiled shakily. "I really am sorry."

"Well, you do have quite a punch there." He grinned, then turned serious, going back to his desk chair. "But I'm afraid I can't help you much with that house."

"Oh?"

"It seems to be owned by a corporation—TCIL. Some sort of import-export company. At least, that's who pays the taxes. There doesn't seem to be anyone living there, though."

"But I was there," Abby insisted. "I talked to a woman there just last night."

Jimmy went back to the computer and turned the monitor around. "Here, I'll show you."

She leaned over the desk and saw that he'd brought up a county tax report. "As you can see, this corporation is listed as the owner. Now, here—" He clicked to another page. "I tried a few other things, including everything available to us as Realtors. No current residents come up for that house."

"But—" Abby sat back down and rubbed her face. The headache was getting worse as the medication wore off.

"Look, don't take this the wrong way," Jimmy said, "but, uh…I don't suppose there's a chance that the medication they gave you in the hospital caused you to get the number wrong?"

She showed him the piece of paper. "I wrote this down long before I was there, and long before I was in the hospital. I'm certain it's right." Abby began to slump in the chair, her energy flagging.

He stood. "Look, see that armchair back there next to the air conditioner? Why don't you go back and relax a few minutes. I've got one more source I can check out."

"I really didn't mean to take up so much of your time," Abby said tiredly. "I should go."

He smiled. "You've got my curiosity going, so you might as well stay. I really want to follow this through."

"But you must have other work to do."

"Oh, there's always something with criminal law. But like I said, it's slow here in the summer. It's as if half the crooks are too hot to do much, so they take a siesta till fall."

"I wish they'd been taking one last night," Abby said, wincing as a sharp pain ran through her head.

"Go," Jimmy said. "It's cooler back there, and if you fall asleep again, that's okay, too. I'll wake you up when I know something."

She hesitated, unsure if she should trust him. His niceness might be an act.

Don't be crazy. You're getting paranoid.

The truth was, she felt that for her own safety she had to suspect everyone now—even those she felt intuitively she could trust. Maybe Angelita, the cabdriver, was with the FBI. Did she "just happen" to pick her up outside the hospital because they told her to? Had Angelita brought her here so that this man, pretending to be her cousin, could find something out from her?

It was all too much. Trust, don't trust. Either way, she could be making a mistake. But when presented with someone she didn't know, versus Ben Schaeffer and Robert Lessing—two men she did know—she might as well take the devil at hand.

16

A sharp pain flew through Abby's torso. She was pinned to a bed by someone's weight, a hand pulling her jeans down, then jamming itself between her thighs. Tears of impotency and rage filled her eyes.

"How does it feel?" a male voice said. "How does it feel to have all that power and not be able to do anything with it?"

She tried with everything she had to shake him off, but her efforts didn't work. An arm held her head in place, and her screams, coming from deep within her throat, made little sound. He began ramming her over and over, so mindlessly and rough she felt pain in her skull. Then, suddenly, a new kind of agony seared through her, robbing her of sanity and will.

"You know how sick I got of hearing how you wanted a baby?" the male voice rasped. "You wanted pain down here, some doctor, some other man, sticking his bloody instruments up you? Well, now you have it. Everything you ever wanted, bitch."

She screamed again, though there was no sound. It

was the last thing she knew till she woke on the hill... the hill...the cross...oh, God, the cross...the car...the handcuffs...

"Abby! Abby, wake up!"

Jimmy was frowning, standing above her. "Thank God. For a minute there, I thought you were unconscious."

She was back in the realty office, drenched in sweat despite the air conditioner that still kicked out its icy breath next to her.

"I was dreaming," she said, her voice weak and her whole body shaking from the memory. *It wasn't real,* she told herself. *It wasn't real, it wasn't...*

But the mantra parried with truth, because it had been real, two years ago.

After all this time...why am I dreaming this now? I thought I was better. They told me I was better.

She freshened up in a cramped but clean bathroom that shared space with large new packages of paper towels and toilet paper. Looking in the white-framed mirror attached to the wall, she saw how tired and drawn her face was. Would she ever be over it? The psychologist had called it post-traumatic stress disorder. The dreams, the fear, the flashbacks even when awake...

The bruises on her lower face made her look harsh, and even a bit scary. What must the man in the outer office think of her, showing up on his doorstep like this? Amazing that he hadn't just called the cops.

She washed her face with a wet paper towel, then tried to style her hair with a damp hand, so that it covered the stitches on her scalp. Her arms quickly became weak, though, and she gave it up as a lost cause.

Sighing, she went back into the outer office just in time to see Jimmy Delgado put her purse back on the desk.

"Looking for something?" she said sharply.

"Uh, no, just moving it…" He shrugged and shoved his hands into his pockets, facing her. "Okay, here's the truth. I was checking the local news while you were in there. You were on it."

"Me? On the news?"

"There's an APB out on you. That's an all points bulletin—"

"I know what an APB is," she snapped. "Why are they looking for me?"

"Well, according to the news, the police say you left the hospital without permission."

"Right. That's true. But people check themselves out of hospitals all the time. They don't get arrested for it—and they certainly don't end up on the news."

"Uh…they do if they're being sought on a murder charge," he said.

She was so shocked, she couldn't come up with words.

Jimmy walked around his desk and turned off the television and computer. "The name was the same, but the photo on the news didn't look much like you. The face was more swollen than yours is now, but the bruises and stitches matched."

He paused and folded his arms. "So, care to share? Who did you kill? They didn't say, on the news."

"I did not kill anyone," Abby said. "*I'm* the one who was attacked and almost killed. Besides, what has this got to do with you rifling through my purse?"

"I did not rifle," he said. "You never told me your last name, and I wanted to check your ID, make sure you were the Abby Northrup they were looking for. I decided not to."

"And if you had? Would I have walked out here to a posse of cops?"

"I'm not sure. I wanted to know what I was getting into, first."

"Well, then, you'll be reassured to hear that you're not getting into anything," Abby said coldly, "because I'm leaving. I won't bother you again."

"I don't think so," he said.

She wasn't sure she had heard him right. "You don't think what?"

"I don't think you're leaving. At least, not alone. As a matter of fact, I have other plans for you."

He reached under his desk for a brown paper bag. "First, though, you need a change of clothes. Angelita brought these by for you."

Abby looked in the bag and found a pair of jeans shorts and a sleeveless white T-shirt. They weren't new, but smelled freshly washed.

"Where—"

"She has her sources," Jimmy said. "You want to put them on?"

"I…yes, of course," she said, surprised at the tears this one small kindness brought to her eyes. She suddenly didn't feel so alone, as she had when she'd woken in the hospital and found that Ben was gone.

It must have been the dream, she thought. *The dreams always make me feel lost and afraid.*

Abby took the clothes into the bathroom and changed. When she came out, Jimmy picked up a summer-weight tan blazer off the back of his chair but didn't put it on.

"Come with me," he said.

"No," Abby said, shaking her head. "Look, I appreciate all this, your help and the clothes and all, but I've been thinking, and I'm not sure—"

Jimmy sighed, but his tone was firm. "Woman, this whole thing has ratcheted up a notch since you walked in here. If I don't turn you in, I could be charged with having harbored a fugitive. For my own protection, I need to know what's going on. And, if you're lucky, I just might represent you."

"Forget it. I don't need you representing me. I did not murder anyone."

"Yeah, well, like they say, tell it to the judge. But you'll be a lot better off with me by your side."

"You don't even know me," Abby said. "How could you possibly think of defending me?"

"Oh, I'll know you all right, by the time we're through. I'll also know every single detail about your trip to Phoenix, how you got those bruises and stitches, and more important, why."

She was silent for a long moment. "Why should I trust you?" she said finally.

"Maybe because I didn't call the cops the minute I heard they were looking for you? Maybe because I told you they were looking for you, instead of keeping you in the dark and letting you walk out of here looking like Herman Munster?"

He walked to the door and pulled down green roller shades against the hot sun, then hung a Closed sign in the window.

"Are you coming?" he called back, opening the door. His voice sounded as if he were mentally tapping an impatient foot.

Abby picked up her small purse and took a quick look inside. Everything seemed to be there.

"I'm coming," she said grudgingly. "But don't think I've decided to trust you."

"Now, why on earth would I think that?" He shook his head, and when she passed through the door, he closed it behind them both with a thud.

17

Abby knew she was losing her mental balance. The beating she'd taken, not to mention the one she'd given herself trying to get out of that car, had taken its toll. Along with everything else, she'd lost her focus on the job at hand. She had to find Alicia. That was the important thing. And she couldn't do that if she was in jail.

Anger and confusion worked their way through her mind. *What are they doing to me? What murder are they trying to pin on me? The one at the Highlands? Instead of Alicia? Or has something else happened?*

"Look, I really do have to be somewhere," she said as Jimmy eased his air-conditioned black Lexus around traffic.

"You said that," he responded. "A couple of times. Three or four, at least."

She looked at him to see if he was being critical, or poking fun at her. There was no way to tell with his eyes hidden behind the aviator-type sunglasses.

"Where are we going?"

"I told you that three or four times, too," he answered. "A place I know."

She opened her mouth to argue, then shut it. The truth was, she'd either have to get out of the car or give up worrying about where he was taking her. And she didn't feel up to walking. She would keep her wits about her as much as possible, though, and go with whatever happened. Even if he were driving her straight to a police station, dumping her and her troubles off there, she could handle it. She'd been through worse. Much worse.

"I do have to call someone," she said, fighting off a growing anger.

He sighed. "You said that—"

"I know, I know!" she snapped. "Three or four times, I'm sure!"

"Actually, only once." This time he grinned.

"Please don't patronize me. I do have to call someone."

"I'm not patronizing you," he said. "It's just that your mind is a little—"

"Off! You don't have to say it, dammit, I know!"

He sighed again and handed her his cell phone, but the main Prayer House number wouldn't come to her. She'd known it for almost two years, but her mind drew a blank. She knew the area code for Carmel, she thought—609. Or had it changed to 83…something?

She dialed 609, but wasn't sure if the Prayer House number started with 464 or 646. Or maybe it was—

"Dammit!" she screamed at the phone, banging it

against the dashboard over and over. "Dammit, dammit, dammit!"

"Hey, easy on the hardware!" Jimmy said, taking the phone from her hands. "Geez. I just got this car."

She didn't even say she was sorry this time, but sat there with her arms folded, staring ahead.

Another few minutes and she couldn't stop herself. "Tell me where we're going right now, or I'm getting out of the car."

He slowed and pulled over to the curb.

"Okay," he said.

"Okay, what?"

"Okay, get out of the car."

"But I—"

"Dammit, get out of the car!" he said.

Turning off the engine, he took the keys out of the ignition and stepped out into the street, slamming the door behind him.

She began to really hate him, and was about to open her door and say so when he opened it for her.

"Are you coming or not?"

"Coming?"

"We're here. Why do you think I stopped?"

She looked beyond him to a building with a flashy neon sign that announced, "Taco en Paraiso."

"Taco in Paradise?" she said.

He took her arm and led her to a carved oak door that reminded her of some of the vintage Spanish ones in the Prayer House. "It's a takeoff on Cheeseburger in Paradise," he said. "My mom's from Maui, where she used to manage the Cheeseburger in Paradise restaurant, named after Jimmy Buffet's song."

"Your mom is Hawaiian? But—"

"My dad's Mexican. I'm kind of a mutt."

He opened the door and they stepped inside. The interior was cool and dark, a welcome change from the hot sidewalk. As Abby's eyes adjusted, she saw red booths against white walls, and tables in the middle of the room that were covered with crisp white tablecloths. Candles were on every table, and a barrage of spicy scents filled her nostrils, making her stomach growl.

"Mama's cooking in the back," Jimmy said. "Getting ready for dinner."

"Cilantro," Abby murmured, inhaling. "I love cilantro."

"Mama!" he called out. "I've brought a friend. Tell Joey we need him, too."

The woman who came from the back was not much over sixty, Abby guessed. She was tall and striking, like her son, with the same kind of angular face that made Abby think of the early royals of Hawaii, now that she knew the woman's background.

Jimmy introduced her to his mother, and to Abby he said, "This is my mom, Ianela." He pronounced it the Hawaiian way, *Ee-ah-nay-lah.*

The woman smiled. "Call me Janella, Abby. It's easier. And welcome to Taco en Paraiso. What can I get you? And you, too, Kime. Are you hungry?"

Kime, Abby noted, was pronounced *Kee-may*, apparently the Hawaiian for Jimmy.

But before he could answer, a burly man of about six foot four joined them. He was nearly as broad as he was tall, and his frown was the opposite of Janella's welcoming smile.

"Hey, Joey," Jimmy said. "I closed the office for the day, and I've brought a friend. We need your help."

He led Abby to a booth near the kitchen, and Joey followed. Janella said, "I'll bring you a mixed platter to share."

Jimmy smiled. "That'd be great, Mama. Thanks."

To Abby, he said, "Go ahead and sit down. I'll get us a pitcher of ice water."

Abby slid into the booth and Joey followed. There were a few awkward moments when she didn't know what to say, but she couldn't help noting that he'd taken a hard look at her stitches.

Jimmy came back with the water and slid in at Abby's other side. Turning over glasses and filling them, he said, "Joey, we have a situation here. I thought you might be able to help us."

"Does this situation have anything to do with the news I just saw on the TV in the kitchen?" Joey asked. "Because if it does, I'd say you have more than a *situation,* brother. You're harboring a suspect in a murder."

"*Suspect,*" Jimmy said. "That's the key word here."

"Always is, with you." Joey gave Abby another of those hard looks. "No offense. I just don't like seeing my little brother get in trouble with the law."

"That's just because Joey *is* the law," his brother said

easily. "He thinks being a cop gives him the right to make judgments."

Abby's fight or flight kicked in. Every muscle went on alert.

"And *he* thinks," Joey said, "that being a lawyer gives him the right to prove me wrong."

Jimmy didn't take the bait, but merely folded his arms and looked at his brother.

"Oh, for God's sake," Joey sighed. "Okay, what do you need?"

"Abby doesn't know why they're looking at her for this murder," Jimmy said. "Can you find out what that's about without raising any suspicions?"

"Sure. You could have called me for that. And?" Joey folded his arms this time.

"And," Jimmy said, "I myself would like to know who's saying she did it."

"I take it you think this is a setup of some kind?"

He shrugged. "I think it's a possibility."

"And you?" Joey asked Abby. "Just out of curiosity and for the sake of my little brother here, how did you get those bruises?"

"I was looking for a friend," Abby said. "At a house here in Phoenix. Someone gave me the address, but the woman at the house last night claimed not to know her. Then I got hit on the head and woke up in a junkyard."

Joey just stared, and Abby sighed. "Look, it's a long story. The point is, I need to find my friend. I think she's in danger, and I really think the woman who was

at the house last night knew her and didn't want me to
find her."

Joey looked at his brother.

"Complicating matters," Jimmy said, "is that there's
no one listed anywhere as living at that address."

"Wait a minute." Joey turned to Abby. "There's no
one living there, but you say you talked to a woman at
the house last night?"

Abby nodded, and Joey fell silent. Before he could
speak again, Janella arrived at the table with a huge platter of steaming food. Jimmy swept the candle and salt
and pepper shakers aside to make room for it. "Mama,
you've outdone yourself," he said, smiling.

"That's right, insult me!" she said. "Acting like you
never saw food like this before!" But she leavened her
words with a kiss on his forehead.

"You don't look well," Janella said to Abby. "Can I
get you something else?"

"I'd love an aspirin," Abby said. What she really
needed was a head transplant. The painkillers from the
hospital were wearing off.

"I'll be right back," Janella said. "Eat first, though.
It's better for your stomach."

As Jimmy and Abby helped themselves to tortillas,
frittatas, enchiladas and a sampling of appetizers, Joey
excused himself. "I have to make a phone call."

Abby put her fork down and watched him go to a pay
phone at the rear.

"What's he doing?" she said, afraid suddenly. "He's
calling them to come pick me up, isn't he?"

"Joey? I doubt it. If he wanted to take you in, he'd do it himself."

"You *doubt* it? If you aren't sure—"

"Relax," Jimmy said. "Nothing's going to happen to you here. How about some of this chimichanga?" He cut the crispy, chicken-and-cheese-filled burrito in half and put one piece on her plate. "Mama puts cilantro in hers."

She was surprised he had heard her about the cilantro, and even more that he'd remembered. Should that make her feel reassured? Or more cautious? Her eyes were still fixed on Joey as she took a bite. He was coming back to the table, and she tried to figure out what he was thinking. He had that cop-look that Ben got when he was hiding something.

"Okay," he said, sliding into the booth, "here's the deal. The house at that address used to belong to the mob. Then, about a year ago, the mob abandoned it, and somewhere around seven months ago, it became a CIA safe house. The corporation you saw listed as the owner is a CIA cover, and the woman you saw there was probably an agent."

Abby's food went down nearly whole and stuck in her throat. She grabbed for her water and swallowed, washing it down the rest of the way.

"You get that from Brownie?" Jimmy guessed.

"Straight from the horse's mouth."

"Who's Brownie?" Abby asked.

"A friend of Joey's in the bureau," Jimmy answered, since his brother's mouth was full.

Joey washed the enchilada down with a tall glass of beer. Folding his arms across his chest, he sat back and said, "Ms. Northrup, I think it's time you told us what's really going on."

Abby tensed. "How did you know my last name? Did your FBI friend tell you that?"

"It was on the news," Jimmy reminded her. "Is that where you heard it, Joey?"

"Sure," Joey said. "That was it—on the news."

Abby pushed away from the table. "Okay, that's it. You seem a nice-enough guy, Joey, but a very bad liar. Jimmy, please thank your mother for the food, but I have to be going."

She stood and turned to the front door.

"Better not go that way," Joey said casually, popping an appetizer into his mouth.

"Why not?" Abby turned back.

"'Cause they'll be out there waiting for you."

18

Abby froze. "*Who* will be out there waiting for me?"

"Local feds, probably, and some police chief from California. They were in the office when I was talking to Brownie."

"Then you did tell them I was here!" she said angrily.

"Of course he didn't," Jimmy said, frowning. "You didn't, right, Joey?"

"Nah, I didn't tell them. But I'm sure Brownie figured out that's why I was calling." He looked at his watch, then at Abby. "That's why they'll be out there by now."

"And you couldn't bother to tell me?" Abby said. "You've just been sitting there stuffing your face?"

Joey winced. "That's pretty offensive. I've been eating my lunch, I have not been 'stuffing' it. Besides, they won't come in here."

"I—" She shook her head, dumbfounded. "How can you possibly know that?"

"Because the local cops wouldn't let them. They respect Mama too much to start anything in here. But you won't be going out there, either. At least, not through that door—or looking like that."

Abby's hand went to her stitches and the pain in her head. She longed for the serenity of the Prayer House, and the life she'd had before Alicia Gerard showed up. Was all this worth it? She was in a strange town with people she didn't know and couldn't really trust.

But Jancy needed her mom, and she'd promised everything would be all right. What if the FBI or CIA caught up with Alicia first? She would be arrested and most likely deported—or worse, sent to prison for treason.

As for Jancy, God only knew what would happen to her. Would she live the rest of her life without a mother?

Abby wasn't sure how she felt about her old friend now, but she couldn't just leave her without some sort of backup. Even if she were guilty of the murder, there had to be something that made her do it, something that had pushed her too far. She was protecting someone, either Jancy, herself or possibly even Gerry.

The terrorist connection was impossible. That was some kind of story made up by those agents, to cover whatever they really wanted her for.

As for Gerry, had the police or FBI in New York contacted him by now? Surely he'd be frantic about Alicia, and even more about Jancy, especially if he thought she was on the run with her mother. And even though Abby had agreed to Alicia's request the other night not to call him, the circumstances were far different now.

She sat back down. First things first. She needed help, and she couldn't be picky about how she got it.

"Okay, I'll tell you as much as I know," she said. "I told you I was looking for my friend at that address. That was the truth."

"But you said she wasn't there."

"She might have been. I wasn't allowed inside."

"Well, if your friend's being held in secret at a CIA safe house, your friend must be in trouble with the government," Joey said reasonably.

"Or," Jimmy pointed out, "she's being *protected* by the government."

"And why would they do that?" Joey asked.

"I have no idea," Abby answered.

But she could guess. *A matter of national security,* Kris Kelley had said, warning her not to tell a soul. But she hadn't actually agreed to that, had she?

A planned attack, Ben had added. Only a week away. And he'd said that a couple of days ago. Were there five days left? Or hadn't he been that precise about the time?

A phone rang, and Joey reached into his hip pocket and pulled his cell out. It was so small, it was almost engulfed by his round face.

"I'm here," he said. "Yeah. I'll tell her."

Putting the phone down, he said to Abby, "Chief Schaeffer says if you come out now with me, nothing will happen to you. They just want to talk to you."

"Like hell," Jimmy said. "Stay where you are."

"And you, brother, just made yourself an accessory," Joey told him sharply.

"Not if I'm her lawyer."

"Aah. You gonna be her lawyer now?"

"I already am," Jimmy said. He turned to Abby. "Right?"

"Right," she said.

"Come with me," Jimmy said, taking her hand and leading her back to the kitchen.

"But—" She looked back at Joey, certain he'd try to stop them. His dark eyes were unreadable slits in the ample folds of his face.

"Never mind him," Jimmy said. "He barks, but I've only been bitten twice."

"Are you sure he won't send them after us?" Abby said.

"I am for now," Jimmy answered. "But we've got to hurry. Once those people outside get to him, that could change everything."

"Wait. Why are you doing this?"

"Let's just say it's downtime in Phoenix and I'm bored," Jimmy said. "Now, come on."

Abby held back. "But you're a lawyer. And Joey's right. If you help me, you're an accessory."

"Wouldn't be the first time," he said. "Nor the last. *Are you coming?*"

He pushed the swinging kitchen door open and pulled her inside. His mother was walking back and forth behind the head chef, checking out his work and making comments about ingredients, how fresh they were and how much to use.

"Mama? May I speak with you a moment?" Jimmy asked.

Janella nodded but didn't stop. When Jimmy got to her, she stood on tiptoe to kiss his cheek.

"Storeroom," she whispered. "It's all there."

He gave her a hug. "Thanks, Mama."

Confused, Abby followed Jimmy to a room by the back door. Along one side were shelves holding linen tablecloths and napkins, candles and silverware. On the opposite wall were assorted cleaning solutions and paper products.

Abby's attention, however, was caught by the chair at the end of the long, pantry-size room. Hanging over the back of it was a man's thin khaki jacket, worn and shabby, a pair of men's faded, torn jeans and a black T-shirt. There was also a crumpled khaki hat. A tackle box, fishing rod and dirty, worn sneakers finished out the outfit.

"Your wardrobe, madam," Jimmy said, pointing to it with a flourish.

"You're kidding," Abby said, but his look told her he wasn't. She shrugged. "Well, I've always wanted to look like the sloppy half of the Odd Couple."

"Hurry," he said. "I'll wait outside the door. Knock when you're ready."

Abby wasted no time asking questions. She stripped down to her underwear and put the clean but tattered clothes on in less than a minute.

She knocked lightly on the door, and when Jimmy opened it, she said, "How's this?"

"Where's the hat?" he asked, stepping in and peering closely at her. "You'll need that to cover the stitches."

"I need something to hold my hair up, first."

"Right." He took a carved wooden box from one of the shelves and opened it, revealing various jars of makeup, bobby pins and an assortment of hair clips.

"How fast can you make yourself look like a man?"

"Watch me," she said. How many times had she done just that for a mom on the run?

Opening a jar of foundation with a suntan tint, she slathered it on thickly. The stitches puckered a bit as the makeup touched them, but it did a reasonably good job of hiding them. Grabbing the clips, she drew her hair up into a knot and shoved the hat down on her head, tilting it slightly in front.

"Okay?" she said.

Jimmy shook his head and said softly. "More than okay. Who would have thought you could ever look like a man?"

She blushed, but said, "Your mother keeps all this on hand?"

"We've had occasion to help people disappear before. Unfortunately, there's no time to get you false papers."

"You do this sort of thing often? Work outside the law, I mean?"

"Only when the law doesn't make sense," he said.

"But who decides that?"

"I do. And whatever happens, it's on me."

Wow, she thought. *A man after her own heart.*

"Well, not to worry about the false papers," Abby said, feeling free at last to be herself. "I'm good."

"All right, then. We'd better go."

Crossing to the back wall, Jimmy pressed a small spot that looked like it had a spider on it from a few feet away. Upon closer inspection, Abby saw that it was a small *painting* of a spider over a button, made, like trompe l'oeil, to look three-dimensional. A door swung open, revealing an empty room. Its storefront windows were covered with brown paper, and a yellowed For Sale sign hung on the door, facing out.

Abby followed Jimmy to a room behind that, where stairs led upward. At the top of the stairs she paused for breath and said, "Where the hell are we going?"

"To the roof," he said. "We can cross over from there to another building, and then take stairs down to the street behind this one."

"So in all the time you've been working outside the law, so to speak, the cops don't know about this?"

He shook his head. "Not even Joey knows. This is Mama's deal. And mine."

She didn't say so, but Joey didn't look all that naive to her. Still, what other choice did she have at this point?

She followed him up the stairs, all the while imagining a truckload of cops and FBI at the top, just waiting to throw a net around her. But they stepped out onto the roof to the cooing of pigeons and an airliner roaring overhead, nothing more.

The surface of the roof was flat, and covered in tar paper and stones. The air was blazing hot, and melting tar bubbled up through the stones, getting on her beat-up sneakers. Come to think of it, there had been old, dried tar on them already. Seemed like they'd seen this roof before.

When they came to the edge of the roof, Jimmy turned to her and said, "Now, here's where you'll have to trust me."

"Oh?" She looked warily over the edge.

It was a two-story fall to the alley below, and between where she stood and the building across from it, was a full three-foot gap.

Not that far, but enough to remind her that she was scared to death of heights.

"I thought you meant that the roofs butted up to each other," she said, stepping back a few feet. "Not this far apart."

"It's not as bad as it looks," Jimmy said. "You can do it."

In her fear, she turned on him. "I can do it? How the hell do you know I can do it? You don't know me at all."

"I know you survived a beating, a very bad rap on the head and almost got turned into scrap metal. Are you telling me you can't jump three feet? I've seen tinier women than you do it!"

"I don't care. I can't do it! You don't understand."

"I understand we might not have much time left before your FBI and cop friends show up and arrest you. Look, I'll go first, and I'll be right there to catch you."

"No! Don't go!"

Her vision went dark and she swayed, then fell to her knees. Bending over, she put her head between them.

"For God's sake, Abby—" Jimmy stood over her, his hand on her shoulder, voice tight with worry. "Abby, get a grip. This is no time to faint!"

"I'm not fainting," she muttered angrily. "It's vaso-vagal."

"What?"

"Just give me a minute!"

He patted her on the shoulder. "Take your time. We'll make it work somehow."

She sighed, sat up for a minute, then got to her feet. "It's vasovagal syndrome. Some kind of nerve pressing on an artery in the neck. It can make you faint, nause-ated, anxious… I've had it a couple of years." *Since that bastard nearly strangled me, in fact.*

Jimmy ran his hands through his hair. "Dammit! How often does this happen?"

"Not much. I never know when—"

"For God's sake, Abby! Why didn't you tell me?"

He ran his fingers through his hair again. "Well, that's it, then. You can't jump. Not if you might pass out on the way."

"I will not pass out," she said firmly. "I was just afraid, and this was sort of like an anxiety attack. I'm not afraid anymore. So let's go."

Before he could say or do anything, she walked back several feet to get a head start, then turned and ran to the edge, flying across the open space to clear the other roof's edge with room to spare.

Jimmy stood where she'd left him, just staring at her.

"You were faking!" he said. "You weren't afraid at all!"

But Abby barely heard him. Once she knew she was still alive, she passed out cold.

19

Janella had arranged for Angelita to pick them up in her cab on the next street over. Abby had no idea where they were going, but was too busy nursing a sore ankle to worry about it.

"You should have seen her," Jimmy said to Angelita. "She was scared to death, and she still jumped off that roof."

"I was not scared," Abby lied. "It was nerves. Besides, I've learned to shut out fear when I have to."

"Oh? How'd you do that?" Angelita asked, looking at her through the rearview mirror.

"Martial arts. It's one of the first things you learn."

Jimmy shook his head. "Why is it that sounds like only half the story?"

Abby didn't answer, and Angelita just shot her a knowing glance. *Men,* the look seemed to say. *The things you have to know, just to protect yourself.*

But Abby had to admit that Ben, at least, was one of the good ones. He had never abused her, never given her any reason to be fearful of him.

They just didn't seem to be on the same track lately. It shocked her that almost overnight she had lost her trust in him. Where was he now, for that matter? Waiting with the FBI and the Phoenix cops to arrest her.

"We're here," Angelita said.

Abby looked out the window and saw that they were at the house she'd been to last night. Turning to Jimmy, she said, "We're doing this *now?*"

"I thought you'd want to. You may not have another chance, if that posse catches up to you."

"I...I guess you're right." She wasn't sure she really wanted to know if Alicia was here, now. What would she say to her, after what had happened last night? *Why did you let them knock me out and leave me for dead in my car?* That might be a good beginning. But did she really want an answer?

Sighing, she stepped out of the car, and then remembered, for the first time since the roof, the way she was dressed.

"No one's going to open the door to me looking like this!"

"That's why I'm going first," Jimmy said. He was still wearing the lightweight sport jacket he'd jumped the roof in. Fastening the middle button, he said, "There, now. Do I look like a lawyer?"

There were scuff marks on the knees of his jeans, and spots of black tar on the jacket and one side of his face.

She rubbed some of the tar off his cheek with a thumb. "No. But I'm not complaining."

"Let's go, then. And you stand behind me, so they

can't get too good a look at you. Pull that hat down over your face."

She tilted the hat and followed him up the walk, while Angelita waited in the cab with the motor idling.

"I feel really stupid," Abby said in a low voice. "Like Harpo Marx. Or some cheap detective in one of those old movies."

"If it makes you feel any better, that's exactly what you look like," Jimmy said with a chuckle.

"Gee, thanks."

He stepped up onto the concrete block that served as a porch and rang the bell.

For a few seconds, no one answered. Then footsteps sounded inside the door and it slowly opened. It wasn't the woman from last night, but a man. Abby stole a look from under the brim of the hat, and couldn't keep her mouth from falling open.

It was one of the FBI agents from that night at the Prayer House. She was sure of it. She'd only had a brief glimpse of him as he stood under the overhead light in the main hall, but this was the same man—light blond hair cut to the scalp, blond eyebrows and a hard mouth. She remembered him because when they all came busting in, she felt like Maria in *The Sound of Music,* with the Nazi soldiers on her tail.

While Jimmy talked to the man, she forced herself not to make a sound, and carefully kept her head down.

"Sorry to bother you," Jimmy said. "I'm an attorney, and a client has asked me to find someone for him. I understand she lives here. Alicia Gerard?"

The man shook his head without missing a beat. "Sorry, there's just me and my wife here. I don't know anyone by that name."

He started to shut the door, but Jimmy leaned in slightly. If the man tried to close it on him, he'd have to use force.

"But I have a phone number that's listed at this address," Jimmy said, pulling a piece of paper from his pocket and studying it with a frown. "Did you just move here?"

"A few months ago," the man said. "That must be the problem. When the person you're looking for moved, the phone would have been disconnected."

"Did you buy this house from a woman named Alicia Gerard?" Jimmy asked.

The man shook his head. "We bought it through a real estate company. I don't remember anyone there by that name. Now, if you'll excuse me, I need to do some work."

As he said this, he was looking around Jimmy to Abby. "Your friend...is he a relative of this woman?"

"Harry?" Jimmy shook his head and touched it with a finger in the age-old way of indicating that his companion was "teched."

"No, Harry's my cousin," he said, smiling. "I'm looking after him today. He sort of follows me around."

The man stared at Abby. "He seems familiar somehow."

"Harry? Oh, everybody knows Harry. You probably saw him in the park by City Hall. He likes to people-watch."

The man stared a moment more, while Abby kept her head down, her hands in her pockets and shuffled her feet.

"About the woman I'm looking for—" Jimmy said.

The man withdrew into the house. "Like I said, I don't know anything about her. I really do have to go now."

He shut the door, and without looking at Abby, Jimmy said softly, "Home run. Now let's get back to the car. But slowly. And watch the way you walk, Cousin Harry."

Abby slouched and dragged her feet in the filthy sneakers. Jimmy went around to the back door of the cab, street side, and Abby slid in from the curb. Angelita, who had kept the motor running, pulled out into the street.

Abby turned to Jimmy and said, "That guy. I know him."

"That guy at the door?"

"Not his name. But he's an FBI agent. He and his pals were at my house the other night, looking for Alicia."

"And I thought *I* had hit a home run," Jimmy said.

"Really? How?"

"Well, it was pretty clear he was lying, just by the way he held himself and wouldn't let me in the door. An innocent person doesn't act that way, even if they don't want to let someone in. Usually, they'll apologize more, smile awkwardly, that sort of thing."

"Oh, he was lying, all right. I'm just not sure—"

"You two want to go anywhere special?" Angelita asked from the front. "I could just keep driving east, but we'd be in Chicago in three or four days."

"Drive anyplace away from the restaurant or the real estate office," Jimmy said, "till we figure this out."

He looked at Abby. "I can talk to Joey, see if he could get a search warrant to get into that house."

Abby shook her head. "When I stood outside that door just now, I had a feeling Alicia wasn't there—or if she was, she's gone."

"Oh? Anything substantial to base this feeling on?"

"Well, today, instead of just pretending no one was home, that FBI agent came to the door and opened it. Seems like he must have seen us coming up the walk, so he'd know we weren't anyone he was expecting."

"True. So why did he open the door?"

"I'm thinking he must have had word from the agents who were outside your mother's restaurant that you and I were on the run. And I'll bet my Cousin Harry disguise didn't fool him a bit. But he didn't grab us and arrest us. Or me, anyway. Don't you think that's a bit strange, when we just had to leap over rooftops to get away from the CIA, the FBI and a passel of Arizona and California cops?"

"Not if he wanted something from us," Jimmy said thoughtfully.

"Exactly. But what?"

"Now, there you've got me."

"Maybe he wanted to know if I'd found Alicia," Abby said, "or if we were there for some other reason.

Once you asked if she was in the house, he wasn't interested in us at all."

Jimmy frowned. "You're right," he said, "and this is looking more and more like some sort of setup."

"With me as the patsy."

"Angelita," Jimmy said to his cousin, "where are we going?"

"You told me to just drive, Kime. We're in Scottsdale now. Next stop Yuma, Mexico City, Rio..."

"Very funny. How about if we mosey on over to a pay phone instead."

"Sure thing."

"Who are you calling?" Abby asked.

"A guy I know downtown. He works for me on missing persons cases."

"You trust him?"

"With my life."

"I don't know about that," Angelita warned. "I remember one time—"

"That was a mistake," Jimmy said shortly. "Here—this gas station. Pull up!"

Angelita jammed on the brakes, hooked a hard right and thumped over the curb. She swore. "You're gonna owe me a new cab one of these days, cousin."

Jimmy got out and crossed to the phone booth while Angelita shook her head and made worried sounds.

"There's something wrong with this guy he's calling?" Abby asked.

"Oh, Juan's nice enough, I guess. He comes over to dinner sometimes, plays with the kids, sort of like an uncle. But there was that one time when I was pretty sure he got Kime in trouble on purpose."

"Really? What kind of trouble?"

"Kime was helping a father from Mexico to get to his children in Texas. The mother had crossed over with the kids a couple of years before, but the dad couldn't. Then the mother died, and there wasn't anybody to take care of the kids. A neighbor in their apartment house looked after them and tried to keep them out of child services, but they really needed their father."

"So Jimmy helped the dad to get into this country illegally?" Abby said.

"He tried to, with the idea that the father would straighten it out with INS after he got his kids. But Juan, who was supposed to drive him from the Arizona border to Texas, messed up and the dad got caught and deported. The kids have been in the system ever since."

"And you think Juan messed up on purpose? Why would he do that?"

"Money." Angelita faced front and folded her arms, sighing. "It's always money, when people don't have any."

"So Juan needs money?"

"All the time. Oh, don't get me wrong. He makes plenty. Juan just likes to spend it." Her laughter was bitter. "On the ladies, on gambling..."

"Then why is Jimmy trusting him now?"

"He probably isn't. But Juan knows his way around, and Jimmy needs somebody like that. Besides, Juan isn't all bad, he just bends the rules. Not that I'm anyone to talk."

Angelita turned again and grinned at Abby. "Like now, for instance. If they caught you with me—"

"If they caught me with you," Abby said, "I'd swear I'd never seen you before in my life. I'm not above bending a few rules myself."

Angelita smiled. "Sure, kid. I know that. But Kime's my cousin, and I worry about him, too."

It didn't take a genius to understand what she was saying. "You're right," Abby agreed. "It's time I got myself a new cabbie," she said firmly. "And a new lawyer."

"You might not need to do that," Jimmy said, getting in beside Abby again.

"Oh?"

"Juan says Alicia Gerard hasn't been reported missing—not here, or anywhere in the country. And neither have you."

"But that's impossible. I was told there had been an APB put out on Alicia back in Carmel. And you told me that according to the news, when I left the hospital, there was one on me, too."

"Well, there isn't anymore. Juan says they must have both been withdrawn."

"But why—"

"I'm thinking that maybe they don't want you found after all. I think they're still hoping that you'll lead them to Alicia."

Abby twisted to look out the back window. There weren't any cars she could remember having seen before today. There was a black sedan behind them now, but then, there were all kinds of black cars on the road.

"I don't get it," she said. "The FBI and CIA must have better ways of finding people than anyone else. Why would they need me to find her?"

"Good question. Juan suggested that somebody may be hiding her. If so, it would have to be someone with plenty of power. Enough power—and probably enough money—to outwit the federal government."

"Gerry!" Abby said immediately. "That would be Gerry, her husband."

"The thought did occur to me. You haven't talked to him, have you?"

"No, Alicia asked me not to. But I've been wondering what he was told. *If* he's been told. If the fact that she's missing is being covered up, and Gerry's not the one hiding her, maybe he hasn't heard anything at all."

Abby leaned forward and said, "Angelita, could you take me to the airport?"

"Sure. You need to pick up your clothes or anything first?"

Abby shook her head. "All I've got is what's on me right now."

Fortunately, that included the shorts and T-shirt she was still wearing under her disguise. She could dump the fisherman's clothes in the airport restroom, and she would still watch to see if she was being followed. But now that the APBs had been lifted on her and Alicia, she saw no reason to go to extreme lengths to hide.

To Jimmy, she said, "I've got Gerry's private cell phone number at home, and I'll call him from there. I think it's time I got back home, anyway, and checked on Jancy, their daughter."

"Would you like me to go with you?"

She studied him. "You'd do that?"

He shrugged and smiled. "Like I said, things are slow in Phoenix in the summer."

It was tempting. Jimmy had stood by her this entire day and had trusted her in the same way Ben once did.

Once being the operative word.

But she, like Angelita, didn't want to bring any more trouble down on him than she already had.

"Thanks," she said. "But this is something I have to do alone."

He raised a brow but didn't argue with her. Instead, he took out a card and wrote a number on the back of it. "This is my private cell number. Call me if I can help."

She hesitated but took it. "Okay."

"That's not a very resounding okay. Promise you'll call?"

She smiled. "*Okay.* I'm sure, though, that this will all be over by the time I get home. Alicia will have been found, she'll tell the authorities what they want to know, and life will go back to normal."

But even to her own ears that sounded false. When had life ever been "normal"? A feeling of impending disaster swept over her, and Abby's hand shook as she put the card away in her purse.

20

H. P. Gerard sat at a tempered glass desk the size of a pool table, staring out at the view. His three-story penthouse on Central Park West was worth more than a billion dollars today, but he'd bought it when it was "cheap" at only fifty-nine mil. He liked living like this, liked the perks and the way maître d's and waiters fell all over him when he walked into a hot new restaurant, issuing him past all the Brad Pitts, Robert Redfords and Julia Robertses who were left standing in line.

It hadn't always been like this. During law school and for years afterward, Gerry Gerard had lived in run-down houses, gone without food and worn beat-up jeans and Ts that made him look more like a college freshman than a lawyer.

Then, ten years ago, a change came over him. He began to look around at the people who were actually getting things done in the world, and one thing came to him loud and clear—they weren't schmucks like him. They were people who lived in penthouses and flew in private jets. They were, for the most part, the "rich white men" people talked about, the ones who ruled the world, who got things done—and not by marching with and defending the homeless, the illegal, the poor. The actual running of the world was done in boardrooms and country clubs, not out there with the people he'd been trying—with little cooperation from the government—to help.

Gerry had made the switch almost overnight, after seeing a bill that was close to his heart get shot down. He'd worked damned hard on that bill. If it had gone through, it would have eased the laws about illegal immigrants, letting them work legally at jobs they would pay taxes on, which—in his opinion and that of many others—could only benefit the country. Instead, illegals worked for employers who paid them peanuts under the table and didn't give them any benefits. They had no health insurance and no sick pay, and no way to take care of their families the way the average middle-class American family was able to—at least, was able to in good times.

The best thing about the bill he'd helped to shape, in his opinion, was that it dealt with the argument that illegal immigrants, most of whom came over the border from Mexico, would take jobs from the average middle-class American family. The truth was, the average middle-class worker either abhorred or hadn't the skills for most of the jobs Mexican immigrants were more than willing to do.

Thank God my parents taught me how to work, he thought. As a kid, Gerry had learned to do jobs most kids wouldn't take these days. There was the usual paper route or stocking shelves in a neighborhood grocery store, and in summers he mowed lawns and cooked burgers in fast-food restaurants. Because he had proved himself to be both a good employee and a smart one, his father had hired him to work at his law office in Gerry's junior and senior years of high school. He'd learned how to handle and get along with clients, and to come up with ideas for making the business run more smoothly and effectively. His mind had been sharpened and tested. And when he went off to college after his senior year, he was already ten steps ahead of many of the freshman kids, who'd only come to party and live off their parents' savings.

The best thing his father had taught him was to expect to be treated as well as any other employee of similar status. As long as he worked hard, showed up on time and didn't ask for special favors, his father had paid him the same as any other assistant in his office. Thus, at the end of each summer in the law office, Gerry had a nice chunk of change, which—except for a few personal expenditures—he gave back to his parents to put toward his tuition. The fairness his father had treated him with had taught him that it was only fair to give back, a lesson that had stuck with him all his life.

It was while sitting at a hotel bar one night, brooding about the failed bill for immigrant workers and missing Alicia and Jancy, that Gerry met Charles Grantham Jr. They had begun a friendship before Gerry even knew that Chuck was a mover and shaker, one of the few men that even the Donald Trumps of the world answered to.

Chuck, who was ten years older than Gerry, was a banker, from a long line of bankers who had escaped Black Thursday, the stock market crash of 1929. Having money at a time when very few did had proved to be an enormous asset, enabling the Grantham family to wield a lot of power. That power had carried over into politics, and it was said that Chuck's father and grandfather had placed more presidents in office than anyone knew or would ever know.

It was through Chuck Grantham that Gerry wound up in politics himself. Not that he'd ever even consider running for office; he was too smart now to think that being president made a man anything but a puppet to the Granthams and others of their ilk.

The word *ilk* gave him a guilty twinge. It sounded contemptuous. And even though Chuck Grantham and his family had let him into their inner sanctum, and his entire business had been built on their goodwill for him, he did have contempt in his heart for the kind of power they wielded. Even as he used it to his own benefit, he hated it—and despised himself for playing their game.

Gerry, at the Granthams' behest, had worked his way into the back rooms, the boardrooms and the private estates, where the decisions were made, the candidates chosen, and—polls and even votes to the contrary—the winner of the next presidential race would be decided. It hadn't taken Gerry long to learn that, with the right combination of money and staff, a president could be made. There was no luck to any of it, just strings being pulled behind the scenes, strings most American voters never saw and few even believed existed.

One day, Gerry knew, he would have to separate himself from their world, before he lost all respect for himself. But not now. Now, he needed all the help he could get.

The phone on his desk rang. Gerry blinked, staring at it as if it were a snake. He had purposely given his assistant the day off, and checking the caller ID, he saw it was the call he'd been waiting for.

He punched the speaker button. "Did you find her?" he said, his voice cold and hard.

For a moment he listened to the caller, frowning. Then he cut the man off. "I told you, no excuses, dammit! You know what to do."

He slammed the receiver down and sat there, thinking. The woman had to be stopped. She was ruining every chance he'd been given, every sacrifice he'd made to get where he was.

No matter the hurt, she had to go.

21

Abby made her way through the dark rose garden and let herself into the Prayer House. Tiptoeing down the hall, she tried to make it to her apartment without waking anyone. But at the far end of the hall stood a tall, dark figure.

Abby gasped, feeling her pulse flutter in her throat. As she neared the figure, however, she could see that the arms were crossed and the figure's left foot was tapping impatiently.

"God, Helen! You scared me to death! I was trying not to wake anyone!"

"Don't say 'God' like that."

"Sorry."

"You thought I wouldn't hear you parking your car?"

"Helen, it's way past midnight. You should be in bed."

"And how could I be, young lady? I haven't slept a wink since you've been gone. Where have you been? Why didn't you call?"

Abby felt as if she were a teenager, sneaking in late to find her mother waiting up.

"I told you I was going to Vegas," Abby said defensively. "And I called you from Phoenix."

"That was yesterday. Where have you been?"

Abby sighed and let herself into her apartment. "For heaven's sake, ease up. There hasn't been a lot of time for phone calls." A small smile curved her lips as she thought of the leap between the two buildings, and the disguise as "Cousin Harry." Well, that adventure in Phoenix had gotten her out of her rut, at least.

The smile disappeared as she realized she'd thought of her life as a "rut." She tossed her overnight bag onto the bed. "How is Jancy? Has she been okay?"

"That depends on what you mean by okay," Helen said disagreeably.

"Meaning?"

"Meaning, she disappeared yesterday and gave us all a fright."

"Disappeared!" Abby's eyes widened. "How long ago? Did she come back?"

Helen rolled her eyes. "Humph."

"She came back, Helen, *right?*"

"I suppose you might say that. Ben's police friend, Arnie, saw her in town and brought her back—complaining and sulking all the way, he said. She's up there in bed now, but she hasn't been talking to any of us since."

Abby sat on the edge of the bed, and motioned Helen to take the chair next to it.

"What happened?" she asked.

"You tell me," the nun answered, sitting heavily.

"Oh, for God's sake, stop trying to be mysterious and just tell me what's been going on!"

"I told you, don't say—"

"Helen!"

"Well, it's her that's being mysterious," Helen snapped. "Maybe now that you're home *at last*, young lady, you can drag something out of the girl."

Abby groaned. Why, why, why had Alicia left *her* with this responsibility? When would there ever be time to just go away somewhere and relax?

"I'm sorry Jancy was trouble for you," Abby said contritely. "I'll talk to her in the morning. How about the others?"

"Well, Narissa's been spending time with Jancy, even though she's not talking. Narissa just sails through everything, takes whatever comes like a freighter in a small breeze. Benicia's worried, though. She says the girl isn't eating."

Abby nodded. "I'll take care of it. Were there any more visits from the law, either local or federal?"

Helen sniffed. "If you're asking whether Chief Ben Schaeffer has been here to see you, no. And none of his cohorts, either."

Abby thought it best not to mention that Ben and the others had all been in Phoenix, either tracking her down or setting her up.

"Anything else?" she asked, yawning.

"No, and I can take a hint." Helen stood. As her knees took on her weight, she groaned.

"You need to get to that doctor for your arthritis," Abby said.

Helen mumbled something incoherent as she walked out and shut the door, but Abby got the usual message: *Butt out.*

She stretched out on the bed fully clothed and stared at the ceiling. What now? And where the hell did Jancy go yesterday? Had she snuck out to make a phone call to her mother? Was that the source of her silence ever since? And what could Allie have said to her—

Abby sat straight up, her tiredness gone.

Did Jancy actually *see* her mother? Had Alicia been here, on the property? Or in town? Was that why Jancy had disappeared, to meet her somewhere?

Her tiredness gone, Abby took a flashlight from her desk and walked quietly through the dim hall to the main stairs and the second floor, then toward the solarium and Jancy's room. Opening the door slightly, she listened for the even breathing of a sleeping person.

Nothing.

Sweeping her flashlight over the bed, she saw a slight shape under the sheets. Crossing over, she reached out a hand and touched the form lightly.

"Jancy? Jancy, it's me, Abby."

The form didn't move, and Abby, somehow knowing all along that it wouldn't, swept back the sheets.

Pillows. No Jancy, just pillows.

22

Though she was tired enough to drop in her tracks, Abby went from Jancy's room into the office in her apartment. Crossing over to a drawer, she opened a small red leather address book and found Gerry Gerard's private phone number, at his penthouse in New York. No one except family and close friends had this number, and Abby hadn't even remembered having it herself until earlier today. It had finally come back to her that Allie had given her the number a couple of years ago in case of "an emergency."

Funny. That was exactly what she'd told Willow when giving her the Phoenix phone number. What kind of emergency had Allie expected, even way back then?

She punched in the number on the desk phone and listened as the one in New York rang several times. Glancing at the small gold-framed clock Ben had given her last year for her thirty-eighth birthday, she saw that it was after 2:00 a.m.—5:00 a.m. in New York. If Gerry was home, he'd still be sleeping now, wouldn't he? Maybe he had this private phone turned off.

But a moment later she heard his voice, sounding rushed, impatient and very much awake. "What?"

"Gerry?" she said, somewhat taken aback. "It's Abby. Abby Northrup."

"Oh. Abby. Sorry, I was in the shower. What's up?" His tone was brusque and not very friendly.

"I'm calling about Alicia," she said. "And Jancy."

"What about them?" Gerry snapped.

"I, uh…wondered if you've heard from them."

"No, I have not. Why?"

"You haven't had any calls from anyone about them?"

"No, of course not. Look, Abby, this is a bad time. I can't talk right now."

"Gerry, wait! Alicia's in trouble with the law. The FBI and the CIA are after her, and no one can find her."

There was a small silence. "Abby…how long has it been since you've seen or talked with Alicia?"

There was something not quite right about his reaction, and she was suddenly on guard. "I don't know, Gerry. A few years?"

"Then you probably don't know how dramatic she can be these days. Alicia has a way of stirring up trouble and then making far too much of it."

"Gerry, she's wanted for murder," Abby said mildly. "I doubt the people who are looking for her are making too much of it."

"See, that's what I mean. In all likelihood she was in the area of a murder but doesn't know a thing about it. She'll straighten it out, Abby, you'll see. Now, if you don't mind—"

"Dammit, I do mind! What about Jancy? You didn't even ask, Gerry."

"What about her?"

"Jancy has disappeared, too."

A small silence. Then, "Jancy is even more of a drama queen than her mother," he said impatiently. "I'm sure she'll turn up sooner or later."

With that, he hung up, leaving Abby to sit there staring at a dead phone.

Abby went to her little kitchen and made herself a single cup of coffee in the pod coffeemaker she kept in there. Then, grabbing one of the homemade cinnamon doughnuts from the plate Binny had left for her, she went back to her desk.

Would Arnie be at the station in Carmel, she wondered, since Ben was off in Phoenix or wherever? She never knew where Ben might be these days, since he'd joined forces with his new blond friend.

She picked up her cell phone and punched in the number for the police station business line. Tess, one of the female dispatchers, answered and told her Arnie was off.

"Probably asleep. Can I take a message? You can leave your number, and I'm sure he'll call you in the morning."

"No, thanks. I'm in Seattle, so I'll just call him when I get back."

Tess was a nice person, but Abby wasn't about to trust anyone except Arnie with the news that she was home. Even though the APB on her had been canceled, she wanted some room to navigate before having to answer questions from a bunch of cops, agents, whomever.

Besides, Arnie used to be Ben's partner, and she knew his home number by heart. Like Gerry's, though, it rang on and on.

"Whoever you are," Arnie said finally in a grouchy, half-awake voice, "go away."

"Wait! Don't hang up, Arnie. It's me, Abby."

"Ab?" She could hear him lighting a cigarette and taking a puff. "Where are you?" he asked.

She ignored the question. "Sorry to wake you, but Jancy's gone again. I need to know where you found her yesterday."

"Walking along Highway 1," he answered. "I was on my way down to Rocky Point to meet somebody for lunch, and there she was on the side of the road. I called the Prayer House, but Sister Helen said you were out of town. You back home now?"

"That's the second time you've asked me that, Arnie. Don't you and Ben collaborate on my whereabouts?"

"Well, I did hear you were in a hospital in Phoenix. You okay? You home?"

"I'm fine, but I'm not home. I'm in a motel in Barstow."

"_Barstow?_ You must be on your way home, then? I mean, geez, no offense to Barstowians, but nobody goes there except to pass through or die."

"Nevertheless, that's where I am," she said. "Arnie, I just talked to Sister Helen a while ago, and like I said,

Jancy's gone again. We need some sort of clue as to where she might be. Was she heading south yesterday? Like, toward L.A.?"

"Nah. Actually, north—toward town."

"Really?"

"I thought that was funny, too. A kid runs away, she should be leaving town, not running toward it."

"Was she actually running?"

"Like the devil himself was on her heels. I was in one of the cruisers, and to tell you the truth, I don't think she'd have gotten in the car with me if she wasn't afraid of something. She kept looking back, and I tried to get it out of her where she'd been, but she wouldn't tell me a thing. And like I said, Sister Helen told me to bring her out to the Prayer House, so I did."

"You know, Arnie, now that I think of it, there's something wrong with all that."

There was a pause at his end of the line. "Okay. Shoot."

"See, Ben and those agents were at the Prayer House looking for Jancy, as well as Alicia, the other night. A woman and a teenager—Alicia and Jancy. But I told them they weren't at the Prayer House. Right?"

"Uh…right, I guess."

"Yet you called the Prayer House yesterday to tell me you'd found Jancy. Why would you do that? And come to think of it, isn't there an APB out on her as well as Alicia?"

"Dammit, Abby, I was just trying to do you and the kid a favor. The kid begged me not to take her in. She said she wanted to go to the Prayer House instead, and she promised to stay put out there if I let her stay with you. And yeah, I knew about the APB. But Abby, she's just a kid. I wouldn't want one of my kids sitting in a holding cell when there wasn't any proof she'd done anything wrong."

"So, there still is an APB out on Jancy and Alicia?"

"I can't really talk about that, Ab."

"Because it's been pulled, right? They've ordered it canceled."

"They?"

"Oh, for heaven's sake, Arnie! The FBI. The CIA. Pat Robertson. Who the hell knows?"

"Like I said, I can't—"

"Never mind. And hey, thanks for taking Jancy out to the Prayer House. You're a real pal."

"Do I detect a note of sarcasm in that?"

"Just wondering how many people are watching the Prayer House now, and following Jancy's every move."

"If that's what's going on, Abby, I swear I don't know about it. Ben's been keeping me pretty much in the dark on this one."

"So I guess he didn't tell you they canceled the APB on me, too."

"Not a word," Arnie said. "How were things in Phoenix?" he added casually, as if asking, "How was the weather?"

"Oh, so-so," Abby said.

"Yeah, I didn't think you'd tell me anything. Had to try, though."

"What about you?" she asked. "Would you tell me how Ben and his cronies happened to find me there?"

"Like I said—"

"You don't know anything," Abby interrupted.

"I swear. All's I know is Ben went off on some special assignment with that CIA person, and he's playing his cards close to the vest on this one."

"CIA person? You mean Lessing? FBI?"

"Him, too, but Ben's mostly working with that woman—Kris Kelley."

"Lovely," Abby said.

So they were together on the same assignment—tracking *her*, to see if she met up with Alicia.

Well, not much chance of that. Alicia was proving a bit too hard to find. And now, it seemed, so was Jancy.

23

Abby tried to nap, but an idea nagged at her, keeping her awake. Finally she got up, took a shower and dressed in clean jeans, a warm sweater, a leather jacket and hiking boots. Grabbing the small kit of tools she sometimes used when helping to relocate the women who came to the Prayer House, she quietly slipped outside. The fog was thick and it was still cold and dark when she got into her car and drove into Carmel.

At Highway 1, after checking to see that no cars had followed her, she turned left and headed south toward Big Sur. At this hour of the morning she had the winding road to herself, except for an occasional truck servicing food to the few inns that dotted the landscape on either side. With nothing but steep cliffs on her left and the ocean crashing against jagged rocks hundreds of feet below on her right, she followed a truck's taillights. Her fingers, gripping the steering wheel, were white, but she felt reassured that as long as that truck stayed on the road, chances were she would, too.

Jancy had told her that Mike and Betty Randolph's

house in Big Sur was the one the Gerards had been borrowing for vacations. Fortunately, she knew where the Randolph house was, having been there a couple of times during her marriage, when Jeffrey was part of the local political crowd. The three men—Mike, Gerry and her husband—had graduated from Yale and had that well-known "men's club" thing going for them—buddies helping buddies, no matter what, for life.

She was pretty sure now that Jancy must have been coming from the Randolph's house the day before, when Arnie found her heading back into town. If Alicia had been in the Carmel area last night, what better place to meet Jancy than a secluded house on a peninsula overlooking the Pacific, ten miles south of town?

For that matter, what better place to hide out than the remote Randolph house?

A memory flew back of the time she'd had to break into the house of an abused woman who was being held prisoner by her own husband. To keep her inside while he was at work, he'd boarded up all the windows of the isolated house, and installed several locks on the outside of the door. Neighbors believed the house had been abandoned, and the woman had been a virtual hostage there for months before she'd finally managed to call her sister for help. The sister had been referred to Abby by a friend who knew about her work with *Paseo*.

"That phone call to me nearly cost Debbie her life," the sister had said.

Debbie Lutz, after one particularly brutal beating, had managed to screw up just enough nerve to smash open the locked cabinet where her husband kept the phone when he was out of the house. That was two months before, the sister had told Abby, and Debbie'd had to end the call abruptly, afraid that her husband had returned. It was the first time the sister had heard from her in months. The sister, who had thought they'd had a falling-out, was shocked to hear what was going on.

The husband, when the sister confronted him, tried to cover by saying his wife was "going through one of those female things, a kind of depression, and the doctors didn't want her disturbed."

The sister didn't buy it. She tried all the legal channels, but was told time after time that if Debbie herself didn't ask them for help they couldn't do a thing. Finally, the sister ended up at Abby's door.

Abby, knowing full well what the consequences might be if she wasn't successful, was too enraged about the situation to care. She knew what it felt like to be abused, and she wouldn't be worthy of the job she was doing if she let this pass.

With the sister standing by, Abby had driven out to the house in Seaside while the husband was at work, torn the boards off a window with a tire jack and broken the glass to get in.

Since they hadn't been able to warn Debbie that they'd be there, she was terrified when she saw daylight for the first time in months—not to mention a woman in jeans, boots and heavy leather work gloves bursting through shards of glass to get to her.

The sister calmed her, though, and they managed to

get Debbie to Abby's car and then a safe place before the husband ever knew what had happened.

Once free, Debbie was able to tell the police what had happened. After her husband had been arrested and jailed, she agreed to talk to reporters. She was asked why she hadn't just screamed for help till it came. "Because my husband sometimes came back and stood out on the porch listening, just to make sure I wasn't 'trying anything funny,'" she told them. The one time she did try to scream for help, her husband was out there hearing it. He'd beaten her up and left her with a broken arm, warning that if she ever tried that again he would cut out her tongue.

Abby shuddered at the memory, and in the fog, she almost missed the Randolphs' drive on the ocean side. The truck she'd been following had turned off at one of the inns, and she'd had to creep along at ten miles per hour since then, her gaze fixed like glue on the barely visible stripe along the narrow road.

It was the old "Survivor" tree that stopped her. A huge Monterey pine, it was famous for having withstood all the mudslides that had taken down parts of this highway over the years. The giant tree, its arms splayed wide as if warding off the winds that had barreled in from offshore over the years, stood at the foot of the Randolphs' drive.

Abby braked and backed up a few feet, then parked just off the highway, out of sight of the house. Trudging up the muddy drive, she shivered in the chill air and buttoned her leather jacket, shoving her hands into the pockets for warmth. The house was about a hundred feet from the highway and around a curve, so she couldn't see it until she was nearly on top of it. Then, what she did see made her catch her breath.

Something new had been added—a tall iron gate with an intercom box, and a high-security fence around the front and side gardens that seemd to extend along the back as well. Along the top were four strands of wire. A sign stated that they were electrified.

Of course, times had changed since she'd been here in '92. People with money had to protect themselves now from home invasions and any number of dangers. But was all this necessary?

Abby hunkered down next to shrubbery and studied the house. There were no lights on, and no sounds coming from it. She looked at her watch. Just after 5:00 a.m. If Jancy was in there, she'd probably still be sleeping. But Alicia? Would she be sleeping, knowing that the law was on her tail?

Or maybe I'm on the wrong track entirely. Maybe the Randolphs are in there. Maybe I'll get caught and arrested for housebreaking.

For that matter, why aren't the cops or the FBI here watching this place, in case Alicia does show up?

Because they don't know about it. Still...it couldn't have been that hard to find out.

Standing, she took a deep breath and released some tension along with it. She was still nervous, though, and her shaking hands were proof of it. Finally she straightened her shoulders and walked toward the gate. This wouldn't be nearly as bad as the case of the abused wife, she reminded herself. All she had to do was ring the bell on the intercom, and see who—if anyone—answered. If the Randolphs were home, she could say in all honesty that she was looking for Jancy.

Or, if Jancy answered, she'd somehow talk her into letting her in. Then, she thought, her mouth tightening into a grim line, she'd find a rope, hogtie the kid and carry her over her shoulder out to the car.

Alicia, of course, was another matter. Abby didn't like to think what she'd do about Alicia, after she'd almost been killed looking for her.

24

None of the scenarios Abby had imagined happened. No one answered the intercom, and the gate, on closer inspection, had been left unlocked.

Odd, unless Jancy forgot to lock it when she ran from here yesterday. *If* she ran from here yesterday.

Once on the porch, she rang the bell next to the door. There was no sound of approaching footsteps or of anyone calling out sleepily.

She knocked several times, but still nothing. The beveled glass in the door bent everything out of shape, and she couldn't tell if there was someone in there or if what she saw was merely a chair. The only thing she knew for certain was that a light was on somewhere inside.

Just for the hell of it, she tried the door. If the gate was unlocked, maybe someone had left the door that way, too.

But no luck. The doorknob didn't even move. And there was still no sign of life inside.

So, Plan B. Abby drew the small burglary kit from

her jacket pocket, found the tool she wanted and after a few moments had the door unlocked. She opened it, then crossed the foyer and entered the living room, where she stood listening for the sound of a security alarm.

Nothing.

So she'd figured that right, at least. If Jancy had been in this house yesterday and was running from it when Arnie came across her, she probably hadn't thought to set the alarm or lock the gate.

Several questions remained unanswered, though. What, or who, had she been running from here? Had someone threatened her? Or was she nearly caught by someone and ran to escape being seen?

Abby stood there getting her bearings. Sweeping the beam of her penlight, she saw before her a massive "great room." To her left was a large living room area with high beams, wall-to-wall windows and a huge stone fireplace. To the right was a sunken family room area with a U-shaped sectional pointing toward a big, black eye that turned out to be a television screen at least seventy inches wide. Straight ahead of her, to the rear, was a kitchen with a long granite-topped island and six light oak stools facing it.

On the far right side of this great room was a hall-way, presumably leading to the bedrooms and baths.

Abby crossed to the kitchen first and opened the refrigerator. The hardwood floors creaked as she walked, making her even more nervous. If anyone was in here, surely they'd hear that.

Stop being paranoid. If there was anyone here, they would already have shown themselves.

Picking up a carton of low-fat milk, Abby opened and sniffed it, making a face. Sour. Putting it back, she noted that the only other food in the fridge was a quarter-pound stick of butter and a moldy loaf of seven-grain bread. Her stomach growled. Bread and butter were her favorite guilty snacks, and she hadn't eaten since the airport in Phoenix, waiting for her plane to take off.

But even if she'd had the time or the inclination to eat here, there were no fixings for a meal, no sweets for dessert. Not even ice cream in the freezer. This did not look like a place where Alicia, Gerry and Jancy had been vacationing—at least, not anytime lately.

Next, she made a quick survey of the entire house, opening doors to bedrooms, closets and, finally, an office. All of the rooms had been nicely decorated, but weren't notable in any particular way until she came to this one. A bank of windows looked out to a slope with a row of evergreen trees at the bottom, and beyond them, the ocean. The trees were just becoming visible now that the fog had begun to lift and dawn had arrived. In the twenty-by-twenty-or-so room, two walls were lined with bookcases from floor to ceiling, while a third held light maple file cabinets and office equipment. On top of the low file cabinets was a combination fax, copy machine and color printer. On either side of that was a desktop computer. Smaller pieces of office equipment were lined up on the cabinets, along with an electric pencil sharpener and a large-screen plasma TV. The TV was hooked up to a VCR, a handheld video camera and a notebook computer.

The computers had been turned off. Abby's first thought was to turn them on and go through all three of them. Then she remembered that, from the first time they'd met, Allie had always had a notebook computer with her even before they were common. She liked working on planes and in airports to pass the time, and liked being able to write out her notes in hotel rooms the night before her speeches.

Thinking it might be the most likely source of recent information, Abby crossed over to the notebook, turning it on. As she waited for the programs to load, she thought she heard a sound somewhere in the house. For a moment she froze, but the sound didn't reoccur. She'd looked in every corner, every closet, every nook and cranny, she reasoned, and there was no one there. The tiny thud she'd heard was probably pinecones falling on the roof, or a squirrel running across it. She was nervous, that was all.

The log-in screen appeared, telling her this was Alicia's computer, and asked for a password.

Damn. What would Alicia use as a password? *Jancy?* Abby tried it. Nothing.

Next she tried *Gerry,* followed by *H. P.* None of them worked.

Thinking back, she tried to remember everything she knew about Alicia. Within minutes, she realized that Alicia had never shared much about her personal life. That came as a shock. Funny how you can "know" someone for years and think you're close, but there are so many things you never share.

It was a stream-of-consciousness exercise that got her in. She'd been feverishly trying any combination of words she thought might apply when she made herself calm down and just let her mind wander. A few moments later, she remembered that Allie had sent her a postcard from Maui a couple of years ago. On it, she'd raved about the island and the beach house she was staying at with Jancy. *"It's called,* Hale Pau Hana," she'd written. *"House of No Work. When I get home, that's just the kind of house I want!"*

The postcard was the last Abby had heard from Alicia, until she and Jancy had come to the Prayer House. She knew that people sometimes used their favorite vacation places for passwords, just as they used their favorite pets' names or colors. Since she hadn't come up with anything else, she typed in "Maui."

Nothing. Well, it was a reach.

"House of No Work" was a bust, too.

Holding out little hope, she tried, *"Hale Pau Hana,"* and almost fell over when the desktop miraculously appeared.

A shiver of excitement went through her, but there was little time to savor the win. Starting with the obvious, she opened Alicia's e-mail and ran down the list of saved mail, looking for something, anything, that might be a clue as to where Alicia was. A letter to someone, a travel itinerary, a confirmation of plane tickets.

At first she looked only at the past week's e-mails, both sent and received. Then she realized that Alicia wouldn't be likely to have a record of where she'd gone this time, since she hadn't expected to be on the run. Abby began to look back a month, then two and three. Four, then five.

Nothing but sales ads from stores, brief notes to a friend saying the weather was good, bad, whatever, and what had *her* family been doing lately? One was a recipe for chocolate cake, and another was to a company, complaining about the quality of their foods.

Abby was about to give up and go to one of the larger computers when she remembered a trick of her own, one she'd developed when she was married, to hide her daily journals from Jeffrey's prying eyes. She'd set up a folder called Household Bills—nothing he'd be likely to care about—and then a subfolder under it for gas, another under that one for electricity, and so on until the seventh or eighth folder down said "Paid Bills." That was the one she always saved her journal to, buried so deep that Jeffrey, who knew almost nothing about computers, would never be likely to find it.

She also remembered sharing this information with Alicia.

Looking through the folders on Alicia's computer, she found one titled Travel, which seemed appropriate but too obvious. It was empty. Another, titled Dogs, drew her attention next, since she had never known Alicia to have a dog.

She hit the plus sign next to it and almost laughed

when the subfolders came up and she saw that Alicia had adopted her idea. Under dogs was cats, then fish, then birds, and so on—a virtual Noah's ark of files. Finally a subfolder named Coyote appeared. Remembering again that the coyote was known to be a trickster, Abby opened that folder. Inside it were several travel confirmations and receipts for airline tickets.

None of them included itineraries, though—no information other than "from" and "to." There were flights once every month to various cities, but no notes about how to reach Alicia in any of them—where she was staying, phone and fax numbers, business contacts.

Abby made one more try, going back over the list of e-mail messages again. There was one that had struck her eye as she'd scanned down them before. On the subject line was one word: Lily. Something about that had nagged at her.

She clicked on the e-mail, thinking it might just be a gardening article, as Alicia had always been an avid gardener. But the only thing on the screen was a photograph of a lily—an Easter lily, if she remembered her Easter Sundays in church as a kid. The pot was wrapped in yellow foil, and imprinted on that was a gold cross.

Abby stared, wondering if the cross meant anything specific. Then, music began in the background. The voice sounded like Glen Campbell's, or possibly the kind of sound-alike singer that e-cards often used. She missed the first words but heard "…sea winds blowing…" What the—

Galveston. The song Glen Campbell used to sing. She remembered it well.

Odd, though—a song like that with a picture of an Easter lily.

Going online, she typed "Easter lily" into Google. Any number of sites came up, but except for the fact that Easter lilies were native to Japan and poisonous to cats, this was all simply information about gardening. One noted that ninety-five percent of all Easter lily bulbs in the world were grown along the California-Oregon border, and Abby rummaged around in her brain to come up with some connection between that area and any of the trips Alicia had taken.

Nothing came, but she made a note to keep it in mind until she could share it with Ben and ask him for his thoughts on it.

That stopped her in her tracks. Share it with Ben? Maybe before, but now? An ache grew in her collarbones, along with a sense of emptiness and loss. There hadn't been time to think much about Ben these past few days, other than to keep one step ahead of him. Instead of backing her up, he seemed to have aligned himself with the "other side" now. She felt completely distanced from him, as if a limb had been cut off.

Shaking her head at herself, she almost closed the Google page, wanting to go home and crawl under her covers and sleep. She could be here all night looking for some kind of clue on all these sites.

Unwilling to give up, though, she decided on one more try. Typing "Encyclopedia Britannica" into

Google, she waited while the online version came up. Then she typed "Easter lily" into the search space. What she saw there made her blink in disbelief.

Out of eighty-some references, the first one listed was "Easter Rising—1916. Republican insurrection in Ireland against the British, which began on Easter Monday, April 24."

Abby lost all sense of time as she dug further into the bowels of the Internet, bringing up article after article about the IRA. One of the things she found was that the Easter lily was the symbol of the 1916 Easter Rising in Dublin.

From her Catholic upbringing, she recalled that the Easter lily, used for years to decorate churches on Easter Sunday, was a symbol of resurrection—new life. But she'd had no idea that IRA members wore the lily in remembrance of those who gave their lives for the cause of Irish independence.

Okay… The lily began to make sense, given what she'd been told about Alicia's father and his connection to the IRA. But "Galveston"? Where did the song fit in?

She ran through the words in her head, recalling that it was about a man in a war, afraid of dying, as he remembered his girl in Galveston. It was a sad song about him missing her and longing to see her again.

Was Alicia's father telling her that he and her mother missed her and that she could find them in Galveston? One of those tickets a month ago had been to Houston, which was only an hour or so north of Galveston.

Could be a stretch, Abby thought, but it seemed worth following up on until something else came to mind.

She sighed and rubbed her face, looking up from the computer. Sunlight was pouring through the windows of the cathedral ceiling, and she was astonished to realize how long she had been standing there. Looking at her watch she saw that it was after 7:00 a.m. Three hours? Her back hurt and her feet felt like she'd been hiking uphill on razor blades.

Stretching, she did a few yoga exercises to get her limbs moving again. Then, straightening, she headed toward the office door, only to jerk to a stop as a noise sounded in another part of the house. The sound was like that of door hinges that needed oiling. A squeak, then an abrupt halt, as if the person opening the door didn't want to be heard.

Abby flattened her back against the wall just inside the office, listening.

Footsteps, hushed and quick. Something falling in the kitchen, thudding on the counter. A dish? A cup? Then the distinct sound of a refrigerator door opening, the little swish of suction it made.

Not Jancy. Not even Allie. This was all too quiet to be someone who belonged here, someone "rattling around" as she made her morning coffee.

Abby inched around the corner of the doorway into the hall, then along the hallway toward the great room and kitchen. Stopping just short of the great room, she paused to listen but heard nothing more. The entire house was now silent.

The hairs on the back of her arms and neck rose. Something was wrong. Nobody went into a kitchen and just stood there without making another move. Had he or she heard her in the hallway? Were they playing their own waiting game?

No longer able to take not knowing, she rounded the corner of the hallway in one swift move, hoping to startle whoever was there.

Instead, her heart jumped into her throat as the cold business end of a gun was jammed against her forehead.

"Stop right there," a voice said coldly. "Don't even breathe."

25

Abby's limbs were shaking. Part of that was from hunger and low blood sugar, she knew, but the rest was from having her life literally flash before her eyes.

She had all but collapsed into a chair at the dining table in the great room. The gun was still in the hand of its owner, who sat in a chair across from her. It was held loosely, but at the ready. Abby noted that the CIA agent's hands were trembling and there were deep dark circles under her eyes. The usually smooth blond hair was disheveled, as if she hadn't bothered to even look at it when she got up—if, indeed, she had slept at all.

Something was terribly wrong.

"Is Alicia Gerard here?" Kris Kelley demanded, her voice harsh.

"No."

"Do you know where she is?"

"No."

"I suppose you don't know, either, that Ben's out at the Prayer House looking for you?"

"I do now that you've told me," Abby said. "So?"

"So, you're in big trouble."

"Wow. As you can see, I'm shaking."

"Abby," Kris said sharply, "do you understand the kind of trouble you're in?"

"Not exactly. Are you taking me in now, locking me up under the Patriot Act or some other un-American law, the way you'd like to do with Alicia?"

"On the contrary. I'm trying to figure out how the hell to keep you from getting locked up."

"Golly, how nice of you. I didn't know the CIA had a heart."

"Believe me, we don't. Now, will you please shut up and listen to me?"

Given the other woman's jumpy state, Abby decided to stop baiting her. "What's going on?" she said.

"Agent Lessing is getting desperate," Kris said. "He wants Alicia Gerard, and he wants her now. If he gets his hands on you, he'll do whatever's necessary to make you tell him where she is."

"Whatever's necessary…" Abby hid a sudden surge of fear. "Are we talking torture? Truth-telling drugs? What?"

"I didn't say that. But, as long as you're imagining, imagine something much, much worse."

"Well, before I'm lashed to a rack and stretched till I'm nine feet tall, would you like to tell me how Alicia Gerard is involved in this terrorist attack Ben told me about?"

Kris's trembling had stopped, but she was obviously still at a breaking point. "I'll tell you, but only because

I've got to trust you, Abby. You can't tell anyone about this."

"We'll see," Abby said, "when I hear what it is."

Kris's mouth tightened. "You are the most—" But she broke off her retort and went on. "We have credible intel that Alicia's father is working with a splinter group of the IRA called The Candlelights. Without going into all the history, Pat Devlin—Alicia's father— is making a doomsday bomb for them, and if we don't get to him fast, millions of lives will be lost."

Abby hid her shock. "This is real? My God. Ben said the attack was planned for a few days from now. And you still don't know where this is supposed to happen?"

"No. Also, Ben wasn't being exact when he said a few days. We have less than three days left now. It's imperative that we get to Alicia's father, arrest him and make him turn that bomb over to us."

Abby looked at her skeptically. "He couldn't just destroy it, huh? Our government wants to study it, right? Back engineer it?"

Kris paused, swallowed, and when she spoke her voice was shaking again. "I don't know, Abby. For God's sake, what does it matter? The point is, we have to find Alicia Gerard. She can lead us to her father, and once we have him, the attack can be averted, at least for now. God only knows how long it'll take them to find someone else to do their dirty work."

Abby narrowed her eyes. "Okay, let me get this straight. You're CIA. The CIA and FBI have been after me because they think I know where Alicia is. But now that you've got me, you aren't taking me in? You're trusting me with all this information because we're such great pals?"

"Of course not," Kris snapped. "I'm trusting you because I don't have a choice. I need you."

"Aah. So, get on with it, then. Obviously, I don't know where Alicia is, or I'd tell you, now that I know what's at stake. Given that, what else could you possibly want from me?"

Kris's voice shook badly now, and Abby was startled to see that her eyes filled with tears. "They've got my son, Abby. My little boy, Danny. He's seven years old, and they've got him!"

Her entire sleek facade crumbled as she burst into tears.

"Who?" Abby demanded, shocked. *"Who's* got him?"

Kris grabbed a paper napkin from the middle of the table and blew her nose. "The IRA. The Candlelights. They've threatened to kill Danny if I don't keep Pat Devlin from being found and stopped."

"Good God, Kris!" Abby's first instinct was empathy for Kris as a mother. Her second was to wonder if what the CIA agent said was the truth. "Why you? Why your son?"

The agent shook her head. "They must know I'm a key player in this case. Abby, it doesn't matter! What matters is that they've got my boy!"

Abby's hand went out to her. "I'm sorry. I truly am."

Kris's voice went from shaky to grim. "They grabbed him from our backyard in San Francisco. Sara, his nanny, turned away from the kitchen window to answer the phone, and when she turned back he was gone. Just like that. Abby, the yard was completely fenced."

She paused, swallowed and began again. "The lock on the gate wasn't even broken. They must have gotten a key somehow."

"The nanny?"

Kris shook her head. "Sara's been with us since Danny was born, and I'd trust her with my life. She's almost as devastated as I am." Kris dug into a pocket of her black jacket and slid a piece of green paper over to Abby. "They left this, stuck between boards in the gate."

Abby reached for the page. Drawn in gold ink on the top left side was a lily. She read the note and studied Kris Kelley. "It says they've taken your son out of the country, and if Pat Devlin is found and his work is stopped, Danny dies. It says if you keep Devlin from being found, they'll let Danny live."

Abby shook her head. "Kris, this is crazy! Let's say you could actually find a way to botch the search for Pat Devlin, you can't honestly believe these people will release Danny when this is all over."

"No. No, of course I don't believe it. But I'm half out of my mind, trying to think what to do. If Devlin isn't stopped, half the people in this country are almost certainly dead. If he is caught and stopped—" She wiped tears from her eyes. "I can't even think what they'll do to Danny...what they might even be doing to him now."

Abby read the note again. "There's something weird about this. In the first place, what makes them think you can do anything about this? Even if you, personally, were to try to keep Pat Devlin from getting arrested, you'd be up against the FBI, the CIA and swarms of other agents who must already be all over this case. There's no way you could get them to back off, not with the lives of millions of people at stake."

"Dammit, don't you think I know that?" Kris's face flamed. "Sorry. I'm just about over the edge, Abby. That's why I need your help."

"My help?"

Kris began to pace, and Abby had a feeling of foreboding. Kris was too desperate, too panicked by Danny's kidnapping. Could she possibly be thinking straight? Could she be trusted?

"The thing is," Kris said, "I can con them. The Candlelights, Lessing, everybody. I'm good at conning people. I've been doing it all my life. And you know what? You are, too, Abby. I knew that the minute I met you."

She waved off Abby's protest. "Don't even bother. Now, look, here's the way it goes down. Let's say I get conveniently sick all of a sudden. Some weird summer virus. I can pretend I'm too sick to work and have to stay in bed. I'll tell them I'm going home to San Francisco for a few days."

"But you'll really be…?"

"Looking for Danny."

"Looking for… But Kris, it says here they've taken

him out of the country. How would you even know where to begin?"

"Leave that to me. I'll work it out. Will you do it?"

"Will I do *what?* You haven't even told me what you want me to do."

"You—" Kris took a deep breath. "You just have to keep looking for Alicia and get to her and Pat Devlin before the feds. You stop Devlin from finishing that bomb, or if he is finished, and, God willing, he hasn't already turned it over to The Candlelights—then stop him from doing that. When I find Danny and have him safe in my hands, I'll call you. That's when you turn Devlin in."

"That's *all?*" Abby said. "Well, then, I can't tell you how relieved I am. I just have to find Pat Devlin before the FBI, the CIA, all seventeen or so of the new security agencies, various police departments and God knows who else…and then all I have to do is chain and padlock him to a chair, throw away the key and hold him hostage till I hear from you." She would have laughed, if the situation hadn't been so serious. "Gee, Kris, not a problem."

She sat staring at Kris until the woman stopped pacing and realized what she'd said. Her voice softened. "I know it's a lot. But think of it, Abby. You'll be a hero."

"My life's dream," Abby said, "to die a hero. Do they have Purple Hearts for citizens?"

Kris's voice caught on a sob. "Please, Abby! Don't think I don't know what I'm asking of you. I just don't know where else to turn. I thought maybe Ben, but he…well, you know…."

"Ben is a stickler for the rules," Abby agreed. "He'd tell Lessing and they'd probably lock you up to keep you from running off in search of Danny and possibly botching the case."

Kris took one of her hands. "I can't promise you, Abby, that the FBI won't find you and lock *you* up. Or that The Candlelights won't grab you and try to finish you off this time—"

"Wait, *this* time? They're the ones who put me in that car in the junkyard? But that house in Phoenix belonged to the CIA. What were The Candlelights doing there?"

"Following you, most likely," Kris said. "It was more than just a warning, Abby. You have to start watching your back better."

Abby stared down at the note. It was handwritten in block letters, which wouldn't be easy to identify, even for a handwriting expert. As for fingerprints, she couldn't ask Arnie or Ben to check for them. They'd ask too many questions, and that would defeat the whole purpose.

"I'm just not sure I can do this," she said. "Kris, I think maybe you've got me all wrong. Sure, I help women who are on the run, but I don't work the streets to do it. There are other people who do that, while I sit behind my desk in my nice little Prayer House ivory tower and write checks, talk to people, provide the moms and kids with a bed for the night. I don't have any special skills in tracking people down."

Kris took her by the shoulders. "For God's sake, Abby, look at yourself! And take a second look while you're at it. You were one step ahead of us all the way, till you showed up at that house in Phoenix."

"Yeah, that went well," Abby said.

"Not your fault. The agents there should have been expecting trouble. If they didn't see The Candlelights grab you, I don't see how you could have, either."

"But that's not the point. I never should have been there. What an idiot I was, tramping around in the dark like some supersleuth who didn't even know which end was up."

Kris sat back down and took Abby's hands. "Please, don't do that. There isn't time now. Look, Abby, you've got good instincts. And you know Alicia Gerard better than anyone on this case. You're the kind of friends that can pick up after not seeing each other for a long time and it's like you've never been apart. And listen, I'm not asking you to save the world. As soon as I know Danny's safe you can call whoever you want—Ben, Lessing, the police. Turn Devlin in, and let them take over. All I need is a little time to find my kid, first."

The woman's hands were freezing, and Abby shivered. *Millions of lives at stake. Three days left. No, two, by the time she figured out where to start looking.* What if she never found Alicia, or she did, and Alicia didn't know where her father was? Or what if she, Abby, found him and he didn't agree to turn the bomb over to the authorities?

Of course he wouldn't agree. Why would he? She'd have to hold a gun to his head. And even then, she didn't know anything about bombs. How could she know he wasn't deceiving her in some way?

Abby put her head in her hands. "Give me a second." Running over her options, she thought of the Easter lily e-mail and the song "Galveston." Hardly anything definite, but it could be a lead. The minute she'd seen it, she'd felt something. A hunch. And it didn't seem Kris or anyone else on her team had discovered it.

Should she just go to Ben or Lessing and tell them about it? With so much at stake, how could she possibly risk doing this all alone?

On the other hand, if the authorities took over now and Pat Devlin was found too soon in Galveston, The Candlelights would think that Kris hadn't followed their orders. They would almost certainly kill her child.

"Abby," Kris said softly. "I told you when we first met that I know you. I know you're strong and capable and smart—"

"You don't know me at all," Abby snapped, feeling pressured and manipulated. "You met me three days ago. You don't know what's in my gut." *Fear. Deep-down, ice-cold fear.*

"Look, I know you have less self-confidence now than two years ago."

Abby paled. "Where did you hear that? Ben?"

"No, Ben never said a word. I got it from my background check on you. You'd be surprised the things we can find out when we need to."

Shit, Abby thought. *George Orwell's Big Brother is alive and well and living in Carmel.*

But despite her fear, Abby still wanted to find Alicia. She wanted her to have an even chance when the authorities did catch up with her. Even more, she wanted to keep her promise to Jancy.

Maybe—with a little help—

Abby met Kris's anxious gaze. "Just one thing. Say I find Pat Devlin. What if he refuses to cooperate? I'll need something to hold over him. Some way to convince him not to turn over that bomb to The Candlelights. Or, if he already has, to tell us where they are."

A strange look passed over Kris Kelley's face as she released Abby's hands.

"No problem," Kris said. "I'm way ahead of you."

"Meaning?"

"Meaning, I have something to trade with our bomb-making friend."

Abby felt confused. "To trade? With Pat Devlin?"

"Not just him. With Alicia, too."

"What could you possibly—"

"I've got Pat Devlin's granddaughter, Abby. Alicia's daughter. I have Jancy."

Abby flew to her feet. "You *what?*"

"You heard me," Kris said, her voice suddenly hard. "And Alicia won't see her again until I get my son back. Alive."

Abby's hands knotted into fists. It was all she could do to keep from strangling Kris Kelley. She had just begun to trust her, and now—

"You're the one Jancy was running from yesterday?"

"That's right. I'd have gotten her, too, if Arnie hadn't shown up. I grabbed her later, though, at a pay phone outside a market in Carmel."

"And you're holding that little girl hostage until—" Abby swallowed hard, feeling sick. "My God. How does that make you any better than the people who have Danny?"

"It doesn't," Kris said with deadly calm. "But in the immortal words of old Rhett, frankly, my dear, I don't give a damn. I've spent seven years protecting that little boy, and I want him back. I'll do anything to make that happen."

"I don't believe you!" Abby said. "You talk tough, but you'd never kill Jancy! You haven't got it in you to kill a child."

"Maybe not, but I can fix it so the Gerards never see her again."

"Impossible! You think Jancy's going to let you get away with keeping her from her parents? She'd take off the minute your back was turned."

"Not if she didn't remember that she even had a mother and father named Gerard," Kris said in a tone that meant business. "Or, if what she 'remembered' was that *I* was her mother."

Abby felt her blood literally run cold. "You're bluffing. You can't do that!"

"We have people on our payroll who can do precisely that," Kris said.

Abby felt faint. "My God. What kind of monster are you?"

"I'm a mother," Kris said. "I would kill to protect my child. And though I'd prefer not to, I *will* kill if Danny is harmed, to avenge my child."

26

It was hot and muggy in Galveston at nine-thirty that night. The highway south from the Houston airport had been clogged with traffic, and a cheap little rental car was all they'd had left. The AC wasn't working right, and within the first ten minutes, Abby's silk blouse had stuck to her skin.

There was no time to waste. Three days till doomsday. Two, now, after tonight. If she and Kris were lucky, Pat Devlin would still have possession of that bomb. If not, and they couldn't find The Candlelights who had it, nothing else would matter in two days' time.

She couldn't believe Alicia knew about this and wouldn't have tried to stop it. After all, her own child could be one of the bomb's victims. Alicia wasn't a monster. Not like Kris Kelley.

Was she?

Abby pulled up to the lobby entrance of a motel with a leaping dolphin on its sign and parked, sliding off the sticky faux-leather seat of the car. Inside the lobby it was cool, and the room she'd reserved online under the name of Katherine Gavney was ready for her. Air-conditioned and nonsmoking, thank God.

She drove to the side of the building and found number thirty-eight alongside a swimming pool that was flanked with nearly dead palm trees. Dragging her tote bag, purse and a map of Galveston into the room with her, Abby flopped on the bed. Staring up at the ceiling, she kicked off her shoes and took a moment to breathe in the cool air.

When on earth had she ever been this tired? The last time she'd slept, other than brief catnaps on airplanes, had been the hospital in Phoenix. Two nights ago? Three?

She hadn't wasted any time getting here, other than making a necessary brief stop at the Prayer House after Big Sur. From there, she had secured these reservations on her computer, made a phone call and taken another five minutes to throw a few things into a tote bag.

Sister Helen had stood by, obviously upset with her. A woman with two children had come to the Prayer House seeking sanctuary through *Paseo* while she was gone.

"I don't know how to do all that as well as you," Helen had complained to Abby as she packed for Galveston. "It's not my thing."

Abby had smiled. "Your *thing?* What *is* your thing, Helen?"

"To be retired!" Helen had grumbled. "Do you realize it's been fifteen years since I retired from teaching? When do I get to act like it?"

Despite her worries, Abby's smile had widened. "I've been trying to slow you down for years! The minute I get you to stop doing one thing, you're on to another."

Abby knew Helen's grumbles were largely for effect, but on the off chance she was serious this time, she'd said, "I can arrange for Narissa to take over all your duties, Hel. And she can sub for me with *Paseo*. She grew up with a lot of siblings, and she's great with kids."

Sister Helen had sighed. "We'll see. I guess I can hold out till this is over. But please don't call me 'Hel.' It makes me think too much of the afterlife."

"Sorry." The afterlife wasn't something Abby wanted to think of at the moment, either.

"How long do you expect to be gone this time?" Helen had asked. "And just where exactly has that Jancy girl gone off to?"

"I don't really know how long I'll be gone," Abby had said. "No more than a few days, I hope. Maybe less. As for Jancy, she's staying with a friend. She's okay."

I pray she's okay, Abby had added to herself. It was something she had to believe in, to trust. But Kris Kelley? Was there anything more formidable than a mother protecting her child?

She had started to fall asleep on the motel bed when a knock sounded at the door. She started, then looked at the bedside clock—2:23 a.m.

Crossing the room in her bare feet, she looked through the peephole, but it was too dark to make out who was on the other side. Speaking softly, she called out, "Who is it?"

Holding her ear to the door, she heard, "The KGB. Who else? Let me in."

She smiled, opened the door and hugged Jimmy Delgado. His return hug lifted her off her feet.

"I don't think there's a KGB anymore," she said. "But thanks for showing up."

"How could I not?" he said, putting her down. "I told you, I was glad to hear from you."

Noticing the small airline bag, she said, "Here, toss that down, and let's talk."

He dropped the bag and looked around the room. "Not the fanciest, but you really want to talk? I thought we were having a rendezvous."

"More like a summit meeting," she said.

Jimmy sighed. "I was afraid of that when you called me earlier. Something about terrorists? Didn't sound very romantic." He grinned. "Unless, of course, that's your idea of a fantasy."

Abby smiled, and felt good for the first time in days—or as good as anyone could feel under the threat of an impending doomsday.

"There's a coffeepot over there," she said. "I'll make some, then we'd better get started."

"So, Joey thinks this is where Devlin could be?" she said ten minutes later, drawing a circle in red on the Galveston map. In a blank space she wrote *Emerald Gardens*.

They were sitting at the small table by the motel window. The drapes were closed so that no one could see in, and they had both moved their rental cars to the back of the motel.

It wasn't much in the way of security, but they'd both also made sure they weren't followed, and had signed in under fake names.

"That's what his contact in the IRA told him," Jimmy said, answering her question. "But you've got to remember, this guy was a double agent. He got washed out of the CIA years ago, and even Joey isn't sure how credible this information is. The other place he mentioned was Los Angeles. This one just seemed more worth checking out because you said Devlin might be in Galveston."

"This guy worked for both the IRA and the CIA? Why did he wash out?"

"Heavy drinker," Jimmy said, tilting his coffee cup to get at the last dregs. He went over to the utility table and got the pot of coffee, bringing it back.

"More?"

Abby nodded. "Keep it coming."

He poured and said, "The CIA was afraid he'd start selling out. This was in the nineties, after the Cold War with Russia was over, and they were cutting back on agents anyway. I guess he didn't seem like much of a loss."

"Is he still with the IRA, though?"

"Joey says no. He just hangs around in the same bars with them. Hears things. There's a large Irish community in Phoenix, you know. They have a festival, all kinds of events, every year."

"That's what I'd heard, which led me to think Joey

might be able to find something out. But if Joey's wrong about this guy, we could be walking into a trap."

"We could," Jimmy agreed. "Do you want to back out?"

"No way. As far as I'm concerned, this is just the beginning. And thanks to you and your brother, I'm ten times further along than I was this afternoon."

"With any luck," Jimmy said.

"Right. With any luck." Abby felt a chill as she remembered all the times her luck had run out.

Joey's friend had given him two pieces of information. The first was Emerald Gardens, which they'd discussed earlier as being the most likely place in Galveston for Pat Devlin to be hiding out. An upscale mobile home park, it had high walls and extreme security. The park was known by the underground to be equivalent to a "safe house" for anyone—legal or not—who had enough money to pay the rent. No one got in or out without the permission of a homeowner, and no homeowner ever gave permission to a stranger. These weren't people expecting the Joneses over to dinner and a night of watching movies. If Pat Devlin was in there, the ex-CIA agent had said, good luck getting to him.

Joey had also gotten out of him the fact that there was, or at least used to be, a warehouse along the waterfront where the IRA often met. If The Candlelights were connected in any way with the IRA, they might be hanging out there.

"He told me," Joey had said, "to check out the lease on that warehouse. If it was still under the name Thomas Rannigan, that was a good sign. The name Thomas Rannigan was one the IRA and their splinter groups used sometimes to rent or purchase property. Came from some old hero of the Troubles," Joey had said.

He and Jimmy had done a search of properties along the waterfront and found one that was, indeed, leased under that name.

Since it was dark and too late to check out Emerald Gardens, they decided to drive by the warehouse and see what it looked like. Finishing up the coffee, they took Jimmy's rental car, grabbed cheeseburgers and fries at a McDonald's and headed down to the waterfront.

"Are you thinking what I am?" Jimmy asked, as he washed down his last bite of burger with a Pepsi.

"What are you thinking?" Abby said.

"This warehouse. What if we find Pat Devlin there tonight, working on that bomb? What if he falls into our lap—" he snapped his fingers "—just like that?"

"I don't know…" Abby said thoughtfully. "From the map, it looks pretty crowded along the waterfront. I can't imagine he'd be building it in a place where anyone could just walk in."

"Maybe nobody *can* just walk in. Maybe it's as protected as that mobile home park."

"Well, we'll know pretty soon."

Abby peered through the side window, looking at street signs. "It should be coming up…three more blocks, on the right. Let's just drive by first, take a look. See if there are any lights, or any activity going on."

"You know," Jimmy said, "for somebody who lives in an abbey, Abby, you sure do have a lot of coplike tricks. I suppose you picked them up from that California cop? The one who was in Phoenix looking for you?"

"If you're talking about Ben Schaeffer," Abby said vaguely, still looking out the window, "I guess after two years, things do rub off."

"So he *is* your boyfriend?"

"Used to be," she said. "Now? Hell, I don't know. Sometimes I think I don't know anything anymore."

"Oh, well, now, I definitely object," Jimmy said.

"You object?"

"To the witness's testimony about herself. Aren't you playing prosecutor now, with you in the defendant's chair?"

Abby gave him a look. "You know what?" she said. "You're weird."

He laughed. "Yeah. Joey keeps telling me that."

"No, really. I mean, I keep forgetting you're a lawyer. For heaven's sake, all you do is break the law all the time."

He pulled over to the curb and turned the engine off. "Isn't that why you called me, instead of him?"

She didn't answer. Instead, she looked at the street sign a few yards in front of them and saw that they still had two blocks to go. "Why are you stopping here?"

"Because," Jimmy said, "I have a few tricks of my own."

* * *

Doing a drive-by, he pointed out, would make them much more suspicious to anyone guarding the place—especially if they went slowly enough to really see anything. Instead, he suggested they get out of the car and walk down the side street at the corner ahead of them, then into an alley at the back of the warehouse.

"How do you know there's an alley?" Abby said as they got out of the car.

"There's always one for deliveries, and there should be addresses on the backs of the buildings."

"You're right," Abby agreed as they entered the alley. She peered at the number on the wide loading bay that served as the only back door to the nearest warehouse. "Here's 307. We want 422. Must be at least halfway down the block."

"Or in the next one," Jimmy said.

"No, look, the numbers are jumping up faster than that. This one says 380."

All the warehouses were dark and closed up for the night—or more likely, Abby thought, abandoned. On the first three, the corrugated roofs were rusted and coming off in places. They flapped and made an eerie slapping, squeaking sound in the cool night breeze off the water.

Without discussing it, they both slowed down and became quiet as they approached number 422. Abby tugged on Jimmy's shirtsleeve to pull him back beside a Dumpster for cover, though it was hardly necessary. The only light in this block was on this warehouse—a dim yellow bulb with a metal cage around it, by a normal-size door. This building had no loading dock or bay.

"Doesn't look like there's a guard or anyone else around," Abby said. "In fact, this whole alley looks dead."

"Like no one's used these buildings in years," Jimmy added.

Quietly, they eased around the side of the building toward the front. There was a door there with the words Cartwright Shipping above it. The green paint on the door had peeled badly, and windows on either side were boarded up. A large sign in an empty lot across the street read, Future Site of the Pirate's Booty Inn.

"I'll be darned," Jimmy said. "They're gentrifying the area. These warehouses'll probably be a parking lot once they get going. That, or a restaurant and shops."

"One thing's sure, it doesn't look like there's any building of bombs going on here," Abby said. "Unless—" She thought a minute, then said, "Let's go back."

Pausing by the door at the rear of the building, she took one of the burglary tools from her back pocket and began to pick the lock.

"What the hell?" Jimmy said worriedly, at the same time moving into position beside her so that she couldn't be seen from the street. "Do you always carry those around?"

"Pretend you don't know," Abby said. "They'll go easier on you if we're caught."

"Oh, right," Jimmy said. *"I had no idea I was dating a common crook, officer. We were out for a nice quiet stroll along the waterfront, when all of a sudden—"*

"Shh... I need to hear when the tumbler clicks."

"You're kidding. I thought they just said that in movies."

Abby leaned her ear against the door and strained to hear as she moved the tool carefully inside the lock. After a couple of attempts accompanied by frustrated curses, she gave a satisfied sigh. "Aah...got it!"

She opened the door and pushed. It scraped along the cement floor as if it had warped from decades of damp air, and then stuck altogether about halfway.

"I don't think anyone's used this door in years," Abby said, batting away a cobweb. Turning back, she saw that Jimmy was hesitating.

"Are you coming?"

"Do I have to?" he said warily. "I don't know whether to be more scared of this place, or you."

"Will you stop? This isn't funny. This whole thing could be a setup, a cover. There could be a whole army in here of...I don't know, someone, something...."

"Rats?" he offered helpfully.

"No, dammit, IRA!" She stared at him. "Oh, my God, don't tell me you're afraid of rats. You can leap tall buildings in a single bound, but you're scared of rats?"

"Only in the dark," he said. "I had one run up my pant leg once."

"Oh. Sorry." She frowned. "Did it, uh...bite anything important?"

"Do you mean, am I disabled in any meaningful way?" he asked, grinning. "I guess I'm kind of flattered that you want to know."

"Oh, for heaven's sake!" Abby said, holding back a smile. "Are you coming or not?"

"Of course I am. I just wanted to be a real man about it and admit my fear, first." He pushed past her. "Stand back, woman. I'll defend you to the last…" He came to a dead stop. "Oh, crap! Cobwebs!"

She couldn't help laughing softly as he grabbed at the ones on his face and tried to clear the tensile strings from his hair. But as they stepped inside, a noise somewhere nearby made her grab his arm for attention, then plant her fingers against her lips.

They both stood motionless for what seemed to Abby like an eternity. There was a strong smell of mold in the warehouse, and her nose itched. She placed her index finger beneath it and pressed to hold back a sneeze.

Finally, when the sound didn't repeat, she whispered, "Let's see what's up there."

She pointed to a second-story room, the shape of which was becoming visible as her eyes grew accustomed to the dark. It was at the opposite end of what now appeared to be a completely empty warehouse, and windows across it looked down on the floor where they stood.

"If anyone's up there, they know we're here," Jimmy said. "That lightbulb shining in from outside would have made us perfect targets when we came through that door."

"Yet they aren't showing themselves."

"Which means they're either hiding, hoping not to be found—"

"Or they're setting a trap," she said.

"Uh-huh. Tell you what, there are stairs leading up to that room. I'll go up, see what's what, and you stay down here. If it looks like I'm in trouble, you can run and call the cops."

"No way," Abby said. "I'll go up and you stay down here. You can call for the cops."

He sighed. "You are the most obstinate—"

"Yeah, I think you said that before. Now, stay here. I'll be right back."

She took off toward the stairs to the upper room. When she reached them, she looked back, but Jimmy wasn't by the door where she'd left him.

Oh, for God's sake.

As she moved silently up the stairs, the room on the second floor still seemed dark. But as she grew closer, she realized that a blackout material of some sort covered all the windows. Between the nails that held the material to the window frames, where the fabric hadn't been drawn tightly enough, slits of light could be seen. And now that she was nearly at the top of the stairs, the faint rumble of a male voice could be heard.

My God, there's someone in there! And these curtains explain why we weren't seen coming in.

But wouldn't they have a guard stationed somewhere, or some sort of alarm letting them know when a stranger came through that back door?

The thought had no sooner left her mind than she heard the sounds of a scuffle below—punches against flesh, and men's voices grunting. A loud metallic crash resounded like a gong through the empty warehouse as something fell.

A moment later, the door to the second-floor room, only three steps above her now, flew open. "Leo? What the hell's going on?" a man hollered.

He was around fifty, his black hair receding, with the stocky frame of someone who'd played football at one time, but who'd gone soft in the belly. As he waited for an answer, he looked down and saw Abby crouching just three steps below him.

In that moment, Abby sprang up the steps and launched herself against him, causing him to stagger backward on the small platform in front of the door. A metal railing surrounded the platform, and he nearly went over it. Abby grabbed him by his black knitted shirt and, using a Kenpo move, shoved him into the room by sheer force of momentum.

He fell, banging his head on the scarred wooden floor. For a moment he lay there, dazed.

Abby called back into the warehouse, "Jimmy! You okay?"

What had happened to him? Had he been injured? Worse? But Jimmy was already coming up the stairs, pushing a redheaded kid of about eighteen ahead of him. The kid looked sullen and embarrassed to have been taken down, but the fight had clearly gone out of him.

When they both were in the room, Abby looked back at the man she'd overcome and said, "Who are you? What are you doing here?"

He was on his feet by now, nursing a sore wrist. "That goes both ways," he said angrily. "Who the hell are you?"

"I'm a friend of Pat Devlin's," Abby said, not sure that was the right answer, but chancing it.

The man's face cleared. "You're Linda? Pat's friend? You the one who's supposed to get the package to us?"

The package. The bomb?

"I am," Abby said. "Me and my friend here. Colin."

He looked at Jimmy. "You're Colin?" He frowned. "You don't look much like the guy Devlin described."

Oh, great, Abby thought. I pick a fake name and it's gotta be one they know. Now what?

"Well, I am," Jimmy said, falling easily into her scam. "And Devlin's not gonna like hearing that your little schoolboy here attacked me."

"You should'na snuck in like that," the kid said sullenly. "I'd'a opened the door if you'd just knocked and gi'n me the password." He seemed to grow bolder with every word. "Besides, I ain't scared of old Devlin. He's not even—"

"Leo, shut up!" the other man snapped. "Shut your stupid mouth and leave this to me."

The kid shot him an angry glance, but did as he was told.

"So, where's the package?" the man asked Abby.

"You need to identify yourself first," she said firmly. "I don't do business with strangers."

"Hardy," the man answered with an edge. "Hardy Boyd. Now, hand it over."

Abby laughed. "I hardly carry it around in my pocket," she said scornfully. "You'll get it when the time comes."

His face grew red. "Wait a minute. *When the time comes?* Lady, you have any idea how little time we have left?"

"I know exactly how little time we have left," Abby said. "And we'll get it to you. Just tell me where to deliver it."

The man's eyes narrowed. "You telling me you don't know?" he said suspiciously.

"No," Abby said calmly, trying to hide the faux pas. "What I'm telling you is, I heard the plans had changed."

"Well, I don't know about no change in plans," he said, moving back a few steps to a desk in the middle of the room. "And if you're a friend of Pat Devlin's, you don't know about no change in plans, either."

Before Abby realized what he was doing, he'd reached under a pile of papers on the desk and picked up a gun. He pointed it directly at her.

"Now, who the hell are you?" he said.

Jimmy stepped up and held his hands palms out, saying quickly, "All right, easy now! Clearly, there's been some miscommunication. The point is, you'll have the package. And you'll have it *on time*. That's what you want, isn't it? After all, I doubt your friends will be very happy with the job you've done if you don't come through for them."

The man appeared to think about it. "You know what?" he said at last, swinging the pistol toward Jimmy. "Me mum always told me to beware of people with silver tongues. They're either thieves or liars, that's what me mum always said."

Jimmy laughed. "So go ahead and shoot me," he said. "Let's see how much that impresses my friends in al-Qaeda."

The man stared. "You're not...nah. That's another lie. You ain't al-Qaeda." He lifted the gun slightly so that it was on an even plane with Jimmy's face.

Jimmy shrugged and said to Abby, "What do you think, Linda? Do I have friends in al-Qaeda? Friends with money? And are my friends keeping a lock on their bank accounts till I report back about the kind of job The Candlelights did with this package?"

"That's what I hear," Abby said. "And you know, it'd just be too damned bad if anything happened to you, and The Candlelights didn't get that money after all."

The man's gun hand wavered. Abby could almost hear him trying to think his way out of making the wrong decision.

"Don't risk it," she said. "Twenty-four hours from now, this will all be over. The Candlelights will have a reputation for being worthy of al-Qaeda money, and you'll be a hero with the IRA."

She began to walk toward him. "So, why don't you

put down the gun. Let's talk about where to deliver the goose that's going to lay that golden egg."

But Hardy had made his decision. He raised the pistol at Abby and began to squeeze the trigger. Before the hammer even connected, Abby flung herself aside in a lightning-quick move and dove for his lower torso, bringing him down. She was standing with her foot on his chest and the gun in her own hand within seconds.

"Who the hell *are* you?" the man said, dumbfounded. "Batwoman?"

Abby turned slightly to check on Jimmy and saw that he had grabbed Leo and shoved him face-first against the wall, his hands behind his back.

"More like Wonder Woman," Jimmy said. "Watch out for that golden lariat."

Abby steadied her breath and took a good look around the office for the first time. It was nearly empty, except for a few straight-back wooden chairs, a plain battered wooden desk, a bare overhead lightbulb and the papers that were scattered on the desk. There was a musty smell over everything, and even the chair at the desk looked as if it had been there since the 1940s.

"You okay with him for a minute?" she asked Jimmy.

"Sure, but I've got a better idea." He bent down to disconnect a telephone cord from the wall. It was at least twenty feet long, and connected to a telephone under the piles of paper on the desk—the only piece of electronic equipment in the room.

"Toss me that other end, will you? I'll tie our friends up so they won't be any more trouble."

"Wait a minute," Abby said. "Leave it connected."

When she was still out on the stairs, she'd heard a man's voice inside here. That had to have been Hardy. But who had he been talking to, since Leo was downstairs?

She lifted the receiver and hit the redial button. The phone at the other end rang, and the person that Hardy had apparently been talking to came on the line.

"Who's this?" a man said.

"Linda," she answered in a low voice.

"Linda? That you? I can't hardly hear you. You take that package over yet?"

"It's not ready yet."

The man cursed. "What're we supposed to do with this kid? He's a fuckin' handful!"

Abby's first reaction was confusion. Then her legs went weak. *This kid.*

Was it Danny? Did the man on the other line have Kris's son?

"What are you—"

He cut her words off.

"Just tell the old man he'd better get that package to us, pronto. We need to get rid of this brat."

The man hung up, and Abby just stood there a moment, feeling numb and unable to think.

"Hey. You okay?" Jimmy said.

She pulled herself back and hung up the phone. "I'm here. Catch."

Pulling the cord from the phone, she tossed it over to him—but not before making note of the exact time and writing it down.

Jimmy had Leo lying on his stomach, and was sitting on him. He took a Swiss Army knife from his back pocket and cut the phone wire in four long pieces. While he tied Leo's wrists and ankles, Abby continued to hold the gun on Hardy. When Jimmy was finished with Hardy, who was cursing steadily and loudly, she sat in the chair. As her mind slowly cleared, she began to go through the papers on the desk. Her fingers shook, and all she wanted to do was get out of here and call Kris. But there might be a clue here, something to lead her to Devlin, or the bomb, or even to Danny.

Most of the papers were shipping receipts and bills, and it didn't take more than a glance at the dates to see that they were all from decades past. Props, she guessed, to make this look like a working office in case anyone stumbled in by accident and didn't get to make a closer inspection.

Abby stared at them a moment and wondered where the real business was being done. At the other end of that phone, where Danny was possibly being held?

And what kind of "package" was Hardy waiting here for? This warehouse, which didn't even have a loading ramp, seemed hardly the place to be delivering a bomb.

In addition, neither Hardy nor Leo seemed very bright. They must have had to write some things down, rather than depend on their memories.

On a hunch, Abby shoved the papers aside until she could see the old green ink blotter beneath them, like the ones they'd had in the ancient library in high school. Abby had often been caught doodling on them by Sister Helen. Most of the kids did that, in fact, which was why the school stopped buying desk pads made of ink blotters in the first place. That, and the fact that, as times changed, four-letter words started appearing on them.

The hunch paid off. There were all kinds of doodles on the ink pad, and in the lower left-hand corner was a ten-digit phone number with a Galveston area code. There was no indication as to whom the number belonged, but Abby wrote it down, anyway. It could be important.

She could ask Hardy about it, but she knew she wasn't likely to get an honest answer. Besides, she'd be giving up her own game, and it was too soon for that. In the event it would come in handy, she was hoping they still thought she was the "Linda" they'd been waiting for.

Abby jotted the number down on the back of one of the shipping receipts, then shoved it into her pocket and looked through the dusty drawers of the desk till she came across a roll of tape. It was only masking tape, and old, but enough layers of it would hold for at least a while.

"Here," she said to Jimmy. "A little something for our friends."

He grabbed it and taped over their mouths and around the backs of their necks, over and over till he had a thick layer. "There, that should hold them."

"Yer a good mon, Colin," she said in the best Irish

accent she could remember from her aunt Maureen Sullivan.

"And yer an amazin' wee one," Colin/Jimmy replied.

She waited until they were outside to laugh. "You sounded like Johnny Depp in that pirate movie, for God's sake."

"Oh, yeah? Well, you sounded Jamaican. *Mon?*" He made a sound like a snort. "Gimme a break."

The minute they were in the car, Abby used her cell phone to call Kris. She told her about the warehouse and the two men there, suggesting Kris have someone on her team pick them up—but not yet.

"Why not yet?"

"Well, I don't want to get your hopes up, but I think I may have just talked to the man who's got Danny."

There was a small silence on the line.

"Kris?"

"Yeah, I'm here. You say you talked to this guy?"

"From that warehouse. I redialed a call this guy Hardy Boyd was on when I first showed up there. Told the man who answered that I was Linda—who, I take it, is supposed to be delivering the bomb, or some package, at least, to the warehouse. Then this guy Hardy was supposed to take it to this person on the phone."

"You say you redialed him. So you don't know what phone number he was at?"

"No, but I wrote down the exact time I talked to him, and if you can trace that call from the phone in the warehouse to this other one—"

"Got it. What's the number of the phone in the warehouse?"

"That's a problem. It wasn't written on the phone, but I figured it has to be listed at that address with the telephone company—"

"Abby, I've got my hands full right now, and I just don't see how I can stop what I'm doing to handle all this."

Abby was silent a moment. "I don't get it. If they have Danny—"

Kris's voice sounded tired and desperate. "I know, but I don't think... Abby, I just don't think it's Danny they've got. Maybe they do this all the time, hold kids hostage. Who knows who this kid might be?"

"But what makes you think it's not Danny? This is the best lead we've had, Kris."

"Abby..." There was a long pause. "Look, this is between us, okay?"

"Uh, sure...I guess."

"No, I mean this. You've got to swear."

"Okay, okay! I won't breathe a word."

"If you ever do..."

"Kris, for God's sake!"

She could hear Kris's deep breath over the phone. "I'm pretty sure Gerry Gerard has my son."

Abby was stunned. "Gerry! You can't be serious."

"I'm quite serious," Kris said. "I've tried all my sources, and no one has heard anything about this Candlelight group, the IRA or al-Qaeda holding a little boy hostage."

"But—"

"Abby, I've talked to the people who would know, people I trust to tell me the truth. That leaves me with just one son of a bitch cruel enough to do what he's done. Gerry Gerard."

"But that doesn't make sense. Why would Gerry—"

"It makes all the sense in the world. I don't know why I didn't think of him in the first place. Gerry is Danny's father, Abby. He's been trying to get him from me for years."

"My God!" For a long moment, Abby didn't know what to say. "Does Alicia know about this?"

"Not from me. And I doubt Gerry ever told her. It was a one-night stand, Abby. I was hired to be his body-guard at a convention one night, and when we got to his hotel, one thing led to another…" She sighed. "It's not like we had a relationship of any kind. He went home to Alicia afterward, and I had Danny and raised him alone. End of story—or almost. He found out about Danny somehow and picked him up from school one day. With a forged note from me, by the way. Took him to New York and kept him for five days. Danny didn't know who he was, just what Gerry told him—that he was a friend of his mother's. It scared him to death."

"But that's terrible! And you didn't know where he was? For five days?"

"Not a thing. While he had him, Gerry had a crony MD of his run a paternity test in record time. His lawyer showed up at my door five days later and told me he'd bring Danny home after I signed papers giving Gerry joint custody. I was outraged, of course, but frightened, too. I already had the police looking for Danny, but Gerry was threatening all kinds of things if I told them what he was doing, like taking him out of the country so I'd never see him again. I knew he'd do it if I didn't think of something, and fast."

"So you gave in to him? You gave him joint custody?"

"Like hell I did. I had a couple of guys on my CIA team find out where he was keeping Danny, bring him home and at the same time scare the hell out of Gerry."

"And since then?"

"Since then, I've practically had to build a moat around Danny, to keep Gerry from grabbing him again."

"He's tried?"

"Oh, yes, he's tried. Twice."

"Can't you get a restraining order against him?"

"I finally did get one, despite all his threats. It might as well be an engraved invitation, for all the good it does."

"Kris, I'm so sorry. Gerry used to be someone I admired, but I guess I really don't know him anymore."

She was remembering that Alicia hadn't wanted him to know what was going on with her, nor did she want him to take care of Jancy while she was away.

She'd denied that he was abusive, though. So there must be other things Alicia knew about Gerry that she was not ready to talk about.

At the very least, she probably hadn't trusted him

enough to tell him about the murder at the Highlands, or that the FBI and CIA were looking for her father, and why.

"Okay, look," Abby said. "I have another source for finding out where that guy on the phone is. You just do what you have to do there. Which reminds me, where are you?"

"I'm in New York. Shadowing Gerard, looking for a chance to get into his apartment. He's got it guarded better than the queen's castle. That, if nothing else, makes me think he's got Danny in there."

"All the more reason why you shouldn't be doing this alone. Gerry sounds like he'd do just about anything to stop you if you went in after Danny."

"I agree, I need help. And, Abby—I don't want you to feel like I'm stepping on your toes here, but I've asked Ben to help me out."

"Ben?"

"Well, he's not part of any of the agencies, and I'm supposed to be out sick, after all. He's the one person I could think of to keep this confidential, at least once he'd heard the whole story."

"So you did tell him about Gerry being Danny's father?"

"I...I had to. I'm sorry, Abby. I know you and Ben have a relationship, and I'm honestly not trying to put myself in the middle of that."

"No... I mean, you're right, of course. Ben's a good choice. But you're not going to tell him what I'm doing, are you?"

"That you're in Galveston chasing down Alicia Gerard and Pat Devlin? Not a chance. Although I must tell you, I'm sure he's figured at least some of it out."

"I'd be surprised if he hadn't," Abby said. "But you still want me to hold off on turning Devlin in—that is, if I find him—till I hear you've got Danny?"

"If you possibly can. I don't think Gerry would actually hurt him. I mean, that note—if he's the one who sent it—was just meant to scare me, I'm sure. On the other hand, I doubt Gerry would hesitate to take Danny out of the country and hide him away someplace where I'd never see him again."

"Kris, about that note. Why would he have made it look like The Candlelights sent it? Does Gerry have some connection to them?"

"Not that I ever knew of. But it does seem too much of a coincidence, all this happening with The Candlelights and Gerry taking Danny at the same time."

"My point exactly," Abby said. Her voice hardened. "What about Jancy? Do you still insist on using her to make Devlin turn the bomb over to the feds?"

"Oh, Abby...I was half out of my mind about Danny when I did that. I've already had her taken back to the Prayer House."

"So she's okay?"

"The only harm she might come to is being spoiled to death by Sister Helen."

Abby breathed a sigh of relief. "Thank God."

"Well, I couldn't really give that poor kid any more grief in her life. She's half the reason I've been keeping Danny's paternity a secret. And before this is over, she and her mother will have all the trouble they can handle. Now, what about you? What are you doing next?"

"We'll be checking out a mobile home park here as soon as the office opens. My informant thinks we might find the Devlins there."

"We?" Kris said.

"I have a friend here helping me."

"A friend. That wouldn't be your partner in crime from Phoenix, would it?"

"It would."

"He's trustworthy?"

"Absolutely."

That's great," Kris said. "We both have backup, then. Call me the minute you have Devlin under control."

"Kris," Abby said worriedly, "I know Danny's got to be your priority, but don't forget…we only have today and tomorrow left. In fact, we don't know how much of tomorrow is left."

"I've hardly forgotten," Kris snapped.

"I know. I just meant…oh, I don't know what I meant. Sorry."

She did know, but couldn't bring herself to say it: while Kris was busy getting her son back, they could be losing the race to find that bomb.

But there had to be thousands of agents all over the country by now, working on finding it. They didn't need Kris, and they sure as hell didn't need her getting in their way.

Still, she couldn't back off now. Even though that note threatening Danny's life might have been a hoax, written by Gerry, they couldn't be sure until Danny was found. Besides, there was her promise to Jancy—that her mother and she would be all right. That might not be a promise she could keep, as far as Alicia, at least, was concerned, but she could try.

She hung up after wishing Kris luck, then turned to Jimmy.

"Kris has her hands full. I'm thinking Joey, for that phone number?"

"Dial for me," he said. "I'll talk to him."

He told her the numbers and she punched them in. Joey answered personally and she handed the phone to Jimmy.

"We need a phone number," he said, "and we need to know where it is. Pronto."

He told Joey the address of the warehouse and explained that they didn't know the number there. Then he gave him the time Abby had made the call, and said that this was the address they needed. Joey said he'd get on it and call back.

They headed back to the motel, Jimmy driving and Abby sitting silently—or so she thought—next to him.

"What was that?" Jimmy said, as he navigated the early morning traffic.

"What?"

"You were thinking out loud. Muttering."

"Oh. Well, one thing I was thinking is that Pat Devlin couldn't have turned the bomb over to The Candlelights yet, because Hardy and his little friend were still there at the warehouse waiting for it."

"If the package is, in fact, the bomb," Jimmy said.

"Right. You think it's something else?"

"Just wondering. This woman, Linda, who's supposed to be delivering it. Unless *she's* Wonder Woman, I can't quite see her lugging a bomb onto a truck, hauling it through the streets of Galveston and then sneaking it into that warehouse. Even if she could hide it somehow, there's no loading dock, remember? No lift or any other kind of loading equipment there."

"Not to mention that there's just that one small door in back and another in front," Abby said. "Of course, we don't know if they're talking about the entire bomb."

"True. Maybe the package is the deadly part of it, the bioweapons or chemicals. I would imagine they might come in a small package, to be loaded into the actual bomb."

"Which could be just about anywhere," Abby said, holding back a groan. "But let's look on the bright side," she added. "If you're right, then the 'package' could very well be right in Devlin's house."

She looked at her watch. "Ten after six. The office at Emerald Gardens doesn't open till nine. We need to get there as soon as we can, in case Devlin isn't there at all."

"Or he is, and we can't get to him," Jimmy said.

"In which case—"

"In which case, we'd better call in the marines," Jimmy said. "Meanwhile, let's try to catch a nap when we get to the motel. This is bound to be a long day— and probably an even longer night."

* * *

By the time they'd settled in—Abby on the bed and Jimmy stretched out on the floor, which he insisted was better for his back than the bed or a chair—Joey was calling back with the address of the redialed number in Galveston.

"The place is over the causeway from Galveston, to- ward NASA and Houston. It's built like a farmhouse, but most of the surrounding land is just swamp," he told Abby. "There's a long dirt road leading to it, and you can't get there any other way, except maybe by chop- per. If you're in a car or walking, they'll be able to see you coming, 'cause there's no trees, no nothin'."

Joey had additional information about Emerald Gar- dens. "If you're hoping to get anything out of the guy in the office, good luck. His job is to steer people away from the place. So number one, don't let Jimmy go in there. He'll be spotted as a lawyer right away. And when you do go in, Abby, wear something dressy. A good suit, maybe. Try to look well-off. It's a mobile home park, but my guy says you've never seen one as classy as this one. Anyway, this is the last address he could find for the Devlins, and it wasn't easy. Or cheap."

"Send me the bill," Abby said.

"You better believe I will. But, Abby, I can't prom- ise you they're still there. I'm just thinking maybe you can find someone who knows where they are now. A neighbor, maybe. Just don't go around asking too many questions, because I'm pretty sure they'll just clam up. Look for clues, instead. Mailboxes, trash, if it's on the curb, cars parked with mail on the dash, that sort of thing."

"I'll remember that," Abby said, wondering just how inconspicuous she could manage to look doing all that in broad daylight. Especially in some "dressy suit." Which, come to think of it, she didn't have with her.

She thanked Joey and told Jimmy what he'd said, adding that she'd have to pick up a suit and heels some-where along the way. "That's going to change our schedule a bit."

"Just a bit?" Jimmy said skeptically. "Since when does a woman take 'just a bit' of time shopping?"

"When that woman is me," she said. "Just watch me."

"And where exactly are you hoping to find this up-scale suit? I haven't seen anything but gas stations, restaurants and motels along the highway."

"Ah, but that's where being a woman comes in handy. I—being a woman—noticed a mall a few miles up the road. It probably doesn't open till ten, but I'm pretty fast at shopping for clothes. I figure we can be at Emerald Gardens by eleven, if not before."

Jimmy sighed. "I guess we'll see if I was right, then."

"Right?"

"Calling you Wonder Woman."

Abby smiled and lay back down on the bed, appre-ciating the cool pillowcases under her head. She would just close her eyes for a minute....

"Wake up, Sleeping Beauty," she heard, as if through a fog. Opening her eyes she saw that Jimmy had showered and dressed in a clean shirt and jeans. He was shaving with a cordless razor as he wandered around the room, now and then pushing the drapes back an inch or two to look out.

"What are you looking at?" she asked.

He shrugged. "Not much."

"What time is it?"

"It's 9:22. I figured time enough for you to get dressed and get to that mall when it opens."

"Sounds right. I'll get ready," she said.

He set the razor down. "We're out of coffee. I'll go down to the office and get us some."

"Sounds great."

At the door he turned back. "By the way, check the news on TV. There's a tropical storm headed this way."

"Please, not a hurricane," she said. "That's about all we need now."

"Just some heavy rain, I think."

He left, and she took a quick shower. Fifteen minutes later she checked herself out in the motel mirror, thinking she'd managed to look upscale from the neck up, at least. Her long dark hair was pulled back in a smart twist, and her makeup was perfect. It showed off her high cheekbones and dark eyes, but was still subtle enough to be considered "tasteful." At the store she'd find pearl earrings and a necklace, possibly a lightweight designer suit and sunglasses.

Since Jimmy hadn't returned yet from the office, she

decided to get his car in back and drive up there. Stepping out of the air-conditioned motel room, though, was like opening the door of a blast furnace. A sign across the street on a bank read 102 degrees, but the heat index had to be at least 115. By the time she'd walked to the back lot where their cars were, Abby was drenched.

"And it hasn't even started raining yet," she muttered. Her "subtle" eye makeup was dripping and her reflection in the car window told her that rather than an upscale society matron, she looked like Dracula's bride.

She unlocked Jimmy's car and slid into the driver's seat, turning on the air-conditioning full blast. Taking a Kleenex from the car's glove box, she wiped as much of the makeup off as she could. Then she drove around to the front office. When she didn't see Jimmy through the office windows, she got out of the car and went in to look for him.

The manager glanced up and asked with a smile, "Good morning. Something I can do for you?"

"I'm looking for my friend," Abby said. "Tall, dark hair…he came down to get coffee…."

Her voice trailed off as she looked around and realized there wasn't a table set up with coffee and doughnuts, as in some motels.

"I'm sorry," the manager said. "We don't offer a continental breakfast. There are coffeepots in every room, though."

"I know, but… My friend must have gotten his signals crossed. He did come in here?"

The manager shook his head. "No one's been in here

in the last hour. Most of our guests pay in advance, then they leave their keys in their rooms."

"I know," she said, confused and still looking around. "I just thought…"

She went back to the car and drove around the motel, checking out the parking lot on every side. It was late, and most people had already checked out. There were only a handful of cars in the lot.

And no Jimmy.

There was a gas station next to the motel, and she drove over there to look for him. Had he walked over here looking for a coffee machine, then used the restroom?

But no one answered her knock on the men's restroom door, and the clerk inside said he hadn't seen anyone matching Jimmy's description.

She was seriously worried now. If Jimmy had intended to go any distance, surely he'd have taken his car. She crossed over to the bank and looked inside. Not there.

For the first time, the thought struck her: Something's happened to him. He wouldn't just disappear like this.

Then she remembered the way he'd been looking out the motel room window when she'd woken up. She'd asked what he was looking at, and he'd said, "Not much." Shortly after that he'd said he was going to the office for coffee. Where was he?

Jimmy's cell phone was on the seat. She scrolled

down to Joey's number and dialed. The phone rang a few times before he answered brusquely. "Yeah?"

"Joey, it's Abby. Have you heard from Jimmy?"

"Since when? Last night, you mean?"

"No, this morning."

"Not a word. Why? Isn't he with you?"

"No. He left our motel room a little while ago, saying he was going to the office for coffee. But now that I think of it, I'm pretty sure he was looking for somebody out there. Joey, he never did show up at the office, and I've looked everywhere around here, but I can't find him. I'm getting worried. I mean, I'm calling you from his car, on his cell phone. He wouldn't have gone far without them. Not intentionally."

"I hate to say it, but knowing what you two are doing there, I think you're right. Where's this motel? In Galveston?"

"No, it's across the causeway, toward Houston. A sign on a car repair place across the street says Texas City Auto."

"Okay, listen. I'll contact the PD in Texas City and ask them to help. Meanwhile, I'll be on the first plane there. What's the name, address and phone number of this motel?"

She gave them to him, and was surprised to find that her voice was shaking. "I'm really worried, Joey. I don't know whether to stay here and keep looking for him, or what."

"If you do, I can guarantee you he'll be pissed," Joey

said. "No, you stick to your original plan. Let me worry about my brother. Just keep his cell phone with you, and I'll let you know what I find out."

"I feel like somebody's got him, Joey. We need to find him."

"Which is why I'm coming down there. And which is also why everything's gonna be okay. Okay?"

"I...okay."

She hung up, and sat there a few minutes, her hands on the wheel. This was way beyond her scope. She had bought into Kris's pep talk about being strong and capable, but the truth was, she wanted to cry. She never should have let Jimmy get involved in any of this. The men at the warehouse must have gotten through to someone in The Candlelights or the IRA, and described him. Her, too, most likely. They might even have been followed from the warehouse. Then, when Jimmy went back out, they grabbed him. While she was showering—useless, a complete and utter failure.

It wasn't until a horn blasted behind her that she realized she was already on the highway, driving in the direction of the mall.

27

The traffic had thinned out for a mile or two on the way to the mall, when Abby first noticed the sleek black Lincoln Town Car following her. As she turned into the mall, the traffic became too dense to try to elude the car. A lighted sign, however, advertised valet parking. That was the kind of information that always stuck in her mind when she was helping women and their children on the run. Now and then the fathers, or detectives they hired, would pick up their trail, no matter how hard everyone along the line worked to keep that from happening. It was helpful to study various methods for throwing them off the track.

Pulling into the underground garage, she left the car with a valet. As she stepped out and crossed over to the glass doors leading into the mall, she noted that the black Town Car had turned in, too. It was hanging back and hadn't yet reached the valet. From a quick sideways glance at the windshield, she thought there might be two figures in the front seat, but she couldn't be sure.

Abby walked as casually as possible to an elevator

and took it up to the main floor. There was a department store on her left, and she entered and picked up speed. Hurrying through the department store, she looked for an exit to a parking lot and a bus stop on the far side of the mall. But either she wasn't on the main level after all, or they simply didn't have exits to the outside from here.

Panic set in. Glancing around quickly, she scanned the other shoppers. And there he was—a tall, well-built man with a pale complexion, reddish hair and wearing sunglasses.

No one familiar, but he stood out like a sore thumb among women's clothes in a department store. His height made him clearly visible over the clothing racks.

Abby grabbed several dresses. Looping a thumb through the hangers, she held them behind her and ducked into the nearest fitting room. The cubicles all had doors that were open at the top and bottom. One at the far end was slightly larger than the others. She slipped into it and locked the door behind her. Hanging the dresses on a hook, she stood with her back against the farthest wall, hoping the cubicle would look empty.

Don't let him find me, she prayed, as a vivid flash of memory brought back that morning in the junkyard. *Don't let him find me.*

But I'm not helpless, she reminded herself. *I'm not helpless anymore.*

For at least five minutes she stood like that, barely breathing. A couple of women came out of another cubicle, talking about how sizes had changed since they were younger, and now you could wear a twelve when you were really a sixteen. They left, and there were no other sounds in the fitting room after that. She was alone.

Which meant that this would be the perfect time for him to come in, looking for her.

She waited, straining her ears to hear, for what seemed like hours but was really only minutes.

Then she heard it. The slight whisper on carpet of stealthy footsteps.

Abby got into position. With one arm upraised at neck height and the other bent by her waist, she took a deep breath and let it out silently, feeling her chi rise.

The footsteps stopped by her cubicle. The curtain moved. She opened her mouth to make a warrior sound and startle the opponent as she took him down.

But what she saw in the split second before attacking her victim sucked the air from her lungs and weakened her knees.

"Oh, my God," she said. "Oh, my God."

28

"Where on earth have you been? I've been so worried about you!"

Abby's words were muffled by the fact that her face was against Alicia's shoulder as they hugged. She pulled back and said, "How did you find me here, Allie?"

"That was me and Dell, my bodyguard, behind you. I knew when you glanced our way that you'd spotted us. I told him to follow you in here and let me know when and where he saw you go."

"That was your bodyguard? The tall, red-haired guy? But how did you know I was in Texas? No, wait." Abby grabbed her arm to pull her out of the cubicle. "We can't talk here."

Alicia pulled back. "It's okay. Dell's barring the door to the fitting room, telling people it's under renovation. We'll have a few minutes before store security starts to question what's going on." She frowned. "Abby, please sit down. You look so damned tired, and I know it's all because of me."

Abby *was* feeling weak and shaky from too little sleep and food. She sat on the floor while Alicia slid into a squat, her back against the side of the cubicle.

"To answer your question, Dell followed you and the man you were with from the warehouse early this morning. He saw where you were staying and came and got me."

"Your bodyguard was at the warehouse? What was he doing there? And how did he know me?"

"It's a long story, Abby. But he has photos of everyone I know, everyone I've ever known. Short and not-so-sweet, that's the story of my life."

Abby hadn't realized until this moment how much she really cared for, and had missed, Alicia. There had been so many years, so many confidences exchanged. Though she'd been angry at her for leaving Jancy without a word, never for a moment had she believed that her old friend had killed the reporter at the Highlands Inn.

Which made this all that much harder. "Do you know the FBI and the CIA are both looking for you, and your father? That there's an all-out manhunt for both of you?"

Alicia hesitated. "Yes. I know that."

"Do you know why?"

"Yes, Abby. I know about the terrorist threat, and I know my father is supposed to be making a bomb for them."

"Then what the hell are you doing, Allie? Why haven't you turned him in?"

Voices sounded from the door of the fitting room, one male, one female, and it seemed Alicia's bodyguard was having trouble maintaining his post.

Alicia lowered her voice and got to her feet. "We've got to go now. Abby, I need you to come with me."

"Come with you?" Abby stood, and felt a moment of fear, hating herself for it. Surely her friend wouldn't lead her into some kind of trap. Would she?

"Where do want me to go?"

"Just come with me. Please. I need someone's help, and right now you're the only one I can trust."

29

Abby left Jimmy's car at the mall and climbed into the back seat of the Town Car with Alicia, hoping she wouldn't regret it. Dell, the red-haired bodyguard, pointed the car south toward Galveston.

"We're going to Emerald Gardens?" she said.

"Eventually," Alicia replied. "First, we make a stop at Trudy's Catering in Galveston."

"A catering service?" Abby said mildly. "Are we throwing a party?"

"Don't I wish," Alicia answered grimly.

At Trudy's, Dell pulled into a lot at the back of the building. He parked the Town Car so that it blocked the view of the rear entrance from the street. Abby followed Alicia's instructions to slide out quickly and go inside. Once they were out, Dell pulled the car off to the side, got out and stood in the lot by the door, his arms folded.

Inside, a short blond woman dressed in white pants and a white jacket smeared with chocolate came up to Abby and Alicia. She didn't speak, and had clearly expected them. She took them into a kitchen, where double-tiered steel carts were being loaded with appetizers that smelled like garlic and butter. Abby's stomach growled loudly, but, before she had a chance to be embarrassed, the woman took a small white plate off a shelf. She put four of the small flaky pastries on it and handed it to Abby. Then she fixed one for Alicia.

"Take these with you," she said in an Irish accent. "You can't be knowin' when you'll have another chance."

She led them into a large room off the kitchen where white uniforms hung neatly against one wall. "Good luck," she said softly, covering both catering carts with white linen cloths and pushing them into the room. She closed the door.

"Find your size and put one on," Alicia said to Abby.

Abby hesitated a moment, but Alicia said, "Trust me," and stripped down to her bra and panties, then put on a uniform with long pants and a white chef's top. Abby followed suit. When they were both dressed, their hair pinned up under short, tight white caps, Alicia pressed a buzzer.

At the other end of the room was the kind of rolling metal door Abby had seen at loading docks. Alicia grabbed one of the catering carts and motioned for Abby to do the same.

"Our transportation from here on," she said, rolling the carts to the metal door.

The door rolled up into the ceiling, and a warm blast

of humid air entered the room. A small white van with the words Trudy's Catering on the side had backed up to the loading dock. Its rear doors opened automatically and Alicia pushed her cart onto the truck. Abby followed Alicia's lead, feeling a bit foolish but unwilling to seem anxious. She wanted to trust Alicia, and she thought she did. Even if her faith in her friend proved unwise, she wanted to see this thing through to the end.

The truck's door slammed shut and everything grew quiet and dark. There was a wall of some kind between this part of the van and the driver. Of course, it was a catering truck. There must be times when it needed to be kept cold, or hot.

Still, small spaces, especially small *dark* spaces, were not her favorite thing.

"Allie?"

No answer.

"Allie!" she said more insistently, panic rising in her throat. God help her if she blacked out now, the way she had on the roof with Jimmy.

Jimmy. She hadn't thought of him in the past hour, or of what had happened to him. And now, instead of being in a position to find and help him, she was in this tiny, pitch-dark closet, being driven God knew where—

She was about to start pounding on one of the rear doors when she heard a quiet *"Shh."*

"Allie?"

"I'm here. You have to be quiet, Abby. We can't talk now—I'll explain later."

Abby sat on the floor, her knees up to her chin and her feet stabilizing the cart. It took all the energy she had to stay that way as the truck swayed and jerked from the sharp turns it was making. She clung to the steel legs of the cart to keep it from falling on her, wondering if it really was necessary to take such a winding route. Her legs, back and arms began to ache, and she felt as if she were on a funhouse ridde called Hell Drive.

Finally, the truck slowed, made a sharp turn and came to a stop.

"Abby," Alicia whispered, "the doors are going to open. When they do, take the cart down the ramp as fast as you can without seeming to be in an abnormal rush. I'll be right behind you."

The truck's rear doors opened, and Abby pushed. The heavy cart tilted slightly as it began its descent down the ramp. She had to hang on tight to keep it from getting away from her, but at the end of the ramp she saw a garage door in an upscale suburban house. The door opened and she saw light and heard loud music and voices, people laughing as if they were having a good time. Party sounds.

"Keep going, Abby, I'm right behind you," Alicia said.

The garage door closed behind them, and all the sounds abruptly stopped. Dell was suddenly at Abby's side. He grabbed her arm and half dragged her through a door into the house.

"What the hell?" Abby said, yanking her arm away. "Let go of me! Allie?"

"Right behind you," Alicia said again.

Abby turned and saw that her friend was indeed right behind her. And she was pointing a gun directly at her head.

30

They stood in a dimly lit kitchen, the two women facing each other.

"I'm getting real tired of this," Abby said, rubbing her arm. "If one more person points a gun at me—"

"I'm sorry," Alicia said, sliding the Glock into a drawer. "But I wasn't pointing it at you…or, at least, not really. Dell's orders were to get you in here fast, and I couldn't take any chances we'd be ambushed from inside."

Dell had gone to stand outside the front door, once he was assured that Abby and Alicia were safely in the house. Another man, dressed in shorts and a T-shirt, stood in the living room, watching them over the breakfast bar.

"Don't mind him," Allie said. "That's Jase, my mom's bodyguard."

She went in and whispered something to him, then came back and said, "My mother's in with my father. I'll take you to them."

"Allie, wait. What the hell is going on? And where's that party I heard?" Except for an odd *whish-whish* issuing from somewhere in the house, it was as silent now as a graveyard.

"The party sounds are on tape," Alicia said. "To provide anyone watching with a reason for the catering carts. The tape turns on when the garage door opens, and goes off when it closes. The houses themselves are soundproofed."

"Geez. And just how many parties do you have in a week?"

Alicia made an apologetic grimace. "This is the second. We didn't need to do this until the past few days. Ready?"

Alicia looked tired and worn, as if bracing herself for something unpleasant. Abby had another moment of anxiety, wondering if she should be walking into whatever this was. There were so many people depending on her to do the right thing. What if—

"It's okay, Abby," Alicia said, sensing her hesitation. "I just want you to meet my father and mother."

"You're sure about that?"

"Yes."

"Are we talking about Pat and Bridget Devlin?"

"We are."

"And you're not afraid I'll turn them in, now that I know where they are?"

Or was it that she, Abby, would never have a chance to tell anyone what she knew? She still couldn't get over the image of Allie with that gun. She was sure that no matter how Allie had shrugged it off, the gun had been pointing straight at her.

The *whish-whishing* noise grew louder as they went down the hall and came to a door. Alicia paused there and tapped softly.

"It's me, Mom," she said.

"Come in," a woman's voice answered.

Alicia opened the door to a room that was dark except for one dim light over a bed. In the bed, which was raised to a half-sitting position, lay a man—or what remained of a man. He looked shriveled and old, so emaciated that she had to wonder how his head could support even the light weight of the respirator cup over his nose and mouth. The *whish-whishing* sound came from the respirator next to his bed. His eyes were closed.

A woman sat on a chair next to him, holding his hand.

"How is he?" Alicia asked.

"He's doing fine," the woman said aloud, though she shook her head at Alicia. Her green eyes were wet with tears, and her hair, though it showed signs of having once been red, was short and sprinkled heavily with gray.

"Mom, this is my friend, Abby. Abby, this is my mother, Bridget."

Bridget Devlin set her husband's hand down gently on the crisp white sheet and rose, crossing over to them.

"Alicia told us you were coming," she said softly. "I assume you know who we are, and why Alicia had to take extraordinary steps to bring you here to the house."

Abby nodded. "I suddenly don't know why I'm here, though. How long has your husband been ill like this?"

Surely Pat Devlin hadn't been making any bombs lately.

"I'm afraid I've lost track of time," Bridget said. "This past three months—"

"It actually started about six months ago," Alicia said. "It's been getting worse each month. Lung cancer."

"I'm sorry," Abby said again, looking at the slight form on the bed. He couldn't have long to live, she thought, not in that condition. Besides the respirator, there were tubes everywhere.

And she couldn't even begin to think what to do now. If she told the authorities where to find the Devlins, they'd come down on them immediately. But to what point? And who in the intelligence agencies had screwed up so badly? Why on earth had they thought Pat Devlin was making that bomb? Were they going on one person's report? Rumor? They had said "credible" intel. Where had it come from? Was it all a mistake, or was there more to it?

No matter what, this was terrible. If Pat Devlin wasn't making a doomsday bomb, was someone else? And if so, how could he ever be caught in time? They'd already wasted far too long on the wrong man.

She turned to Alicia. "Can we talk?"

Alicia nodded. She went over to her father's bedside and stood there a minute, looking down and touching his hand. His eyes remained closed, and when Alicia turned back, she was crying silently.

Her mother hugged her, and Alicia said, "I'll be back to relieve you."

"It was nice to meet you, Abby," Bridget said. "I hope…I mean, you have to do what you feel is right, of course. But until this whole thing is over, I hope you understand that we can't possibly let you leave here."

31

Dell escorted Abby into Alicia's bedroom. He was courteous but firm, and Abby was too shocked to resist.

"I'd like your cell phone, please," he said, holding out a hand. She grudgingly turned it over.

So, it had turned out that she couldn't trust her old friend after all. She was to be held prisoner here until… *"until this whole thing is over."* What whole thing? Did she mean the attack? Or something else?

As Dell left, Alicia entered the room. Abby turned on her angrily. "I can't believe you're doing this."

"I had to, Abby. You don't understand."

"You're damned right I don't understand! You're obviously using me. For starters, why don't you ask me why I'm here?"

"All right, then! Why *are* you here?"

"Among other reasons, for Jancy," Abby said.

"Jancy? What about her? She's all right, isn't she?"

"Nice of you to ask. And sure, she's fine. Since you left her with me, she's run away twice and been kidnapped once. But not to worry, Allie. Jancy's just fine."

"Oh, my God. I thought…I was sure she'd be all right with *you*."

"I guess you haven't noticed that Jancy has a mind of her own?"

"Well, yes, but—"

"Look, it doesn't matter. She's at the Prayer House now, she's fine, and we don't have time for this. Allie, you've got to call the CIA or the FBI and tell them your father is here. They need to know where that bomb is, and they need to stop him from turning it over to The Candlelights."

"Abby, my father is on his deathbed! Surely they can't believe he'd be involved in anything like that, in his condition!"

"Still, he must know something about it. He may be ill, Allie, but if he can still talk—"

Alicia covered her eyes and began to cry. "I can't, I just can't. Abby, you don't understand!"

"Then tell me," Abby said. "Start at the beginning, with the murder at the Highlands, and tell me everything. But, for God's sake, get on with it, Allie! We've only got hours left now."

Or minutes, possibly, before various government agents came streaming in. And she still hadn't heard from Kris, so she must not have Danny yet. The timing would be delicate: convince Allie to turn her father in, but get her to wait until Kris called with the go-ahead—assuming she managed to get her cell phone back. And manage all of this before the feds showed up.

That didn't allow much time for idle chatter.

Alicia sat on the bed, her shoulders slumping. "That

reporter at the Highlands, Duff? He knew about my parents' background with the IRA, and he heard that Gerry had been asked to run for the presidency in the next election. He figured he could get some money out of us to keep quiet about my parents' illegal status and whereabouts. I gave him some, but of course he wanted more, and I knew it would never end."

She lay down, pulled the comforter up to her chin and hugged it as a child would. "So it made sense that the police might think I killed him to shut him up. Even as shaken as I was, standing there looking at all that blood, with Jancy scared and sobbing her eyes out next to me, I could see that. I panicked, Abby. Instead of calling the police, I came to you. I felt sure you'd take in Jancy, if nothing else."

"While you jetted off to Galveston to warn your parents that their story might come out during the investigation of Duff's murder?"

"I…yes. I didn't know what else to do."

"Well, I understand your reasoning, even if I don't agree with it. But why didn't you just tell me what was going on? I'd have taken in Jancy regardless, and you could have trusted me not to tell any of this to the police—at least till we could sort it all out."

"But I didn't know that, Abby. How could I? We haven't talked in ages, and I'd heard you and the police in Carmel were pretty thick."

"Oh? How did you hear a thing like that?"

"You remember those news reports about the attack on you two years ago? After your friend Marti was killed? They mentioned what happened to you, too, and how you had helped the police to find your friend's killer."

It was true, Abby thought, that the story had hit all the wire services. Tabloids had picked up on the more salacious news, like the fact that Ben and Abby were living together. Living together might not be salacious these days, but the crude details they made up were.

"So, you left Jancy with me and took a roundabout route to Galveston to throw the cops and the horde of government agents off," Abby said. "Alicia, didn't you think I'd come after you? In fact, didn't it even strike you that The Candlelights might try to kill me if I came after you? Anything, to keep me from finding your mother and father?"

Alicia's eyes widened. "My God, Abby, if that's what happened, I'm so sorry! But I truly never thought you'd get involved in any of this."

"By any of this, you mean the fact that your father was building them a bomb?"

"Oh, Abby, I really am sorry. It never entered my mind that you'd find out what this was all about, or that you'd come looking for me. I just knew you were devoted to helping kids, and I thought it was the most I could hope for, that you'd take care of Jancy."

"So, you get to Galveston," Abby said, "and find your father with possibly hours to live. And you say he's been in and out of the hospital for the past five weeks. If that's the case, he can't have been working on that bomb after all."

Alicia looked away.

"He hasn't, has he?" Abby said. "Well, they could still formally charge him with being in the country illegally, and he and your mother would probably be deported. But as I see it, that's the worst that could happen—at least, to them. The murder charges against you are another matter. But the sooner they know your father has been too ill to work with The Candlelights, the sooner they can start hunting for whoever is."

"No," Alicia said, shaking her head and wiping her eyes with the backs of her hands.

"No?"

"They'd still come here to question him, Abby. And you've seen him. He goes in and out of that state, and he might get confused and say something he shouldn't."

"You mean he might name somebody in The Candlelights or the IRA? What do you care? The police could provide all of you with protection."

Alicia didn't answer.

Abby grabbed one of her shoulders and half shook her. "For God's sake, we're talking about stopping a terrorist organization from killing millions of people. *Hours* from now, Allie! If you think 9/11 was bad, this—" She let her go, then wiped her hands on her pants, as if to remove dirt from them. "You don't want to be responsible for this."

Alicia started to cry. "I know. I just can't—"

"Stop it! I'm sick of hearing that! What the hell are you holding back?"

Alicia looked at her with all the misery of the world

written in her eyes. "It's not my dad," she said softly. "It's my mom."

Abby felt confused. "Your mother? Bridget? What about her?"

"She's the one, Abby. The one who…" Alicia broke off and swallowed as if the words had stuck in her throat.

Abby's heart sank. "You don't mean…oh, God, Allie. You can't mean she's the one making the bomb!"

"They threatened her, Abby. They said if she didn't, they'd kill me and Jancy. She tried to tell them she didn't know anything about chemicals, but they already knew somehow…."

"Knew what?"

Allie shook her head and looked away.

"C'mon, Allie! Knew *what?*"

Alicia's chin went up. "All right, dammit! But you've got to understand that it wasn't her fault. Times were different, forty, fifty years ago in Ireland when she was young. She had to choose sides."

"You're saying she chose the IRA? She and your father? I already know that, Allie. And I do understand. But what about now? What about today?"

"Okay, I'll tell you. But you've got to promise to listen without interrupting me till I'm done."

"I'm not promising a damn thing," Abby said angrily. "But you'd better start talking before I shake it out of you."

Alicia took a deep breath. "The Candlelights, Abby, are a group consisting mostly of women. Their roots go back a couple of centuries, when middle- and upper-class women were responsible for taking care of the poor. Charity was an actual job for women then, and it was how they became part of the political process. But eventually, their work became less abut charity and more about extreme political measures."

Abby couldn't hold back her scorn. "So you're saying she's still in the IRA? And she thinks that creating a bomb to wipe out half of the United States, and maybe the world, will improve the situation in Ireland?"

"No! God, no! She hasn't been involved in any of that since they came to this country when I was little. My mom and dad are good people, Abby. They've made it their life's work to do penance for their past wrongs by helping people in need."

"Until now, you mean."

"No, until a few months ago. Abby, I swear I didn't know anything about this until I got here this time. I was just coming to see my dad, the way I've been doing every month since he got sick. But this time, I guess because he's so near the end, my mom decided to tell me what's been going on."

"Nice of her to foist that off on you."

"No, I made her tell me, Abby. That's what I meant by you not understanding. My mom's near the breaking point. I could see she was holding something in, and it was making her sick. So I forced it out of her."

"Okay. Go on."

"The daughter of an old friend of hers, she said, someone she grew up with, showed up here a few months ago. She's in The Candlelights in Ireland, and she somehow learned that my mom and dad were living here. This woman came here and threatened my father. She was sent here with a message—work for The Candlelights. Do what they want, or they'd kill me and Jancy."

Alicia began to shake. She threw off the comforter and stood and paced, as if trying to work off her fear. "Abby, The Candlelights have devolved into a terrorist bunch of women *and* men. They bear almost no resemblance to the earlier Candlelights. These are no longer middle- and upper-class philanthropists. They have very little money, and they're willing to do anything to get it."

"In this case," Abby said, "by proving themselves worthy of being funded by al-Qaeda."

"Precisely. I dread to think what they plan to do with all that money. But, Abby, the point is, my mother doesn't belong to them and doesn't want anything to do with them. That school bus bombing back when I was little was more than she and my father could take, and the way they've been living… I really meant it when I said it's like they've been doing penance ever since."

"Do The Candlelights know it's your mother who's actually working on the bomb?"

"It was their idea," Alicia said. "My mother tried to get my father out of it at first, by telling them he was ill. She pleaded with them to find someone else. But The Candlelights knew that she had learned about chemicals from my father all those years ago. They said it didn't matter how sick he was—she could do it, and he could show her anything she didn't know."

"So, it's the bioweapons she's been working on? Not the actual bomb?"

"Yes. The bomb is being stored somewhere else. She doesn't know where, and she isn't really working on the chemicals at all. She's faking the work, doing just enough so they'll believe she's making progress. This woman—the one who came here before—she comes around every now and then to check on her. We don't know when to expect her, so my mom has to have something new ready every time. Fortunately, this woman doesn't know enough about chemicals to know whether they're the real thing or not."

"That's pretty stupid," Abby said. "Even drug dealers test a product before they buy it, to make sure it's real."

"My mom's been afraid of that. She thinks there must be someone who will do that after the package is delivered."

"The *package?*"

"That's what the woman who comes here calls it."

"Is this woman's name Linda, by any chance?"

"Yes. How did you know?"

"Let's just say I was mistaken for her." *Which could be useful at some point. I'll just have to figure out how.*

"The Candlelights must be getting anxious for this package," Abby said. "Their target date is tomorrow, and today is half over. What is your mother telling her?"

"That my father's gotten worse and he hasn't been able to help her with it."

"Meanwhile, they're threatening to kill you and Jancy," Abby said, "unless she has it ready to go by... when?"

"Tonight."

"Tonight. Is Linda the one picking it up?"

"That's what she said."

And the man on the phone was waiting for it to be delivered. By Linda. Furthermore, he was holding some "kid" at that house out on the marshlands until she arrived.

What kid? And why was he holding him? If Gerry Gerard had Danny, and Jancy was at the Prayer House—

Abby turned to ice. She grabbed Alicia's arm. "I need to make a call, Allie. I need to make it right now."

Alicia shook her head. "Dell told me not to let you talk to anyone outside this house."

"And you listen to him? All the time?"

"He's keeping us safe."

"Safe from who?"

Alicia shrugged. "The authorities...I don't know. The police, the INS, whoever might want to arrest my mom and dad."

"Allie, wake up! There will be government agents all over this place any minute now. Your dad is too sick to run, and your mom probably won't leave his side. So it's over. The best thing you can do for them—and you—is to turn them in yourself."

"Do you know what you're saying?" Alicia cried. "I can't turn my own parents in! There has to be another way."

"There is," Abby said. "But you have to be willing."

"What do you mean?"

"I could do it for you. I could tell them where your mother and father are. When they hear the true story, especially about your father's condition and your mother's unwillingness to work on the bomb—in fact, the way she's faked her work on the bomb—I don't think they'll be too hard on them."

"No! Abby, they'd take us away from one another. They'd split us up and put him in some government hospital. He wouldn't have either of us, and we've got to be with him when he…" She began to cry. "He's only got a few more days, Abby—if that. A few more days."

A few more days might give Alicia more time with her father, but who would The Candlelights harm when they realized they'd been duped? The child they held hostage? Jancy?

"They gave up so much for me," Alicia said. "They went into hiding to keep *me* safe, you know, not them." She dried her eyes and blew her nose on the tissue Abby handed her. Folding her arms, she rocked back and forth, as if the motion itself could ease her pain. Abby remembered her mother doing that in hard times, and she'd been told "rocking" was the Irish way of dealing with grief. She sat quietly as Alicia went on, hoping that once she got out the pain she might see more clearly what she needed to do.

"After they came to this country," Alicia said, "they couldn't find work at first, and the little money they'd brought with them didn't last long. My mother said I cried myself to sleep every night for a week from hunger, and it broke her heart. She had to make 'pancakes' for me out of flour and water when they ran out of food, just to fill my stomach. She did everything to protect me."

Alicia took a deep breath. "Abby, I know that what these people are doing now is wrong. God, wrong? It's monstrous! There aren't really any words strong enough to describe it. But my mother has been determined to protect me and Jancy by doing whatever they ask, at least right up to the very last minute. I've pleaded with her for the past three days to go to the police or the FBI. I've tried to convince her that Jancy is in a safe place, and not to worry about me. I've even threatened to go to the police myself. She just keeps saying 'no.' Over and over, sometimes, like a mantra. 'No…no…no…' Abby, she has the most desperate look in her eyes. How can I do that to her at the very time my father—her husband—is dying?"

"Your mother is overwhelmed by your father's illness, Allie. She isn't thinking straight."

Alicia turned a pale, tearstained face to Abby. "I don't know, Ab. I just don't know what to do."

Abby patted her shoulder. "Don't worry," she said. "We'll work it out."

In fact, she already had an idea. It would require a little act of deception, but she was getting used to that.

First, though, she had to get her hands on a phone and confirm her worst and latest fear: that Jancy was no longer at the Prayer House.

32

It was several minutes before midnight. In his penthouse high above Central Park, H. P. Gerard sat with six men and four women around a polished teak table. Privately delivered memos had gone out to each member of the Matalene Trust early in the morning, calling them here to a meeting "of utmost confidentially and urgency."

Each member lived within three hours via plane from New York City, and each had formerly been a CEO and board director of their own company. Their portfolios were a stockbroker's dream. Members of the Matalene Trust could afford to retire and do whatever they wished for the rest of their lives. Money was no object.

The Matalene Trust, however, consumed their days, nights, weekends and would-be family holidays. All the members had lost family or friends in the war against Iraq. One woman's eighteen-year-old son was killed by friendly fire when the jeep he was driving, one he had commandeered from insurgents, was shot at by U.S. soldiers. Another member, a man, had lost twin sons who had joined the army when their local recruiter promised them a college education.

The man's grief, and guilt, stemmed in part from the fact that he could have easily provided both of his sons with an education. Instead, in an effort to teach them to be strong and independent, he had told them they were on their own after high school. He had worked his way through college, and toughing it out had prepared him for the real world. Now, he'd told his sons, the "real world" was *surreal,* and they would be all the better for their experience.

Except that they had turned the tables on him and, instead of getting jobs, had joined the army without even telling him they were going to. And every time Lawrence Jessup passed Harvard now—the school he had hoped his sons would attend—his eyes teared up without warning. Being part of Matalene was the only thing that helped to fill the emptiness in his heart.

At H. P. Gerard's invitation, each of the people here had come together and formed a watchdog group. Its mission statement was to make sure the kinds of bad intelligence and poor decisions that had led to the war with Iraq never happened again. The name Matalene came from a former New York City jeweler who had designed and sold high-quality watches. H. P. Gerard was a collector of antique and unusual watches; when a name was being discussed in the beginning, he had glanced down at his wrist and come up with the name Matalene, as befitting a "watch" dog group.

Now he folded his hands and looked at each person in turn. "Thank you for coming. I see we're all here."

A tall, thin man spoke. "I had to cancel an important meeting. Hopefully, this will be quick."

"When I tell you why you're here, Gordon, you won't be thinking of business," Gerard said. "At least, not the oil business."

"Only if the world is coming to an end," someone cracked.

"It very well could be," Gerard said in a low, solemn voice.

"What's going on?" a man with graying black hair and a muscular body asked.

"I'll get right to the point. I've had word that the U.S. is in imminent danger of a bioterrorist attack. This is not rumor, and it's not just chatter. This is solid information, and it comes from the top."

A heavy air of tension filled the room, but no one spoke.

"We need to find out where this attack is designed to take place," Gerard continued. "It could be here on the eastern seaboard. It could be in California or New Mexico. Or, it could be some damned small town in the Midwest that we haven't even thought of."

"You're saying it's a needle in a haystack," a man with a Spanish accent commented. "I take it Homeland Security knows about this?"

"They know the 'what.' But so far, they don't know the 'where.' I don't have to tell you that this is the most important presidential commission we've had since we formed Matalene Trust. Fortunately, we were able to fend off the planned attack on Los Angeles last spring, as well as the one on Montreal two years ago, and on Japan before that. This one, however, is the big one. I don't mean to sound dramatic, but in all truth, it could decimate the world as we know it."

After a small silence, another man asked, "How much time do we have?"

"Until tomorrow," Gerard said. "If we're lucky."

There were shocked sounds around the table. "Even with our connections—"

"With our connections," Gerard interrupted briskly, "we *will* find out where this is set to happen. If we don't…" He paused and shrugged. "Odds are, some of us won't be here next week."

He scanned the faces around the table and wondered if they believed him. Had he done a good enough job?

He stood. "This is what I know." Using his hands for emphasis, he laid out the information he said he'd been given two days before by the director of the CIA, the director of the FBI and the president himself.

The meeting had taken place in the Oval Office, he said, and the only other person in attendance was the director of Homeland Security. Gerard told the members of Matalene about the importance of finding Pat Devlin, and he revealed that Devlin was his own father-in-law.

"This IRA guy? The one who bombed the kids' school bus in the seventies?" one man said disbelievingly.

"He's Alicia's father," Gerard confirmed. "I didn't know. But speaking of which, any word on Alicia yet?"

A pale man at the end of the table shook his head. "Since we lost track of her at the airport in Phoenix, she seems to have disappeared into thin air. We have to assume someone is helping her."

"Any idea who?"

"Not yet. Could be that friend of hers, Abby Northrup. After Phoenix, she went back to that place in Carmel Valley where she lives with those nuns. The Prayer House, it's called. Then, tonight…" He paused.

"Go on," Gerard prompted.

"Well, Ms. Northrup flew into Houston tonight and drove south. Our investigator, uh, lost her on I-45, but we think she may have been heading for Galveston. That could mean that your wife is there."

"But you don't know, right? You don't know because your investigators lost Abby Northrup on the road! Just what use are they to us?" Gerard said with sudden anger. "They're supposed to be the best in the world, and they can't follow a car on a highway?"

"I didn't say they wouldn't find them, Gerry," the other man said calmly. "Sometimes things go wrong. They take time."

"We haven't got time!" Gerry said, his voice rising. "Christ, man! Haven't you been listening? We have no time!"

Nor can I have Alicia and her nosy friend Abby messing around in this. They could ruin everything.

He rubbed a hand over his face and slumped his

shoulders. "I apologize. But you *must* find Alicia—*and* Abby Northrup."

"I agree that Galveston is our best lead," a woman with short red hair said. "After all, there was that tip that Pat Devlin might be there, then Alicia showed up, and now Abby Northrup. It would figure she went down there because she had some lead on Alicia and her father. And what about that mobile home park?"

Gerard thought for a minute. "I doubt that it's important. Someone who's been hiding out as long as Pat Devlin isn't going to be living in a mobile home park. Have you ever seen how those people peek through their curtains at their neighbors?" He laughed scornfully.

"I guess you've forgotten, Gerry," the red-haired woman said mildly. "My company makes modular homes—which is what we call them these days. They're really quite nice, and so are most of the people who live in them."

Gerry waved a hand as if to brush off a fly. "Yes, yes, I've heard that. Sorry. Now, let's get back to business. I want an investigator at every motel in Galveston— *tonight*—and I want every door knocked on and every room checked out *personally,* until someone comes up with either Alicia or Abby Northrup."

"Gerry, have you any idea how long that could take?" Paul Rogers said. "By the time we get all the search warrants we'll need to do that, it'll be too late."

"Screw the search warrants!" Gerard said. "Tell them to proceed as if they've got them, and not to take no for an answer from anyone."

"Hell, Gerry. Need I point out that we could go to jail for that? The FBI—"

"The FBI," Gerard said tersely, "is powerless against the approval I have. The highest authorities have given me permission to act in any way I deem necessary."

He stood. "You all know what to do. Thank you for coming. This meeting is adjourned."

A few of the Matalene members talked among themselves in the hallway, making plans to meet later. Paul Rogers, however, stayed behind.

Gerard looked up from the table, where he had begun to pore through papers. "Something I can do for you?" he asked, though his tone was clearly one of dismissal. He had hoped to avoid a confrontation with the vice president of Matalene tonight.

"You damn well can," Rogers said. "I want to know how much of this is about Alicia—and you."

Gerard frowned. "Are you crazy, Paul? We've got the possible end of the world on our hands here. You think I'm playing games with this?"

"Look, Gerry, I know you. I've known you since Yale. Sure, we've got a genuine and very scary emergency on our hands. But you are just too damned anxious to track down Alicia. Sure, she could lead us to Pat Devlin, but there are plenty of other ways—"

"All of which the FBI and CIA are doing," Gerry snapped. "And as you well know, we have other, more persuasive methods."

Rogers blanched. "Vancouver was a mistake. I thought we'd put that behind us."

"Vancouver would be rubble by now if we'd listened to you. And, no—I, for one, have not 'put that behind us.' You honestly think I could ever forget what happened there?"

He remembered back to the early days... Vancouver. *The Prime Minister's life had been saved, but not before an innocent clerk had been set up, his life sacrificed "for the cause." Matalene had needed a boost, something to prove its value to the president and his Intelligence cronies.*

Rogers's eyes narrowed. "What's going on, Gerry? Don't try to tell me you haven't got your own agenda this time. May I remind you that when we formed Matalene, we all vowed never to use the organization or the people in it for personal reasons?"

"I'm not doing that, Paul."

Rogers stood. "The hell you're not! Have you and Alicia split? Is that the real reason she's disappeared? Did she take Jancy with her? I have a right to know, Gerry!"

"I'm telling you, Paul, it's not like that!" Gerry threw up his hands in a gesture of frustration. "As Jancy's godfather, you would be the first to know if Alicia and I split up."

"All right, then. How about this? You're pulling some power play to take all the credit when these terrorists are caught, and Alicia's got something to do with that."

"Like hell. You want the credit, Paul?"

"No. But it sure wouldn't hurt your run for the presidency."

"You think I want to run for president?" Gerry laughed. "I don't know how these rumors get started, but have you taken a good look at our president lately? Presidents don't have any power, Paul. More often than not, they're laughingstocks."

Paul Rogers rubbed his eyes, shaking his head wearily. "Then I can't imagine what you're up to."

"The only thing I'm up to," Gerry said, "is stopping Pat Devlin from turning that bomb over to the terrorists."

"Then you'd better be playing this straight," Rogers said. "Because think of it, Gerry. What happens if we don't stop these guys?"

"What happens is that you pray they haven't targeted your hometown."

"But we're— I mean, all of us in Matalene—"

"Are from cities with millions of people," Gerard agreed. "New York, Washington, Philadelphia, Los Angeles… Paul, if this thing happens, it's not just the cities. The air will be poisoned everywhere in between. It will drift. And depending on the way the wind blows, it could cross the United States—perhaps the whole planet—within days."

He shook his head and closed his eyes as if warding off a terrible vision. "We should pray together, Paul, that this never happens."

33

Except for the *whish-whishing* of Pat Devlin's respirator, it was deadly quiet in the home of Alicia's parents. The only sign of anyone being alive was the shifting light beneath the bedroom door every time Dell moved his feet. It seemed he never slept, and Abby wondered if that would make him easier to handle should the need arise.

They had locked her up in the room next to Alicia's. She'd been lying here awake and meditating, clearing her mind for what she needed to do. At one point she'd had to sit up in order to stay awake, but she kept meditating, keeping her mind as blank as possible, just letting the inevitable thoughts flow and move on.

Finally, she heard it—the faint knock at the front door and voices, muted. One a woman's. The door opened, closed, and there was silence again. Then, from Alicia's room came a soft tap, then two, on her bedroom wall.

Allie's sign that Linda had picked up the package.

Abby looked at the clock on the nightstand—12:34.

She tried not to make a sound as she pulled on the jeans and T-shirt Allie had loaned her. Tiptoeing to the double-hung window that overlooked the backyard, she cautiously unlocked it. Pushing it up, she steeled herself for an alarm to go off.

Silence. Her nerves flashed, like a jolt from a short in an electric cord, then settled back into the earlier calm. Alicia had bypassed this window on the alarm, just as she'd promised. Abby relaxed and slung a leg over the sill, then the other. Dropping to the ground, she looked around.

Her eyes were accustomed to the dark from lying awake in the dark bedroom. But the eight-foot cement-block wall around the backyard looked like Mount Everest compared to her height of five foot four.

"Once you're over it," Alicia had said, "head for the trees behind the office. Stay near the outside perimeter of the trees where you can still see the houses. Give it about ten minutes, and then follow the tree line to the left. You'll come to the end of this street. It's a dead end, and you'll find my car there."

She had handed Abby her keys. "It's a dark blue BMW. Drive as quietly as you can past this house and out the gate. Then you can push it all you want. It'll do 140, easy."

Running over to the cement wall, Abby grabbed the thickest flowering vine she could find and pulled with all her strength, testing it. It held, and she hauled herself up, hand over hand, to the top. She could see over it now—the greenbelt, the trees off in the distance. She let out a sigh of relief and dropped to the ground.

A spotlight big enough to light up Red Square came on, pinning her against the ground. At the same time, an alarm like a shriek from all the souls in hell blasted throughout the park.

Abby scrambled to her feet and ran. She was halfway to the line of trees when she tripped over a fallen limb and fell again, twisting an ankle. Ignoring the pain, she got to her feet and ran as fast as she could, staying clear of the closed park office. She knew they were following her, could hear the pounding of their feet on the hard grassy lawn. She looked back once, saw Dell and, behind him, the other guard—close, too close. She imagined "space" around her ankle, a yoga trick, and after a few moments the pain disappeared. Running faster, she made it to the trees and raced through them, not stopping until she was on the other side.

But ahead of her lay open ground. There was no place to hide here, and no buildings or people in sight. She could almost feel their breath on her neck as she paused a second, wondering which way to turn. Her chest felt tight, her legs numb, and she cursed herself for not eating that day. This was like the nightmare she sometimes had, where no matter how fast she ran, "they" always caught her. In her dream, she would finally be too tired to run farther. She'd try to fly then, to get away, but she never could get high enough. They would grab her arm or leg and pull her down.

In her dreams, though, that was when she woke up. No such luck now.

Knowing that she could go no farther, she fell to her

knees, then crumpled on the ground, pretending to stumble. She could feel their footsteps pounding harder now, the vibration through the hard-packed earth getting stronger and stronger. She could even feel the change in energy, growing darker and heavier as the first one grew closer and then stopped above her.

"I thought you'd learned to mind your own business in Phoenix," Dell said, breathing heavily. She sensed his hand, reaching for her.

Phoenix? Kris had said that was The Candlelights. Allie's bodyguard was a Candlelight? Pretending to protect them, and all the while he was actually a spy in the house?

The memory of her hands cuffed to the car steering wheel filled her with rage. In a move that she'd never gotten right before, she turned over, planted a kick in his groin and then flew to her feet, letting loose with a kick to the chest. The bodyguard doubled over, groaning and gasping for breath.

Abby turned to run again, but felt something cold and metallic against the back of her neck.

"Don't move."

Once they've got you, it's all over, Ben had said in an exercise.

Without even thinking, she cross-stepped to seven o'clock, then pivoted one-hundred-eighty degrees clockwise to six. Her right arm shot up with her hand open, palm facing in, and shoved the gun past the right side of her head. Quickly, she jabbed with her left fingertips to strike the second bodyguard's eyes. Stopping just short of plucking them out, she used the jab to inflict pain. He cried out, covered his eyes with his hands and stumbled. But just when she thought he was down, he came at her again. She didn't try to duck the right punch, but blocked it with her left hand, grabbing his right wrist. Striking down with her right forearm, she hit his punching hand and again went for the eyes.

This time she didn't hold back. Her fingertips jabbed his eyeballs hard, and he screamed and fell to the ground. His hands covered his face, and she could see that blood seeped from between the fingers.

Pausing for breath, she realized that she was still calm. She had defended herself and even gone on the attack, but there had been no hatred behind it as she so often had felt during practice. Her mind had stayed clear, and she'd known exactly what to do. *Damn.* Jancy and Davis would be proud.

But Dell was on his feet again and coming at her. Grabbing his right arm, she twisted it clockwise, then circled down the arm. Her right hand grabbed his right wrist from the outside, and she drew back with her left foot and into a right cat stance facing twelve o'clock. Pulling forward with her right hand against his right arm, she leveled a kick to the groin. He went down again, and a quick check showed that he was no longer conscious.

With both men down and out, Abby swept up the second bodyguard's gun and ran.

Allie's car was right where she'd said it would be. Abby slipped into it, started the engine and drove slowly away from the house toward the Emerald Gardens' main gate. Stopping short there, she was stumped. The gate was locked, of course. Why hadn't she thought of that? Why hadn't Allie?

For a minute, she wondered if Allie had set a trap for her after all.

Then her mind cleared, and she realized how exhausted she must be. Exhausted, screwed up and ravenous. Her thinking was off, to suspect Allie of that sort of thing. Reaching up to the sun visor, she found the remote she should have known was there from the first. Pushing the only button on it, she watched the gate open. It was slow, slow as maple syrup at the North Pole, and she wanted to jump out of the car and push it. Even more than that, she wanted to scream.

On the road to the freeway, she picked up speed. At the freeway entrance she paused and set Allie's GPS to find the house in the marshlands. It directed her north on 45, and after 6.8 miles, right on Mathers Road. After that there were no turns at all—just one long, straight line to the house, as Joey had said.

Allie had left her own cell phone on the passenger's seat, and before entering the freeway, Abby used it to call the Prayer House. It was late, but Sister Helen answered right away and gave her the information she had expected to hear.

Damn, damn, damn, she muttered under her breath as she jammed her foot down on the accelerator and pulled onto the freeway, nearly running several cars off the road. *Why couldn't I have been wrong?*

By the time she reached Mathers Road, it had started raining. A different rain, not the kind that snuck up on you in Carmel, starting with a wisp of fog over the hills and followed by a few gentle drops that turned into what they called a "mizzle" in England—a cross between a mist and a drizzle. This rain was a downpour from the first. The heavens opened up with a loud clap of thunder and a bolt of lightning that streaked across the sky like an angry blast from a shotgun. Abby could almost hear the words from *The Movie Network:* "God is mad, and He's not gonna take it anymore!"

Or something like that. Remembering quotes began not to matter as the rain pelted the windshield and the wipers became all but useless. Abby gave up trying to see the road and followed the red taillights of cars ahead. She almost went off the road twice, trying to find the right button to push for the heat to dry the steam from the inside windows. Somewhere along the way, she realized she was chewing the inside of her mouth, a nervous tic.

The Mathers Road sign was bent over and lying in the dirt, apparently the result of some other storm, but the GPS alerted her when she was nearly upon the street. Slowing down, she saw that it really was nothing more than a dirt road. And now, thanks to the rain, it was a muddy dirt road.

She turned off her headlights and parked on the side of Mathers, though there was little space. If another car turned onto the road, they'd see the BMW and know someone was here who shouldn't be here. A few feet more off the mud, though, and the car would be in the swamp.

Why on earth would anyone build a house out here like this?

So they wouldn't be bothered by the likes of you, she heard her aunt Kate say. Then, just as quickly, her mother would add, *Or because they're nuts in the head, like you.*

Upon which they'd all laugh, including Abby, and the visit would be off to a great start. She missed her mom and Aunt Kate. It was time to go home for a while.

First, though, she had a job to do. Stepping out of the car into the slick mud, Abby hung on to the open car door to make sure she didn't slip and fall on her face. Then, reaching back in, she picked the bodyguard's gun off the seat and stuck it into her belt. The tiny flashlight she usually carried was in her back jeans pocket on the left, and her mini burglary kit was in the right back pocket. Not that she expected to need it. Allie's cell phone was next, and she turned it to vibrate and stuck it in the back of her belt, along with the gun.

Closing the car door, she slid onto her knees in the mud, then onto her stomach. With her elbows bent, she belly-crawled along the road toward the house soldier-style, as they'd taught her to do at Ben's survival camp. The house was at least three city blocks away, and the rain beat down and blinded her. Mud went up her nose and into her mouth, and there were times when she thought she didn't have another ounce of strength in her, but she kept going. Even the creepy, crawling things on her bare arms, neck and face didn't stop her. She pretended she was in a mud bath at a spa, being massaged.

It worked, until something long and squiggly slithered up the leg of her jeans. Smothering a scream, she reached down and grabbed it from her calf before it went any higher. Holding it up, she could barely see it but could tell from the way it moved and felt that it was probably nothing more than a harmless baby snake. She tossed it over into the swamp.

The house, as she neared it, looked like one Hitchcock might have rejected for the original *Psycho*, but only because it was far too scary out here for a camera crew. The rain clouds had covered the moon, and the house was a dark, ominous outline against an even darker sky.

There was a light downstairs, though, which she saw as she wiped her eyes and her vision cleared. It seemed to be coming from a front window, and there might be one on the side as well.

She was covered completely in mud, and that was good; it made for excellent camouflage. She took time to pick a bug out of her ear, but stayed on her belly until she was within feet of the house. There's probably a dog, she thought, and she prepared herself—at least in her mind—for a possible attack. But there wasn't even a warning bark.

These people must feel pretty confident about their security out here, she thought.

But why? Were there alarms inside that told them when someone was coming up the drive?

The house seemed to have been built on a small piece of solid land. The yard around it, if it could be called a yard, was circled with white-painted rocks. Abby assumed that the rocks were to show where the solid land ended and the marsh began. At the moment, however, there was little delineation, since the winds and rain had blown mud and vegetation all around the yard, turning it into a six-inch-deep bog.

Abby crept to the lighted front window, and pulled herself up on the outside sill to see in. The window was streaked with rainwater, which made everything blurry, and her arm muscles almost screamed aloud from holding up her weight. Her fingers were raw from scratching through the mud, which had mixed with the sharp gravel of the road bed beneath it. She tried to hang on, but lasted only a few seconds. In that time she was able to see that there were two men in what seemed to be a living room straight out of the Depression years. Flowered wallpaper was stained and peeling, while an overstuffed brown couch was tattered and had springs sticking up out of a cushion.

One of the men was Hardy Boyd, from the warehouse, and the other was someone she didn't recognize. They sat slouched on armchairs that were frayed and faded, drinking beer as if they hadn't a care in the world. On the floor between the two men were several empty beer cans, and in the middle of the room a card table had been set up. On it was what could only be "the package."

It was approximately two feet wide by one foot high,

and wrapped in brown paper, then secured with mailing tape.

So Linda had made her delivery. They must be waiting now for the Candlelights person they were supposed to turn it over to. But who?

Abby crept to the next window, lifting herself up again to see in. She had to stifle a gasp. Tied to a straight-back wooden chair was Jimmy, and a wave of relief swept over her. It grew when she saw that on another chair was the reason she'd crawled through all that muck and mire: Jancy. Both had tape over their mouths, but both seemed awake and, thankfully, alive.

Since her telephone conversation from the warehouse to the number at this house, Abby had been afraid that Jancy might be the "kid" they were holding. And when Sister Helen confirmed that Jancy had disappeared yet again from the Prayer House, she was sure of it. Since Danny was in New York with Kris, it was the only thing that made sense.

Except that it *didn't* make sense. Not really. What on earth could they possibly want from Jancy? To hold her over Pat and Bridget Devlin's heads until they turned over the bioweapons? But Alicia and Bridget didn't seem to know that Jancy was here. And how did they get her here? She would have had to be unconscious, or she'd have kicked and screamed all the way.

As for Jimmy, had they grabbed him outside the motel that morning? And what did they want with him?

Before her muscles gave out, Abby let go of the sill with one hand, just long enough to tap lightly on the window. Jancy was the first to hear it. She saw Abby, and must have signaled Jimmy with some sound. He looked at her, and when she nodded toward the window, he turned his head and saw Abby. His eyes widened. Then he shook his head rapidly, as if telling her to get away, and fast.

There was no way for Abby to respond. The most she could do was place one hand against the window in an expression of comfort before she became too weak and slid to the ground. Kneeling there in the dark, she paused, trying to decide what her next move should be.

There was nothing to keep her from walking right up to the front door. She was armed, and she could knock and say she was Linda. If she muffled her voice, the men in the front room probably wouldn't question it—until they saw her. And the gun she was pointing at them.

But what good would that do? She could free Jancy and Jimmy, but the two men in the front room didn't seem in charge of anything. In fact, just the opposite—they appeared to be waiting for a boss, someone to tell them what to do with that package, or someone to hand it over to. If she took them on too soon, she might in some way send a warning to the people at the top, the ones who planned to take what they thought was a lethal mix and put it into a bomb.

Those were the ones who should be caught, and then grilled for information, to prevent this from happening again—as well as to protect the Devlins.

But let's face it. This really isn't my job anymore. It's way beyond me, and I'm smart enough to know it.

Backing off quietly until she was twenty feet or so

from the house, she pulled out Allie's cell phone and called Joey, having memorized his number. He didn't answer, and for the first time she felt truly worried about what she was doing. Until now, she had simply trusted that there would be backup when she needed it.

She left a message on his voice mail, telling him she was at the house on Mathers Road, and that Jimmy was being held hostage here, along with Jancy Gerard. She told him the package was here—the bioweapons for the bomb that was scheduled to be detonated sometime, somewhere, today. She had no idea when someone would be here to pick it up, and they were running out of time to find and round up all the conspirators.

So, now what? she wondered, hanging up. Since she hadn't been able to reach Joey, she had no idea when he, the local police or the feds might show up here. Should she call Lessing? Ben? Kris?

No. Not yet. All she needed was for a passel of military choppers to suddenly come swarming over the house. Jimmy and Jancy would be dead within minutes; they'd never be left alive to testify against the men inside or reveal anything they might have learned here.

First Things First was her usual motto. Do Your Best and Leave the Rest was another, and that was what decided her. Stomping up the front steps to the rickety porch, she knocked loudly on the door. At the same time she pulled the Glock 9 mm out of her belt. A man's voice said cautiously, "Who is it?"

"Linda," Abby replied in a low voice.

There was a moment or two of hesitation. Too long,

Abby thought. *Something's wrong. They know it isn't Linda. Get ready.*

She braced herself. When the door opened a crack she kicked it in, raising the gun at the same time so that it was level with the head of the man who stumbled back from the door and onto the floor.

The other man, a shocked expression on his face, began to rise from his chair.

"Sit!" Abby yelled, moving the gun back and forth between both men. "Both of you! Back in the chairs!"

Make plenty of noise, she'd heard the instructor at the survival school say. *Scare the bejeezus out of 'em.*

By the expressions on the two men's faces, she thought she must have succeeded.

The smell in here was horrible. Enough mold, she guessed, to wipe out an army. She tried not to gag.

"Who are you waiting here for?" she demanded in the tone of a drill sergeant. "When is he coming?"

Both men shook their heads, as if their voices had left them. Only then did Abby realize what she must look like, smeared from head to toe with mud, debris, bugs, worms. The Creature from the Black Lagoon had arrived.

"Take a good look," she said coldly. "You'll be dying out in those swamps if you don't start talking soon."

Hardy, the man from the warehouse, was closest to her. He spoke first. "We're not waitin' for nobody. We've just been sittin' here, talkin'."

"Liar!" She kicked him in the left shin, hard enough to make him yell out. Then she shoved the gun barrel against his neck, so deep that it made a dimple in the thick, fatty flesh. She could see his carotid pulsing against the metal.

"Somebody's coming here to pick up that package," she said. "When are they coming?"

Hardy began to sweat. "I don't know, I swear! I was just told to wait here and keep an eye on it!"

She looked at the other man, who was younger. He was already shaking his head. "I don't know anything, either. I'm just the caretaker here. I don't know what anybody does. Honest!"

"Honest, huh?" She crossed over to him and smacked him in the face with the back of her free hand. "Is taking care of human beings part of your job?"

He cringed. "I...I don't know what you mean."

"The man and girl in the other room, that's what I mean! What the hell were you planning to do to them?"

"Nothin', honest! I didn't plan nothin'!"

He was wearing old canvas Nikes, and she stomped on his foot, putting all her weight behind it. He yelled and doubled over, moaning.

"Oops, sorry. I didn't plan that, either," Abby said.

"My, my," another voice boomed as a blast of cold, wet rain entered through the front door. "I don't remember you being so mean, Abby."

She whirled around and came face-to-face with Gerry Gerard.

A jumble of explanations ran through her mind: Gerry was looking for Jancy and had tracked her here, after learning she'd been kidnapped. He was working

with the feds to help find Pat Devlin and make a name
for himself as a hero before the elections came up.

"I'm the UPS guy," Gerry said, smiling. "Here to
pick up a little package."

He came closer. "You can put the gun down now,
Abby. This hasn't anything to do with you. Put the gun
down and you can leave. No harm, no foul."

"Back off," she said, still confused but not giving an
inch. "Stop right there."

"Are you going to shoot me, Abby? After all Allie
and I have done for you? I don't think so. Besides, my
partner—who just came in through the back, by the
way—would have to kill your friends back there."

"*My friends?* One of those people is your daughter,
Gerry! Do you know that?"

"Know it? I arranged it," Gerry said, the smile still
on his face. "Jancy is what you might call my insurance
that this whole thing comes off today."

"You mean the bomb? No! You can't be behind that!"

"Oh, Abby," he said with mock sadness. "I thought
you would have figured it out by now. You were always
so sharp. It's that Prayer House, of course. Living there
has turned your mind to mush."

"You may actually be right about that," Abby
conceded, recovering. "Because I sure don't see
what good having Jancy bound and gagged will do
you…unless, of course, your plan was to scare the kid
to death."

*Keep him talking. Give Joey and the cavalry time to
get here.*

He chuckled. "Scare Jancy? Have you seen her lately? Oh, that's right, I forgot—I found her at your Prayer House. In fact, that's where I convinced her to come with me. For Alicia's sake, I told her. Fierce little kid! Loves her mom like crazy, though you wouldn't know it half the time. At any rate, she couldn't get into the car fast enough. And it's all your fault, Abby. Yours and Kris's."

"Really. How do you figure that, Gerry?"

He had come a step closer as he talked, and all her senses went on alert. At the same time she stayed calm, unemotional. When he made his move, she would have to be ready. Gerry was a large man. He could easily take a woman down.

And there were still the other two men to watch out for. If Gerry got the upper hand with her, they'd pile in just for the fun of it.

"Why is it your fault Jancy's here?" Gerry said. "Well, when I grabbed Danny, it was to keep Kris under control. Of course, she's ruined all that now. Kidnapped him, right out from under the noses of my so-called security experts."

Gerry shook his head. "That woman is something else. I'd almost applaud her, except that once Danny was gone, I needed a stand-in, of course. And who else but tough, impervious-to-everything little Jancy?"

"A stand-in," Abby said, feeling chilled and loathing him more with every word. She had the feeling she was talking with a madman. "Why a stand-in, Gerry?"

"Isn't it obvious? The only thing that'll stop the feds

in their tracks is the safety of a child. And I needed them far, far away in order to bring my plan off."

Abby shook her head. "I don't get it, Gerry. You've put your own son and daughter in danger. They're going to hate you. And for what? Why are you doing this? It goes against everything you always believed in."

A shrug. "I was a kid back then, Abby. A foolish, know-nothing kid. I didn't realize that power's the only thing that really matters in this world. And when I finally did realize it, I set up a secret organization, thinking we could make the world a better place." He frowned. "My one screwup. Turns out the people I've been working with are a bunch of kindergartners. They aren't willing to go the extra mile."

"The extra mile. Is this so-called terrorist attack 'going the extra mile'?"

"So-called?" he said sharply.

"Because you're behind it, not The Candlelights. They're just going to take the fall, right?"

He smiled. "Again, I thought you were smarter than that."

"You know, Gerry, I thought you were, too. You've worked all your life to get into a position of power, and now you're going to destroy half the country, maybe the world. You're not going to leave much to have power over—

"Oh, my God." She stopped short, completely stunned. When she could speak again, she continued. "You wouldn't do that. Of course you wouldn't do that! But I used the right word, didn't I? It's a *so-called* attack. A hoax, to terrify the country. There never were any terrorists. At least, not anyone important."

"Hell, no, it's not a hoax, Abby! Not in the sense you mean. When the morning papers come out, and when people tune in to CNN and Fox, the entire country will learn that an Armageddon bomb is set to go off in the U.S. today. Worse, they'll learn that no one knows where or when. There will be chaos—people wanting to run from it but not knowing where to go, whether it's in their town or the one they're heading for. They'll hear that there's no escape, so they'll be paralyzed with fear. That's better than any paralysis caused by a chemical."

Gerry's face lit up, as if he'd found the Holy Grail and couldn't wait to tell the world. "Remember the hurricanes in New Orleans and Florida? Remember the gridlocks on the freeways? That happened here, too, Abby, in Galveston and Houston. People trying to get out of the storm's way, running out of gas, food, water, and having to sit in boiling-hot cars for hours. You think they aren't scared to death that'll happen again? Watch, Abby. Next time they won't even evacuate. They'll be too damned afraid."

His voice rose as his excitement grew. "Dirty bombs are already obsolete, Abby—at least as a threat. The chaos and fear—the *belief* that a dirty bomb is about to strike—is all we need anymore to control people. And before this day is over, the powers that be will know what *real* power is. What's more, they'll know that I've got it. *I* sent the warnings out. *I* was the 'credible intel.'"

"But, Gerry, if you've already got enough power to do that—"

"One can never have *enough* power, Abby. *Never.* And you know when I'll have it? At the end of the day, when I've saved the whole damned country from the worst holocaust imaginable."

"That's it, then? You're going to 'save the country' single-handedly? Brilliant, Gerry. You'll have some kind of story, of course, about stopping The Candlelights and destroying the 'Armageddon' bomb. And all the while, the *real* Candlelights don't even know why the hell they're being rounded up and arrested, I suppose."

"Congratulations, Abby!" he said, giving a mock tip of an invisible hat. "Finally, that brain of yours comes alive."

"Okay, then, why The Candlelights?" she asked. "Why not al-Qaeda?"

"Because The Candlelights were the one group I could tie to my dear wife's father, Pat Devlin," he said. "Master bomb maker. Give the feds something credible to chew on while I went about my business."

"And you chose a dirty bomb because…"

"Shock and awe, Abby. Shock and awe. What is the American public most afraid of since 9/11?"

"Terrorists?"

"You got it."

"So, how far back does this scam of yours go? To when this woman Linda first talked to the Devlins and threatened Allie and Jancy's lives? Was she working for you?"

He smiled. "You'd be surprised, Abby. Everybody works for me. *Everybody.*"

"Not me," she said.

His voice grew hard. "Which is why I need you to give me that gun."

He took two more steps and reached for the Glock. Abby brought it cracking down on his wrist, then swiveled to the side. With her left hand she made a chopping motion, connecting with his neck, while her left foot swung up and got him in the groin. He bent over, groaning, and fell to the floor.

"Geez, Gerry, you disappoint me," Abby said, stepping back a few paces. "A man with all that power, and you couldn't even stop a little thing like me from taking you down."

She swung the Glock in the direction of the two men, who were both halfway out of their chairs. "No way," she said. "Don't even breathe."

There was a closet under the stairs to the second floor, and she crossed over to it and looked inside. Except for a few old rolls of faded wallpaper, it was empty.

"Get over here," she ordered. "All three of you. Move it!"

Hardy and his pal scrambled to obey, and she heard Hardy whisper to the other guy something about "Wonder Woman."

She almost laughed. Clearly, none of these men were familiar with martial arts, and thank God for that; it gave her an edge.

Gerry glared at her, struggling to his feet. She didn't trust him for a second, and she kept the Glock leveled at him as she hustled him into the closet after the other two, telling them to move to the back and sit on the floor. The closet was even more musty smelling than the room, and there was black mold on the walls. She held her breath to keep from inhaling it, but felt a sense of satisfaction for putting these lowlifes where they belonged.

Next, she slid both heavy armchairs across the wooden floor and pushed them against the door, since there was no lock. She would need something to keep them from just sliding back, though, when the men tried to get out. There was a ratty old gray rug, about nine by twelve, in the middle of the room. She rolled it up with its rubber pad on the outside, and pushed it against the chairs, hoping the rubber would stick to the wooden floor and keep them from sliding. Then she piled everything heavy she could find in the room on top of the chairs—irons from the fireplace, a rusted metal doorstop in the shape of a cat and the few pieces of smaller furniture that were scattered around helterskelter.

Satisfied that the men were safely locked in the closet, at least for the time it would take them to push all that stuff out of the way, she went into the back room where she'd seen Jimmy and Jancy.

They were gone.

34

The ropes they'd been tied with hung loosely over the chairs, and pieces of duct tape lay on the floor.

By the way, my partner came in the back way, Gerry had said. *If you shoot me, he'll have to kill them.*

She'd thought Gerry was bluffing. *Stupid! Stupid, stupid!*

Is that why he'd taken them, to kill them? *Dear God, no.*

Where the hell were Joey and the local law? She couldn't just leave to look for Jimmy and Jancy, with the three men so poorly contained, but she couldn't just sit here, either, waiting for help to arrive.

She went through the kitchen and, leaving the lights off, opened the back door. Standing there, she saw nothing but darkness—dark sky, dark marshlands—and the little line of white rocks around the yard. She began to call out softly for Jimmy, then Jancy. When they didn't answer, she raised her voice—loathe to do it, because if they answered her louder call, it could mean they were not in the inner circle, but out in the swamps.

No one answered, though. The only thing to break the silence was the amazingly loud chirping of crickets. Or were they *cicadas* down here? And what was the difference? She didn't know, but they were so loud, her imagination ran wild about how big they must be. Big enough to tie down a five-foot-four woman and chomp her to death?

Focus, Abby. She felt on the edge of losing it. No food, no sleep and now no Jancy or Jimmy. The whole thing was a nightmare.

She put the Glock back in her belt and pulled out the cell phone. As she dialed Joey, she breathed a prayer that he'd answer in person this time. She needed that contact, some steadying influence.

But no, it was still his voice mail. And she hated how shaky and vulnerable her own voice sounded.

"Joey, where are you? I'm still at the Mathers Road house, and I've got three guys locked up in a very flimsy closet. Jimmy and Jancy have disappeared, and I've got to go find them."

What else? "Gerry Gerard, Alicia Gerard's husband, is one of the guys locked in the closet. It seems the doomsday bomb was a hoax to scare the American public. It was all a scam cooked up by Gerry, so he could "find" the bomb and "save the world.""

She paused again. She should be telling Kris all this, or Lessing, or Ben. But who knew when she'd be able to reach them? When she finished this call, she'd try Kris.

"Let's see…the bioweapons," she went on. "I've got

the package that's supposed to hold them right here, but Alicia told me her parents had faked them, so they shouldn't be dangerous. The one bright spot in all this is that Gerard doesn't seem to know they're fake. I can't wait to see what happens when he—and the rest of the world—finds out he's not a hero."

A beep sounded and her message was cut off.

"Son of a bitch!"

She almost fell out the door as a voice behind her in the kitchen said, "If that's me you're calling names, I'm right here."

She swung around, her hand on the gun, the other arm already in attack mode.

"Jimmy!" Her hand came off the gun and her arm went around his neck instead. He lifted her into a hug, and she'd never been so glad to have someone's arms around her.

"Thank God you're safe!" she said against his neck. "I was just imagining you out there in the swamp, being eaten by crocodiles."

She looked around and behind him. "Where's Jancy?"

He put her down. "I just got the Master Manipulator to a safe place, down the highway. Left her with a nice waitress named Millie who's hiding her in the back of her diner, and who promised to stuff her with pancakes and applesauce."

"Applesauce?"

"Her favorite food. Didn't you know?"

"No. Just how did you find that out?"

"She told me."

"She actually talked to you? Civilly?"

"Sure. She likes me. In fact, she likes me *and* you. Together."

"*What?* The kid is matchmaking now?"

He grinned. "You sound disapproving. Is that because she's matchmaking, or because of that particular match?"

Abby frowned. "You know what? My head is swimming. I could use some pancakes and applesauce myself."

"I recognize that you're changing the subject," he said, "but I'm not in the least offended. So let's go. To Millie's, it is."

"Hold on a minute there," she said. "I've got a maniac who thinks he's God in the closet with two dumbos who should be working in a circus. One of these days they'll figure out that all they have to do is push hard enough, and that door will open. Meanwhile, I can't leave till the cops, or someone in authority, gets here. Which reminds me, why did you come back?"

"To get you, of course. You didn't really think I'd leave you to fend for yourself with God and the dumbos, did you?"

"Well, since I thought you'd been taken somewhere else and possibly even killed, I didn't know. Who untied you two?"

"Your friend," he said. "The cop."

"Ben?"

"That would be the one."

"You mean, he knew I was all alone there in the front room with those three, and he just left me there? Same as you?"

Jimmy shrugged. "I guess we both have a great respect for your abilities, Abby."

"Gee, thanks. Is he all right?"

"The boyfriend?"

"Whatever."

"Yeah, he's fine."

"Thank God. Where is he?"

"I don't know. He drove us out to the highway, left us with an officer and a squad car, then took off with a horde of police and other authority types. I think they were heading for Emerald Gardens."

"Was Joey with them?"

"No, I haven't seen hide nor hair of my brother. Should I have?"

"He said he was flying down here, Jimmy. He should have been here hours ago."

"His flight may have been delayed."

"But he's not answering his cell phone, and he hasn't returned my calls. I'm getting worried."

"Joey's pretty good at taking care of himself," he said, though he looked worried as well. "What do you say we find some rope to tie the evil warlord and his henchman up, and then go get some food and tons of hot coffee? You can tell me all about what's been going on here since I fell for the charms of a fourteen-year-old."

He'd begun to look through the lower kitchen cabinets. Abby started on the upper ones.

"Jancy?" she said. "What happened?"

"I went out to the parking lot this morning to see why a particular car kept circling the lot. The car slowed down and this kid waved at me from the back seat. I'd never seen her, remember, and didn't have a clue. I just thought she wanted to ask directions or something. I went over to the car and the door swung open. Something weighing at least three tons came up behind me and shoved me into the car. They clamped something with a real bad smell over my nose, and next thing I knew I was waking up here." He grinned. "And that cute little girl was tied up next to me, cussing like a marine."

"Was there another man here? Somebody who came in through the back door while I was in front?"

"No, why?"

"Just checking. I was pretty sure Gerry was bluffing. Here!" she said. She had found a pantry, and in it, aside from dusty cans of beans and corn, were several lengths of clothesline. It was old, but made in a day when clothesline lasted forever.

"Let's go get 'em," she said. "I can't wait much longer for food."

"Here, throw me that," Jimmy said. "Just lead me to 'em."

Abby tossed the heavy coils over to him and started out the door.

Then she felt it—air brushing over her face as the rope came down over her head and settled around her neck.

She tried to scream, but no sound came out. She

clawed at the rope, trying to get a finger under it, but he'd had the element of shock going for him, and there was no space. She tried to kick back, but he was ready for that, too. Then her arms were bound to her sides, and her ankles tied together. She fell to the floor, but not before she was able to look into his eyes.

They were not eyes she had ever seen before. They were in Jimmy's face, but he wasn't Jimmy anymore. He was someone else, someone hard and cold, someone focused on a mission.

A mission to see her dead?

The rain had stopped, and the sky was as clear as glass. The stars were brighter than she'd ever seen them. She felt something crawling on her arm and looked down. A tarantula. No, a scorpion.

Dear God, what do I know about scorpions?
They're poisonous. That's all you need to know.
Don't move.

No question of that. She was bound so tight, her arms had gone dead.

Dead.

Wouldn't be long now. The sun would come up. The damned sun. How long would it be before vultures began to circle overhead? Were there vultures in Texas? No matter, there were always predators.

She was lying in muck somewhere behind the house, close to the white rocks. Mud oozed up through her clothes and into her hair and ears. It was alive with the same kinds of crawly things as the mud in the road.

Then, she'd been able to keep moving and not think about them. Here, it was all she could think of.

No, that wasn't true. She couldn't shake that image of Jimmy standing over her, knotting those ropes around her.

She tried not to, but couldn't help crying. How could she have gone so wrong? If anyone had asked, she'd have said she trusted him with her life.

But she'd done that before, with another man, and that had ended badly, too.

What was wrong with her? Why did she keep trusting the wrong people? Tears ran in torrents down her cheeks.

Why had he done this to her? She had lain on the kitchen floor while he took the Glock and the cell phone, then went into the living room with the remaining rope. He had done all that without saying a word, but she could hear him in there, tying up the three men. Or maybe not all three. Had he taken Gerry with him? Was he in on this whole thing with Gerry? And if so, for how long had he been in it? Since she first met him? How long had he been betraying her?

A faint tickle on her wrist. With her other hand she tried to get the tiny flashlight out of her back jeans pocket. Though she was trussed up like a Thanksgiving turkey, there was a little wiggle room by her hips. If she sucked her stomach in, there was an inch or two more.

She felt the flashlight through the denim, and pushed at it until it was nearly out of her pocket. Then, by straining the only two fingers that weren't numb, she could reach just far enough to grab it. *Easy, now. Easy.*

It fell into the muck beneath her. She tried to reach it, but that only seemed to drive it farther into the mud. She was trying too hard. Jancy had said that. *You try too hard.*

She forced herself to relax. To "see" the flashlight in her hand, already there, easy as pie.

Her two good fingers found it and closed slowly around it. Moving carefully, she brought it up as far as possible, over her hips and a little more. Then she pressed the button that turned it on and looked at her other wrist.

A spider. A tiny brown spider with long legs was crabbing its way up her arm. She could see, as it grew closer, the dark shape of a violin on its head and back.

God, she hated spiders. And this one—what did she remember about it? Something specific about that violin shape.

A brown recluse, she remembered with a chill.

"You can identify the brown recluse," she remembered Sister Anne Marie saying in biology class, "by the violin shape on its head and back, actually called the cephalothorax."

She had gone on to say that brown recluse spiders did not reside in California. "There are spiders here with vague violin shapes on their backs, but they aren't brown recluses. If they're in California, they've been misidentified."

"Do they kill you?" Marti had asked.

"Not immediately, but their bite is dangerous. It causes the victim's tissues to die and decay. He or she might get a fever, nausea, joint pain. Gangrene can set in. In some cases, the bite area may have to be cut away."

"You mean amputated?" Abby had asked.

Sister Anne Marie hadn't answered.

But where had Sister Anne Marie told them that the brown recluses were found?

In the Midwest and the Southeast. Throughout Texas. Great.

Fear consumed her, and she tried to pray but couldn't think of the words. After all those years of Catholic school and the convent, none of the formal prayers would come to her.

But her angels were always there. That much she knew for a fact. Her angels had saved her more than once.

Help me, please, she prayed. *Just help me get through this.*

At least Danny and Jancy were safe.

Or *was* Jancy safe?

A cold shiver ran along her back, having nothing to do with the rotten damp beneath her. She had only Jimmy's word that he'd taken Jancy to that diner, a "safe place," he had called it.

What if that wasn't true?

Dear God. Children were so expendable these days. What had happened to the "Gentle Shepherd"? The one who'd tried to teach the world that children were valuable and should be treated with love and care?

I've accepted that I'll never have a child of my own, she prayed, *but let me at least live to help as many as I can.*

Tears coursed down the sides of her face, soaking into her hair. She hadn't really prayed, or even cried, this hard in years.

And then she felt it—the thing she'd been trying not to think of. A prick at her inner arm, just above the elbow.

Abby's head jerked around. *The brown recluse,* Sister Anne Marie had said, *may not bite if you don't move.*

But she could actually see the bite. She tried to shake the spider off, but it was too late. How long did it take for symptoms to set in?

The pain from the bite was already intense, and waves of nausea gripped her. How long could she last? She thought she had read that with any insect bite it was best to remain as calm and still as possible, to slow its progress through the bloodstream. Myth or truth? She didn't know. But she closed her eyes and didn't move a thing—other than her lips, which were busy whispering prayers.

35

She didn't know how long she was unconscious, but when he picked her up, she screamed. Every joint in her body hurt, every bone, every muscle. She thought she might break in two, but his movements were gentle, and when he put her on the stretcher, he leaned over and kissed her forehead.

"We're taking you to the hospital," he said. "You'll be all right."

Her vision was blurry, but she knew the voice. "Ben?"

"Yeah, it's me."

"Need to talk."

"Not right now. Just sleep, let the medicine take over."

"But—"

"Shh."

He sat beside her and held her hand all the way to the hospital. When the ambulance hit a bump, she cried out from the pain. He stroked her forehead and said, "Shh," over and over—the same way he had two years ago when she'd nearly been killed on that hill.

"Got to stop meeting like this," she said as they rolled her into the emergency room.

He smiled, but in his eyes was a world of sadness. "I've been thinking the same thing."

He was leaving her. She'd known it from that first night, after the paintball exercise. It was what he'd been keeping from her. He was leaving.

A strong, flowery scent made her open her eyes. The first thing she did was look at her arm. Was it still there? Had they been forced to amputate?

Oh, God! Tears puddled, then covered her cheeks. *Thank you, angels. Thank you.* Her arm was bandaged, but still there. She could see her fingers sticking out at the end of the bandage. She wiggled them. They still worked.

Her relief was enormous. She didn't know till that moment how afraid she had been.

Her gaze drifted over to a chest of drawers against the hospital room wall. The heavy perfumelike scent was coming from a huge vase of pink day lilies and white roses.

A nurse came in and adjusted the IV tube where it hung by her side. "Hi," she said. "Do you know who you are?"

She smiled. "Abby. Abby Northrup." Her mouth was dry, so it came out "Norfrup."

"Great," the nurse said. "Now, do you know *where* you are?"

"Not exactly."

"You had a brown recluse bite," the nurse said. "They brought you here to Methodist Hospital in Houston for treatment."

"Am I okay?" Abby asked.

The nurse didn't answer immediately. Maybe she didn't hear.

"Am I okay?" Abby asked again, her stomach starting to tighten.

The nurse held a straw up to her mouth and urged her to take a sip of water. "The doctor would like to talk to you himself."

That can't be good.

The nurse left. Twenty long minutes later, the doctor came in.

"Abby? I'm Dr. Mueller. Sorry it took me so long to get here. I was in the middle of an emergency."

"No hurry here," Abby said. "I take it I'm not leaving just yet?"

He sat on the edge of the bed. *Another bad sign.* They were teaching doctors to do that these days, like waiters at the Outback restaurant sitting at your booth. It was supposed to make it easier to connect, to make everything seem real friendly. At the Outback, it was in case your steak came out overdone. Here, it was to ease the telling of bad news.

"The good news," Dr. Mueller said, as if reading her mind, "is that we were able to save your arm."

"Right." She waited.

"The not-so-good news is that a large area of your flesh, from the elbow to the wrist, was destroyed by the venom. It's called necrosis. In your case, there's a hole in the flesh left from the tissue having become gangrenous."

"A hole," she said, feeling numb. "In my arm."

"The dead tissue will gradually slough away, but you'll have an ulcerated sore that could last weeks. Eventually, it will heal, but I'm afraid you'll be left with a rather large scar."

"Plastic surgery?" she asked.

"Possibly, but it could take several painful surgeries. And there's more bad news."

"Great. Hit me with it, Doc."

"Right now you're on a heavy dose of medication. But the venom attacked your joints, and I'm afraid you've been left with a great deal of pain. Something on the order of a severe case of arthritis."

Could it get any worse? "How long does that take to go away?"

He sighed. "I'm afraid it doesn't. Go away, that is. I'm very, very sorry."

"But there's some sort of cure for it, right?"

"We can use the same kinds of treatment as for other kinds of arthritis—medications, heat treatments, massage. I'm afraid we don't really have a cure for it yet."

For some strange, crazy reason, she wanted to laugh. "That's why old people drink," she said, remembering something her mother had told her about their elderly neighbor, Miss Grace, when she was little.

"Sorry?" the doctor said.

"They can't afford the medicines, and there's nothing else for the pain, really, but alcohol. In the retirement communities, vodka's the number-one seller, I hear."

Keep talking, don't think.

"I'm sorry," the doctor said again. He shook his head. "I keep saying that, don't I? I just don't know what else to say when there's no cure to offer a patient. I'd suggest walking as much as you can, perhaps regular swimming…"

"What about martial arts?"

He smiled, as if she were joking. "I don't think I'd go quite that far."

So let's see now, what's left in my life? Oh, I know…Sister Helen and I can compete to see who can limp the fastest from the front door to the kitchen.

"Excuse me, Doctor," the nurse said, sticking her head in the door. "There's someone in the hallway waiting to see the patient. Shall I send him in?"

"No," Abby said.

The last thing she wanted was a visitor. That was what she disliked most about hospitals. You had no privacy at all. People could just walk in on you at any time, and they all assumed you'd be happy as hell to see them.

"Are you sure?" the nurse said. "Might do you good."

Oh, for cripe's sake. "Yeah, I guess. Send him in." It was probably just Ben, coming to say goodbye. She might as well get all the bad news today. Then maybe tomorrow would be better.

The doctor stood and patted her on the shoulder

lightly, as if knowing anything more would hurt. "I'll be back later on."

"Would you like to freshen up a little before your visitor comes in?" the nurse asked. "Comb your hair? And how about some makeup?"

"Why bother?" Abby said. "I've got a hole in my arm, for God's sake, and I'll be shuffling out of here like my grandmother. Who cares what my face looks like?"

"I do, for one," Jimmy said, coming into the room. "And it looks as beautiful as ever."

"What the hell are you doing here?" she half yelled. "Nurse, get him out of here! No, wait. Call Security, tell them to get the police, and don't let him get away."

The nurse looked confused. "I'm not sure…"

Abby picked up a water glass and threw it at him. Her entire arm blazed with pain, and it missed him by inches. But when it hit the door, the water splattered all over his white shirt and khaki pants.

"Why aren't you in jail?" she demanded. "Does anyone know what you did to me?"

He came to the side of her bed. "That's why I'm here. I couldn't let you think I'd turned on you. Abby, I'm so sorry about the spider bite. I had no idea there was anything poisonous out there. The plan—"

"Plan? What plan? What the hell are you talking about?"

He pulled up a chair and sat. "It was Kris Kelley's idea. She called me in Phoenix shortly after you left, and asked me if I was willing to be deputized. It meant being near you, so I said sure. Even if you hadn't called and asked me to come to Galveston, I'd have been there. I was supposed to stick close and make sure nothing happened to you."

"You were *babysitting* me? That's what she hired you as, a *babysitter*?"

He had the grace to flush. "Well, no, that wasn't all of it. She liked the way we handled ourselves in Phoenix. She thought we made a good team, and that together we'd have a better chance of finding Alicia and the Devlins than the other agents would."

"And you didn't see fit to tell me this?"

"Abby, I had to swear not to."

"You had to swear? Didn't you think that was a little weird?"

"As a matter of fact, I did. But then we were at that house on Mathers Road and I had a chance to get close to H. P. Gerard. Abby, when I tied you up I needed a true response from you. If you'd known I wasn't really turning on you, you wouldn't have come across as afraid. Gerard would have suspected something."

"You idiot!" Abby said angrily. "You damn near got me killed! Did you know that? Are you expecting me to just understand why you did that to me? Am I supposed to forgive you?"

His dark eyes pooled with unshed tears. "No, Abby. I didn't come here today to ask you to forgive me. I know you can't ever do that. I just wanted to say how sorry I am. I thought if Gerard believed I was on his side—if I untied him and let him out of there—I could follow him and find out where The Candlelights were keeping that bomb."

"But there never was a bomb!" Abby said. "It was all a hoax. Didn't you know that?"

"I do now. I didn't at the time."

Of course not. He hadn't been there when Gerry admitted to the hoax. He thought he was doing the right thing.

So many mistakes, so many lies. So much hurt.

She leaned back against the pillows, her anger dissolving. But there was one thing she didn't think she could ever get over. "You left me there to die, Jimmy. I was completely helpless to defend myself, and you just…you left me there."

"For a half hour," he said. "No longer. And Gerard wanted you dumped in the swamp. I didn't do that—I couldn't—but I had to pretend to. That's why I took you out there."

"Wait a minute, what half hour? You never came back."

"No. I sent Ben. I thought you would want him, not me."

She had no answer for that.

"I'll go now," Jimmy said, standing. "Abby, if there's ever anything I can do…"

She turned her face away so he wouldn't see her tears. He stood there a moment, and then he left.

36

Alicia Gerard's father died that night, and Alicia turned herself in to the FBI in Houston. She claimed not to know where her mother was, but she did tell them the truth about her parents, the threat from The Candlelights—or what she had believed to be The Candlelights—and how her mother and father had faked the bioweapons in order to keep Alicia and Jancy safe. Once their work was done and Jancy was in a safe place, they had planned to turn themselves and the splinter group in.

Alicia gave the FBI agents a key to a safety deposit box that held what was purported to be the authentic plans—given to them by the supposed Candlelight woman, Linda—for the "Easter Lily Bomb" hardware. Now that they knew Gerry was behind the whole thing, though, and there weren't any Candlelights involved, she couldn't guarantee that these plans, too, weren't just part of the hoax.

After hearing Abby's story, the FBI had turned their attention to finding H. P. Gerard. They sent agents to watch his penthouse, and within twenty-four hours, he showed up, determined to bluff his way out of all charges. He had the ear of the president, after all. No one in their right mind would believe he'd had anything to do with perpetrating a hoax on the American public. And let's face it, all they had was the account of a woman half out of her mind from a spider bite, who was still clearly hallucinating about what had happened to her at the house on Mathers Road.

"Speaking of which," Gerry had said, looking bewildered, "I don't think I've ever even heard of a Mathers Road. Jerry Mathers, maybe. You know, the Beaver?" He'd smiled jovially and patted the investigating agent on the back. "But no, no Mathers Road. Where did you say that was?"

Kris called Abby in her hospital room early the next day. "Have you heard what Gerry is saying?"

"I have."

"They're buying it, aren't they?"

"They are."

"We can't let him get away with that, can we?"

"We can't."

"Okay, listen, can you meet me? Back in Carmel, at the Prayer House? Are you well enough?"

"That depends. When?"

"I'm flying out of Houston with the team at ten this morning. We're going back to Carmel together to wrap this up with the authorities there. Abby, I checked, and there's another flight out of Houston to San Francisco at eleven. Are you well enough to be on it?"

"Yes." Her body hurt like a thousand fiery hells, but hey, a few more pumps of morphine and she could still move.

"Okay, listen," Kris said in a low voice. "Figure a four-hour flight to SFO, then a two-hour drive to Carmel. Lessing's decided we'll all drive down together. Three cars—a damned caravan. That means...let me check my watch...I can be out at the Prayer House by early evening."

"I'll see you then," Abby said. "And don't worry. I promise you, we'll make the bastard pay."

37

Abby and Kris were in the living room of Abby's apartment at the Prayer House. Jancy was staying at the Prayer House until Alicia was released. She was asleep on the second floor, and Danny, who had arrived safe and well with Kris, was asleep in the room next to her. Narissa, the young ex-novice, was sitting in the hallway outside their doors, keeping watch.

Kris began to pace nervously. "I can't stand this waiting," she said. "Dammit, I want to kill that man!"

"No way. You can't have all the fun."

"Don't worry, I may want to, but he's not worth it."

"We'll get him," Abby said gently. "We'll get him, don't worry."

"And when we do, I promise you, I'm going to make that son of a bitch wish he'd never laid a hand on Danny or Jancy."

"Is Alicia going to be charged with anything?" Abby asked.

"Not anything to do with the terrorists, since it turns out there weren't any. And security photos have cleared her of that murder at the Highlands Inn. She and Jancy were still in the restaurant at the time it occurred. Alicia could still have a problem with her illegal status, though. I was told her lawyer's trying to make a deal with the INS."

"That's a relief. Maybe now life can go back to normal for Jancy—whatever normal is. So, when are they letting Alicia go?"

"Pretty soon, I'd imagine. For now, though, she's still in custody in Houston. The last I heard, she wasn't allowed any contact with the outside world until they've finished questioning all the suspects."

"What suspects? So far as I could see, all Gerry had was a meager little band of hoodlums playing guard dogs for him."

"Well, the feds got inside the Matalene Trust somehow," Kris said. "That's Gerry's secret organization to 'save the world.' It's no longer a secret, and every single member is being questioned and their backgrounds thoroughly checked."

"Gerry called them kindergartners. He said they wouldn't go 'the extra mile,' so I doubt they'll find anything illegal to charge them with."

"Gerry Gerard has no conscience," Kris said. "If nothing else, we know that about him."

"So he really did snatch Danny just to make you botch the search for Alicia and the Devlins? It wasn't that he wanted custody of him, after all?"

"Doesn't give a damn about him, actually," Kris said with a snort. "But if Pat Devlin had been found too soon—before he could finish the bioweapons and Gerry could conveniently find them on his doorstep and turn them over to the feds—he wouldn't have had a chance to become a hero."

She laughed. "I just can't wait for the government scientists they've got working on those 'bioweapons' to tell the press they're fakes. If I have anything to do with it, you can be damned sure the talking heads will be after Gerard for months."

Binny arrived with the tea and sandwiches they'd asked for after Jancy and Danny had been fed and were safely in bed. The roast beef sandwiches were consumed without conversation as Kris and Abby purposely stocked up on carbs and protein. Side salads of pasta were in cups on the sandwich plate, and they chowed down on them, too.

"You sure you don't want coffee?" Abby asked when they were finished.

Kris shook her head. "I get more energy from tea. I'm Irish, you know."

"I kind of assumed as much. And speaking of which, what happened to Alicia's mother?"

Kris smiled. "Funny thing, she wasn't at the house in Emerald Gardens when the FBI got there. And no one seems to know where she's gone."

"Ah…the disappearing Devlin act, again."

"With a few false IDs and some money from me this time," Kris said.

"Oh, really? Just please don't tell me you're a member of an IRA splinter group."

"No, I just felt I had to do something to make up for taking Jancy. The fact that I couldn't go through with it makes me only a half level up from Gerry. Besides, from what you told me, it sounds like the Devlins have lived a pretty clean life the past thirty years. Bridget deserves to start a new life."

"True. Even so, Kris, I'm impressed. And to think I didn't like you the first time I saw you."

"No offense. Nobody likes me when I bust into their house and flash a warrant." She smiled. "Oh, by the way, that wasn't a real warrant."

"What? But it looked—"

"Official? I made it up on a computer at the police station before we came over here that night. In fact, that's how I made up Bridget Devlin's papers. Amazing what you can do on a computer these days."

Abby started to laugh, then sobered as the antique clock on her mantel sounded a single chime. *Eleven-thirty*. Gerry would be here soon.

38

The nuns and other women of the Prayer House had been asked to stay on the second floor for the rest of the night, and since they were usually in bed by this time, it wasn't a problem. Abby had told them not to worry if they heard any unusual noises. Above all, they were not to call the police.

Narissa, being young, energetic and therefore needing little sleep, had been asked to keep an eye on the two younger guests. If either one left his or her room, she was to keep them from coming downstairs.

The downstairs was dimly lit, and Abby stood at a window looking out at the grounds. At exactly midnight, headlights swept up the driveway. Good. Joey was right on time.

"He's out on bail, so I'll bring him to you," he'd said, "and I'll drop him off. Just don't tell me what you're doin'. I don't want to know. And remember, this is just a favor for leaving you high and dry in Houston when my flight was grounded."

Abby opened the door and Joey "escorted" Gerry

into the foyer with a firm push. "Gerry!" she said with a false tone of pleasure. "Good to see you again. I'm sorry it's not under better circumstances."

He didn't bother with the amenities. "What do you want, Abby? I've already got plenty of charges pending. There's nothing more you can do to me."

"I'm sure you're right," she said, smiling at Joey. "I think you had something to do?"

Joey nodded. "Don't worry about me. I'm outta here."

"Wait—" Gerry looked around as if searching the shadows for ghosts. "You're not leaving me alone here, are you?"

"Hey, man, you'll be all right," Joey said. "Abby here, she's a fine woman."

Gerard made a scornful sound, and Joey left. The hallway became very quiet. Abby let the silence become uncomfortable.

"You might as well get on with it," Gerry said at last. "Whatever it is you want. I know you can't kill me, because that was a cop and he's probably still out there. I'd better stay alive and well."

"No problem, Gerry. As I told you on the phone, this is about Jancy. Your daughter."

"Jancy? What about her?"

"She's sick, and she's been asking for you."

"So, what's wrong with her?" His tone let her know that this was an inconvenience, and Jancy had better be damned sick to have dragged him all the way out here just to see her. "Where is she?"

"We put her out in the infirmary," Abby answered, "in case whatever she has is contagious."

"Infirmary?"

"Our little hospital. We have two sisters who were registered nurses before they came here."

"Let's get this over with, then. Where's this infirmary?"

"It's behind the gardens," Abby said, "next to the new Women's Center for Learning."

"You mean, she's not here in the house? You've put her outdoors somewhere? I guess that tells me something about you people and how you run this place."

"Gerry, she's hardly outdoors," Abby said mildly. "And I haven't just 'put' her there. The infirmary is a brand-new building, top-of-the-line, and Jancy's getting excellent care."

"Then get on with it! Let's go," he said in a clipped, impatient tone that said he was accustomed to ordering people around.

"Of course," Abby said, reaching for her denim jacket by the door. "Let's go."

39

The sky had clouded over, smearing the moonlight into a vague blur. The air was chill. The closer Abby and Gerry Gerard got to the old chapel, the more she shivered and the more her joints began to hurt. She started to limp.

"This is damned far out," Gerry complained as he caught his toe on a root in the path. He righted himself with a curse.

"We manage to stay in touch," Abby said.

"I'd like to know just exactly *how* you stay in touch," Gerry said irritably, "if people have to use this path all the time. You haven't even paved it."

"We have intercoms," Abby said. "Walkie-talkies, cell phones, land phones, e-mail…as I told you, this is a new facility. The woman who was director here before me was wealthy, and she left us an excellent inheritance to build whatever we thought we needed. I added my money to it, and we were able to do a great deal."

"Is that the infirmary?" he asked, as if he hadn't been listening. "That building over there? It looks dark."

"No, that's the Women's Center for Learning. We bring teachers out here and offer classes for women who need help reentering the business world."

Gerry, obviously not interested, didn't respond.

They were coming up to the old chapel, which was no more than a crumbling tower and three walls, with the entire back side open to the surrounding forest. Along the right-hand wall was a large tree with branches so low they had to duck to pass under them.

"Wait!" Gerry said. He stopped walking.

Abby nearly jumped. "What?"

"I heard something."

"It's just the horses," she said. "At night, when it's quiet, you can hear them moving around in the barn."

"No, it was something else." He turned his head from side to side, like a hound on the hunt.

"Gerry, there are all kinds of sounds in the country that you probably never hear in New York City. It's a whole different world out here."

"I suppose—" he began.

It was the last sound he uttered before he was flattened to the ground by Kris, who had dropped from a branch of the tree and landed smack on him.

She lost her balance as she got to her feet, and he pushed her away and managed to stand. But Kris flew at him as Abby grabbed his right arm and stuck a foot behind his legs, making him land on his back again. Using all the strength she could muster, she rolled him onto his stomach, then sat on him while Kris tied his hands together, then his feet.

Abby was panting loudly, and she couldn't believe how tired she was. She had done everything so far on adrenaline, but oh, God, she hurt now. The bandaged arm had struck something, probably a tree branch, and it felt on fire. Blood was seeping through the bandage, and her entire body shrieked with pain.

"You will never come near my son again," Kris said, her breath short and rasping as she fastened the knots. "You will never even drive by my house, or talk to him in the school play yard, or even speak his name again."

"You bitch!" he muttered, showing no sign of fear. And to Abby, "Get off me! You'll both pay for this!"

"Say it, you monster. Say you are sorry that you kidnapped Danny and you will never come near him again."

This time Kris's voice was steady and cold. She stood above him, holding a gun in both hands, pointing it straight at him.

"Kris!" Abby said anxiously. "We were only supposed to scare him. You promised, no violence!"

"Shut up, Abby, and get off him. This is my show now."

She kneed Abby in the shoulder. "Off! Now!"

Abby half fell to the ground next to Gerard.

"I can't let you do this!" she said, painfully rising to her feet.

Kris pointed the gun at her. "Your job is over, Abby. Go back to the house."

"No!"

"I mean it!"

"This is my home, Kris. No way in hell am I leaving."

Kris shrugged. "Suit yourself. But if you get in my way, or try to stop me, I won't hesitate to take you out along with him."

Abby watched as Kris, with what seemed like superhuman strength, yanked Gerry up by his shirt with one hand. Buttons popped, and Gerry swore. "You crazy bitch, I'll get you for this."

"Move!" she ordered, pushing him toward the inside shell of the chapel. Step by step, with the gun pressed to his neck, she made him hobble, stumbling from the ropes around his ankles. When they reached the table-size stone where the altar used to be, she shoved the gun into his back.

"Up there!" she ordered.

A Coleman lantern rested on a small table to the left of the stone. Next to it, gleaming in the flickering light, was a knife.

Gerard saw it and went weak. He tripped on the first step and fell to his knees. "Look, you don't want to do this—"

"Now!" she said.

His voice shook, but he got to his feet. "You'll lose Danny for good if you kill me," he said. "You'll spend the rest of your life on death row."

Kris slammed him against the stone. He let out a cry as his head hit against it. Blood ran down his face from temple to cheek.

"Kris, please!" Abby said. "You're going too far—"

"I told you to shut up! Do you think I give a damn what you have to say, when this monster stole my son?"

Kris's face was illuminated by the lantern's light, and Abby could see it was twisted and pale.

Kris held the gun to Gerard's ear. "I'll give you to the count of five to get up there. One…two…three…four…"

"All right, all right!" He climbed up onto the stone table.

"Lie down on your back," Kris said coldly. "And say the words, 'I am sorry I kidnapped Kris's son Danny, and I will never go near him again.'"

"Go to hell!" he said.

She hit him on the temple with the butt of the gun. "Say it!"

He began to whimper. "Damn you—"

She raised the gun again.

"All right, dammit! I'm sorry I kidnapped Kris's son, Danny…and I will never go near him again." The whimper turned to anger. "There! Are you satisfied?"

"Hell, no," Kris said. "I have lots more in store for you."

He began to plead with Abby. "I know you don't want this. Think what it would do to the Prayer House, all the bad publicity if it comes out what she did here. And think of Alicia. She's your friend, for God's sake! And Jancy! What about Jancy?"

"So, now you care about your daughter?" Abby said. "Well, not to worry. Jancy's fine. She's asleep in the house."

"Asleep?" He looked dazed. Confused. "You said she was sick."

"Just one of those little lies you big CEO types use all the time in negotiations," Abby said. "It is okay to use whatever will get the job done, right?"

Abby picked up the knife.

"But, I heard you!" Gerry cried. "You told her no violence. You wanted her to stop!"

"Actually, that was just a little practice for the community theater tryouts. Did I do good?"

She slid around Kris and stuck her face close to Gerard's, leaning her arms on his chest. The knife was still in her right hand, and the point of it was close to his neck. There wasn't a sign of pain on her face, though the hole in her arm felt as if a hot poker were being held to it.

"See, Gerry, it's not nice to use little kids as hostages," Abby said. "You know how that makes me feel? It makes me feel mad. And when I get mad I'm like one of those abused kids you hear about who need to cut themselves. Only in my case, you know what, Gerry? I like cutting someone else."

She raised the knife and studied it, as if gauging its sharpness. "I put this out here before you came," she said. "Sister Binny uses it to cut meat. It's so sharp, she can dissect an entire pig, guts and all, with this knife."

"Oh, God." He began to visibly tremble. "You're both crazy! You're both fucking crazy!"

"You may be right," Abby said. "So, Gerry, this is what we're going to do." She laid the knife alongside his head. "Kris and I are going to take turns dissecting little pieces of you. I'm going to start with an ear, and then she's going to carve out an eye. Little by little we'll work our way down, and unless you pass out from shock…you know what, Gerry? You'll still be alive and able to feel it when we get…here."

She rested the knife point against his crotch.

Tears fell from his eyes, but he still tried to plead. "You don't have it in you, Abby. You'd never do a thing like that. Just let me up—"

"You think I should let you go?"

"Yes! Please, Abby. We'll forget this ever happened."

"Oh, I know what you're thinking, Gerry," Kris said. "You're thinking that once you get away from here, you'll hire someone to kill me. Abby, too, I suppose. But you know what? There's a camera in here."

His head swung side to side, and on his face was an expression of shock.

"Oh, don't bother to look for it," Kris said. "You'd never find it in a million years. The point is, I've been taping all this. I have your confession now that you kidnapped my son. And my nice little tape is going into a safety deposit box that you'll never find." She smiled. "The CIA will, though. And they'll come after you like bats out of hell for harming one of their own. You'll be ruined, Gerry. And gee, you know what? You might even be dead."

40

After Kris left, Abby sat in the chapel until the fog wore off and the sun came up, then far into the afternoon. Gerry's mouth was taped, and he was bound to the altar with rope.

Finally, the call came through on her cell phone. Abby moved away from Gerard and spoke softly. "All's well on the Carmel front."

"Great," Kris said. "Thanks for doing this, Abby. We're all moved. I found a nice condo for the two of us on the tenth floor, with a doorman and locked gates all over the place. Danny loves it. There's a safe, enclosed patio, and he can see the Golden Gate Bridge from here. And there's no way Gerry will ever find us. I've swept our tracks clean."

"Thank God. I take it I can let our friend go now?"

"Is he sufficiently humbled?" Kris asked.

"He peed his pants," Abby said. "Is that humble enough?"

Kris laughed softly. "I really wanted to kill him, but I'm glad all it took was the threat of torture."

"At least he'll think twice," Abby said, "before he goes after Danny or Jancy again."

Abby hung up, then untied Gerry with one hand, all the while holding Kris's gun on him with the other. She told him he could go, but it didn't seem to her he appreciated her kindness.

"If it wasn't for that goddamn tape," he said, rubbing his wrists and mumbling as if his lips had gone numb, "I'd ruin you, bitch. You and her, too."

"Isn't it lucky we women have learned to protect ourselves, then," Abby said. "And by the way, I'm keeping Jancy until Alicia can come and get her. Don't mess with that. You won't win."

He held himself stiffly as he left, spine straight, chin high. There he goes, Abby thought. Mover and shaker... adviser to presidents...man with the world on a string. If only people knew.

And they will, as word gets around.

Abby gathered up the night's gear, putting ropes, tape, knife and camcorder into a cardboard box. Glancing around, she vowed to redo the chapel first chance she got. Never again did she want to see this place and be reminded of this night.

Before Ben came to her apartment the next day, Abby wasn't sure what she was going to say. When he arrived, however, it all came clear. He was loving and solicitous. He had been worried about her. He was sorry he couldn't have been with her and helped her more.

He was everything she'd always wanted in a man. And yet...

She'd been thinking that since she was nearly killed two years ago, she'd been on a journey of healing. For a long time she had leaned on Ben, and that had been good. But leaning had a way of bending a person, like a young sapling, out of shape. She'd lost some of her own strength in the process, at least until the past few days. The moment she'd taken charge of the two bodyguards on the field at Emerald Gardens that night, she had felt something new rising in her. A new energy, a sense of personal power.

On the way home from Houston she had realized, too, that the paintball exercises with Ben had been her way of fighting with him, of getting her anger out at feeling diminished as a woman because of what had happened to her that night two years ago—even though he'd had nothing to do with it. She knew now that she'd been using Ben, and that what she had thought was love, was not.

The sex afterward? It had been fun, but she'd always known that for both of them it had been largely a way of using up the adrenaline they'd amassed from the hunt.

Nothing wrong with that. Ben was a good man. She just didn't want to do this to him anymore.

So when Ben came and told her how bored he'd been in Carmel and that he wanted to quit the force and work for the FBI in San Francisco, she congratulated him on the decision. And when he asked her to put someone else in charge of the Prayer House and *Paseo*, and come with him, the answer leapt to her lips without hesitation.

"I think this is the end of the road for us, Ben. Don't you?"

It was a difficult goodbye, but Ben had agreed that he, too, had felt them growing apart, each of them going their separate ways. They made promises, of course.

Let's stay close...let's keep in touch...let's talk on the phone. And they both professed that they would always love each other—as friends.

Abby accompanied Ben through the rose garden to his car, and sat there waving as he drove off. If she shed a tear or two, it was only natural, after all this time. But she felt a burden lifting, and knew she'd made the right decision.

In her apartment again she packed a bag with a few things and spoke with Sister Helen, Sister Binny and Narissa about taking care of Jancy and anyone else who might show up looking for sanctuary. In effect, she turned her work over to them. Then she met Jancy in the kitchen and told her she'd be gone for a while.

"I'm sorry to leave you again right away," she said, "but I have to make this a priority or I'll never do it."

Satisfied that everything would run smoothly without her, Abby got into her car and headed north on I-5. A few hours later she was in Berkeley. Turning onto a street she hadn't seen in far too long, she pulled up to a two-story condo. Parking, she stepped out—painfully—and went along a flowered path to the front door. When a woman with dark hair streaked with gray opened the door, Abby smiled. Just before collapsing in her mother's arms, she said, "You keep complaining I never visit, Mom. This goes under the heading of 'Be careful what you ask for.'"

"I don't know why you can't stay longer," her mother said three days later over bacon, eggs, English muffins and jam. "Your aunt Kate will be here tomorrow."

Abby dabbed at her mouth with a French linen napkin. "You know what Benjamin Franklin said, Mom. Fish and company stink after three days."

"Well, I haven't noticed you stinking yet," her mother said.

"That's what you always say."

And that, in fact, was one of the reasons she hadn't been home for a while. No matter how long she stayed, it was never long enough for her mom.

She had to admit that this time was a bit different, though. For a change, she actually hated leaving. Especially with Aunt Kate coming.

But she had to get on with her life. That was what she'd promised herself the day she'd left the hospital in Houston. *A new life.*

"To be honest, Mom," she said, "I have a date."

"Really? With Ben Schaeffer?"

"No...it's not with a person. Well, it is, but not exactly."

"Are you going to tell me who, what, when and where?" her mother asked. "Or are you trying to make me crazy?"

"I think I'll save you from impending insanity," Abby said. "The 'where' is Phoenix. And the 'who' is a lawyer."

Her mother, who looked and acted more like thirty than the sixty she was, chuckled. "Is this serious? Tell all."

So Abby told her. "It's not serious, Mom, not the way you mean. There's a clinic down there that specializes in the kind of physical therapy I need from that spider bite, and this lawyer—well, let's just say he wants to help me out, and I think he deserves the chance to do that. You know how sometimes we have to let people do something for us, but it's really for them?"

"He's that Jimmy Delgado you told me about, isn't

he?" her mom said. "The one that landed you in this mess. So he needs to salve his guilt?"

"Something like that, Mom. To tell the truth, I don't really care." She tapped the arm of her wheelchair. "I only need this now and then. Right now, my muscles are weak because I overdid things a bit. Tomorrow, I could be doing cartwheels." She grinned. "Well, not exactly, but I do need to start working out so that hopefully I won't hurt so much. That's what this clinic can do for me."

She rolled the wheelchair away from the kitchen table and took her coffee cup to the sink. In Phoenix, she'd have water therapy, massages and plenty of sunshine.

She would probably never do Kenpo again. That left her with a hole in her heart that was worse than the one in her arm.

But hey, life wasn't too bad. She still had the Prayer House, and she had enough money to buy a plane ticket now and then to get away from her small, isolated apartment and exercise her mind.

Maybe this was just the push she'd needed. *Everything happens for a reason,* her aunt Kate always said. Her mom might follow it up with, *God never closes a door without opening two windows.*

And the best one: *Clichés become clichés because they're true.*

Well, God only knew what she'd been missing the past two years in her Prayer House ivory tower. But right or wrong, good or bad, wise or not so wise— Abby was about to find out.

New York Times bestselling author

STEPHANIE LAURENS

A successful horse breeder and self-proclaimed rake,
Harry Lester samples women like wines. But after having
his heart trampled upon by someone he actually loved,
he has no intention of falling for a woman again,
let alone being ensnared by the trap of marriage.

Harry heads for the racing town of Newmarket, only
to encounter Mrs. Lucinda Babbacombe, a beautiful,
independent widow. And before he knows it, Harry vows
to protect Lucinda from the town full of lonely gambling
men, despite her refusal to accept his countless offers of
help. But will Harry let himself be taken prisoner in this
most passionate of traps?

An Unwilling Conquest

MEG O'BRIEN

66932	CRIMSON RAIN	___$6.50 U.S.	___$7.99 CAN.
66723	THE LAST CHEERLEADER	___$6.50 U.S.	___$7.99 CAN.

(limited quantities available)

TOTAL AMOUNT	$_____
POSTAGE & HANDLING	$_____
($1.00 FOR 1 BOOK, 50¢ for each additional}	
APPLICABLE TAXES*	$_____
TOTAL PAYABLE	$_____

(check or money order—please do not send cash}

To order, complete this form and send it, along with a check or money order for the total above, payable to MIRA Books, to: **In the U.S.:** 3010 Walden Avenue, P.O. Box 9077, Buffalo, NY 14269-9077; **In Canada:** P.O. Box 636, Fort Erie, Ontario, L2A 5X3.

Name: _____
Address: _____ City: _____
State/Prov.: _____ Zip/Postal Code: _____
Account Number (if applicable): _____

075 CSAS

*New York residents remit applicable sales taxes.
*Canadian residents remit applicable GST and provincial taxes.

MIRA®

www.MIRABooks.com

MMO0506BL

Psychotherapy
A Personal Approach

Psychotherapy
A Personal Approach

D. J. Smail

J. M. Dent & Sons Ltd
London, Melbourne and Toronto

First published 1978
© D. J. Smail 1978

Printed in Great Britain by
Biddles Ltd, Guildford, Surrey
and bound at the
Aldine Press, Letchworth, Herts
for
J. M. Dent & Sons Ltd,
Aldine House, Albemarle Street, London

This book is set in 10 on 12pt Compugraphic English

British Library Cataloguing in Publication Data
Smail, David John
   Psychotherapy.
   1.Psychotherapy
   I. Title
   616.8'914   RC480

   ISBN 0-460-12027-1

Contents

Acknowledgments

The author and publisher wish to thank the following for permission to reproduce copyright material:

Feyerabend, P. To New Left Books for an extract from *Against Method* (1975).

Fingarette, H. To Routledge and Kegan Paul Ltd and Humanities Press for an extract from *Self-Deception* (1969).

Freud, S. For an extract from 'The Unconscious', to the Hogarth Press Ltd (*Standard Edition of the Complete Psychological Works of Sigmund Freud*, 1915. Trans. and ed. James Strachey. Vol. XIV) and to Basic Books, Inc. (*The Collected Papers of Sigmund Freud*, Vol. IV, edited by Ernest Jones, M.D., authorized translation under the supervision of Joan Riviere, published by Basic Books, Inc., Publishers, New York, by arrangement with the Hogarth Press Ltd and the Institute of Psycho-Analysis, London).

For an extract from 'Femininity' to the Hogarth Press Ltd (*Standard Edition*, Vol. XXII) and to W. W. Norton, Inc. (*New Introductory Lectures on Psychoanalysis*, 1965).

Hayek, F. A. To the Hutchinson Publishing Group Ltd and Random House, Inc., for extracts from 'The Primacy of the Abstract' in A. Koestler and J. R. Smythies (eds.) *Beyond Reductionism* (1972).

Jung, C. G. To Routledge and Kegan Paul Ltd and Princeton University Press for extracts from *The Practice of Psychotherapy* (1954).

Koch, S. To the *Journal of Humanistic Psychology* for an extract from 'The Image of Man Implicit in Encounter Group Therapy' (Fall 1971).

Landfield, A. W. To John Wiley and Sons Ltd, for an extract from the chapter by Landfield in D. Bannister (ed.) *Issues and Approaches in the Psychological Therapies* (1975).

Polanyi, M. To Routledge and Kegan Paul Ltd and University of Chicago Press for an extract from *Personal Knowledge* (1958).

Sartre, J.-P. To Methuen and Co. Ltd and Librairie Gallimard, and to Philosophical Library, Inc., for extracts from *Being and Nothingness*. Reprinted by permission of Philosophical Library, Inc. Copyright © 1956 by Philosophical Library, Inc.

1

The Context of Psychotherapy

There tends to be a certain mystique surrounding psychotherapy. This often occasions in the uninitiated that attitude of almost reluctant reverence—easily turning to derision—which is usually to be found in situations in which we invest others (priests, gurus, doctors) with powers and abilities more advanced than our own. With some notable exceptions, psychotherapists themselves have done little to puncture this mystique, and indeed many continue to further by all means possible an image of themselves as expert technicians in the alteration of human behaviour and psychological suffering, or as possessors of some kind of ultimate knowledge of how human beings should be, and how to get them to-be it.

Our culture is saturated through and through with beliefs about human nature and society which provide a rich nutrient on which the psychotherapy industry can feed. Men and women should be happy—anxiety, depression, fear, panic and confusion are in no way acceptable, and, where they do arise, are to be banished as quickly as possible from the psychological scene. People must be *competent* to achieve those—largely materialistic—aims which fall within the range of possibilities determined by their social position. People must *get on with* other people. Love is good and hate is terrible. People must be sexually 'adjusted' and must *enjoy* sex. Families must be harmonious. People must find out what their 'full potential' as human beings is, and then realize it. People by and large cannot help the way they are: they are moulded by genetic endowment, the physical world and their relations (particularly in childhood) with others. You need an expert to see what's gone wrong and to put it right.

The experts, certainly, are ready and waiting, and the credibility of their role is immeasurably reinforced by the confidence in its own institutions our society generates. Social institutions, indeed, are often scarcely seen as human creations, and hardly at all as the frail and fallible, transitory structures they are. They are seen rather as enduring *realities*, as tangible proof of the correctness of our social

1

vision, as validations of our ideas about our own nature and conduct. And the claims to expertise of our experts are upheld by the very fact that they hold a position in the institutional network. For example, the very existence of schools and universities, professional teachers' organizations, hierarchies of academic rank, and so on, tends to be taken by all but a handful of critics as a kind of tacit justification of our fundamental ideas about the nature of education (e.g. that knowledge is *taught to* pupils by teachers).

This kind of attitude is well exemplified by the remarks of a student psychiatric nurse which demonstrated her readiness to abandon her own experience in the face of institutional disconfirmation. Her impression of her patients was that their problems stemmed from social and material difficulties, but not from illness; but they *must* be ill, she concluded, 'otherwise they wouldn't be in hospital'. Obviously absurd, you might think, and representative of a kind of thinking scarcely worthy of consideration as a serious component in the formation of most people's attitudes. And yet, look at the institution of 'training' and the ready acceptance given by even the most discriminating in our society to 'trained' experts. Just as the fact that somebody is in hospital means that he must be ill, the fact that somebody is trained means that respectable procedures must exist in which to have trained him. As long as your teacher, lawyer, doctor, psychotherapist has satisfactorily emerged from an official training, you can accept that he knows something worth knowing, something which gives him some kind of special authority to interpret the realities of his subject more competently than others. And yet no more than three-quarters of a century ago physicians, no less respected then than in the present day, were on the whole, despite their training, likely to achieve little more than a somewhat swifter demise for their weaker patients than might have occurred without their ministrations. (There are, of course, those who argue that in fact the situation is not so different today.[1])

The point, anyway, is that, not always wisely, we accept a great deal from our experts on trust. I do not want to suggest that there is ultimately anything very much else we can do, but I do want to examine upon what, in the field of psychotherapy, that trust can be based, and above all I hope that, by means of such an examination, the nature of psychotherapy and the character of its practitioners can be rendered a good deal less mysterious.

The nature of psychotherapy has not been determined by scientific insights into the objective realities of human functioning.

Nor could it be. It has on the whole been determined by a somewhat incoherent mixture of assumptions about what constitutes human health and happiness, combined with ideas about how one person can set about understanding, influencing and changing others. It is with these assumptions and ideas that this book will be centrally concerned, offering criticism as well as alternative conceptions.

The first task in this enterprise is to attempt an initial understanding of what is meant by 'psychotherapy', and to indicate the particular areas of our interest.

There is, in fact, no such thing as 'psychotherapy', and to assume that there is is to make a mistake which, as we shall see later, has in the past caused a good deal of misunderstanding about the nature and value of psychological methods of treatment. The field loosely covered by the term 'psychotherapy' comprises, on the contrary, a wide range of philosophies, theories and techniques which are frequently in marked opposition to each other, and are defended and attacked from deeply entrenched, and contrasting, ideological positions. A closer look at some of these positions will be taken in the next chapter. For the moment we should note that 'psychotherapy' can range from the intricate and closely woven theories of human personality and mental functioning which led Sigmund Freud and his followers to develop the techniques of psychoanalysis, to brief commonsensical chats between medical practitioners and their patients ('supportive psychotherapy') which consist of little more than sympathetic listening and more-or-less considered advice. The aims of 'psychotherapy' can vary between the 'cure' of neurotic or other disturbances in individuals thought to be mentally ill, and the acquisition by mentally well-adapted and socially successful people of heightened states of self-awareness, 'transpersonal consciousness', 'individuation', and so on. The theoretical mechanisms of change which psychological therapists postulate to account for their practical activities can similarly vary from the operation of unconscious mental dynamics, to the conditioning of physiological reflexes, to which latter process the 'mind' is thought to be irrelevant. Psychotherapists may claim to be able to treat people individually, in families, in groups, or even by correspondence course. The arena could be a mental hospital, a private consulting room, your own home, a 'growth centre' for week-end 'encounters', or almost anywhere else. Psychotherapists themselves may be medically trained psychiatrists, psychologists (who do not have medical qualifications), social workers, or in general any of a wide range of people to be found in the 'helping professions'; or they may be people who have trained in some particular psychotherapeutic creed without any other basic training, lay counsellors, or simply people who have bestowed upon themselves the title 'psychotherapist' and nailed a brass plate to their front door.

Faced with such divergence, we shall for the purposes of this book inevitably have to be selective. Most of the serious thinking and research which has gone on in the field of psychotherapy has been in the context of the treatment of mental disorder, and that mainly concerned with so-called neurotic illness. Recent years have seen an explosion in the 'growth', 'humanistic', and 'encounter' approaches which often concentrate more on ideals of human psychological functioning than on the removal of neurotic symptoms. While we cannot afford to ignore the latter, we shall concentrate mainly on the former: because it is here that the issues concerning psychological disturbance, its causes and its treatment, are in sharpest relief; because this, at the present time at least, is the area of greater social significance; and, not least, because it is in this area that my own experience has largely been acquired.

It is not my intention in this book simply to educate the interested reader—even if I could—in the current status and background of psychological therapies, to put him or her in touch, as it were, with the most advanced thinking on the subject, or to offer a privileged insight into recent developments of the medico-psychological and social/behavioural sciences. On the whole, as already suggested, we tend to approach the subject-matter of our intellectual and scientific institutions with reverence, in the tacit belief that the very most we could hope to achieve would be to *learn from* them. In the case of psychological theories and therapies, the natural tendency to accept what experts say as valid (or at least as *more* valid than one's own opinion) is reinforced by the enormous prestige that medicine and science command in our culture—and it is in medicine and science that most psychotherapies claim to have their roots. Science and medicine are endowed—and not only in the popular conception, but by many medics and scientists—with an *authority* which rivals that of mediaeval scholastic theology. It is my view, and one which I shall attempt to elaborate later, that this authority is ill founded, and indeed its acceptance perverts the development of human knowledge and undermines human experience. However this may be, what does seem absolutely clear to me is that, as things stand at present, the more or less *unquestioning* acceptance of the intellectual respectability, scientific soundness and clinical value of any of the psychological therapies cannot be justified on any grounds. For this reason, then, I feel that educating (or training) a person in 'psychotherapy' is not enough: such an approach could, and indeed does, (a) result in the creation of 'experts', semi-experts and technologists who promulgate theories or apply therapeutic techniques with very little critical understanding of the dubious nature of their conceptual foundations, and (b) reinforce a cultural attitude in which, in matters with which they are not acquainted at first hand, people simply accept what they find.

It is surely not possible for any disinterested observer to survey the contemporary scene in psychotherapy without, at least, bewilderment, or, at most, despair. There are so many approaches, so many competing claims, such differing appeals to scientific or moral authority, that we cannot simply take what we find and hope that sense will emerge from it all in the course of time. We have no alternative but to return at some stage to first principles, to examine critically the scientific and moral ideologies which underpin psychotherapy in its many forms.

In the course of this book, then, I shall be very critical of many current approaches to psychotherapy, and, in advocating the substitution of currently dominant conceptions of medical and scientific authority with the authority of the *personal* experience of those involved in psychotherapy (to be elaborated in later chapters), if I do not lay myself open to charges of mindless iconoclasm, I am at least likely to incur the displeasure of much of the psychotherapy 'establishment'. This is unfortunate, but the risk must be taken.

Since the central focus of this book is to be theory and practice in the psychotherapeutic treatment of neurosis, it is necessary at this stage to sketch in the general background in which such treatment takes place.

Although psychotherapy has its roots in medicine, most modern psychotherapies are in many respects opposed to purely medical approaches to mental or behavioural disorders: few psychotherapists, for example, would believe that the main causes of neurosis are physiological, but would see them rather as residing in the individual's acquired experience. Psychotherapy, again, is not, in Britain at least, the dominant approach to the treatment even of purely neurotic disorders (this would not so much be the case in the United States). The anxieties, phobias, obsessions and depressions which are held to constitute the symptoms of neurosis are most frequently treated by the use of tranquillizing and anti-depressive drugs, and the medically trained psychiatrists who prescribe such treatment see themselves most frequently as physicians, whose primary approach to the alteration of behaviour is via the body. It is perhaps true that few psychiatrists would claim that the neuroses are primarily physical disorders, and most would pay lip-service to the 'influence of the environment'. This passing acknowledgment of environmental influence does not, however, alter the fact that the treatment they offer is most often exclusively physical in nature. The sheer extent of the problem of psychological disturbance coupled with the fundamentally medical nature of psychiatry means that, in the British National Health Service, psychotherapy is hard to come by, and where it is to be found, tends to be reserved for the more articulate and middle-class patients for whom research on the whole suggests it is most useful. Outside the context of the National Health Service, psychotherapy is often, though not always, a lengthy and expensive business, and its patients are far more likely to be found among an affluent middle class than elsewhere. In America, psychotherapy is seen as a more integral part of psychiatry, and this, combined with a much greater commitment to private practice, means that it is more readily available. However, it is important to realize that, in a global context, psychotherapy as an approach to psychological suffering plays only a very minor role, and is largely restricted to the more socially privileged sections of society.

Despite its opposition, in many respects, to medicine, it is important to examine the legacy which psychotherapy has inherited from it, and the influence that medical assumptions have had on psychotherapeutic approaches. Some of that inheritance will already have become apparent in the early pages of this book: so far I have been using terms like 'treatment', 'neurosis', 'patient' largely uncritically, except for some use of inverted commas or qualifying clauses. These are, of course, terms which make no attempt to hide their medical origins. This is not the place to document the process by which medicine made the field of psychological disturbance its own—others, like Thomas Szasz, have done so very satisfactorily:[2] it may for our purposes be sufficient to note that the founding fathers of psychotherapy and their intellectual mentors were doctors, and were imbued with an unshakable confidence in the conceptions of medical science prevalent at the end of the last century. You do not, for example, have to explore the writings of Sigmund Freud very far before stumbling across the most sweeping—indeed arrogant— assertions of the intellectually unassailable nature of mechanistic scientific inquiry and its primacy over all other forms of human spiritual endeavour.

Thus, a system of classifying psychological problems was rapidly constructed which reflected approaches which had proved useful in physical medicine, and the relation of the sufferer to his sufferings was modelled on the relation of the patient to his symptoms. Even today, psychiatry has little hesitation in characterizing psychological disturbance as 'mental illness', and indeed we are encouraged by the medical profession and the health authorities to think of mental illnesses as 'illnesses like any other'. Partly, no doubt, some of the impetus behind this campaign is humanitarian, and it may be feared that the alternative to regarding somebody as mentally ill is to regard him as in some way intrinsically evil, stupid, or *responsible* for his condition.

There has been much criticism in recent years of the concept of mental illness (the main critic being Thomas Szasz, whose major work has already been referred to), yet nevertheless the concept has become deeply and concretely embedded in our society, and shows no signs of becoming less so. Psychological disturbance is mental *illness*, it is *treated* in *outpatient clinics* or mental *hospitals*, by *doctors* and mental *nurses*. The methods of treatment are, as already pointed out, largely physical in nature: mainly drugs, but also electro-convulsive therapy, which necessitates a general anaesthetic, and even brain surgery. Psychological disorder has given rise, in short, to a gigantic medical and pharmacological industry. For this reason alone it takes considerable nerve to suggest that alternative views of psychological disorder are possible.

In many respects it is towards alternative views that psychotherapy, in its various versions, points. Many therapists, for instance, reject at least some of the terminology of medicine—they prefer to speak, for example, of 'clients' rather than 'patients'. Most psychotherapists have little or nothing to do with physical treatments, and prefer to see their clients as far as possible outside medical settings such as hospitals and clinics. Some forms of psychological treatment have their theoretical roots in entirely non-medical disciplines: those techniques loosely grouped under the heading 'behaviour therapy', for example, draw their inspiration from experimental psychology and the study of learning, although most have accepted to some extent the diagnostic classification built by the early psychiatrists and psychoanalysts.

It is hoped that it will prove possible in this book to crystallize an alternative to the dominant medical approach to psychological suffering, and to highlight those aspects of psychotherapeutic thinking which help us to do so. The task will be, then, to provide an account of how somebody can be 'neurotic' without being ill, stupid, evil or deliberately wayward. Our task will, however, be made doubly difficult by the additional contention that, while being none of these things, the neurotic individual is also *not helpless*.

So far I have betrayed clearly enough my objection to the medical approach, but I have not made clear the reason for that objection. It lies, in fact, precisely in the centrality to the illness conception of the *helplessness* of the person supposed to be mentally ill. The medical approach is par excellence a *mechanistic* approach to psychological disturbance: it characterizes the patient as a passive, helpless mechanism, whose only hope for recovery lies in the expert readjustment of the faulty parts.

In the first place, I object to this view because it seems to me simply to be wrong, and in later chapters I shall try to persuade the reader also that it is wrong. Second, because it is wrong, the view of man as helpless mechanism seems to me to have disastrous consequences. From a general point of view it generates social institutions which are designed to organize, manipulate and mould people to *institutional* ends and obscures from them that they can manipulate social institutions to their own ends. From a specific point of view it has the result that the psychologically disturbed individual is denied, at least from the viewpoint of 'official' theory, the one most effective avenue to coping with his disturbance, i.e. helping himself. In practical terms, this most often means that he is left to fester psychologically in his fears, confusions and painful personal relations, while somebody tinkers with his body chemistry or stuns him periodically with electric shocks. Patients in the average mental hospital are *dis*couraged from facing their psychological problems or questioning the values of the (usually) benevolently authoritarian régime which takes them in its charge and claims responsibility for their future psychological health. The patient is thus denied access to the means of helping himself, or at least his access to it is discouraged. For, to help himself, he must be able to examine, understand and change his psychological predicament. He may indeed need help in doing this, but that help will certainly not consist in diverting his attention from his predicament.

It is of course in this area that the psychotherapies hold out their promise. Superficially, at least, they seem to offer ways in which the individual can come to an understanding of his predicament and in which the predicament itself can be changed. And indeed it will be an argument of this book that from the psychotherapies can be distilled a way of conceptualizing how the individual can take charge of his own psychological functioning even when subjectively at his most helpless and 'ill'.

And yet, if psychotherapies hold out hope of achieving such a liberating view of man and his psychological problems, it is often in the teeth of their own theoretical leanings. If psychotherapy has escaped from some of the more limiting medical assumptions touched on above, it still in large part shares with medicine about the most limiting assumption of all: that is, the assumption of mechanism. Psychotherapists of many, though not all, persuasions tend to have taken over unthinkingly the view common to early medicine and academic psychology that to be scientific you have to accept some mechanistic (though they might not actually use the word) constraints. The acceptance of some form of determinism, for example, is widespread among psychotherapists, and indeed is as central to psychoanalysis as it is to behavioural psychotherapy. Similarly, the doctor-patient, expert repairer-faulty machine relationship is characteristic of many forms of psychotherapy. Where therapists have departed from these models, they have often done so hesitantly and nervously—making ritual obeisance to determinism, perhaps, by speaking of the patient's 'sense of mastery' rather than his freedom, and so on. In the next chapter the theoretical background of some of the major psychotherapies will be examined in much greater detail, and later in the book we shall hope to provide reasons for therapists to make the break from mechanistic assumptions more boldly. But it is important at this stage to note one particular consequence of the insidious invasion of psychotherapy by medico-scientific mechanism: namely, that even psychotherapists run into conceptual difficulties when they try to help patients with their helplessness.

Most patients—and certainly those who fall into the 'neurotic' class with which we are mainly concerned—come to the therapeutic situation equipped with a theory, or theories, about themselves which are not so different from those of the professional experts. Partly because of the expectations engendered by our culture and its social institutions, and partly because it is the most *convenient* belief for them to hold (since the unacceptable alternatives seem to be malice or stupidity), patients tend to see their psychological problems as outside their own control. They may find themselves in the grip of behaviours they seem unable to resist—for example, compulsions to keep clean and free of various kinds of contamination, or an irresistible urge to engage in repetitive checking that they have not committed some careless and potentially dangerous act; or they may feel unaccountably assailed by apparently baseless feelings of anxiety or panic; or such intense fears of apparently harmless objects or situations that they have to organize their lives round avoiding them. Or they may feel a pervasive depression and lack of interest in life without being able to identify its source; or perhaps an inability sexually to consummate an otherwise apparently satisfactory relationship. The complaints, in fact, which people bring to their doctor or therapist can vary over an almost infinite range—from being compelled to eat coal to feeling sexually attracted to horses—but they tend to have in common that the person feels at their mercy and unable to help himself. The theory a patient holds, tacitly or explicitly, to account for his predicament may appeal to a mechanical disorder of his body, a childhood trauma, financial problems or stresses at work, the malice of others, and so on; and in this he may find a ready echo in the theoretical beliefs of his therapist. Everything, including the very fact that his therapist *exists* as a socially accredited expert in his problems, suggests to the patient that he may submit himself to the therapist much as the host of appendicitis submits himself to the surgeon. Yet he will soon discover that, far from being the passive recipient of various technical procedures, he is engaged in a taxing struggle with his problems which makes great demands on his personal, active resources. The therapist also, while embodying the role of technical expert, will in fact (and possibly with an uncomfortable recognition of the dimly implied contradiction) be making demands upon his patient's resources, and requiring of him his active participation in treatment.

This is one of the most puzzling and difficult of the theoretical problems which psychotherapy has to deal with, and one which may well cause the patient a lot of grief. He is encouraged by the mechanistic temper of the age to look for 'the cause' of his psychological problems. He no more knows why he is neurotic than I know why I am a psychologist, but the bits and pieces of popular medicine or psychoanalysis he has picked up will set him off in a diligent search for causal events, childhood experiences, etc., which he expects to 'explain' his condition, which in turn, having been explained, will presumably vanish. It may well become a source of anxiety, and even anger to him to discover that this approach proves fruitless, and it only confuses and further angers him that his therapist, while professing beliefs which apparently support his mechanistic strategies, in actuality seems to be demanding of him something else. We are here anticipating themes which will be developed in greater detail at a later stage. We can note, however, that the anxiety, anger and confusion which tends to arise in this situation frequently results in patients' terminating psychotherapy and departing in disgust or despair, thereby adding to the statistics which demonstrate that, whatever else it is (and it is much else!) psychotherapy is not a sure-fire technical method of curing 'neurotic illness'.

Much of the language, and some of the concepts, which the medical approach has contributed to the understanding of psychological disturbance is hard to dispense with without artificiality. The terms 'neurosis', 'treatment', 'patient', and indeed 'therapy' itself, as well as many others, cannot easily be separated from their medical connotations, and tend almost unavoidably to foster mechanistic assumptions about the nature of psychotherapy. The dilemma of the writer who wishes, as I do, to reject these assumptions without straining the reader's patience by inventing an entirely new vocabulary is not easily solved. 'Neurosis', if it can be thought of without the implication it carries of being a medical diagnosis, a type of disease entity, can be usefully retained as a shorthand to describe a kind of strategy by which a person can deceive himself about the reasons for and aims of his conduct (a view to be elaborated later). If I could think of an equally succinct term which expressed what I mean and carried no medical implications, I should use it. Since I cannot, I shall continue to use the term in the slightly idiosyncratic sense given above, and hope that I am not too frequently misunderstood. The substitution of 'client' for 'patient' now frequently made by psychotherapists I do not myself feel to be particularly satisfactory. It is true that 'client' avoids the directly medical flavour of 'patient', but it does not escape—indeed it in some ways furthers—a view of the therapeutic relationship as one of professional expert and passive recipient. Further, while being in this respect no less mystifying and mechanizing than 'patient', it introduces a commercial tone to the therapeutic 'transaction' which, though many therapists feel the commercial aspect to be of central (rather than incidental) importance to therapeutic effectiveness, I for one find mildly unfortunate. Because of this, and because the repetitive use of the words 'person' or 'individual' tends to become irritating after a time, though basically I prefer them, I shall not shrink from using the familiar 'patient'. 'Treatment', 'therapy', and so on, could I think be more usefully, and accurately, called something like 'psychological guidance' or simply 'help', but here again to do so single-mindedly would inevitably seem artificial. In time perhaps the context in which these words are used will establish their detachment from medicine and medical assumptions, and their presence in the language will depend simply on their convenience. That, anyway, is why I use them. I shall certainly *not* be talking about 'mental illness'.

1 Illich, Ivan. (1975). *Medical Nemesis*. London: Calder & Boyars.
2 Szasz, T. (1962). *The Myth of Mental Illness*. London: Secker & Warburg.

2

Approaches to Psychotherapy

The approaches to therapy to be discussed in this chapter have been selected first for their general importance and influence, and secondly because they exemplify in one way or another theoretical, or even ideological positions which it is our aim to understand and make explicit. It is not the purpose of this book to provide a comprehensive review of the various kinds of psychotherapy practised today, or a full history of their development. The reader looking for this kind of information should consult one of the texts already available which are aimed at fulfilling this purpose.[1] There is a particular class of approaches to psychotherapy—those involving groups of patients, families and marital couples—which I shall not be considering in this chapter. Their omission reflects a concern for economy of space and, more cogently perhaps, my belief that the central issues in psychotherapy can be raised by a consideration of individual therapy alone; it does not, however, carry any implication of relative therapeutic unimportance for these methods, many of which have great potential usefulness.

It is important to emphasize that in this chapter I am considering therapy from the point of view of what therapists *say* they do, and not from that of what they *do* do. In other words, my perspective is theoretical. As we shall see in Chapter 3, it is by no means the case that what therapists say they do always matches or describes accurately what they actually do. In that case, it may be asked, why concentrate on a theoretical perspective? Why not just describe what actually happens in therapy? My reason is that, though theories are often not (indeed, in some cases because of their fundamental absurdity *could* not be) put into therapeutic practice, they nevertheless have consequences for our view of ourselves and our relations with each other which are very far-reaching. I hope to demonstrate this later in this chapter.

One cannot, then, afford to ignore theory, however much it departs from practice, and however much practitioners may feel contemptuous of it. Ours is becoming a largely technological, rather

13

than a scientific, culture. We are concerned with *whether* things 'work', not with how and why they do; we are more concerned with cost-effectiveness than with truth. In the field of psychotherapy this leads, particularly in some camps, to a Philistine dismissal of theoretical considerations; what matters to these therapists is simply whether or not the patient 'gets better'. It so happens that many of the therapists of this persuasion belong to the 'behaviour therapy' school (to be discussed below), which in origin springs from a theoretical position which is very easily demolished. Despite behavioural theory being in ruins, behavioural therapeutic technologists will happily carry on, because they believe that what they are doing 'works'. If you attack their theoretical position, as it is so easy to do, they will accuse you of attacking a straw man, gaining a hollow victory, etc., as they no longer really subscribe to that, or any other, theory. This would be all very well if it were not for the fact that the theory has not been abandoned at all, but carries on under cover, so to speak. For in the field of psychotherapy, in which by adopting some criterion or other of human health or happiness the therapist is putting forward *values*, he simply cannot escape having a theory about human nature and what is good for it. There is just no way of saying whether a patient is 'better' without having a theory about how people ought to *be*, any more than there is a way of trying to change people without having a theory about how to do it. The fact that therapists exist who are unaware of their therapeutic theory is considerably more frightening than the existence of therapists who consciously subscribe to a theory which is, for example, absurd or self-contradictory. The latter, at least, are answerable for their values, while the former promulgate theirs without knowing what they are. This is no merely abstract intellectual problem, as we shall see shortly.

Psychotherapy as a formal procedure appealing for its justification to the accepted principles of science has its origins in Freud's psychoanalysis. Psychotherapy is of course not to be confused with psychoanalysis: the former is a much broader term than the latter, which refers specifically to the theoretical beliefs and therapeutic practices of Freud and his followers.

Most of the many variants of psychotherapy have moved very far indeed from psychoanalysis, and in not many of them would it now be felt that they owed all that much to it. There are also, certainly, many more psychotherapists—of various persuasions—than there are psychoanalysts, and there is little doubt that psychoanalysis is no longer the power it once was in this field. But although 'pure culture' psychoanalysts may be relatively thin on the ground nowadays, Freud's ideas have had an enormous impact on our culture, and in the public mind Freudian analysis is often more or less synonymous with psychotherapy. In fact, in the professional spheres of psychiatry and psychology, Freudian psychoanalysis has probably had less influence than outside, but even so there can be few areas of professional concern which have not at least been touched by some aspect of Freud's thought.

It would be both arrogant and foolish to attempt to condense an adequate account of psychoanalysis into the space available in this chapter, but perhaps enough can be said to convey the general tenor of some of the debates within psychoanalysis and to indicate to the reader where further information might be found.[2]

The range and extent of Freud's output was vast. Among other things, he bequeathed to posterity a theory of the development of personality, a theory of psychological (mental) functioning, and a theory of neurosis together with a technique for its treatment. None of these would today be accepted without qualification by any but a small handful of highly orthodox psychoanalysts, but in the course of developing his position Freud elaborated a number of technical concepts which are still extremely influential.

Freud subscribed to a brand of mechanistic rationalism which was in his day thought by many to be characteristic of science, and he saw the 'discoveries' of psychoanalysis as opening the way to a more or less final understanding of the nature of man. Human nature could thus be *reduced* to a relatively small set of mechanisms, the nature of which it was the business of psychoanalysis to reveal. In this way, man could in principle be scientifically understood as an *object*, in much the same way as physical objects could be understood by the natural sciences. From this alone it is possible to appreciate how easily a mystique could come to be attached to psychoanalysis: the analyst becomes a subject whose knowledge encompasses and explains the conduct of those objects—people—to whom he turns his attention. Despite a certain mock modesty, it is evident from much of Freud's writing that to a great extent he revelled in this mystique.)

One could caricature Freud's conception of psychological functioning as a whole, as a kind of vast steam engine, in which the motive power of 'libido'—sexual and aggressive energy—is forced through various valves (defence mechanisms) and chambers (levels of consciousness) until it is finally converted into observable activity. In many respects Freud does seem to have had this kind of model in mind. Behaviour is indeed reduced in the end to the way the individual has managed to deal with his sexual and aggressive energy, from the early vicissitudes of breast feeding and toilet training (the famous oral and anal stages of infantile development) to the full flowering of genital sexuality, not to mention the enormous challenge of the Oedipal stage, at which the child has to cope with the threats posed by its sexual attraction to its parent of opposite sex. All later development, and in particular the formation of neurotic symptoms, was seen as hinging on the conscious and unconscious manoeuvres which were brought to bear in the attempted resolution of these sexual problems. In some ways the individual was seen as the embodiment of a moral struggle between the opposing forces of his psyche, his unconscious, preconscious and conscious minds providing the arena for battles between his 'id' (the naked impulse to sexual and aggressive satisfaction), his 'ego' (roughly corresponding to a consciously aware self) and his 'superego', or conscience. Through psychoanalysis the individual could become aware of some of the unconscious springs of his problems, particularly as these centred in his sexual relations in childhood with his parents, and by working through them and their consequences in his relationship with his analyst, bring them under the conscious control of his ego. Since the problems were deeply rooted in the first place in the unconscious mind, the techniques of psychoanalysis were to focus on ways of reaching this inaccessible stratum. Having tried, and abandoned, hypnosis, Freud concentrated instead on free association and the analysis of dreams. For although the unconscious mind could clearly not be expressed directly by the patient, its influence, Freud felt, could be detected in the unmonitored drift of his associations, and in his dreams, where again the vigilance of conscious censorship was relaxed. The processes by which consciousness tries to exclude what is to it the very threatening nature of the unconscious sexual and aggressive impulses, were elaborated in great technical detail and with considerable sophistication by Freud. These are the defence mechanisms, of which the most important is 'repression', which is best characterized, perhaps, as a kind of intentional forgetting: the individual succeeds either in actively ejecting sexually or aggressively charged material from consciousness, or in preventing its initial entry into consciousness.

The nature of unconscious mental contents could often only be divined from the symbolic distortions they had undergone in dreams or free associations, and for this reason Freud developed what now appears to be a rather simplistic lexicon of symbolism, which, among other things, could be of service in the analyst's 'interpretation' to the patient of the meaning of his unconscious (dream and free-associative) productions. In this sense, the analyst would be able to tell the patient what his thoughts, fantasies and dreams *really meant*. This is a point we shall certainly be returning to, but it is scarcely any wonder that in the early days of psychoanalysis the hint of powers of this kind attracted to it, from some quarters anyway, a quality of almost religious awe.

A central belief of psychoanalysis and many of its later derivatives is that a person's perception of his present relationships—and in particular that with his analyst—is determined unconsciously by his earlier relationship with his parents. The role of the analyst in therapy therefore, at least in part, becomes one of providing a 'screen' onto which the patient can 'project' largely fantasized attributes which betray the psychological structure of his childhood parental relationships. To facilitate this process, the analyst excludes as far as possible any revelation of personal characteristics: he contrives to remain 'neutral'. This is one of the reasons why, in classical psychoanalysis, the analyst sits behind the prone patient, where the latter cannot see him. Feelings the patient has for or about the analyst are thus characterized as the 'transference' onto a neutral figure of qualities which have their origin in the patient's infantile past. The therapist's analysis of this transference, his demonstration to the patient by means of interpretation, etc., of the real significance of the latter's feelings about him, is the central plank in psychoanalytic technique.

There is much in Freud's original formulations which only a tiny minority of his present-day followers would be prepared to defend. His sexual reductionism, for example, cannot, in its more extreme form, command the serious attention of modern psychological theorists. Consider the following quotation from a paper of his on femininity,[3] which, incidentally, makes the modern male chauvinist look like Joan of Arc:

The effect of penis-envy has a share . . . in the physical vanity of women, since they are bound to value their charms more highly as a late compensation for their original sexual inferiority. Shame, which is considered to be a feminine characteristic *par excellence* but is far more a matter of convention than might be supposed, has as its purpose, we believe, concealment of genital deficiency. We are not forgetting that at a later time shame takes on other functions. It seems that women have made few contributions to the discoveries and inventions in the history of civilization;

there is, however, one technique which they may have invented—that of plaiting and weaving. If that is so, we should be tempted to guess the unconscious motive for the achievement. Nature herself would seem to have given the model which this achievement imitates by causing the growth at maturity of the pubic hair that conceals the genitals. The step that remained to be taken lay in making the threads adhere to one another, while on the body they stick into the skin and are only matted together. If you reject this idea as fantastic and regard my belief in the influence of lack of a penis on the configuration of femininity as an *idée fixe*, I am of course defenceless.

However, despite what now appear to be obvious weaknesses in Freud's original ideas, there are many aspects of his elaboration of theory and practice in psychoanalysis which are still highly influential in psychotherapy. If his conception of infantile development in terms of an oversimplified set of crucial psycho-sexual stages has largely been rejected, his formulation of the nature of consciousness (and unconsciousness), repression and other defence mechanisms, has proved to be of fundamental importance.

Freud's view of science committed him to a theory which is, as has been pointed out, reductionist, determinist and mechanistic, and to a view of the therapist's role in analysis as neutral and impersonal. These are features which orthodox psychoanalysis shares with other brands of psychological therapy which place a similar emphasis on the 'scientific' nature of their foundations. It is to orthodox versions of these which we shall turn next, even though chronologically they belong to a much more recent period. We shall return a little later to the variations and developments which have occurred in the broadly psychoanalytic field.

One of the most influential approaches to the treatment of neurosis in the present day is that of 'behaviour therapy'. The theoretical pedigree of behaviour therapy is different from that of psychoanalysis, and it owes little to turn-of-the-century medical thinking. There are perhaps two main theoretical sources of behaviour therapy which can be clearly identified. The first is Pavlov's work in the earlier years of this century on physiological reflexes and the acquisition of conditioned responses in laboratory animals, and the second is the anti-mentalism of J. B. Watson. The development within experimental psychology—largely a pre-occupation of academic institutions—of the tenets of behaviourism, for the origination of which Watson is usually held to be responsible, will be familiar to most readers of this book, and to chronicle them yet again here would be tedious in the extreme. For the uninitiated reader, however, a few words on the scientific ideology of behaviourism might not be out of place.

Behaviourism was a reaction to what many psychologists saw as the hopelessly subjective entanglements into which psychology as an academic discipline had got itself. Disputes over whether people thought with or without the use of visual images, how many instincts could be identified as motivating human behaviour, and so on, made use of techniques of argument and research which seemed uncomfortably distant from those which were being used with such apparent success in the natural sciences. Science, it was felt, must deal only with observables, and the experimental procedures of psychological scientists must be clearly specifiable in terms of what they do, and what the outcome is. If only psychologists could get away from talking about what went on *inside* people (where no one but the subject himself could see—and not even he necessarily reliably) and measure their activity in terms of some *objective* criterion, psychology stood a chance of becoming really scientific. The objective criterion is, of course, behaviour. With great excitement, psychologists discovered that instead of talking about what people felt and thought, which was liable to subjective error, they could talk about, and actually *measure* (quantifiability being another worthy scientific aim) what they *did*. They could then specify their own experimental operations upon the subject (or 'organism', as he came to be called), and measure the result in terms of his reaction. It thus dawned on the behaviourists that you didn't have to talk about 'minds' at all. All pre-scientific, occult nonsense about thoughts, feelings, ideas and purposes could be scrapped and replaced by behavioural responses to experimental stimuli. Here at least was an exact, objective, quantitative psychological science which could, head held high, proclaim that its aim was 'the prediction and control of behaviour'. In place of mind the behaviourists put the reflex arc, which they borrowed from Pavlov. What happens when a human being *learns*, then, is that a behavioural response becomes conditioned to an environmental stimulus. The way it becomes conditioned is through 'reinforcement'; that is, the conditioned reflex between stimulus and response is established through the association of the latter with (usually) reward.

Much of the work of behaviourist psychologists was in the experimental study of learning. Because, for them, consciousness did not exist as a 'scientific' possibility, because the control and manipulation of experimental variables was essential to their model of experimental science, because in general it seemed the easiest thing to do, most of their work in this area was carried out with animals, particularly laboratory rats. A typical learning experiment would thus consist of rewarding an animal by means of food for achieving some goal (such as running correctly through a simple maze) previously determined by the experimenter. Ingenious permutations and manipulations of this basic situation have filled libraries, and the theoretical implications drawn from them held sway in academic psychology for decades. Incredible as it might seem, a view of man without mind, a model of learning built on procedures which, however ingenious, were no more than techniques of training performing animals, seemed an acceptable price to pay for a 'scientific' psychology.

Behaviourism is now no longer the force it once was in academic psychology, but many of its scientific assumptions go marching on, particularly in its psychotherapeutic aspect, i.e. behaviour therapy. Although it is impossible to avoid questioning some of its practical defects, behaviourism has so dominated the psychological scene that psychologists tend to overlook the fact that the behaviourist theoretical principles which they took in with their mother's milk can be equally called into question. Thus, the aims of mechanistic reductionism (to stimulus and response), determinism (which permits 'prediction and control of behaviour') and objectivity still seem self-evidently necessary to many psychologists, and to many of those who are engaged in the treatment of neurosis. The behaviourist's antipathy for 'mentalism' expresses itself among behaviour therapists as a contemptuous hostility towards the ideas of psychoanalysis, with which, as has been said, it otherwise shares rather similar scientific aims. Unseen, unobservable things like unconscious minds are for obvious reasons anathema to the behaviourist.

In their original conception and purest form the techniques of behaviour therapy closely reflect behaviourist scientific ideology. Reasoning from his own, and others', experiments with animal conditioning, Joseph Wolpe, one of the founding fathers of behaviour therapy, concluded that neurotic behaviour was the result of anxiety responses having become conditioned to otherwise neutral stimuli. Due to some quirk in the history of his reinforcement contingencies, the phobic patient, for example, behaves neurotically (anxiously) in the presence of stimuli (e.g. travelling on public transport) which in the normal course of events do not evoke anxiety. The neurosis, therefore, can be understood as no more than its symptoms: one need no longer appeal to the mysterious operation of unconscious complexes or unresolved, and unobservable, sexual conflicts. Remove the symptoms, and you have removed the neurosis. The removal of symptoms is, naturally enough, achieved by the conditioning of a non-anxious response to the offending stimuli. This reasoning gave birth to the technique, widely practised by present-day behaviour therapists, of 'systematic desensitization'. This technique, originally established as viable by Wolpe with cats, relies upon teaching patients to relax, and then conditioning the physical responses of relaxation, which are held to inhibit anxiety, to a graded series of stimuli which represent—often in imagination only—the situations most feared by the patient. Thus the claustrophobic patient, for example, will be asked to imagine, in a relaxed state, a series of situations involving increasing degrees of enclosure or confinement. At the end of the series he will be imagining those situations which in actuality cause him most alarm. If successful, his anxiety will thus be inhibited, and the process of re-conditioning will be complete. The relaxation responses which have been conditioned in imagination will, by the process of 'generalization' (a construct invented by behaviourists to account for the fact that a behavioural response learned in one particular situation will also be evoked in other relevant situations), also obtain in actual, '*in vivo*', situations. Wolpe claimed considerable success for this technique, a point which we shall return to in a later chapter when we come to consider scientific evidence for the efficacy of psychotherapeutic approaches.

'Aversive' techniques of behaviour therapy have also been arrived at on the basis of the conditioning model. In this case punishment (as opposed to the 'positive reinforcement' of reward) has been used to associate an unpleasant, aversive outcome with behaviours which are deemed 'maladaptive'. Deviant sexual behaviour—homosexuality, transvestism, etc.—and alcoholism have been the most frequent targets for this kind of approach. Thus homosexuals may be administered painful electric shocks when they show signs of arousal to homosexual stimuli, or alcoholics are given drugs which react with alcohol and bring about nausea and vomiting.

'Operant conditioning', the brainchild of one of the foremost apologists of behaviourism, B. F. Skinner provides the rationale for a further collection of behaviour therapy techniques (often known as 'behaviour modification', or 'behaviour shaping') which have been widely practised on chronic patients in mental institutions as well as with mentally handicapped or severely disturbed children. In these, reward is made contingent upon 'desirable' behaviours and the absence of reward upon 'undesirable' behaviours. First, an analysis might be made of what an individual patient finds rewarding. This might take the form of sweets, cigarettes, going for a walk, listening to music, having a bath or any one of a number of events or activities. These rewards will then be withheld until the patient 'emits' the behaviour which is to be reinforced (e.g. talking rather than remaining mute, controlling bladder or bowel functions, behaving sociably rather than unsociably, and so on). His behaviour will thus be 'shaped' to acquire new standards of acceptability. The reader who wishes to pursue further the theory and practice of behaviour therapy will find a voluminous literature awaiting him. [4]

As behavioural psychology reduces the person, so behaviour therapy reduces the individual patient to a mindless focus of stimuli and responses, a manipulable object to be predicted, controlled, and shaped to conform to current social norms.

There are crippling objections to behaviourism. Where there is no consciousness, no purpose, there can be no meaning, no values. How can the behaviour therapist *decide* what to do when he is, on his own theory, no more than the helpless result of his reinforcement history—how, indeed, can he account for his own behaviour as subject-scientist when only objectivity is possible? He can only do so, of course, because he shuts his eyes to those aspects of his activity which fail to fit in with his scientific philosophy; he ignores his own experience, distorts that of others, and ends up as a kind of psychological fraud. This is not the place to develop a full critique of behaviourism. That has been done very adequately by others. [5] Although greatly weakening the general acceptance of behaviourism in psychology as a whole, such attacks have not resulted in its total demise. The behaviourist reaction is often simply to shout louder its scientific credo, or, as often in the case of behaviour therapists, to retire into a kind of technological obscurantism which simply insists that, because behaviour therapy works, behavioural theory must be true. To object to behaviourism and its practical applications in terms of its implications for the freedom and dignity of man is liable to meet with sneering accusations of tender-mindedness and an inability to take one's scientific medicine: maybe people are reduced to junction boxes where stimulus meets response, but if that's what science reveals, that's just too bad.

And it is just this question of the *scientific* status of behaviour therapy which seems to mesmerize its proponents, who do not seem to recognize that it is scarcely scientific to hold on to beliefs which contradict fundamental human experience, involve their holders in self-contradiction and fly in the face of rationality. It is by no means my intention to argue here that behaviour therapy techniques do not 'work'—indeed I am convinced that they often do. What the behaviourist cannot provide, and what it seems to me we must earnestly seek, is a theory which explains *why* such techniques work.

For people for whom values are presumably mentalistic cobwebs, behaviour therapists often seem to exude an almost evangelistic zeal:

The reason for the effectiveness of behaviour modification lies in its derivation from the experimental analysis of behaviour. No other approach in the history of psychology has demonstrated such refined prediction and control over its subject-matter with such scientific rigour, replicability and generality. It should not be surprising therefore that an effective behavioural technology emerges which is based on a powerful science of behaviour.

The cumulative evidence is now sufficient to justify the conclusion that any approach to behaviour change, training, rehabilitation, teaching or education should be informed by operant principles. This means that practical wisdom which many trainers, teachers, rehabilitators and therapists have gathered, with experience in whatever framework they had available to them, can probably be applied more effectively when the laws of behaviour are explicitly recognized and implemented. [6]

But what are we to do with this powerful technology? Who is to decide to what human ills its attentions should be directed? Where at last are we to find a subjective *person* who is able to make decisions of this kind? It may be self-evident that people who don't want to be homosexual shouldn't be, and that a reasonable way of changing them is to ask them to masturbate to pictures of nude men, and electrically shock them when they ejaculate, but how can such self-evidence reveal itself to the blind product of environmental reinforcement? These are questions which cannot be answered by the behaviourist without self-contradiction or sophistry.

In his relationship with his patient, the behaviour therapist, from a purely theoretical point of view, finds himself in the uneasy company of the orthodox psychoanalyst, for, like him, he believes that it is the *technique* of therapy which is important, not the person of the therapist. Whereas the analyst is the vehicle of projected, transference reactions, the behaviour therapist is the scientific technician who juggles stimuli. As long as the juggling is done correctly, the identity of the juggler is immaterial. Many of the early behaviour therapists explicitly espoused this view, and indeed 'automated behaviour therapy', where the therapist is replaced by a machine, is a logical extension of it which some have not shied away from.

Like orthodox psychoanalysis, in short, behaviour therapy has done its level best to remain true to the inspiration of its conception of science. It is reductive, mechanistic, deterministic and impersonal. The practitioners of these forms of psychotherapy are, nevertheless, people, and their saving grace is that what they do in psychotherapy may bear little relation to what they say they do. Unfortunately for them, their conception of what it is to be 'scientific' makes it impossible for them to take into consideration those aspects of their own and their patients' activity which cannot be accommodated within a restricted and simplistic theoretical model. In these as in many other areas of psychology and psychotherapy, we seem in fact to have arrived at a curious inversion of scientific values. If science arose to confront theological dogma with what men actually *experienced*, psychological science these days too often ignores, distorts or denies experience because it does not square with the dogmatic principles of that science.

But by no means all psychotherapists have been afraid to this extent of permitting their personal experience to dictate their theoretical stance. The reductionism and impersonality of Freud's views quickly bred dissent in his own day, and psychoanalysis soon split into a variety of camps representing objections to one or another aspect of the orthodoxy. It is of course not possible fully to document these developments here, but it might be of interest to glance at some of their more salient features.

Carl Jung and Alfred Adler are of course the best known of the dissenters among Freud's contemporaries. Between them, they objected to the sweeping sexual reductionism, as well as the determinism and impersonality of Freud's psychoanalysis, and both formed well-established schools of their own—Jung's 'analytical psychology', and Adler's 'individual psychology'. Neither, however, has had an influence comparable to Freud's on the field of psychotherapy as a whole, although Adler's views had a significant impact in the United States, especially in the area of child guidance.

Adler is probably chiefly remembered for the emphasis he placed on the importance of feelings of inferiority for an understanding of neurosis, and the compensatory activity in which the person engages in order to overcome them. Hence the pomposity of the short man, the verbosity of the stammerer, and so on. In this, of course, can be seen the same kind of reductionism to which Freud appealed. Also, however, Adler placed great emphasis on the individual's *responsibility* for his actions and for changing them: for Adler, thus, the person is no longer solely determined by unconscious forces, but has the opportunity of consciously changing himself and recognizing that his actions are directed towards an end.

Jung was for a time Freud's closest collaborator, and in many ways his conceptual formulations are very similar to Freud's, and no less complex and far-reaching. However, he objected strongly to Freud's all-embracing sexual reductionism, and laid much more emphasis on the spiritual strivings of men to make sense of their lives and to develop fully their individuality. For this reason, a central focus of his interest was on religion and mythology, in which he felt he detected the most fundamental and pervasive of mankind's concerns, and he used his religious and anthropological studies as a basis for the elaboration of a view of the unconscious mind which emphasized the common spiritual foundations of man's experience (the 'collective unconscious'). In focusing in this way on what the person is to make of himself, how he is to grow to self-fulfilment, Jung anticipated by decades some of the present preoccupations of the 'growth movement' in psychotherapy. Jung also reacted to the impersonality of the analyst-patient relationship as conceived by Freud, and chose rather to characterize the situation as follows:

. . . twist and turn the matter as we may, the relation between doctor and patient remains a personal one within the impersonal framework of professional treatment. By no device can the treatment be anything but the product of mutual influence, in which the whole being of the doctor as well as that of his patient plays its part. . . . For two personalities to meet is like mixing two different chemical substances: if there is any combination at all, both are transformed. In any effective psychological treatment the doctor is bound to influence the patient; but this influence can only take place if the patient has a reciprocal influence on the doctor. You can exert no influence if you are not susceptible to influence. It is futile for the doctor to shield himself from the influence of the patient and to surround himself with a smokescreen of fatherly and professional authority. By so doing he only denies himself the use of a highly important organ of information. The patient influences him unconsciously none the less.[7]

Further, Jung clearly felt uncomfortable with the mechanistic over-generalizations in which many psychoanalysts seemed tempted to engage:

It is enough to drive me to despair that in practical psychology there are no universally valid recipes and rules. There are only individual cases with the most heterogeneous needs and demands—so heterogeneous that we can virtually never know in advance what course a given case will take, for which reason it is better for the doctor to abandon all preconceived opinions. This does not mean that he should throw them overboard, but that in any given case he should use them merely as hypotheses for a possible explanation.[8]

Jung was less interested than either Freud or Adler in the influences upon the individual which determine (or through which he determines) his character, and for elaborations of this area we have to turn to later variants of psychoanalysis.

It soon became apparent that the more or less exclusive focus on a few particularly salient features of infantile development (the oral and anal stages, etc.) was found wanting by thinkers and practitioners in the broad area of psychoanalysis. In America, H. S. Sullivan's 'interpersonal psychiatry', and in Britain Melanie Klein's 'object relations' theory paved the way for a much more minute and exhaustive analysis of the relations between children and those around them, and the mutual influences to which these give rise. Not only is a far wider range of *events* seen as important in influencing the child's development, but also an increasing awareness dawns of the importance of the *meaning* of these events for the individuals in whose world they occur: what is a psychologically significant event in one family may not be in another, this being determined by the construction which is placed upon it by those involved.

This major step in the demechanization of psychoanalysis is matched by changes in the way such theorists tend to view the nature of the relationship between therapist and patient: the child acquires its view of itself in the context of its relations with its parents; that view can be changed only in the context of new relationships, in particular that with the therapist. Thus Guntrip,[9] a modern exponent of the object relations approach, saw the effective factor in psychotherapy as 'not a "technique of treatment" but a "quality of relationship"'. It is interesting to note, however, that, far though they are from Freud's original formulations, there is often still more than a hint of mechanism and determinism to be found in the writings of these therapists. For example Guntrip, in the same paper, wrote that the unconscious 'is the accumulated experience of our entire infancy and early childhood at the hands of the all-powerful adults who formed us. We have no choice about its creation . . .' This formulation ushers onto the scene the psychotherapist in his familiar guise as expert; for the answer, Guntrip felt, is for our culture to become imbued with the findings of depth psychology concerning the 'basic necessities in the personal care of children at all age levels'. He sees hopeful signs that 'this process has already begun in the increasing education of all the social work professions in the principles of psychodynamics'. However, he warns against this being done amateurishly, though 'expertly done it can nip in the bud a tremendous lot of trouble'.

This brief look at some of the developments and divergencies that have occurred in the broad area of psychoanalysis does scant justice to the range and complexity of ideas which are to be found in the literature, and I am aware that there are a number of important themes and people that have not been touched on. However, I hope that this discussion may prove useful in orienting the reader for the later development of themes which have been raised here. But before passing on to consider other major psychotherapeutic schools, we should perhaps pause to reflect upon the changes which have taken place in the sphere of behavioural psychotherapy. In some ways these are parallel to those in psychoanalysis.

Behaviour therapy has not, of course, been on the scene as long as psychoanalysis, and so has not had as long, not only to change, but, more important, to reflect upon its changes and assimilate them theoretically. The major problem which faces the behaviour therapist is how to accommodate changes which are forced upon him by practical experience within a scientific dogma which is woefully inadequate for dealing with them. The close identification of behaviourism with science itself makes this problem particularly acute, for the behaviour therapist cannot simply abandon his behaviourism (discordant as it is with his experience) without risking the loss of his *raison d'être* as a scientist.

The way that some behaviour therapists seem to be coping with this problem is by hanging on to a scientistic behavioural jargon while at the same time quietly shuffling away from the basic principles of behaviourism. Thus, without any reference being made to the familiar mechanics of stimulus and response, conditioned reflex, and so on, 'modelling' will be invoked to explain learning by imitation, and 'cognitive restructuring' may be offered as an acceptable term for what seems to be more or less conventional non-behavioural psychotherapy. In this way the behaviour therapist is able to keep his scientific credentials while abandoning his principles, though not all have been quite as furtive about this as I may have suggested. Lazarus,[10] for example, quite explicitly recognizes that the simplified models of behaviour offered by Wolpe and Skinner have proved inadequate for his therapeutic practices, and this despite the fact that Lazarus himself started out as an enthusiastic conventional behaviourist. Many behaviour therapists

are willing now to admit that the nature of the relationship between
therapist and patient is of considerable importance to the outcome
of treatment, but this once again moves them, potentially, into areas
of theoretical complexity which they are ill-equipped to handle.
Behaviour therapy can, as has been suggested, carry on quite
successfully as a more or less useful collection of treatment
procedures, but when such therapists seek to legitimate their
activities by an appeal to their scientific foundations, that appeal
must be spurious. Still less does the success of their procedures
legitimate their theories.

There also exist important schools of psychotherapy, particularly
perhaps that of the American psychologist Carl Rogers, which have
started out from far less conventional scientific premises than either
psychoanalysis or behavioural psychotherapy. Rogers, whose work
has had an increasing impact on the whole field of psychotherapy in
recent decades, puts forward a view of man as a self-creating,
growing individuality who is far from being the helpless victim of
deterministic forces or unconscious conflicts. Rogers' views [11] are on
the whole optimistic: the man who is open to his own experience and
feelings, and those of others, will naturally grow in a psychologically
healthy and fulfilling way. If this growth becomes blocked, if for one
reason or another he is unable to remain open to his experience,
perhaps because it conflicts with some kind of standards he has
internalized (so that his 'self' and 'ideal self' are in conflict), then the
kind of therapeutic help which will prove most useful to him will be
from a therapist who encourages him to trust once again his own
potentialities and to allow the natural processès of growth to reassert
themselves. Thus therapy becomes a matter of sympathetic, 'non-
directive' exploration with the patient of his own experience and its
meaning *for him*. Rogerian 'non-directive' or 'client-centred'
therapy is quite clear about what the nature of the therapist's role in
the therapeutic process should be, and this contrasts sharply with
the traditional 'expert mechanic' role we have considered earlier.
Far from being there to fit the patient, one way or another, into his
own conceptual framework, the Rogerian therapist is there to fit
himself in with his client's. The latter will improve by elaborating his
own solutions to his own problems in his own way, and the
therapist's job is to help him to do so in his own terms, not to impose
upon him an irrelevant (to him) psychological system which can only
confuse or divert the course of his own experience. With this in
mind, Rogers [12] elaborated the conditions he felt necessary and
sufficient for therapeutic change, among which were the empathy

and genuineness of the therapist, as well as the 'unconditional positive regard' in which he holds the patient. In other words, the therapist must understand the patient *from the latter's viewpoint*, and be able to communicate this understanding to him; he must be a genuine *person* in the relationship, not merely a professional mask; and he must respect and accept the patient warmly and non-judgmentally ('unconditional positive regard' is often shortened simply to 'warmth').

Rogers' work is thus particularly important for its central focus on the *personal* nature of the therapist's involvement in therapy—not, one should note, that this had escaped the notice of Jung and of some other therapists in the more psychoanalytic tradition—and his views probably gained currency through his concern to back them with quantitative research. Being a psychologist himself, not only was he committed to providing some kind of 'hard evidence' for his views, but he also knew what kind of evidence would be countenanced by the social scientists whose background he shared, and it is largely the Rogerian school we have to thank for the impetus which gave rise to much of the research evidence to be discussed in the next chapter.

Rogers quite explicitly rejects mechanism, determinism and reductionism in his psychological theorizing, and yet in developing a view of psychology which will conceptualize man as 'a subjectively free, choosing, responsible architect of self',[13] he still appears to hanker after generalities, seeking 'lawful and orderly relationships' in the 'private worlds of inner personal meanings'. It may be unfair to accuse Rogers, on this evidence, of attempting to subjugate subjectivity by means of the tools of objectivity, or at least of hoping to be able to do so. Nevertheless, there does seem to be something slightly inconsistent about studying subjectivity in order to render it objective in the form of laws which can be 'put to empirical test'. In many ways this kind of inconsistency is even more apparent among some of Rogers' followers. For example, observation of the importance of the therapist's empathy and genuineness in psychotherapy has encouraged some to attempt to *train* therapists to be genuine and empathetic, and thus, inevitably I should have thought, to convert personal qualities into impersonal acquisitions. Again, modern work in the Rogerian field[14] seems to be focusing on a linkage of some of Rogers' ideas with findings from the study of information-processing machines as models of psychological operation. There is of course no reason why this should not be done, except that it seems a strange direction for Rogers' anti-mechanism to take.

There are several schools of psychotherapy which, as with Rogers, emphasize the importance of the individual's own conception of his world and the necessity for taking this as the starting point for understanding him. Some of these are rooted squarely in the tradition of European existentialism, others represent distillations of a number of psychological and philosophical influences into a more or less original theoretical position. The work of Ludwig Binswanger, for example, takes an approach to 'existential analysis' which owes much to, among others, Martin Heidegger. Binswanger's approach is interesting for the thorough-going seriousness with which it treats the patient's subjectivity[15] and attempts to unravel the patient's world in terms of his own meanings. Binswanger's work is, however, almost unknown in Britain, though he has probably had more widespread influence in the United States.

Viktor Frankl is another psychotherapist whose approach—'logotherapy'—owes much to existential philosophy. Frankl, whose influence in the English-speaking world is again largely confined to the United States, makes several points of importance to psychotherapy as a whole which once again demonstrate the contrast between this and more traditional kinds of approach. He is, for example, concerned to stress the *freedom* of the individual and his ultimate responsibility for himself, as well as the importance of an *unself-conscious* kind of engagement with the world. In this latter respect Frankl is to be contrasted with those therapists who have as a central therapeutic aim *increasing* patients' self-awareness. This is a theme which we shall take up in much greater detail later.

Frankl, perhaps because of his long association with the pragmatic culture of the USA, does, despite his existential affiliations, show here and there the same kind of tendency to mechanism which we have already noted in the case of Rogerians. For example, his observation of the disruptive nature of self-consciousness led him to advocate a technique ('paradoxical intention') by means of which the neurotic can disrupt his own neurotic behaviour by trying to perform it deliberately and consciously. In 'logotherapy' and 'paradoxical intention', I am afraid we may be seeing the foundations of yet another of the would-be patented 'systems' with which psychotherapy abounds, making technical claims which contrast sharply with the existential values which are supposed to provide their basis.

The 'personal construct' psychology of George Kelly[16] provides the theoretical backing to a brand of psychotherapy which also stresses the freedom of the person to determine his own nature.

Kelly's basic position bears a strong resemblance to the phenomenological school of philosophy: men build their world out of their personal experience, and the construction arrived at reflects a series of personal choices of ways in which to make sense of immediate experience. In other words, reality is not 'given' to us in some absolute and external sense, but constructed out of the interpretations we place upon our fundamental experience. These interpretations may vary within the individual at different times, and will certainly vary between individuals, since they are operating from different perspectives. Thus there is no single, objective reality, but a variety of constructions of reality which may be more or less satisfactory to the 'construers'. Kelly's is certainly the most profound and sophisticated attempt so far to elaborate the phenomenological position in psychological terms, and his writings have been particularly influential in British social and clinical psychology. It is not possible to do justice to his theoretical views here, but we should not pass on without trying to convey a flavour of the kind of psychotherapy they give rise to.

Since Kelly sees the basic activity of man in terms of his trying, rather in the same way as scientists are acknowledged to do, to make sense of his experience and increase his understanding and control of the events around him, it is not surprising that he likens the therapist-patient situation to that of the scientific research supervisor and his student. Therapy, for the patient, becomes a situation in which he seeks to increase his understanding of his experience and behaviour through reflection and experiment. The therapist's job is to facilitate this process of elaboration and experimentation as best he can. As with the Rogerians, the 'personal construct psychotherapist' will have no fixed idea about how people should *be*, and the course of therapy in this respect will be determined by what the patient believes, and discovers, about himself. In contrast with the Rogerians, however, there is perhaps a little more emphasis on the *technical* nature of the therapist's role (as opposed—though not totally—to its *personal* quality). Since in Kellian psychotherapy the therapist's job is to help the patient investigate, elaborate, and experiment with his personal construction of his world, he needs to build a repertoire of skills which, like those of a research supervisor, will help this process along, and this inevitably implies a degree of expertise not available to his patients in the procedures of therapeutic 'research'. The therapist may use his ingenuity in what procedures he devises, though some are suggested by Kelly himself as likely to be of value in some cases at least. One such technique is 'fixed role therapy', in which the patient is invited to construct a role for himself which departs from his usual self-characterization in certain important respects. He is then asked to play this role in real life for a certain period of time (perhaps a week or two). This is, of course, to be seen as an experiment in which the patient exposes himself to new experiences which may enable him to reassess certain assumptions that he had about himself and his world, and not simply as an attempt to change people through play-acting. In order successfully to facilitate such experimentation, the therapist must, in Kelly's view as in Freud's, keep himself as a *person* resolutely in the background: if he is not exactly a Freudian 'screen for projections', he is something rather like it, and should be sure that he is 'interpretable by the client in a variety of ways'.[17] The difference between him and the psychoanalyst is that he may potentiate examination of these interpretations through the deliberate use of role-play; he may produce, that is, different personalities for different occasions, depending upon his judgment of the individual's experimental needs at the time.

This picture of the therapist operating, so to speak, 'within himself', consciously varying his self-presentation, together with the more general emphasis on role-playing in therapy, illustrates the important part played by consciously directed behaviour in Kelly's system. The central aim of therapy thus becomes one of increasing the person's *awareness* of what he is doing and how he is constructing his world. The ability to become aware of oneself and one's 'constructs', and hence to become more skilled in the elaboration of a complex and sensitive set of interpretations through which one's world can be ordered, is thus a fundamental value of personal construct psychotherapy. It is, however, important to recognize that self-conscious skills of this kind can only be used in a context, as a means to an end, and it is easy to slip into a view of them as ends in themselves. There can be no point in becoming more and more aware, more skilful in your construing of your world, if you are not increasing your skill and your awareness *for* something. Failure to recognize this—in any form of psychotherapy—leads to difficulties which will be discussed in a later chapter.

Most brands of psychotherapy which we have not so far considered—and there are still well over a hundred of them—rely for their credibility on focusing on one aspect or area of human psychology and making it central to their system. In this they are aided by the infinite variety of human concerns: whatever esoteric aspect of behaviour or motivation you annex for the basis of your very own patent therapy, there is bound to be someone to whom it makes sense and who will make a satisfactory disciple, if not a patient. The more important variants of psychotherapy, however, may gain impetus and influence by virtue of the fact that, though the same basic process is at work, the area of human psychology they highlight is one which has wide appeal and potential explanatory value, and yet has been so far neglected. Thus, though perhaps limited in terms of their general applicability, such therapies may combine novelty with insight in a way which promises considerable psychological utility. Though lightweight in relation to the monoliths of psychoanalysis and behaviourism, they are nevertheless forces to be reckoned with.

Berne's 'transactional analysis' provides an example of one such therapeutic school.[18] While there are some aspects of Berne's theory which seem to be little more than slightly modified and diluted psychoanalytic concepts, his central achievement was to bring to the attention of psychotherapists the importance of *interpersonal strategy* for an understanding of many of their patients' problems. (This was not, of course, a *discovery* of Berne's, but a view which he was particularly successful in articulating.) In essence, the kind of interpersonal strategies, or 'games', which Berne focused upon are those in which a person, through the covert manipulation of a social relationship, may arrive at a 'payoff' in which he extorts public acknowledgment of a role he is anxious to adopt. Martyrdom, for example, is particularly easy to achieve by means of suitable provocation, and, despite its necessary discomforts, offers rich rewards in terms of moral unassailability and self-righteousness. As with other modern variants of psychotherapy, transactional analysts emphasize the importance of the patient's *taking responsibility* for himself and his actions as part of the process of change.

'Rational-emotive psychotherapy', the creation of Albert Ellis,[19] seems to consist of an almost unbelievably eclectic set of techniques and theoretical justifications which Ellis nevertheless manages to organize around one or two more central ideas. In particular, he emphasizes the role played in neurotic behaviour by the inappropriate (irrational) standards and values the patient holds, and to which, consequently, he over-reacts emotionally. Thus Ellis's aim is to attack 'magical' personal philosophies with the weapons of 'logico-empiricism'. His somewhat optimistic theory is that 'emotional disturbance is little more than another name for devout religiosity, intolerance, whining, dogmatism, magical thinking and anti-scientism; and if people rigorously follow the logical-empirical approach and forego all forms of magic and absolutism it is virtually impossible for them to be seriously disturbed'.

Ellis's therapeutic technique is to confront the patient's irrational beliefs and values in the most direct manner possible, even hectoring or ridiculing him if this seems the only way in which he can be made to see reason. Thus the patient who feels that sexual rejection is a catastrophe of major proportions and is thereby led to despair and impotence, may be exposed to the full blast of Ellis's rational scorn as he is persuaded that such rejection, though unfortunate and frustrating perhaps, has nothing to say about him as a whole person. We are here a very long way indeed from the neutral, opaque psychoanalyst, or the concerned and yet non-directive Rogerian. Ellis represents instead the embodiment of a supremely confident view of man, certain of its aims and its ethics, and ready to proclaim its values by any means at its disposal which can remotely be considered rational. Such means vary from argument to behaviour-shaping of the Skinnerian variety, from ridicule to 'shame-attacking' assignments which require patients to behave foolishly or absurdly in order to demonstrate that doing so in fact results in no great catastrophe. In rational-emotive psychotherapy we again meet factors which are common to several of the recently developed psychotherapies: the belief, for example, that the patient gets *himself* into a situation which only he can get himself out of, and that effective or convincing personal experience will be arrived at, often, only through the patient's actually getting into certain situations and, so to speak, rehearsing them behaviourally. Self-awareness is less of an aim for Ellis than the banishment of self-delusion.

'Gestalt therapy', the parentage of which is again attributable to one man—Fritz Perls,[20] moves us further from the treatment of neurosis and more towards psychological 'growth'. Gestalt therapists are as concerned for the total well-being of the normal individual as they are with the cure of neurosis, and the therapeutic techniques they have devised are aimed at a number of areas of human functioning which are felt to be particularly important in the attainment of such well-being. Among these are a belief in the importance of bringing into awareness the *present* experience of the person as a *whole*. Thus not only what the person is thinking and feeling, but what he is doing with his body (how it feels to him, what he is expressing through it) *now*, in the present, will be the focus of therapeutic work. Again, there is a great deal of emphasis on the person's responsibility for himself, as well as upon the importance for him of self-acceptance, of allowing himself to become what he is. Much of the therapist's activity will thus consist of devising activities and experiences which will put the individual in the position of discovering what he is doing and intending in the immediately present therapeutic situation.

Gestalt therapy is perhaps the most influential of a wide variety of approaches which tend currently to be assembled under the headings 'humanistic psychology' or the 'growth movement'. These are too many and varied even to be enumerated here, and attack psychological problems from widely differing angles. There are the 'body therapies', for example, which attempt to relieve psychological blocks and tensions by concentrating upon and manipulating their supposed foci of emotional and nervous energy in the body, perhaps by means of various types of massage and movement; there are also the myriad kinds of 'encounter group', in which 'authentic' meeting between individuals is engineered by a wide range of techniques, from verbal confrontation to, literally, naked exposure to the gaze of others. The rationale of these approaches usually appeals to some variety of Western or Eastern thinking, or a combination of the two, which stresses the importance of immediate experience, authentic, genuine relationships, and freedom. They tend to share a contempt for the narrow objectivism of orthodox Western psychology and philosophy, but beyond this, identification of common theoretical strands is difficult. Certainly, many of these approaches betray a fierce moralism which makes no secret of its aims for mankind. As Rowan[21] states them: 'Self-understanding, greater autonomy, increased spontaneity and creativity, a higher ethical awareness, lowered defensiveness, clearer perception, greater ability to take risks.' One might be forgiven for thinking that such a programme marks a radical departure from the traditional scientism of behaviourism and psychoanalysis; that we have found at last a way out of the mechanism and determinism which is the hallmark of so much of psychology and psychotherapy.

And yet, curiously, this does not often seem to be the case, and the aspirations of humanistic psychology seem to reflect more a modification of the message than a change in the medium. There is, for example, a certain paradoxical quality about the work of Abraham Maslow,[22] one of the high priests of the humanistic camp. For, having noted that some individuals seem to have achieved higher planes of psychological 'being' and creativeness than others, he goes on to suggest that a study of their methods, so to speak, will enable the rest of us to reach the same peaks. This uncovers a kind of crude, mechanistic pragmatism which surely, in fact, makes nonsense of human achievement. Again, the lofty aspirations in terms of human goals one finds in humanistic psychological literature are sometimes found to mask a strangely contrasting materialism. This, for example, is betrayed in a remark of Maslow's which Rowan quotes in his book. Having gone some way towards identifying his ideal person, Maslow suggests that 'the society which can turn out such people will survive; the societies which *cannot* turn out such people will die.' One is almost left wondering why Maslow did not enlist the support of B. F. Skinner in 'turning out' such people by means of conditioning techniques.

Neither are we, in the growth movement, freed from the mystique of the experts and their superior vision of what is good for us: they are always ready, it seems, to tell us what is, as Rowan puts it, 'more healthy and truly human than the average'. Malcolm Brown, for example, in a paper on 'the new body psychotherapies',[23] informs us that: 'Any person who cannot acknowledge the importance, and directly listen to, the wisdom of his own body is psychologically crippled and neurotic.' A slightly longer quotation from this paper, in which Brown discusses Reichian therapy, will serve usefully to illustrate the extraordinary quality of mixed mysticism and mechanism which is often to be found in such approaches:

Reich discovered that the curtailment of the longitudinal life-energy flow went hand in hand with the active maintenance of the repressive forces of the ego-defences within the neurotic psyche, and that one very effective way to loosen these repressive forces was to directly attack the seven rings of muscular armouring which pervaded the tension-racked body of the neurotic. By systematically attacking each ring by various direct body-contact techniques the Reichian therapist discovered that the patient's ego-defence system could rapidly be blasted open from underneath.

Sigmund Koch, one of the most thoughtful observers of the psychological scene, states a view of this kind of approach in psychotherapy with which it is hard not to agree:

. . . the group movement is the most extreme excursion so far of man's talent for reducing, distorting, evading, and vulgarizing his own reality. It is also the most poignant exercise of that talent, for it seeks and promises to do the very reverse. It is adept at the image-making manoeuvre of evading human reality in the very process of seeking to discover and enhance it. It seeks to court spontaneity and authenticity by artifice; to combat instrumentalism instrumentally; to provide access to experience by reducing it to a packaged commodity; to engineer autonomy by group pressure; to liberate individuality by group shaping. Within the lexicon of its concepts and methods, openness becomes transparency; love, caring and sharing become a barter of 'reinforcements' or perhaps mutual ego-titillation; aesthetic receptivity or immediacy becomes 'sensory awareness'. It can provide only a grotesque simulacrum of every noble quality it courts. It provides, in effect, a convenient psychic whorehouse for the purchase of a gamut of well-advertised existential 'goodies': authenticity, freedom, wholeness, flexibility, community, love, joy. One enters for such liberating consummations but inevitably settles for psychic strip-tease.[24]

The sad thing is that, having identified, so it seems, some of the major ills of traditional approaches in psychology and psychotherapy, humanistic psychologists have lacked the intellectual discipline and moral sensitivity to provide a carefully worked-out alternative. While deploring the fruits of traditional psychology, they have not been sufficiently critical of its methods, and indeed have often mindlessly applied the same mechanistic and deterministic assumptions in pursuit of their own goals, without apparently becoming aware of the paradox involved in doing so. Thus the psychotherapist in search of a scientific formulation of what he is doing is likely to find in the humanistic psychologies either a disguised version of orthodox mechanism, etc., or a contemptuous dismissal of all intellectual discipline combined with an untrammelled moral fervour. The emphasis placed by humanistic psychotherapists on the significance of relationships, the importance of immediate experience to understanding and change, the responsibility of the individual, and so on, is undoubtedly valuable, and continues a tradition in modern psychotherapy which started with Jung. But the methods used to exploit these insights, and to reach towards the moral goals which seem so self-evident to the humanistic therapists, are too often simple-minded and artificial, and typify just that mechanistic use of technique to which one would expect their authors most to object. (I am thinking here, for example, of such things as the use of nudity as a token of psychological self-exposure; the ventilation of anger at somebody by hitting a pillow which represents him; the self-conscious use of embrace or eye-contact as a means of generating intimacy between strangers, and so on and on.)

Though theoreticians of psychotherapy of the stature of Rogers and Kelly have gone a long way towards issuing a fundamental challenge to the traditional psychotherapies, the implications of what they have said for a change in the basic scientific structure of psychotherapy do not seem to have been accepted and elaborated, often even by their own followers, enough to lay the ghosts of objectivist impersonality, mechanism and determinism in psychotherapy. And even the challengers themselves may not always have seen where their insights were leading them to, or, if they did, may have taken fright at the extent to which a rejection of traditional scientific values in psychology would have to go. For if he is to become personal, subjective, dynamic and indeterminist, to give up the general for the particular, is there any sense at all in which the therapist can still consider himself scientific? If you see science as a *method*, the answer is probably 'no'. If, on the other hand, you see science as a certain kind of *stance* towards your own observation and experience, the answer may yet be 'yes'. My own view, already stated earlier, is that scientific method originated as a means whereby scientists could free their own experience from (largely religious) dogma. That means has, in psychology, now itself become dogmatic, and places a barrier between the psychologist and his subject-matter, such that he can no longer take it *seriously*, but must distort what he sees in order to maintain the relevance of his methodology. Much of the rest of this book will constitute an attempt to suggest what changes we shall have to make in our view of scientific method if we are to regain a relationship of good faith with our *experience* as psychologists. In other words, I hope to explore some of the conclusions psychotherapists may have to draw about the nature of psychotherapy if they are to take their experience with their patients seriously.

For there is no doubt that, despite the inroads that psychotherapists have made into some of the more constricting assumptions of orthodox psychoanalysis and behaviourism, the dogmas of traditional science still haunt psychotherapy. But, to return to a question I have already raised earlier, why does all this matter? If, as is probably the case, psychotherapists have recognized that what they do may benefit their patients no matter what they *say* they do, why should we need to become so concerned with their scientific theorizing and the implicit values it contains? Am I not simply involved in attacking straw men and obtusely failing to acknowledge the great pragmatic advances which therapists of all kinds have made?

My answer is that these dogmatic scientific values, implicit and deeply buried in the infrastructure of psychotherapy as they often are, can, and sometimes do, wreak havoc in what we actually do to patients. I shall illustrate this answer with a cautionary tale.

In a paper entitled 'Septal Stimulation of the Initiation of Heterosexual Behavior in a Homosexual Male', Moan and Heath report a form of behavioural treatment for homosexuality which was published in the *Journal of Behaviour Therapy and Experimental Psychiatry* in 1972, and reprinted in *Psychotherapy and Behavior Change 1972*, an annual publication of the Aldine Publishing Company, Chicago, whose editors evidently thought the paper sufficiently important for inclusion among 'the most significant literature published in the field of psychotherapy' for that year.

'Patient B-19', as the authors named him, was a young man with a long record of disturbed behaviour, drug abuse and homosexual activity. Among many other things, the authors describe him as 'hypersensitive to criticism and unreasonably self-conscious in public', 'disdainful, arrogant and grandiose', demonstrating paranoia 'often of true psychotic proportions', 'a severe procrastinator', depressed and preoccupied with suicidal ideas. He was also diagnosed as suffering from temporal lobe epilepsy. The authors' aim was to change B-19's homosexual behaviour by reinforcing (rewarding) heterosexual responses—a procedure they took to be reasonable on the grounds of 'the large number of studies reporting the effectiveness of various operational forms of pleasure in altering or "counterconditioning" undesired human behaviors'. The reinforcing stimulus was achieved by implanting electrodes into the septal region of the patient's brain; a number of electrodes were planted into other brain areas at the same time. Electrical stimulation of the electrodes in the septal region brought about subjectively pleasurable sensations for B-19.

Suitably wired up in this way, B-19 was next snown 'a 15-min. 8mm "stag" film featuring sexual intercourse and related activities between a male and a female'—an experience he did not appear to enjoy. Following this, he was introduced to septal stimulation, controlled both by the experimenters and himself. 'He likened these responses to the pleasurable states he had sought and experienced through the use of amphetamines', and indeed during self-stimulation sessions 'B-19 stimulated himself to a point that, both behaviourally and introspectively, he was experiencing an almost overwhelming euphoria and elation and had to be disconnected, despite his vigorous protests'. Following this experience B-19 showed a 'notable improvement in disposition and behaviour, was less recalcitrant and more co-operative . . . and reported increasing interest in female personnel and feelings of arousal with a compulsion to masturbate'. On being shown the stag film for a second time, discreetly watched through one-way glass by the experimenters, he became sexually aroused during the performance, 'had an erection, and masturbated to orgasm'. For the next few days the patient showed increased interest in women and preoccupation with sex. In view of the success of the programme so far, the therapist/experimenters moved on to the next phase of the treatment, which was to introduce B-19 to 'a 21-year-old prostitute' for a two-hour encounter (carefully described by the authors) in a specially prepared laboratory, towards the end of which time he was able to reach orgasm in sexual intercourse 'despite the milieu and the encumbrance of the electrode wires', which latter enabled the experimenters to make physiological recordings of the proceedings.

The outcome of this treatment is viewed favourably by the authors, despite the fact that B-19, 'while he looks and is apparently functioning better ... still has a complaining disposition which does not permit him readily to admit his progress'. He subsequently had a ten-month sexual relationship with a married woman, whereas, they report, 'homosexual behaviour has occurred only twice, when he needed money and "hustling" was a quick way to get it when he was out of work'. The authors feel that 'the success reported points toward future effective use of septal activation for reinforcing desired behavior and extinguishing undesired behavior', and they comment that 'plans for such treatment programs are under way . . . and will be activated in the near future'.

The reader will, I hope, be able to draw his own conclusions from this rather bizarre story, and will be able to relate the account of it to the discussion preceding it. What is quite plain is that a passion for objectivity and impersonality, leading, for example, to the pointless use of the designation 'B-19' and the provision of details of the gauge and duration of the pornographic film, the age of the prostitute, etc., results in an almost total blindness to the human significance of the procedures used. We are not told, for example, why this patient's general homosexuality was considered 'undesirable' when, by contrast, homosexual 'hustling' for money is passed over as more or less all right. There is no discussion in the paper of how the experiment (which necessitated a potentially dangerous brain operation) was presented and justified to the patient, and indeed his apparent feeling that it had not done him much good is dismissed as characteristic of a 'complaining disposition'. Again, his former drug abuse is mentioned disapprovingly in his history as evidence, presumably, of more 'undesirable behaviour', and yet part of the cure consists in providing him with a direct means of stimulating his brain, which in fact reminds him most of the joys of amphetamine. We are, in other words, lost in a technological fairyland (or nightmare), the mechanistic and impersonal values of which are taken as self-evidently valid, and in which the individual's subjective experience is overlooked as of no consequence. The occupants of this technological world, since it precludes consideration of such things, have only an astoundingly crude and rudimentary understanding of human experience and ethics, and hence no possibility of being self-critical in these respects. It is no surprise, therefore, that they can unblushingly betray the extraordinary poverty of their own values, themselves totally untouched by any kind of rational scrutiny, in speaking of 'undesirable' or 'desirable' behaviour, or in preferring their own judgment of whether a patient 'looks better' to what he himself resists 'admitting'. What we are dealing with, it seems to me, is not science, but a set of dogmatic principles which shows signs of running riot and crushing our capacity to think. The above example may be extreme, but it is not atypical of a significant proportion of what passes for psychotherapy.

We already have, then, some hints of what an alternative scientific philosophy for psychotherapy must be: in contrast to the present dogmatic orthodoxy it must take account of the personal, the subjective, the dynamic and the non-deterministic. Before we explore whether such a scientific philosophy is possible, and how it might change the appearance of psychotherapy, we should perhaps look to the research literature on psychotherapy to see what lessons it may have to offer us. This will be the task of the following chapter.

1 For the current spectrum in psychotherapy see D. Bannister (ed.). (1975). *Issues and Approaches in the Psychological Therapies.* New York and London: Wiley. For an historical perspective see D. Wyss. (1966). *Depth Psychology: a Critical History.* London: Allen & Unwin.

2 A satisfactory initial source is J. A. C. Brown. (1964). *Freud and the Post-Freudians.* Harmondsworth: Penguin Books. The writings of Freud himself are by no means as impenetrable as the non-professional reader might suspect. The *Introductory Lectures to Psychoanalysis* and the *New Introductory Lectures to Psychoanalysis*, and *The Interpretation of Dreams*—perhaps Freud's major work—are titles available in a number of editions.

3 Freud, S. (1933). Femininity. In *New Introductory Lectures on Psycho-Analysis.* Published by W. W. Norton, Inc., 1965 (p. 132) and in Penguin Books, 1973. *Standard Edition of the Complete Works of Sigmund*

Freud (1915). Trans. and ed. James Strachey. Vol. XXII. London: the Hogarth Press.

4 A readable initial source is V. Meyer and E. Chesser. (1970). *Behaviour Therapy in Clinical Psychiatry.* Harmondsworth: Penguin Books.

5 Criticisms of behaviourism in general psychology have been made by S. Koch. (1964). Psychology and emerging conceptions of knowledge as unitary. In T. W. Wann (ed.) *Behaviorism and Phenomenology.* Chicago: Univ. Chicago Press. For a more recent work embodying similar criticism see R. Poole. (1972). *Towards Deep Subjectivity.* Harmondsworth: Allen Lane, The Penguin Press. In the field of psychotherapy particularly cogent criticisms have been put by L. Breger and J. L. McGaugh. (1965). Critique and reformulation of 'learning theory' approaches to psychotherapy and neurosis. *Psychological Bulletin.* **63**, 338.

6 Cliffe, M. J., Gathercole, C. and Epling, W. F. (1974). Some implications of the experimental analysis of behaviour for behaviour modification. *Bulletin of the British Psychological Society,* **27**, 390.

7 Jung, C. G. (1954). *The Practice of Psychotherapy.* Collected Works, Vol. XVI, p. 71. London: Routledge & Kegan Paul.

8 ibid.

9 Guntrip, H. (1971). The ego psychology of Freud and Adler re-examined in the 1970s. *British Journal of Medical Psychology,* **44**, 305.

10 Lazarus, A. (1971). *Behavior Therapy and Beyond.* New York: McGraw Hill.

11 A good account can be found in C. Rogers. (1961). *On Becoming a Person.* London: Constable.

12 Rogers, C. R. (1957). The necessary and sufficient conditions of therapeutic personality change. *Journal of Consulting Psychology,* **21**, 95.

13 Rogers, C. R. (1964). Toward a science of the person. In T. W. Wann (ed.) *Behaviorism and Phenomenology.* Chicago: Univ. Chicago Press.

14 Wexler, D. A. and Rice, L. N. (1974). *Innovations in Client-Centred Therapy.* New York: Wiley.

15 See the chapters by Ludwig Binswanger in R. May (ed.). (1958). *Existence.* New York: Basic Books.

16 Kelly, G. A. (1955). *The Psychology of Personal Constructs.* Vols. I and II. New York: Norton. See also D. Bannister and F. Fransella. (1971). *Inquiring Man.* Harmondsworth: Penguin Books.

17 Kelly, G. A. op. cit., Vol. II, p. 620.

18 For an entertaining introduction to 'transactional analysis' see E. Berne. (1964). *Games People Play.* New York: Grove Press.

19 See, for example, A. Ellis (1975). Rational-emotive psychotherapy. In D. Bannister (ed.) *Issues and Approaches in the Psychological Therapies.* London and New York: Wiley.

20 Perls, F. S. (1969). *Gestalt Therapy Verbatim.* Lafayette: Real People Press.

21 Rowan, J. (1976). *Ordinary Ecstasy. Humanistic Psychology in Action.* London: Routledge & Kegan Paul.

22 Maslow, A. H. (1962). *Toward a Psychology of Being.* Princeton: Van Nostrand.

23 Brown, M. (1973). The new body psychotherapies. *Psychotherapy: Theory, Research and Practice,* **10**, 98.

24 Koch, S. (1971). The image of man implicit in encounter group theory. *Journal of Humanistic Psychology,* **11**, 109.

3

Research in Psychotherapy

It is unfortunately not possible simply to detail research findings in psychotherapy as if they were established 'scientific facts'. This is so, if for no other reason, because such 'facts' as there are more often than not tend to contradict one another, and also because research in psychotherapy is not carried out by disinterested, 'objective' automata, but by psychologists and psychotherapists who have a stake, not only in what they 'discover', but also in where they start looking. If, for example, your primary interest is to ascertain the degree to which your clients reach a higher state of 'being', your research strategies are likely to be very different from those you would adopt if your only aim is to rid patients of the neurotic 'symptoms' they complain of at their initial interview. Pyscho-therapists, in other words, have widely differing values, and these determine the context of their research.

In recent years there has been an explosion in research into psychotherapy which has resulted in a very extensive literature, a thorough review of which would not be feasible for this book. I shall therefore limit myself to a discussion of some of the problems which face the research worker in this area, together with an examination of some of the research results which are most germane to the central preoccupations of this work. Extensive reviews of the psychotherapy research literature are available elsewhere.[1]

For many years—most of the first half of this century—research publications on the nature and effectiveness of psychotherapy consisted for the most part of individual case reports written by practitioners of the more or less orthodox psychoanalytic school and its derivatives. A typical paper of this kind would thus consist of a description of the patient and a formulation of his problems, together with an account of the course of treatment and an assessment of the outcome. Quite clearly such reports must be selective in the sense that the analyst's view of what are the important events in therapy will be determined by what he is looking for, and by the theoretical framework in which he places his activity.

For this reason, case histories of the kind we are considering are not (indeed, *could* not be) purely objective descriptions of what happened between the analyst and his patient during the course of therapy and what befell the patient as the result (such a description would involve an infinity of observations, most of them trivial and boring in the extreme); rather, they assume the validity of a particular theoretical standpoint, and describe the events of therapy in the terms allowed by that standpoint. In this way, a psychoanalytic case report would take for granted the validity of psychoanalytic thinking in some important and central respects— they might focus, for example, on the 'Oedipal conflict' evident in the 'transference relationship', feeling it unnecessary, in view of the work already carried out by Freud and others, to pause in their account in order to justify the use of such concepts.

The model on which this kind of research was based is obviously a medical one, and makes the same kind of assumptions that would be made, for example, in a report of the treatment of a case of tuberculosis. It assumes that a diagnosis (or formulation) has been made which is reliably similar to diagnoses which can be made in a significant number of other cases; it assumes that an established treatment procedure has been carried out which could be reliably replicated by others, and which bears upon (in this case psychological) structures which the patient shares with others to an identifiable extent. It further assumes that the technical language used and the experiences described are shared by other professional workers to an extent sufficient to make their communication worthwhile. Now all these assumptions, and others like them, may be justifiable in an account of the treatment of tuberculosis (though this, as we shall see, is debatable), but even a cursory exploration of the psychotherapy literature suggests that their justifiability does not extend to the psychological sphere. There are two sets of reasons for this, one of which I shall call radical, and the other non-radical. I shall deal first with the non-radical objections to the individual case report kind of research which we have so far discussed, since these are the ones which specifically apply to it. Radical objections apply both to the case study research and to the research methodology which has largely replaced it, and I shall consider these a little later on.

The main point of non-radical objections to the psychoanalytic case study approach is simply that it is not succeeding in what it sets out to do—not (which is the radical objection) that its aims are misconceived in the first place. Thus the non-radical critic will accept that the proper aim of research into psychotherapy is to arrive at findings which are generalizable to certain (possibly diagnostic) groups of patients in terms of the treatment techniques which must be applied to bring about amelioration or cure; he will not accept, however, that the proper approach to such generalizable findings is through the study and report of individual cases. His objections, furthermore, will have more or less equal application in physical as well as psychological disorder, and centre on the lack of objectivity inevitably involved in the case study approach.

The psychoanalyst, it might be argued, has an emotional stake in what he is doing, and hence may be biased in his perception of a patient's improvement. His view of what happens, therefore, needs to be backed up by objective measurement. The theoretical assumptions he makes have themselves not been objectively validated, and may (indeed, fairly obviously do) vary from those of his colleagues, so that different therapists only *appear* to be talking about the same things. The diagnostic criteria he uses may well be largely personal, unless the contrary can be objectively demonstrated, and so his results will not be comparable with those of others. He has no way of knowing whether what happens to his patient is the result of his intervention, or is due to other factors entirely; this could only be established through the use of a proper experimental methodology which makes use, for example, of matched groups of patients in which a treated group is compared with an untreated control group according to measurable criteria. The therapist who relies on anecdotal accounts of what happens to individual patients in psychotherapy for the advancement of his knowledge has, in short, missed the scientific boat. To save himself, he must adopt more rigorously objective methods and submit his procedures to far more searching experimental scrutiny.

The type of research methodology relevant to these non-radical criticisms is in principle readily to hand in experimental psychology, which has long been concerned with just these kinds of problems. And it is to behavioural scientists trained in the academic discipline of psychology that we largely owe the bulk of research findings, such as they are, in psychotherapy. Many of these people are, it is true, clinical psychologists engaged in the practice of psychotherapy; nevertheless, they owe a scientific allegiance to their parent discipline, and it is this which determines their approach to research. Before turning to some of the broader and more radical criticisms which can be made of psychotherapeutic research strategies as a whole, we should consider what the experimentally more rigorous and objective approaches have unearthed.

In a now famous (or notorious, depending on your perspective) paper in the early 1950s, H. J. Eysenck[2] launched an attack on psychotherapy which was probably in large part responsible for the explosion in research work in this area which followed. Critical of the subjective nature of most reports upholding the effectiveness of psychotherapy, Eysenck showed that a consideration of such objective research studies as there were suggested no evidence in favour of a positive outcome, and indeed it seemed that psychotherapy could not be assumed to show any more beneficial effect than no treatment at all. Eysenck, whose preference is for treatment methods based on behaviourist approaches to learning theory, tended to use his findings as a basis for rejecting psychotherapy altogether as a valid undertaking (and by 'psychotherapy' he mainly meant broadly psychoanalytic methods). Other research workers,[3] however, were quick to point out that even from the objectivist point of view that Eysenck himself adopted, this conclusion is not justified by his observations. While it was clear that, taking 'psychotherapy' as a broadly uniform procedure, and assuming comparability of patients across rather diverse research studies, psychotherapy could not be shown to 'work' better than no treatment at all, to *make* these assumptions of uniformity and comparability itself involved an inadequate degree of objectivity and experimental rigour. What was needed, so it was argued, was to make a much finer differentiation between the kinds of techniques used, the kinds of therapists practising them and the kinds of patients they applied them to. One could not simply take, for example, 'psychoanalysts' and see if their 'neurotic patients' 'improved' more than patients who had merely been kept on a waiting list. The reasons why this cannot be done are obvious: psychoanalysts vary amongst themselves both personally and in terms of the techniques they use; patients differ from each other, and diagnosis is more an art than a science; 'improving' involves a wide range of criteria which will vary from therapist to therapist and research study to research study—some might focus on the subjective feelings of the patients, others on a more objective criterion such as vocational, social or sexual adequacy.

It thus came to be recognized that any research study in this area should focus *at least* on the following: the personal as well as the technical and theoretical differences between therapists; the personal as well as the diagnostic differences between patients; differences in criteria for successful outcome; differences in the environmental circumstances of patients during treatment, and so on.

The initial flood of research reports claiming greater objectivity than the psychoanalytic case report approach came largely from the behaviour therapy camp. Flushed with what they saw as the success of Eysenck's damnation of conventional psychotherapy, it was not long before behaviour therapists were publishing strikingly dramatic claims for the success of their methods. Wolpe, for example, claimed a success rate of 90 per cent in the treatment by systematic desensitization of anxiety neurotics.[4] However, it soon became apparent that many of these claims were based less on the sober use of a thoroughly objective research methodology than on a kind of scientific virtue-by-association, as it were, with the behaviourist philosophy underlying the treatment methods, and it was not long before such claims were modified. At the same time, more and more voices were being raised in criticism of a crude 'outcome' approach to research in psychotherapy, and a proper respect for the kinds of problems mentioned in the last paragraph began to develop.

The unfolding of research strategies and findings cannot be traced in detail here, but it may be of interest to consider some of the most salient features to emerge.

What seems particularly evident is that, as I suggested at the beginning of Chapter 2, what therapists *say* they do in psychotherapy is less relevant, in terms of what actually happens, than what they *do* do (this, however, is most emphatically *not* to say that what they say they do is unimportant in a general sense, as I hope I have shown in the previous chapter). A number of studies, for example, suggest that experienced therapists of *different* theoretical persuasions are more likely to behave similarly in their relations with their patients than are inexperienced compared to experienced therapists of the *same* theoretical school.[5] Much of the work in this area was carried out in response to the criticisms and claims of the behaviour therapists, who can be seen (from the perspective of the non-radical critic) to have goaded their more 'mentalistic' colleagues into a more responsible research attitude. Again, however much therapists may focus on the *technical* aspects of their procedures, an increasing body of evidence suggests that it is the *personal* relationship between themselves and their patients which is experienced by the latter as the most potent therapeutic force. Whitehorn and Betz carried out a pioneering study in this area[6] which showed that therapists of a particular personality type were more successful in the treatment of schizophrenics than therapists of a contrasting personality type. Research workers in the Rogerian camp similarly demonstrated in some detail[7] that therapists who offered the therapeutic 'conditions' of warmth, empathy and genuineness tended to be more successful in Rogers' client-centred therapy than those who did not—the latter, indeed, could be positively harmful to their clients. Even some psychotherapists of the more orthodox psychoanalytic variety found in their research[8] that technical procedures seemed relatively less important than personal factors. Such findings have been reinforced, if only indirectly, by further research evidence[9] that the very orientation a professional therapist adopts is likely to be determined as much by factors related to his personal characteristics and social attitudes as by any cool scientific assessment of its validity.

In this way, some of the more obviously constricting mechanistic assumptions underlying psychotherapy have been subjected to great strain—indeed, can be said to have been cracked—by empirical scrutiny. Not, of course, that the debate has been carried on without rancour. Whatever may be the case in the natural sciences (and it may not be so different), psychological research certainly does not proceed in a uniformly disinterested spirit of scientific inquiry: almost any research study can be questioned on methodological grounds, and alternative hypotheses for its findings can be advanced. Because of this, few psychoanalysts will have abandoned their theoretical beliefs on the evidence mentioned above, nor will many behaviour therapists feel that the aseptic rigour of their scientific dogma will not emerge triumphant in the end. There is little doubt, however, that the fervour of both sides has been modified by such findings, as is witnessed by the somewhat more temperate language in which they tend these days to express their views in the scientific literature.

The personal qualities of patients have perhaps received rather less attention in the research literature than those of their therapists. This relative lack of attention may perhaps reflect the passive position which patients still tend to occupy in the therapeutic equation. The therapist is active, and hence his personal contribution is likely to come into focus; the patient is to be acted upon, and hence his personal features are likely to be rather less salient. Even so, most research studies make some effort at describing patients in greater detail than would be afforded by the bare allocation of a diagnosis. Most psychotherapists are probably agreed in rejecting the inappropriate medical framework implied by purely diagnostic preoccupations, and will tend to look at their patients in terms of objective descriptions of their sex, age and socio-economic status, as well as a more or less factual description of the kinds of problems and behaviours they present. In this way such terms as 'anxious', 'phobic', 'obsessional', etc., may be used more as broad descriptions of behaviour than as imputations of distinct types of illness.

Looking at patients in these respects has in a number of studies revealed a trend which is frequently noted by research workers with some concern, if not alarm, and that is that the kind of patient to enter psychotherapy with the best chance of success can be loosely characterized as (relatively) young, attractive, verbal, intelligent and successful. This leads many therapists to feel that their best efforts are spent upon those who least need them. There seems to be little agreement among research workers as to why such patients should do better than others, though these findings lead to the speculation that psychotherapies tend to be middle-class undertakings with middle-class values, and hence are likely to appeal most to those who are most like their originators and practitioners. There are indeed suggestions in the research literature that psychotherapy is most effective where values are shared between therapist and patient, but the business of matching one to the other on these grounds has not been taken far as yet. It does however seem possible that, just as the therapist may choose his orientation on the basis of what he finds appealing to his personal values and characteristics, so the patient may, so to speak, choose his 'symptoms' in accordance with his personal stance towards the world. In this respect a number of studies suggest[10] that whether or not a patient experiences his problems as primarily psychological distress on the one hand or somatic discomfort on the other may depend upon a more generally 'psychological' or 'objective' personal orientation to the world. The implications this might have for matching patient to treatment may well prove to be a central feature of future orthodox research in psychotherapy.[11]

In general, the findings of research workers in the field of psychotherapy tend not to provide the kind of answers which one might naïvely have hoped they would. It is not possible, for example, to say whether Freudian psychoanalysis works better than Jungian analytical psychology, whether encounter groups are better than individual psychotherapy, whether systematic desensitization is more effective than interpretations of the transference (see page 17). Not that studies have not been carried out to attempt such answers: they have simply failed to produce any consistent picture, in part at least because of the enormous complexity of the psychotherapeutic situation. What we have instead is a number of suggestions that what looked to be important in psychotherapy—the technique adopted, the orientation of the therapist—is in fact less important than the operation of factors, such as the personal qualities of the therapist, previously thought by many psychotherapists to be of no account.

In fact there is no indication that any one kind of therapeutic approach is overwhelmingly more beneficial than any other. All approaches, from the psychoanalytic to the behavioural, tend to result in an improvement of about two-thirds of the clientèle and a lack of improvement in about one-third. This is, of course, about the average for a great many studies, using widely different methods of assessing improvement; while individual studies may differ significantly from the two-thirds/one-third ratio, there is no overall trend to support any particular technique or orientation against others.

Perhaps this finding, as well as some of the other points that have been made, could best be illustrated by referring in a little more detail to one of the most recent, and in many ways one of the most adequate (of its kind) research studies to have been carried out.

The study in question was carried out by R. B. Sloane and colleagues, and subsequently published as a book.[12] The central comparison made was between analytically oriented and behaviourally oriented therapists in terms of the effectiveness of their treatments with a group of patients typical of those requesting help at an outpatient clinic. The research was well designed in a number of respects: the therapists were experienced and respected representatives of their orientation; the patients were also genuinely representative of their group (many research studies rely on only mildly disturbed undergraduate volunteers for their subjects); the treated groups were compared to an untreated, waiting-list group; judgments of improvement were made from ratings given by psychiatrists who were not themselves involved in treating the patients; a number of objective measurements of symptoms and personality were made, as were measurements of the personal style of the therapists; patients were followed up over a period of two years. In short, the investigators took into account very nearly all the factors which previous research had suggested may be of importance to therapeutic effectiveness.

A thorough analysis by the investigators of the influence of all these measured factors on therapeutic outcome revealed only relatively minor differences between the two types of treatment. In fact, both kinds of therapy proved effective, and indeed more effective than previous research has often suggested. About 90 per cent of the total group of patients improved in respect of the main symptoms of which they originally complained, 75 per cent improved in their social adjustment, and 70 per cent in their work adjustment. There were measurable differences between therapists in terms of the style of their work—how 'directive' they were, etc.—but these proved to have little effect on the overall outcome. Measurement of the personal qualities of therapists thought by Rogers and his associates to be important (warmth, empathy and genuineness) also failed to show significant effects on final outcome. In this respect, however, it is of interest to note that patients who *perceived* their therapists to be warm and genuine (irrespective, that is, of how warm and genuine they could be *measured* to be objectively) improved more than patients who saw these qualities as less characteristic of their therapists.

Thus, neither the technical approach of the therapists nor their personal characteristics as measured objectively showed any signs of making much difference to the degree of improvement of the patients, who, however, did improve significantly more than the untreated group. This kind of finding does, of course, leave the mechanistic psychologist in rather a quandary, hopeful though it is in many respects for the future of psychotherapy. His problem is that he still does not know what it is about psychotherapy that is effective. His natural reaction is that it must be some kind of 'non-specific' component of the therapeutic situation which he has so far failed to identify, something encompassed neither by the technical operations of the therapist nor by enduring and measurable features of his personality, but nevertheless something that diligent search cannot fail in the end to unearth.

The research workers in this case did not fail to ask the patients themselves what they found to be helpful in their treatment, though, not surprisingly (in view of their orthodox scientific scruples), they are somewhat reluctant to take the answers seriously. Nevertheless, the answers they did get, 'subjective' though they may be, are interesting. At least 70 per cent of the successfully treated patients, regardless of whether their treatment was analytic or behavioural, rated the following items as extremely, or very important: (1) the personality of your doctor; (2) his helping you to understand your problems; (3) encouraging you gradually to practise facing the things that bother you; (4) being able to talk to an understanding person;

(5) helping you to understand yourself. Patients who did well in analytically oriented therapy also felt the following items to be important: (1) encouraging you to shoulder your own responsibilities by restoring confidence in yourself; (2) the skill of your therapist; (3) his confidence that you will improve.

It is inevitable that issues such as these—issues of relationship, understanding, encouragement, responsibility, and so on—should be treated with caution by conventional behavioural scientists (and there is no doubt that Sloane *et al* treat them cautiously). They certainly do not fit snugly into the orthodox categories of psychology and psychotherapy, challenging as they do any conception of psychotherapy as a procedure whereby the expert therapist 'changes' the passive patient. These are issues which must, if they are to be taken seriously, be translated into a language which takes due account of the necessary rigours of mechanism and determinism, and which consequently enables them to be identified objectively and measurably as 'variables' in the behavioural equation. Only after such identification could they be manipulated precisely enough to be of consistent benefit to patients. Whether or not such a translation should be undertaken, furthermore, must depend upon the reliance which can be placed on what patients think to have been important in their treatment. What is important, from the standpoint of conventional psychology, is what has objectively taken place; what the patient *thinks* has taken place is, relatively speaking, neither here nor there.

Not all commentators on the psychotherapeutic scene, by any means, have failed to face the more obvious implications of the findings of this kind of research, even though they might not have seen just how far-reaching they could be. In what can perhaps best be described as an extremely sensible book on psychotherapy,[13] Jerome Frank considers therapeutic methods as just some among many approaches to *persuasion*. What these approaches have in common, he feels, are precisely those 'non-specific' factors which such studies as that of Sloane *et al* tend to reveal. Some of these factors Frank identifies as, for example, the trust the patient has in his therapist, his expectation of positive results, his emotional commitment to the therapeutic process, the stamp of social approval which therapeutic procedures carry, the fact that therapy makes certain demands on patients that they change themselves by active response to therapeutic directions, and so on. He also takes (as indeed do several other theorists of psychotherapy) a *relational* view of neurotic symptomatology: the patient uses his symptoms, in a manner which he conceals from himself, to control the behaviour of the 'significant others' around him. 'The aim of therapy then becomes', says Frank, 'to support the patient until he gets the courage to face what he is up to. This may then enable him to modify his goals in a healthier direction or change his behaviour in such a way that he gains them more effectively.' In a nutshell, Frank believes that: 'Psychotherapeutic procedures can be viewed as forms of personal influence that aim to provide the patient with morale-enhancing experiences that enable him to shed maladaptive patterns and adopt more successful ones.'

Frank's view of neurosis as a strategy for attempting to control others while evading the *responsibility* for so doing, his conceptualization of the process of therapy as one in which the patient gains the *courage* to alter his behaviour, and his assertion of the therapist's role as one of *personal influence*, are, I would feel, likely to evoke a sympathetic response in most psychotherapists who take their experience seriously. These, certainly, are some of the factors which seem to me most central, and they have the added merit of according closely with what patients themselves seem to feel to be of importance in their therapeutic experience. In view of this, it is curious that Frank does not, as far as I can see, draw the obvious conclusion: that a thoroughgoing science of psychotherapy must take these 'non-specific' factors as absolutely central to its field of inquiry. It must, that is, make them 'specific'. The reason why Frank does not draw this conclusion is presumably because, like so many others in this field, he is hamstrung by his conception of what it is to be 'scientific'. In the context of mechanism, determinism and objectivism, it is simply not possible to provide an adequate treatment of such factors as courage, responsibility and personal influence (impersonal influence would be all right). The result, for Frank, is that he is left with psychotherapy as one of the 'healing arts' of medicine, unable to fit it into a truly scientific framework until, for example, neurotic symptomatology has yielded an increased understanding of its biological bases. How, on his own account of such symptomatology, it could do this, remains an enigma. Nowhere in his book does Frank's consideration of the research findings in psychotherapy lead to a critical evaluation of the research methods themselves, nor does he question the relevance of the assumptions they make. Conventional research methodology aims at identifying the precise, 'specific' factors which can be shown to be operating mechanically and determinately in psychotherapy. The fact that it has failed to do so does not lead to a re-examination of the expectation that they *can* be identified, but to a vague dissatisfaction with psychotherapy as a scientifically understandable undertaking. Nor does a consideration of what findings there are in such research lead to the formulation of a theory that would account for them.

These observations lead us into what I called earlier a radical criticism of research methodology in the field of psychotherapy. The reason why psychotherapeutic writers and research workers are reluctant to undertake such a radical critique is because it is likely to change our conception of what it is to be scientific in this field. To many, the idea that this conception *can* be changed may appear merely ludicrous; to others it may seem to be a course that should be adopted only in the gravest extremity. In my judgment, that extreme has been reached. But before moving on to a consideration of what such an altered conception of science might look like, I should first indicate what my radical criticisms of psychotherapeutic research methodology are. They are not, I hasten to add, startlingly new or original. I merely wish them to be taken seriously.

Both the main orthodox approaches to research into psychotherapy—the individual case study as well as the group comparison approaches—make certain assumptions which, if they did not make them, would make nonsense of their own activity in the first place. It may be enough for our purpose to consider only three of these assumptions: (1) that the findings of research are generalizable; (2) that the subjects of research are static; (3) that the relation between researcher and researched is non-reflexive (i.e. the subjects of research must be manipulable by the research worker, but the latter must be immune to a similar kind of influence from the former).

It seems clear that if what you find to be the case with one patient could not be assumed to be the case with similar patients in similar circumstances, if what you find to be the case with a patient today is no longer found to be the case tomorrow, and if what you find to be the case with a patient leads him to *change* what is the case with him, then there seems very little point to your research enterprise in the first place. And yet precisely these are the problems which face all research workers in this area. So far, most of them have dealt with the problems by shutting their eyes tight and carrying on as before.

The central problem, of course, is that psychotherapy does not involve one set of rational, intelligent creatures dealing with another set of inanimate objects, but does involve one set of people dealing with another set of people who are in turn having to deal with the first set! Furthermore, people deal in *meanings* as well as purely physical, determinate events. Thus the significance of what a therapist does to a patient will depend, at least in part, upon the way the patient *interprets* what he does. And patients interpret things differently. To complicate matters further, the therapist will himself interpret the patient's interpretation, which may (or may not) lead him to modify his original action, and so on. To treat this kind of process, for research purposes, as if it were an operation in physics or chemistry is simply absurd. What happens to one person in psychotherapy cannot be generalized (except with the greatest caution) to others, because one person's psychotherapy involves a unique combination of two people's sets of meanings (his own and his therapist's). Patients do not remain static and psychologically inert while therapists tinker with their 'behaviour': they manoeuvre in response to their therapists' manoeuvres, and two different patients will respond to the same therapeutic manoeuvre differently. There is no way that the difficulties presented by this kind of situation can be reduced to the structural simplicity required by conventional research methodology. Don Bannister puts the problem well:[14]

The master chemist has finally produced a bubbling green slime in his test-tube, the potential of which is great but the properties of which are mysterious. He sits alone in his laboratory, test-tube in hand, brooding about what to do with the bubbling green slime. Then it slowly dawns on him that the bubbling green slime is sitting alone in the test-tube brooding about what to do with him. This special nightmare of the chemist is the permanent work-a-day world of the psychologist—the bubbling green slime is always wondering what to do about you.

The individual case report approach to research at least has the merit that some detailed consideration is given to the patient's individuality and special circumstances; but the view given is almost inevitably the view of one person (the writer of the report) who assumes that he is describing something 'objective', without taking into account the perspective which he describes it from, and assumes, wrongly, that another person in a similar 'objective' situation will reach similar conclusions. This is not to say that individual case reports are not *interesting*—they can be extremely illuminating in showing the *kind* of things which can happen in psychotherapy. What they cannot do is establish a particular procedure as correct for others; they cannot, that is, show people what to do in psychotherapy.

The group comparison approach to research, despite, or perhaps because of, the greater sophistication of its methodology of experimental design, is the more simplistic in terms of the assumptions made about people. People, that is, become exchangeable units, passively reacting to the various sorts of stimuli manipulated by the experimenter. In so far as your interest in people is precisely *as* exchangeable units (e.g. as election fodder, or consumers of instant coffee), this approach to research may have its uses, but as a potential method of clarifying what goes on in psychotherapy it is a disaster. This assumption of 'exchangeability' has led in the past to some glaringly silly research efforts, in which it was felt, for example, that a therapy for neurosis could be tested on students with fears of public speaking rather than genuine patients, or, again, in which therapists of one persuasion are trained in the techniques of another so that results of the two 'different' approaches can be compared.

But even in the absence of such crude mistakes as these, the methodological assumptions of such research mean that it can only be interested in the mechanical operation of certain invariant features of the therapeutic situation—ideally the techniques of the therapist, but if all else fails some invariant feature of his personality would do. This means that even if some insight *is* gained into the therapeutic process, it is quickly trivialized and rendered self-contradictory. The 'genuineness' of therapists is a good example: because this form of research must assume that 'genuineness' is an invariant quality that therapists do or do not 'have', research workers will, having discovered 'it' (in the first instance from what patients tell them), then set about training therapists to have it. Just to be sure of when its there and when it's not, they will then devise methods of measuring objectively the invariant property of genuineness they have (like ZX 14 in toothpaste) now isolated. In reality, of course, we then have a group of therapists trained in ingenuine genuineness (which nevertheless must be 'real' because it's measurable), but who, lo and behold!, are no longer thought by their patients to be genuine. Sadly, their now objectively demonstrable genuineness (never mind what their patients think) no longer proves to be therapeutically potent. Objective research has now shown that the whole idea of genuineness as therapeutically important was wrong in the first place! Thus, if such research stumbles across an important feature of psychotherapy which is in fact *not* invariant and mechanical— such as the personal relationship between patient and therapist—it can deal with it only by turning it into nonsense of one kind or another, and ultimately losing it.

The repeated failure of conventional research in psychotherapy to come up with anything like what it expects it should be able to come up with has resulted in a kind of chronic frustration which expresses itself in what one might describe as scientifically degenerate squabbles over research methodology. Countless authorities can be cited for any particular view, countless hypotheses can be advanced to account for any set of data, countless errors of research design and statistical analysis can be advanced to destroy opponents' claims. Somewhere underlying this endless and singularly fruitless process is the myth of the 'crucial experiment': the belief that one day a study will be carried out of such perfect design, such faultless mathematical precision, such impeccable logic and such compelling empirical content as to silence all critics, who will instead be forced into mute reverence for the therapeutic truths revealed.

What psychotherapy research has done, then, is to draw attention to a number of phenomena with which it is not itself equipped to deal. As already stated, these are the phenomena centring on the *personal* nature of the relation between patient and therapist. If these personal themes are to be successfully pursued, it would seem that our research assumptions will have to be modified. Among other things, we shall have to recognize that strict objectivity is impossible, and that what happens in psychotherapy is a function of the perspectives of those involved in it. We shall also have to take account of the fact that therapist, patient, and research worker are all capable of functioning at the same conceptual level and may mutually influence each other. In the absence of any evidence that it is a viable concept in the arena of human affairs, we are also forced to abandon determinism, and we must grapple directly with the complexity of human *meanings* rather than trying to reduce them to scientifically attractive but entirely misleading behavioural or physiological stimuli.

To anticipate later themes for a moment, what this means is that the process of research in psychotherapy, just as the process of therapy itself, is to be seen as one of *co-operation* between researcher and researched (or therapist and patient) in the *negotiation* of a view of therapy which both can share. In the course of our inquiry into these processes we shall be encountering just those 'non-specific' factors in psychotherapy which are thought by patients, and by therapists like Frank, to be of significance: understanding, responsibility, courage, personal influence, and so on.

The scientist is, of course, usually seen as the possessor of great power, the unlocker of secrets which he can then use to bring Nature to her knees. He is not usually seen as having to co-operate with his subject-matter in order to negotiate the 'truth' with it. But then the situation in psychotherapy, and indeed in much of psychology generally, is not a usual one in this sense, and it may be that we have to change our idea of scientific methodology, and, even more drastic, modify our scientific aspirations of 'prediction and control', if we are to remain true to the higher-order scientific ideal of doing justice to our experience, of taking what we find in psychotherapy seriously. It will be our task in the next chapter to consider whether such an undertaking could be considered in any sense scientifically valid.

1 See, for example, A. E. Bergin and S. L. Garfield. (1971). *Handbook of Psychotherapy and Behavior Change.* New York & London: Wiley. Also, J. Meltzoff and M. Kornreich. (1970). *Research in Psychotherapy.* New York: Atherton Press.

2 Eysenck, H. J. (1952). The effects of psychotherapy: an evaluation. *Journal of Consulting Psychology,* **16**, 319.

3 See papers by A. E. Bergin. (1966). Some implications of psychotherapy research for therapeutic practice. *Journal of Abnormal Psychology,* **71**, 235; D. J. Kiesler. (1966). Some myths of psychotherapy research and the search for a paradigm. *Psychological Bulletin,* **65**, 110; S. Rosenzweig. (1954). A transvaluation of psychotherapy: a reply to Hans Eysenck. *Journal of Abnormal and Social Psychology,* **49**, 298.

4 Wolpe, J. (1962). The experimental foundations of some new psychotherapeutic models. In A. J. Bachrach (ed.) *Experimental Foundations of Clinical Psychology.* New York: Basic Books.

5 Fiedler, F. E. (1951). Factor analyses of psychoanalytic, non-directive and Adlerian therapeutic relationships. *Journal of Consulting Psychology,* **15**, 32.

6 Whitehorn, J. C. and Betz, B. J. (1954). A study of the psychotherapeutic relationships between physicians and schizophrenic patients. *American Journal of Psychiatry,* **111**, 321.

7 Much of this work is summarized in C. B. Truax and R. R. Carkhuff. (1967). *Towards Effective Counselling and Psychotherapy: Training and Practice.* Chicago: Aldine.

8 Strupp, H. H., Wallach, M. S. and Wogan, M. (1964). Psychotherapy experience in retrospect: questionnaire survey of former patients and their therapists. *Psychological Monographs,* **78**, no. 11, whole no. 588.

9 See T. M. Caine and D. J. Smail. (1969). *The Treatment of Mental Illness.* London: University of London Press. Also, N. Kreitman. (1962). Psychiatric orientation: a study of attitudes among psychiatrists. *Journal of Mental Science,* **108**, 317; D. J. Pallis and B. E. Stoffelmayr. (1973).

Social attitudes and treatment orientation among psychiatrists. *British Journal of Medical Psychology*, **46**, 75.

10 See for example D. J. Smail. (1970). Neurotic symptoms, personality and personal constructs. *British Journal of Psychiatry*, **117**, 645; F. M. McPherson and A. Gray. (1976). Psychological construing and psychological symptoms. *British Journal of Medical Psychology*, **49**, 73.

11 An interesting start in this direction has been made by T. M. Caine, B. Wijesinghe and R. R. Wood. (1973). Personality and psychiatric treatment expectancies. *British Journal of Psychiatry*, **122**, 87.

12 Sloane, R. B., Staples, F. R., Cristoll, A. H., Yorkston, N. J. and Whipple, K. (1975). *Psychotherapy Versus Behavior Therapy.* Cambridge, Mass. and London: Harvard University Press.

13 Frank, J. D. (1973). *Persuasion and Healing.* Baltimore and London: Johns Hopkins University Press.

14 Bannister, D. (1966). Psychology as an exercise in paradox. *Bulletin of the British Psychological Society*, **19**, 21.

4

The Scientific Philosophy
of Psychotherapy

We inherited, say at the beginning of this century, a notion of the physical world as a causal one, in which every event could be accounted for if we were ingenious, a world characterized by number, where everything interesting could be measured and quantified, a determinist world, a world in which there was no use or room for individuality, in which the object of study was simply there and how you studied it did not affect the object, it did not affect the kind of description you gave of it, a world in which objectifiability went far beyond merely our own agreement on what we meant by words and what we are talking about, in which objectification was meaningful irrespective of any attempt to study the system under consideration. It was just the given real object; there it was, and there was nothing for you to worry about of an epistemological character. This extremely rigid picture left out a great deal of common sense.

The writer of these words,[1] written in 1956, prefaced them with the warning that 'the worst of all possible misunderstandings would be that psychology be influenced to model itself after a physics which is not there any more, which has been quite outdated'. These were not, moreover, the words of some disaffected critic of the scientific orthodoxy, disillusioned with his failure to find a productive corner for himself in the intellectual establishment; they were written in fact by Robert Oppenheimer, prestigious physicist, 'father' of that most awesome example of scientific achievement, the atomic bomb. And yet his warning, like the arguments on which it was based, has largely gone unheeded by behavioural scientists, and, as we have seen in the earlier chapters of this book, the model of science which Oppenheimer characterized as outdated even for physics continues to exercise great, and sometimes damaging, influence on the theory and practice of psychotherapy.

Over and over again, the most compelling features of psycho-therapy are passed over because they do not easily fit in with our conception of what it is to be scientific—we cannot reconcile them with the objective, mechanical, determinate principles with which we feel we must comply if our activities are to be licenced by the authority of Science. As we have seen, this uneasy fit between the experience of psychotherapy and the orthodox scientific framework results in a number of strategies, none of them particularly helpful in furthering our understanding of psychotherapy. One course is simply to crush the phenomena of therapy into their constricting scientific mould, ignore the violence thereby done to them, and recite your scientific credo loudly enough to drown all protests. This, more or less, is the manner of orthodox behaviourism. Or, alternatively, you could decide sadly that psychotherapy cannot really be understood scientifically at all, and relegate it, as Frank appears to do, to the realm of the 'healing arts', awaiting the day when advances in biochemistry or physiology will render the whole business unnecessary anyway. Or again, one can lose patience with the whole intellectual 'scene', decide that science is hopelessly impersonal and dehumanizing anyway, and get on with the job of curing people and fostering their growth unencumbered by any rationalistic claptrap. A number of the 'humanist' psychologists appear to favour this course. Alternatively, and not all that different from this caricature of the 'humanist' solution, one can take what could be called a 'naïve technological' stance, and simply support any therapeutic procedure which seems to 'work', rejecting as tiresome and irrelevant questions about *why* they work, how you know they are *good* for people, and so on. These alternatives exemplify fairly accurately what has happened in the field of psychotherapy, and it is interesting to reflect that the resulting shambles is due almost entirely to the uncritical acceptance of precisely that model of science to which Robert Oppenheimer objects.

But if this is so, why has this scientific model not been abandoned long ago, especially since its weaknesses can seem obvious even to non-psychological scientists like Oppenheimer?

I think it at least plausible that the mechanist/determinist scientific model has dominated, and largely continues to dominate, psychology principally because of the *authority* it confers upon the psychologist. As we saw in the previous chapter, the psychologist, unlike his counterpart in the natural sciences, is dealing with a subject-matter (people) which is capable of answering him back. Not only is he open, as are all scientists, to the questioning and criticism of his expert colleagues, but he is also exposed to the scepticism of the very things he is supposed to be an expert about. One way he can make himself invulnerable to this form of attack is to espouse a philosophy of science which *objectifies* the people he is studying and renders them amenable to prediction and control. Any answering back they then do can easily be dismissed as a failure on their part to recognize the 'true' scientific state of affairs, and he will put his faith in 'behavioural laws' which he feels to be every bit as powerful as the laws of natural science on which, he feels, they are modelled. In other words, in order to escape his fallibility as a *person*—to which he cannot claim to be any less prone than the persons he is studying—he has to associate himself with a body of knowledge which is *im*personal. Having succeeded, in theory, in this enterprise, the psychologist is then caught in the dilemma that he can no longer deal adequately with his subject-matter, which *is* personal.

Perhaps, however, the project to objectify science could be made less attractive to the psychologist if it could be demonstrated that it is in any case not possible, even in the physical sciences; for then he need not feel quite so bad about having to work out an alternative. If, that is, science can be shown *not* to be dealing in cast-iron certainties, its methods *not* sanctioned by the stamp of impersonal reality, we may begin to see ways in which we can come to terms with our personal fallibility.

At this juncture, there are a number of philosophers of science who come to our rescue. Foremost among these is Michael Polanyi, whose book, *Personal Knowledge*,[2] deals precisely with these problems in the context of science generally. In this book, Polanyi demonstrates how all attempts to ground the scientific enterprise on some formal, objective method have failed. The reasoning behind such attempts runs something like this: the universe, or at least enough of it for our purposes, is determined according to the law of cause and effect. If we can find out enough about it at any one point in time, we can then calculate what it will look like at future points. Science then becomes the refinement of the *methods* by which such calculations can be made, and 'being scientific' means rigorously applying these methods to the 'facts' of the universe which are revealed to us. Thus, all we need to do is to discover the rules by which deductions from hypotheses can be tested, proper measurements made, and so on. However, Polanyi shows that none of the rules yet advanced as embodying the scientific method accounts satisfactorily for all of the scientific discoveries we have made. What all of them leave out of account is the *personal activity of the scientist himself.* That such oversights should have been made by 'men of great intellectual distinction' can be explained, Polanyi suggests, by their 'desperate craving to represent scientific knowledge as impersonal'. But, just as we have already noted in the case of the psychologist, the more the scientist succeeds in this project, the more he fails in the total scientific enterprise. As Polanyi puts it: [3]

This is how a philosophic movement guided by aspirations of scientific severity has come to threaten the position of science itself. This self-contradiction stems from a misguided intellectual passion—a passion for achieving absolutely impersonal knowledge which, being unable to recognize any persons, presents us with a picture of the universe in which we ourselves are absent. In such a universe there is no one capable of creating and upholding scientific values; hence there is no science.

The very word 'scientific' is still frequently used to convey a total freedom from values, a noble state of pure objectivity from which our wants, wishes, beliefs and prejudices have been purged by a disinfecting exposure to the rigorous checks of an impersonal reality. The white-coated scientist is seen as a kind of high priest of truth, toughened by his exposure to the cold blast of actuality, immune to the subjective errors of bias and sentimentality to which the rest of us are prone.

Another philosopher of science, Feyerabend, suggests that this picture is a fairy tale: [4]

But the fairy tale is false. . . . There is no special method which guarantees success or makes it probable. Scientists do not solve problems because they possess a magic wand—methodology, or a theory of rationality—but because they have studied a problem for a long time, because they know the situation fairly well, because they are not too dumb (though that is rather doubtful nowadays when almost anyone can become a scientist), and because the excesses of one scientific school are almost always balanced by the excesses of some other school. (Besides, scientists only rarely solve their problems, they make lots of mistakes, and many of their solutions are quite useless.) Basically there is hardly any difference between the process that leads to the announcement of a new scientific law and the process preceding passage of a new law in society: one informs either all citizens or those immediately concerned, one collects 'facts' and prejudices, one discusses the matter, and one finally votes.

The solution to these problems is, then, for the scientist to put himself back into his picture of the world, and to recognize the essential part played in it by his own values, beliefs and commitments. As Polanyi says: [5]

For, as human beings, we must inevitably see the universe from a centre lying within ourselves and speak about it in terms of a human language shaped by the exigencies of human discourse. Any attempt rigorously to eliminate our human perspective from our picture of the world must lead to absurdity.

And again:[6]

If man died, his undeciphered script would convey nothing. Seen in the round, man stands at the beginning and at the end, as begetter and child of his own thought.

It is of course hard for the 'man in the street' to shake off the conviction that the world he perceives around him consists entirely of 'things in themselves', existing completely independently and objectively, and it is perhaps, therefore, not surprising that he is ready to grant the scientist, who appears to be able to penetrate this objective reality, a special kind of knowledge, a knowledge of things as they really are. Once the realization has been made, however, that the way things are cannot sensibly be detached from the way we see them (as Kant also reminded us), we can begin to see that the scientist's knowledge is not an especially privileged insight into reality, but a certain *kind* of knowledge, a particular way (and a particularly human way) of looking at the world.

Science, then, cannot be separated from the people who carry it out, nor can its methods and precepts. The nature of the world is not imposed upon man by virtue of its independent, objective characteristics, but men create a world within which they can perform their scientific operations. In an important sense, the world is man made; the scientist is *responsible* for his picture of the world. The world is discovered in the experience of men, not in the revelation of some kind of final actuality.

What makes the scientific community different from other kinds of human association is the set of values shared by scientists. These probably cannot be stated formally in any very precise way, and almost certainly drift and change with the passage of time. For the most part, scientific values seem to focus on the ways in which *personal* knowledge can be shared and elaborated within the scientific community. Such personal knowledge is not acquired entirely passively through reading books or attending lectures, but rests, as Polanyi points out, on the *active acquaintance* of the scientist with his subject-matter—indeed, the very basis of his knowledge may be quite impossible to verbalize in any adequate manner. In this way the scientist may 'know' something in the same sense that one can be said to 'know' what honey tastes like: such knowledge cannot be acquired or transmitted outside the sphere of personal acquaintance, although it can be shared, and discussed, by those who have experienced it. What allows scientists to construct the intellectual edifice of science is their shared acquaintance with its subject-matter, and their shared evaluation of how to develop their understanding of it. Partly, no doubt, this may involve the use of certain *methods* to which scientists may give their assent, perhaps because, as with the principles of logic or mathematics, they find them *personally* compelling. But science cannot be identified with these methods: logic gives no guarantee of truth, and can be (and has been) associated with extremely unscientific undertakings.

There is, naturally, a sense in which objectivity and agreement are indeed important parts of the scientific value system, but this is not the dogmatic objectivity of behaviourist psychology, which is used as an attempt to *force* a consensus among psychologists. It is, rather, a kind of shared subjectivity. Oppenheimer suggests that the criterion of scientific truth:

... must come from analysis, it must come from experience, and from that very special kind of objectivity which characterizes science, namely that we are quite sure that we understand one another and that we can check up on one another.

For another physicist of great distinction, P. Bridgman,[7] even agreement of this kind becomes problematic, and the core of scientific activity becomes a matter of explaining the relations of individuals to each other:

I believe that in society as at present constituted the possibility of consensus, except with respect to the simplest situations and as a first approximation, is a mirage. There is no such thing as true consensus, and any ostensible reality supposed to be revealed by the consensus does not exist. To my mind this only underlines the importance of the individual and the importance of understanding the relations of individuals to each other. It also underlines the necessity of making my own report in the first person.

However hard it is to achieve, a central feature of the scientist's personal commitment is what Polanyi calls his 'universal intent', i.e. a commitment to a view of the world as shared. Thus scientists seek and work for objectivity on the basis of their personal acquaintance with their subject-matter; it is not imposed upon them from without, and cannot be set up as a *test* of the validity of scientific statements.

Specifying what scientific, as opposed say to religious, artistic, or indeed technological, values are is in any case by no means a simple task. A significant point seems to be that science seeks ultimately to convince us of a proposition's truth by referring us to evidence which we cannot in good faith deny, and that involves reference to a perceptual and experiential world which we find we have in common. The methodology of science seems, again in part, to be aimed at boiling down our more complex and questionable conceptions to simple and compelling ones.

If we are not to abandon psychology, and the procedures which, like psychotherapy, follow from it, to an undilutedly ethical domain in which theories are believed and practices practised simply because theorists and practitioners like or approve of them, it seems that we must indeed try very hard to find a *scientific* framework for them. And this because scientific statements seem to carry a special kind of conviction which is not arrived at by other routes. If this conviction is not attainable through the formal application of objective, mechanistic methodology, what is its source?

As I have already implied, the conviction which scientific statements carry seems to me to stem not from checking them against evidence from an outside, objective 'reality', but from internal experience. We are convinced because we may, to test our agreement with a scientific proposition, freely and unconstrainedly consult our experience (from 'ourselves as centre', as Bridgman puts it); we are not asked to accept it on faith, or on outside authority. What we do find compelling about scientific statements with which we agree is that we cannot in good faith deny the evidence of our own experience, and this is an experience which takes place *within* ourselves. And what makes this process so attractive is that we are compelled by nothing but our free acceptance of our experience; we *choose* to be bound by it. Just because of this, scientific inquiry carries with it a marked quality of freedom. We do not have to submit to a tyrannical intellectual authority, as in magical or religious systems, nor indeed do we have to accept the overbearing demands of an absolute objectivity. Our commitment to the values of science follows from the trust we have in the evidence of our experience and is willingly self-imposed. Not, of course, that there is anything infallible about personal experience, and it certainly cannot be used as a guarantee of any kind of objective truth or certainty. It does, however, constitute the permission we give ourselves to assent to or dissent from scientific statements.

The authority which the mechanistic psychologist seeks for his pronouncements is, then, a chimera, because the 'objective' world he wants to ground his authority in cannot in any case be divorced from the world of his *personal* experience. He keeps his 'objective' authority at the expense of inventing an impossible world and a pseudo-science.

So that we can understand better the process of psychotherapy, and how it can be investigated scientifically, it is also important to examine a little further what is involved in the kind of objectivity which we *can* accept as valid and this, as we have seen, turns upon the ability of people who are involved in the scientific/ psychotherapeutic exercise being able to agree with each other. Scientists seek consensus, and make conditions for it as favourable as they can by, for example, using the same systems of measurement and agreeing on a common language.

But although consensus is clearly a highly important part of the scientific process, and without it, presumably, there would be no science, it also cannot be made a *criterion* of scientific truth. If, in the case of the natural sciences, our sensory impressions did not *happen* to match (if, for example, we did not all see, even after debate and argument, the same number of coloured patches on a microscopic slide) scientific progress would presumably be impossible; but that does not mean that such progress could be brought about by insisting on a consensus of some artificial kind. Science capitalizes on the happy accident that, in some important respects, human beings share a common experience of the world, and can build an intellectual understanding of it on that basis. If you are wondering who in their right mind would try to bring about an artificial consensus as a substitute for common experience, you do not, unfortunately, have to look far for examples. Much of the dogmatic insistence on 'measurement' in psychology and psychiatry is directed precisely at this end. There are systems of psychiatric diagnosis, for example, which seek a monopoly of the kind of questions people can be asked: thus if *everybody* used a certain diagnostic inventory in precisely the same way, the answers obtained, which of course could only vary within the range set by the questions, would be taken to reflect the presence of real disease entities. Again, there is the personality theorist who appears to try to extend the validity of the dimensions of personality he feels he has isolated by giving them a number in a 'universal index' (which he has in fact created himself). In other words, because one can measure what one can agree about, many psychologists and psychiatrists seem to feel that one can find something to agree about by inventing a system of measurement first and insisting thereafter that people fit their disparate experience into it.

Thus, one does not bring about a scientific result by insisting on consensus, but the consensus comes about through an honest assessment of the degree to which one man's experience coincides with another's. Consensus is in this way a *personal* discovery; we *find* that we agree. Of course, if I see what you do not see, I do not at the outset have to conclude that either of us is wrong: I may first check my own experience to make sure that I am not being misled by some (relatively) fleeting illusion or hallucination. I may even negotiate with you concerning our respective perceptions. But my ultimate check will be against further experience of my own. If I were to abandon my own experience in favour of a wider consensus (based perhaps on a dogmatic assertion of what is 'scientific'), if I were to deny what I see because others say they do not see it, or because in some sense I am not supposed to see it, I should thereby *cease* being scientific.

Truth becomes possible as a concept because we *happen to* share certain important areas of our experience. It is thus a social concept, a way of saying what we have in common; it is to be found in the areas of our private worlds which overlap.

How we come to acquire the rather fundamental kinds of experience which we seem able to share (in particular our experience of the physical world) is obviously an exceedingly complex question, and it is certainly not my intention to suggest that they just happen to be present in some neatly finished form in every new-born infant. They may in fact be the result of complex negotiations between mother and child,[8] and they may vary from culture to culture. On the whole they seem to be relatively stable, and there is a limit set on the degree to which they are negotiable. That limit (though it may vary over time) is defined by the individual's personal acquiescence in them on the basis of what he finds at 'himself as centre'.

One reason, then, why the natural sciences have proved so powerful is because they are built on areas of human experience (basically sense experience) in which it has proved possible to find wide consensus on the basis of personal consent. For science to flourish, however, it is also necessary for men to *value* this approach. If I value scientific truth, I value your free discovery that your experience overlaps mine, and if I value scientific method in a wider sense, I will value the possibilities for communication which this discovery affords us, and the fruits it bears in terms of further elaborations of our experience which we can, at least potentially, share.

I may of course not value these things. I may instead wish to make my views absolute by *insisting* that you see things my way, I may try to impose my 'reality' upon you either by force or by appealing to some other kind of value which I think may persuade you—for example, that my system is effective, or economical, or will achieve the greatest happiness for the greatest number. Appeals of this kind, as we have seen, are often enough to be detected at the heart of various psychotherapeutic approaches, which is all very well as long as they do not continue surreptitiously to be put forward as 'scientific'.

This discussion of the nature of the scientific enterprise introduces no revolutionary new concepts. It simply reasserts a view of science which has been advanced often in the past, frequently, as we have seen, by natural scientists themselves. This view, which can be summed up as making the *personal* role of the scientist *central* to an understanding of his activity has, however, been almost entirely neglected in psychology and psychotherapy, with consequences we have noted already often enough. That such a view of science exists does however suggest that the student or practitioner of psychotherapy can cease glancing nervously over his shoulder at the tablets of the psychological law on which are engraved the dogmas of mechanism, and get on with the business of taking what he finds in his own experience, and that of his patients, seriously.

In many ways this means a depressingly fresh start, in which almost all the assumptions of traditional psychology, whether cherished or simply taken for granted, must be re-examined for the polluting effects they may be having on our psychological understanding and our ability to get to grips with our subject-matter. Because people are people and not things, the science we end up with may well not look very much like what we have come to expect, even if naïvely, from the natural sciences, and we may well find that we have to abandon all hopes of the control and predictability which once looked such an exciting prospect. But if there is disappointment at the failure of the original projects of 'scientific psychology', there may also be relief that we can be freed of its demands for objectivity, generality, and so on, and still remain scientific.

As far as psychotherapy is concerned, the most we can hope for, perhaps, is some understanding of our activities as people in relation to each other (patients and therapists); not, certainly, to predict and control them, but to provide a basis on which we can share experience, talk about what we are doing, and define the limits of our understanding.

Because our experience of ourselves, other people, and of society and the values it enshrines is infinitely more complicated than our experience of the physical world, we cannot expect quickly to find a common language in which we can discuss these issues, or more or less ready-made instruments with which we can measure them. This demands a tolerance of different perspectives, a good will towards the experience of others, a patient groping after shared understandings, which will require a very different spirit from that in which psychological inquiry has largely been carried out in recent decades.

Even if what is required is a fresh start, it is fortunately not so necessary to make it with an entirely clean slate. The methodology of traditional approaches to research and practice in psychotherapy may have blinded many of those involved to the content of what they were dealing with, but the content is nevertheless there, and has, even if often passed over as 'non-specific', occasionally been examined with painstaking care by some observers.

In the chapters which follow an attempt will be made to draw together some of these observations, many of which are not to be found clearly stated in the mainstream of psychotherapeutic inquiry, and to add some of my own. The guiding aim of this inquiry will be to stay as close as possible to psychotherapy as a *personal* activity (and hence to be 'scientific' in the sense advocated in this chapter), and to arrive at an explication of some of its more puzzling features without resorting to the kind of mechanistic dogma which destroys understanding and undercuts experience. I certainly do not have a patented system, or a ready-made methodology, or a final solution to offer. More, I hope, a contribution to a scientific conversation about some aspects of psychotherapy.

1 Oppenheimer, R. (1956). Analogy in science. *American Psychologist*, **11**, 127.
2 Polanyi, M. (1958). *Personal Knowledge*. London: Routledge & Kegan Paul.
3 ibid., p. 142.
4 Feyerabend, P. (1975). *Against Method*. London: NLB.
5 op. cit., p. 3.
6 op. cit., p. 265.
7 Bridgman, P. W. (1959). *The Way Things Are*. Cambridge, Mass.: Harvard University Press.
8 See, for example, J. Shotter. (1974). The development of personal powers. In M. P. M. Richards (ed.). *The Integration of the Child into a Social World*. London: Cambridge University Press.

5

Freedom and Responsibility

If people were no more than complicated machines, it would be reasonable to seek to 'cure' their neuroses by operating technically on whatever caused them. In other words, a mechanistic and deterministic stance towards psychotherapy would be appropriate. Such a stance has, however, been rejected repeatedly in this book. It is now time that the somewhat abstract arguments which have been used to support that rejection are substantiated with rather more concrete suggestions about how we may view the processes of psychotherapy in positive terms. The particular concern of this chapter will be to provide an alternative to determinist explanations of how neurosis comes into being, and how it may be changed. The alternative offered is basically very simple: that is, that neurotic behaviour represents the personal strategies of those who enact it, and is based on free choice. This is by no means a startlingly novel view—we have already seen in Chapter 2 that several psychotherapies hold it in one form or another—but it does confront the thoughtful critic with a number of puzzling problems. For example, neurosis involves psychological distress—nobody could *want* to be overcome with panic every time he or she leaves the front door or gets on a bus; nobody could see hour-long rituals of compulsive hand-washing as something he has *chosen* to do. And if these and other neurotic behaviours are something that the person is *responsible* for, why can he not simply 'pull himself together'?

The difficulty with these problems and questions is, I think, that they rest on some grossly over-simplified assumptions contained in our culture. The most blatant of these is that if I do something deliberately and successfully, I am to be congratulated for the actions which I am happy to be responsible for. If, on the other hand, I do things which turn out badly or, more important, which cause me distress, I look for 'causes' outside my own agency which will make my actions 'not my fault'. Again, if I do something bad or distressing, the alternative to its being caused by something outside my control is for it to be seen precisely as being my *fault*. If the neurotic is not ill, he must be a liar, a coward or a con-man.

The task of this chapter, then, is to suggest a way in which we can conceive of neurotic behaviour as the personal responsibility of the individual who enacts it without involving ourselves in simplistic accusations of blame and guilt: for there is one thing which almost (though not quite) all psychotherapists are agreed upon, and that is that blame and exhortation are just about the most fruitless ways to approach psychological disturbance.

The point of this inquiry is no idle philosophical exercise simply to justify a personal dislike of mechanism and determinism. It is, on the contrary, vital to the resolution of one of the most confusing paradoxes of psychotherapy, and one which must surely have puzzled any experienced psychotherapist. For, billed as an expert in the treatment of psychological 'illness', the therapist finds himself occupying a social position—quite possibly in some kind of official institution—in which he is expected to 'do something about' the problems patients bring to him. His very *raison d'être* is based upon what may reasonably be expected of him as a skilled technician. He has degrees and diplomas, and it is considered just that he should be paid for his services. He exists in a culture which defines psychological disturbance as illness, and his very title suggests that it is in the cure of illness that his professional competence lies. And illness is, of course, something for which people can scarcely be held responsible. And yet the therapist soon finds that one of his most central concerns in his activity with his patients is to negotiate with them a view that only they (the patients) can change themselves: he has no psychological spanners with which he can adjust their misery. If they are to change they must *do* something.

Most psychotherapists have to some extent recognized this problem in one form or another, even when they themselves have subscribed to a basically determinist psychology. Freudian psychoanalysis, for example, is greatly preoccupied with the phenomena of 'resistance': the ways, that is, in which patients sabotage and evade the analyst's attempts to interpret their infantile aims and fantasies in a manner which will make open to them the possibility of behaving maturely and responsibly. In dealing with this 'resistance', however, the analyst has a problem, because he has to square what he experiences as the resistance of a *person* with the necessity of staying within the bounds of determinist science. A contemporary psychoanalytic paper[1] states the case for psychological determinism very clearly:

In the first place Freud took over the idea of determinism from the physical sciences and applied it to the psychological sphere. The assumption of psychological determinism is still a cornerstone of psychoanalytic thinking. Briefly, it is the belief that every aspect of behaviour or subjective experience, and every aspect of the functioning of the mental apparatus, can be seen as the outcome of the events (psychological as well as non-psychological) which precede it. It implies that *theoretically* it should be possible to predict and to understand a psychological 'event' in terms of all the forces operative at the time and which have operated in the past. While this is theoretically so, *practically* such precision is impossible, although psychoanalytic psychologists make the assumption that every psychological manifestation or experience stands in a definite and theoretically explicable relationship to the whole of the person's psychological life. Psychological determinism has sometimes been referred to as the principle of *causality*. Determinism is, of course, an assumption which has been generally made in science.

And:

Psychological determinism has sometimes been seen as being in conflict with the idea of 'free will'. This conflict has, on the whole, been exaggerated. An individual may possess a high degree of internal security, and be in a position to exercise his judgment consciously in regard to which of a number of courses he will pursue. Nevertheless, the assumption of psychological determinism could still apply to his final decision, in that one could regard that decision as the outcome of the operation of many factors, including those entering into his assessment and judgment of the situation. However, because of the existence of unconscious mental functioning . . . the psychoanalyst would still take the view that many actions which appear on the surface to be a consequence of free acts of will are inevitably determined by the influence of unconscious psychological forces acting on the individual.

It would be surprising if this formulation did not place the analyst and his patient in an almost impossibly paradoxical situation. If the patient's behaviour is seen as being determined by '*forces*' operating '*on*' him, it seems scarcely reasonable for the analyst to characterize this to him as 'resistance'. And the patient himself might justifiably feel aggrieved at imputations of resistance to his *conduct*, when the theory itself suggests that his conduct is not conduct at all, but reaction to forces operating on him. Of the two, the psychoanalytic concept·of resistance is far more valuable than that of psychological determinism, but to be useful it must be seen in the context of conduct, or activity, for which the patient is responsible. How it can be seen as such will, I hope, become clear as we proceed.

Patients themselves, once they have been through a psychotherapeutic experience, seem less embarrassed about acknowledging
their behaviour as responsible action than is often the case with their
therapists. We have already noted in Chapter 3 that successful
therapy patients accept the importance of 'facing' problems and
'shouldering responsibility'. Writers on the psychotherapeutic
process, even when they agree with this view, are often more
cautious, presumably because of their scientific scruples. Frank, in
the book already referred to, speaks of the importance in therapy of
enhancing the patient's 'sense of mastery', apparently baulking at
the prospect of *actual* mastery. Even behaviour therapists have
become concerned with the conditioning of 'self-control' responses—
showing thereby, perhaps, an admirable regard for the pragmatics
of therapy, even if a blithe disregard for theoretical consistency.

In many ways, of course, the Unconscious of psychoanalysis and
the conditioned reflex of behaviourism have been created precisely
in order to preserve determinism in psychology and psychotherapy.
If the psychologist or therapist is to be an expert in something, it
must be something in which his subjects or patients are not expert,
something which can be known and manipulated by the expert for
purposes of prediction and control. Thus, when the analytic patient
claims that he is acting for some conscious purpose, he can be told
that his actions are 'really' the result of some unconscious wish; he
cannot successfully challenge the analyst's view, because only the
latter understands the mechanics of unconscious processes.
Similarly, the behavioural expert controls the patient by controlling
the 'reinforcement contingencies' (the rewards and punishments)
which operate upon him.

These theoretical positions are, of course, no more than scientistic
bluff. We have already seen that the psychological scientist is not in
the same position as he imagines the natural scientist to be. If he
attempts to predict and control his subject-matter (people), the latter
is perfectly free to observe his operations and out-manoeuvre him.
The psychologist can only possibly maintain his position by keeping
his scientific theory and method absolutely secret: his predictions
can only avoid deliberate refutation by being kept from their objects;
his measuring instruments (intelligence and personality tests, etc.)
can only be effective if potential subjects are kept in ignorance of
their contents. While psychologists can, and do, manage to keep a
measure of secrecy about their operations, this is not easy in face-to-
face, relatively unstructured procedures like psychotherapy, and
patients quickly learn what their therapists are up to. If the therapist

resorts to bluff in this situation, if he attempts, as it were, to render his patients amenable to control by suggesting that they are unconscious in a way in which he is not, he is liable rapidly to find his bluff being called. The bluff can most easily be called by the response: 'all right, then, cure me'.

The idea of psychotherapy as a technical operation on the causes of neurosis can in some ways, then, be seen as the upshot of a collusion between treaters and treated. It suits therapists because it accords with their social accreditation as experts, as well as with their idea of what it is to be scientific; it suits patients because the alternative would be for them to feel that their neurosis was their *fault*. This collusive idea is, however, negated in the actual course of psychotherapy, in which therapists find themselves, willy nilly, appealing in some way or other to their patients to take responsibility for themselves and *change* their behaviour, and patients, correspondingly, find themselves with the prospect of having to *do* something.

Partly because of social and cultural expectations, many of which have been deliberately fostered by psychotherapists themselves, and partly because it suits them, patients tend, on initial contact, to present their therapists with *problems*, in the anticipation that the therapist will find the corresponding causes and remove them through technical intervention. The problems which patients present vary in specific terms over a wide range, but in general terms they can perhaps be split into two or three broad categories. Most patients come to the psychotherapist via a chain of medical referrals, originating with the general practitioner and progressing through various contacts with psychiatry. This inevitably means that many of them will have every justification for seeing their problems in terms of illness, and they are likely to couch their description of them in terms of more or less physical symptoms. Anxiety, depression and fear are naturally describable in terms of their physical expression, and these somatic aspects of psychological distress are often what the psychotherapist first hears about. Stomach pains and nausea, headaches, dizziness, dryness of the mouth, palpitations and tension, inexplicable feelings of panic arising apparently out of the blue, uncontrollable weeping, all these are symptoms which may seem relevant to a primarily medical frame of reference, and patients may present them in the expectation that some kind of medical intervention will prove effective. By the time they reach the psychotherapist, however, it is likely that purely medical remedies, such as the use of drugs, will have proved more or less useless. In cases where the problem is cast directly in terms of psychological distress—fear, compulsion, lack of control, etc.—patients are likely to adopt a further hypothesis offered them by the experts: namely, that there is something causing their problem and that, if 'it' can be discovered, the problem will somehow go away. In this respect, they may expect the therapist to discover some forgotten childhood trauma buried deep in 'the subconscious', some psychological violence done them by their family, some deep-seated fear of which they are unaware, the unearthing of which will, like lancing a boil, cause the distress to evaporate.

It is, therefore, often with surprise and resentment that patients learn that matters are not that simple; that, for instance, an understanding of the history and origination of a complaint does not automatically remove it, or that there is no wonder-drug for the removal of their symptoms. They may be puzzled and hostile if the therapist responds to their presentation of the problem by probing into its meaning for them, rather than by accepting it at face value and launching straight into a course of 'treatment'. If, further, he suggests that the significance of the problem may lie in what it is *achieving* for them, hostility may turn to outrage, and rejection of the whole therapeutic enterprise. As Landfield puts it:[2]

A psychotherapist who wishes to convince people that each person must bear some responsibility for his problems as well as his cure works against heavy odds. His underprivileged patients learn early that life has limitations. They also learn that treatment for them is largely custodial and medical. His more privileged clients do learn that professionals will talk with them about their problems. However, they also learn from the pamphlets circulated by associations for mental health that an emotional problem is sickness . . . for which the person is often not responsible. A corollary to this type of logic suggests that if one is not responsible for one's problem, then one assuredly cannot be held responsible for one's own cure. To further complicate the therapist's task of encouraging his clients to assume more responsibility for their lives, the 'body' theorists attribute the cause of behaviour to genetics and spleen, while the 'environmentalists' attribute cause to external circumstances.

This, then, is the predicament commonly faced by the psychotherapist who is willing to remain true to his experience. He has to convince his patients that their neurosis is something to do with their own agency, something which can only be changed through their acceptance of responsibility for it.

The predicament has not gone unrecognized. One approach quite widely adopted by therapists is to negotiate some kind of 'contract' with patients, in which the aims of treatment, as well as their own responsibilities, are stated as clearly as possible at the outset. In the hospital setting, for example, Cooklin[3] has suggested how staff and patients may initiate the therapeutic process by examining and exposing any unrealistic expectations of passive 'cure', and agreeing aims of treatment which, with his active participation, it may be possible for the patient to achieve. Scott[4] gives an account of the problems presented by the 'medical' expectations which patients often have. He sees these as bearing closely upon patients' wishes to see themselves as not responsible for their problems, but rather as victims of illness, of society, or of the family. He suggests ways in which the hospital ward setting can be designed to counter these expectations, or 'barriers to treatment', as he calls them, and lead to more adaptive and successful strategies. Staff may, for example, avoid 'doing things for' patients *as if* they were ill, or not responsible, and may resist also any attempt made by patients' families to define the hospitalized member's behaviour as 'sick' rather than, in some sense, intentional.

Which brings us back to the problem we must now face squarely. How can somebody want, or intend, to be psychologically disturbed? Can we justify a rejection of the humane notion of 'mental illness' and its replacement by a notion of personal responsibility?

No one, I think, would wish to maintain that an individual is neurotic 'on purpose', in the naïve meaning of that expression. It is, nevertheless, a common experience of psychotherapists that patients *resist* getting better, and it is greatly to Freud's credit that he gave so much attention to this phenomenon. The resistance may be encountered, for example, in the form of patients failing to conform with suggestions from the therapist about how their treatment might be furthered (such suggestions might centre on things they *could* do easily enough, like keeping a diary of troubling events or symptoms, or learning relaxation techniques at home), or might simply be experienced in patients' failure to keep appointments, especially at times when some improvement seemed to the therapist to be imminent. Yet this does not seem to be a matter of simple dishonesty: there seems somehow to be *both* an apparently genuine wish to 'get better' *and* an apparently genuine resistance to getting better when it seems possible to do so. While the resistance may be *denied* by the patient (again apparently genuinely) his actions appear *undeniably* to be aimed intelligently, and often tenaciously, at just such resistance.

Perhaps a concrete example might at this stage help to clarify much of what has been said so far, as well as aid subsequent discussion. As in other clinical examples used in this book, it is based on my own experience, but for obvious reasons does not constitute an accurate account of the problems or circumstances of any one particular individual.

A young, attractive woman complains that she is sexually frigid. She has three small children (conceived in the interests of procreation only) and a husband who is sympathetic and understanding, and whom she 'loves very, very much'. He is the only person she has ever slept with, and they were married at an early age. She has never enjoyed sex positively, either before or since marriage, although once, when they were on holiday in the Canary Isles, it was half-way bearable. Apart from getting no pleasure from sex, she finds it painful. Her first explanatory hypothesis is a physical one: she believes that she must be 'too small inside'. She goes to her general practitioner, who sends her to a gynaecologist. The latter examines her and assures her that she is anatomically normal. She goes back to her general practitioner who prescribes drugs 'to help her relax'. These are to no avail, so her doctor sends her to a psychiatrist, who prescribes different drugs. These do not help either. The psychiatrist now refers her to a psychotherapist who suggests that she come to a therapeutic group. She attends the group for six months. Both she and the group members are puzzled by her complaint: she is not unduly prudish or sexually inhibited in any obvious way, though she reflects that her parents are on the puritanical side, and that sex was a taboo subject at home. Examination of this in the group is exhaustive, but discussion of the problem, in which she herself shows no undue embarrassment, leads to no improvement. A few weeks later she reveals, with considerable hesitancy and pain, that she was 'interfered with' by an elderly male relative at the age of five or six. The group members accept this revelation sympathetically, and one or two of the other women in the group confess to similar experiences. For some weeks this new information is examined for its significance in terms of what it may have done to her relations with men, and some discussion attaches to the rather seductive and yet rejecting, 'teasing' way she relates to the men in the group. This seems to clear the air a lot, but there is still no change in her sex life with her husband. After six months, the patient, the group and the therapist all feel that the best approach would be for her to have some marital counselling, together with her husband. The method to be tried involves discussion, as well as some quite practical counselling on sexual technique, as pioneered by Masters and Johnson.[5] She is enthusiastic about this, and consequently the therapist meets her and her husband for weekly sessions.

At this point, having in previous months run through a series of hypotheses about what 'it' could be, the first signs of resistance begin to emerge. The patient finds reasons why the sexual exercises to be conducted with her husband cannot take place, although there is a week between therapy sessions in which to find time for them. Her husband strikes the therapist as an exceptionally tolerant and understanding man, who is doing conscientiously everything he can to co-operate in treatment. He is somewhat bemused by the development of his wife's apparent lack of enthusiasm, especially after her initial keenness. The therapist encourages the couple to continue, feeling that the wife's problem may simply be some fleeting embarrassment about the project. The following week she telephones the therapist asking him to see her on her own, to which he agrees. At this interview she bursts into tears (which she has never done before) and says that she has come to see her problem in an entirely new light. She is not sexually frigid and, she now realizes, never was. She does not love her husband, and never has. She finds him physically repulsive. She does love the next door neighbour, however, and always has. Nothing has passed between them, but whenever she sees him, her knees 'turn to jelly'. She realizes that she kept herself from recognizing the problem because of what it entailed: she does not want to become involved in the upheaval of breaking up her marriage—she has nowhere to go (as far as she can tell the next door neighbour is quite happy as he is), and she does not want to destroy the happiness of her three children, who love their father.

Suddenly, then, a 'symptom' becomes an acknowledged problem of relationship, an agonizing difficulty, but in no way a mechanical breakdown—either physical or psychological. Moreover, the realization of her predicament burst upon this woman like a bomb—up to that point her search for 'causes' had been as diligent as that of all those who, for a total of seven or eight months, had been therapeutically involved with her, and only the threatening 'cure' of her frigidity with her husband led to her recognition of the true state of her affairs. The 'cure', naturally, had to be resisted, as there was no real problem to which it corresponded: she was not 'frigid' at all. Her 'frigidity', as long as it was left in peace, did, however, serve to keep her from an infinitely more difficult, though in no way pathological, predicament. Somehow or other, her left hand had managed to keep her right hand from getting to grips with that predicament, until the strategy became exposed by the direct challenge posed by marital counselling.

Somehow, then, and often in neurosis, a person may conceal from himself the motives of his own behaviour: he can attribute to external causes behaviour which is in fact purposive or intentional, and so escape responsibility for it.

To understand how this is possible, we have to correct the idea that *actions* are things which we perform in the full light of awareness, things to which *conscious* intentions and motives are particularly appropriate, while things we do 'without knowing why' are the automatic products of causes which we carry round like stones inside us, or which are imposed upon us by outside influences, and for which we cannot be answerable. In fact, satisfactory elucidations of this problem are readily available in the work of a number of philosophers, particularly those of the existentialist school. Much of what follows leans heavily on these ideas, and in particular on the views expressed by Jean-Paul Sartre in his *Being and Nothingness*.

The central point made in this context by Sartre, and others, is that human activity cannot be divorced from its *meaning*, and its meaning involves its *intention*. An action without a meaning ceases to be an action at all, but becomes simply a meaningless movement. Actions, moreover, do not have to be carried out consciously—indeed, much of our meaningful, intentional activity is carried out without any conscious deliberation on our part. This is fairly obvious with trivial activities like combing one's hair or changing gear while driving, but is also true of the much broader 'projects' in which one might be engaged—I live my life as though it had meaning, but would be hard put to it to say what the meaning was. Movements have a quite different quality from voluntary action. If you jog my elbow, my spilling coffee on your carpet can scarcely be seen as involving intentional behaviour on my part. Acts are intentional, movements are caused. If, then, you wish to replace intentions with causes (as, for example, the behaviourist would) you render action meaningless. This, in many respects, is precisely what the neurotic tries to do: to negotiate a view of his activity as meaningless movement. Such a strategy is only persuasive if we insist that activity has to be consciously acknowledged.

To say that activity need not be consciously acknowledged is not to say that it must therefore be unconsciously caused. The activity *is* its meaning and its intention. We split off our intentions from our actions only when we reflect about them, and this is in many ways an artificial process. It is only when we reflect upon our activity that we ascribe conscious motives and intentions to it; we treat what is in fact an integral part of our action as if it were an antecedent cause of it because, after we have done something, we can see that we had reasons for doing it. Sartre states the case as follows: [6]

> ... it is in fact impossible to find an act without a motive but ... this does not mean that we must conclude that the motive causes the act; the motive is an integral part of the act. For as the resolute project toward a change is not distinct from the act, the motive, the act, and the end are all constituted in a single upsurge. Each of these three structures claims the two others as its meaning. But the organized totality of the three is no longer explained by any particular structure...

Conscious motives and intentions are, then, constructs we invent to account for what we *have* done, they are not things which we necessarily have to consider *before* we can act. (I have on several occasions found it of practical help to make this point to patients who are poised on the edge of a rather anxiety-arousing course of action, but who interpose between themselves and it the necessity for 'making a decision', which they then find they are unable to do; which perhaps goes to show that philosophical points are not necessarily irrelevant to immediate practical concerns.) Action, in fact, must come before deliberation in at least one important sense, as Shotter makes clear: [7]

> ... before anything can be done with reason and deliberation it must first be done spontaneously; it is only as natural agents, not as self-directing persons, that we could discover any entirely new potential within ourselves. We cannot direct ourselves towards their discovery, as there is no way of knowing, before they are actualized, what our potentialities are. It takes what we have always suspected it takes ... courage. For to actualize new potentials we have to cast ourselves into new situations, suffer the effects they have upon us, and counter them as best we can—all the time, as mere spectators, observing ourselves and noting the results, being determined the next time the situation arises to do deliberately that which in this situation was successful spontaneously.

Here, then, is an observation fundamental to our problem: viz., that, despite superficial subjective impressions, human action does not always follow deliberation, and quite often the explanations we give for our actions have to be found (almost invented) after the event. In this way, we frequently cast around for reasons for our actions much as we might for reasons for the actions of others. We arrest ourselves in mid flight in order to justify our course so far, and, having done so, we delude ourselves if we are not careful that our justifications are causes, and that our behaviour has all along been consciously planned. Of course, it *is* possible to plan one's behaviour before enacting it, but that does not mean that one always does, neither does it make the plan a cause. And even in the case of planned activity, the *reasons* for planning it this way or that need not be, and indeed often are not themselves clear or explicit (in the case of obsessional behaviour, for example, long chains of carefully planned activity can be carried out for reasons which are totally obscured).

As Sartre points out, deliberation, far from being the ultimate source of our activity, the mainspring lying at its centre, need be no more than a relatively unimportant stage in our reflecting over our actions. And even when we do appear to will an action deliberately, there lies behind that will, as he says, 'a more profound intention' of which we are not aware. Consciousness of one's actions is always in the setting of a 'project' which is not conscious of itself in the same sort of way. Our ultimate projects are achieved, Sartre argues, by our living them, not reflecting about them. Much of *Being and Nothingness* makes somewhat impenetrable reading. The following passage, however, makes the point clearly enough:

I can assume consciousness of myself only as a particular man engaged in this or that enterprise, anticipating this or that success, fearing this or that result, and by means of the ensemble of these anticipations, outlining his whole *figure*. Indeed it is thus that I am apprehending myself at this moment when I am writing; I am not the simple perceptive consciousness of my hand which is making marks on the paper. I am well in advance of this hand all the way to the completion of the book and to the meaning of this book—and of philosophical activity in general—in my life. It is within the compass of this project (i.e. within the compass of what I am) that there are inserted certain projects toward more restricted possibilities such as that of presenting this or that idea in this or that way or of ceasing to write for a moment or of paging through a volume in which I am looking for this or that reference, etc. Nevertheless it would be an error to believe that there is an analytical and differentiated consciousness corresponding to this global choice. My ultimate and initial project—for these are but one—is, as we shall see, always the outline of a solution of the problem of being. But this solution is not first conceived and then realized; we *are* this solution. We make it exist by means of our very engagement, and therefore we shall be able to apprehend it only by living it. Thus we are always wholly present to ourselves; but precisely because we are wholly present, we cannot hope to have an analytical and detailed consciousness of what we are. [8]

Our activity, then, in so far as it is activity and not meaningless movement, is saturated everywhere with intention, as an integral part of it, whether or not we recognize it consciously.

The therapist's first task must then be to decide whether his patient's behaviour is activity or merely movement. The latter alternative is certainly not impossible—it may be that the nervous tic which a patient complains of is the result of organic disease interfering with his motor activity and thereby rendering aspects of it meaningless. If, however, the therapist decides that the patient's behaviour does indeed represent activity, his job then becomes one of helping the patient to investigate what he is *intending* by it, and to see that his conscious protestations and justifications, when these conflict with the intention of his actions, have in fact no impelling claim to be considered as more real or more genuine than, or in any way necessarily prior to or invalidating, the 'intending behaviour'.

A patient's activity, then, whether or not he is aware of it, has a meaning which can only be understood in terms of its intention. He has *reasons* for behaving the way he does, and while reasons may be a certain kind of cause, they are not causes in the sense of inexorable forces operating on the individual—they are causes he chooses. Passive reflection is by no means the best method of discovering what one's intentions are—one has to learn to read off the meaning of one's activity (its intention) in much the same way as one reads the intentions of others, i.e. by observing the effects of their behaviour on the world around them. The relation between action and reflection is of course a complex one, and in our observation of ourselves we are constantly interpreting and reinterpreting the meaning of our actions (especially when they do not turn out very successfully). We shall be examining this problem in a little more detail in the next chapter, largely because it is a problem which lies at the very heart of neurosis: it is in the way we explain to ourselves the meaning of our actions that we have the greatest opportunities for self-deception. But for the moment, enough may have been said for us at least to be able to accept that it is by no means obvious that we can expect to *know* what the intentions of our actions are.

Of course the neurotic does not *want* the distressing mental and physical experiences to which his anxiety gives rise, but at the same time it is necessary to recognize that they are the result of strategies which he is carrying out, and which are directed at a certain end. This is by no means to say that he wants to suffer for, say, masochistic reasons, but rather that the broader intention of his activity inevitably involves suffering. In order to avoid social confrontations (an aim which, for one reason or another, he is unable to acknowledge), he, as it were, makes use of the bodily accompaniments of anxiety (tension, gastric pain, etc.) to turn his fear into an *illness* which provides a social justification for not going to parties, facing difficult situations at work, and so on. Absence of the physical distress he experiences would, in other words, bring him face to face with a kind of distress he would be much less willing to experience. He clings on to his symptoms not out of any bloody-minded stubbornness (which perhaps the notion of 'resistance' is liable to evoke) but because he has very good reasons to do so. In order to change, he must find equally good reasons for abandoning his symptoms, and that is why he cannot simply 'pull himself together'. Being unable to change at the drop of a hat does not, therefore, imply that your behaviour is hopelessly determined by leaden causes, but that you have very good reasons—of which you do not have to be aware—for staying the way you are.

It is of course true that *seeing* that you have good reasons for being the way you are may go some way to convincing you of the *possibility* of change, and this presumably is the value of 'insight' in psychotherapy. But on its own it is not enough. Moreover, seeing what your reasons are may not even be essential to change. Accepting that you *have* reasons, even though you can't identify them, may be the more essential first step towards change. This can, I think, be cast in terms of *accepting responsibility* for your conduct, even though you don't know *why* you do it.

In some ways, to ask somebody to accept responsibility for conduct they do not themselves understand may not be such an unusual request as it appears. It is not uncommon, for example, for a person to accept responsibility for a *mistake*. Mistakes are not something we make *on purpose*, and yet we still make them—if we are not ourselves responsible for them, who is? Again, if babies and small children were not held responsible for their actions, they would be unlikely to develop the kinds of skills we expect from them as adults.

In this way, perhaps, we can draw an analogy between neurotic behaviour and the behaviour of children which may go some way to clarifying the relation between responsibility and blame. This is particularly important if we are to provide an acceptable alternative to the 'illness' model of neurosis, that is, one which does not result in inhumane (and obviously inaccurate) accusations that neurosis is the individual's 'own fault'.

We do not expect small children to develop motor co-ordination and social skill without practice. We therefore do not *blame* them for being physically clumsy or socially gauche. And yet we *do* expect them to identify the source of such behaviour (as their own), and in this respect to acknowledge responsibility for it. A child who breaks a teapot because he is more interested in looking out of the window than attending to the angle of the tray (involved, that is, in a broader project than that of clearing the table, but one which nevertheless has consequences for the success with which the latter is done) may not be blamed for breaking it, but nevertheless may be forcefully reminded that it was he who did it. In this way, too, the adult readily recognizes the absurdity of the child's claim that 'it wasn't me', and will probably reflect that that claim stems from a fear of blame. In many ways this is precisely the position of the neurotic who fears that his behaviour, if seen as *his*, will carry an immediate imputation of blame. And yet, of course, he cannot be blamed any more than the child for behaviour over which, though he is responsible for it, he has not yet gained mastery.

The person, then, is responsible for his neurotic behaviour, and has good reasons for it. Having accepted this, he then has to *do* something about it; as well as developing reasons for abandoning it, he will have to involve himself actively in overcoming it, in mastering it.

Just as it is possible, through reflection, to delude oneself about one's intentions, so it is possible to delude oneself that one can change one's intentions reflectively in a way which will result in new activity. 'Knowing what the problem is' does not, in other words, automatically enable the person to deal effectively with it. The foundering of New Year resolutions provides a common example of this observation. To challenge his symptoms, face his fears, learn new social skills, requires that the neurotic confront them *bodily*, and no amount of rumination can achieve this for him. And what he needs above all for this is *courage*.

If we were simply the victims of causes operating upon us, we should not need courage to deal with what we find psychologically distressing—we should simply need to seek out technical help in getting the causes of our behaviour identified and changed. Since, however, neurotic behaviour involves intentional activity, only the person himself can change it, and that requires effort (courage) on his part. The therapist's role in this then becomes not one of technical manipulation—*he* does not change the patient—but one of *encouragement* (here again one is reminded of the words used by patients themselves when describing what they find useful in psychotherapy).

In many respects this provides a more satisfactory theoretical framework in which to place what have largely been seen as therapeutic techniques than that afforded by traditional psychotherapeutic and behavioural theories, since it reflects more closely what actually happens in therapy. The methods of behaviour therapy—systematic desensitization, social skills training, and so on—can in this way be seen as procedures of encouragement rather than as conditioning techniques, and indeed in this respect behaviour therapy has a great deal to offer. Such methods open up to the patient ways in which he can confront his problems bodily and deal with them actively and directly. Once we have jettisoned the simplistic dogma of science it is supposed to support, the behaviour therapist's emphasis on *behaviour* is in this way crucial, since it enables us to recognize the therapeutic necessity for the patient actually to do something, to operate actively on his experience. This is certainly an important advance on the idea that changes are made by juggling with the intrapsychic contents of the person's 'unconscious'.

There is perhaps a sense in which the procedures whereby a therapist may encourage a patient to get to grips with his predicament, to challenge his fears and actively to experience their resolution, may be seen as technical, but technical in a weak sense. They do not reflect laws of behaviour or the determining influence of conditioned reflexes, but may be seen as flexible strategies which may or may not prove useful to the individual, and they must always be set in the context of the meaning he attaches to them. The bather may deal with the cold sea either by inching into it gradually (behavioural 'systematic desensitization') or by plunging in headlong (behavioural 'implosion'). The method he chooses depends on him, and to elevate either to *the* method would cause a lot of people a good deal of discomfort (not to mention the fact that it is also possible to stay on the beach, or to reserve one's bathing for heated swimming pools).

The therapist who sees his role as purely technical is likely to approach his patients with a kind of psychological tool-kit which, once he has exhausted its capabilities without success, will leave him despairingly bereft of ideas. On the other hand, the therapist who sees his 'technical' activity as flexibly in the service of the general aim of encouragement, will be able to adapt his strategies to the unique set of meanings generated in the relationship between himself and his patient—he will be able to make new tools without, for example, worrying about whether they conform to specifications established by the 'laws of behavioural science'. As long as they fit in with the patient's personal set of meanings, as long as *he* can use them, they will fill the bill quite adequately.

The patient who has the courage to face his problems, to confront them bodily, will discover his freedom to change in his own experience, and will acquire reasons for behaving in ways that he had formerly felt not to be possible. He may also, of course, opt for staying as he was before, but if so he can no longer deceive himself that he is not responsible for doing so—the choice is freely his.

All this, naturally enough, has implications also for the ethics of psychotherapy. If both therapist and patient are looked upon as each independently responsible for their own conduct—whether or not they are able consciously to specify their aims—it becomes, as we have seen, impossible to characterize psychotherapy as a technical procedure. The therapist becomes a guide rather than an expert, a fellow investigator rather than an authority. While he will certainly have influence, his job is not to influence his patients towards any *particular* ends, but to help them acknowledge their own freedom, to recognize that the responsibility for what they do resides with them, and not him. It is unlikely that anyone who accepts the validity of this standpoint will be particularly concerned with the removal of 'symptoms'. 'Illness' behaviour is likely to be seen as strategic, and the therapist will be much more interested in what the patient *means by* his symptoms than he will in simply removing them mechanically. Indeed, he will recognize that, unless there are compelling reasons to believe that the patient's symptoms are in the strict sense unintentional and without meaning (because physically caused, for example), it would be absurd for him to try to remove them.

The therapist must also recognize that he is himself inevitably subscribing to a moral standpoint, i.e. that it is *right* for him to lead people towards a recognition of their freedom. Whether this is a worthier aim than that of, say, conditioning people to being contented and productive members of society, 'adjusted' in their work and play, is entirely debatable. But it is not a less *valid* aim in the sense of being less scientifically respectable or credible. Indeed, that people *are* free, that their behaviour is not simply determined by their biochemistry or conditioned through their 'reinforcement history', conforms more closely to the experience of psychotherapy, and hence to the model of science developed in the previous chapter, than do many competing views.

The therapist who adopts this viewpoint and this moral position is likely to be less concerned than many about what patients do *with* their freedom, and will be prepared for therapeutic outcomes which a few years ago, if not now, might have been frowned upon in more conventional psychiatric circles. A patient may, for example, come to see his or her marriage as hopeless, and get divorced; a person who expresses a wish initially to be 'rid' of homosexual feelings or behaviour may come to accept and value them.

Because of his belief that people's 'wants' and 'needs' are not necessarily a total account of their intentions, such a therapist is unlikely to accept patients' initial versions of their predicament at face value, and he will always run the risk of events unfolding during therapy which were not foreseeable. The most alarming possibility he has to envisage is perhaps that of a patient's suicide. It is clearly possible that a person could come, through therapy, to see that his 'neurosis' was hiding from him a set of circumstances which he now finds unbearable, and that suicide is a solution within the range of his capabilities. Few therapists are likely to see a patient's choice of suicide as a satisfactory solution, however, and this suggests that there may be more to therapy than *just* encouraging people to accept responsibility for themselves. In recognizing that he is responsible for his own conduct as much as patients are for theirs, the therapist is likely to make use of his experience to arrive at judgments about what a patient might do with his freedom in cases where a highly negative outcome seems possible, and to decide whether or not he should enter into therapy with him. He does not, after all, have to apply his theoretical and moral position absolutely inflexibly, and where neurosis hides a predicament of possibly unbearable proportions, he may decide that practical help and support may be of greater value than encouraging its recognition.

The suggestion here that therapists are not responsible *for* their patients, but only for their own conduct towards them, by no means lets them off any moral hooks. Indeed, feeling that you are responsible for what you do with people may make you considerably more concerned and cautious than feeling that you are directly responsible for them or for what they do. In the latter case you would place your trust in your technical skill in controlling the patient manipulatively; in the former you have to recognize that he is free to use your influence in ways you might not be able to anticipate.

1 Sandler, J., Dare, C. and Holder, A. (1972). Frames of reference in psychoanalytic psychology. III A note on the basic assumptions. *British Journal of Medical Psychology*, **45**, 143.
2 Landfield, A. W. (1975). The complaint: a confrontation of personal urgency and professional construction. In D. Bannister (ed.). *Issues and Approaches in the Psychological Therapies*. London and New York: Wiley.
3 Cooklin, A. I. (1974). Exploration of the staff-patient 'contract' in an acute female admission ward. *British Journal of Medical Psychology*, **47**, 321.
4 Scott, R. D. (1973). The treatment barrier. *British Journal of Medical Psychology*, **46**, 45.
5 Masters, W. H. and Johnson, V. E. (1970). *Human Sexual Inadequacy*. Boston: Little Brown.
6 Sartre, J.-P. (1969). *Being and Nothingness*. Trans. H. E. Barnes. London: Methuen, p. 437. Reprinted by permission of Philosophical Library, Inc. Copyright © 1956 by Philosophical Library, Inc.
7 This quotation is taken from an article (*Psychology and Psychotherapy Association Forum*, 1974) which is not generally available. Shotter has however written a very readable book which covers this and related issues in philosophical psychology: Shotter, J. (1975). *Images of Man*. Methuen Essential Psychology series.
8 op. cit., p. 462.

6

Self-Awareness and
Self-Deception

In the previous chapter we considered how a person may be engaged in intentional activity while genuinely believing that his behaviour is due to causal factors beyond his control. In this way, there is a contrast between his actual activity and what he tells himself about the reasons for it. In this chapter we shall consider a related phenomenon: instead of looking at the reasons *why* a person behaves the way he does, we shall look at *what* he does, and how what he does appears to him as he reflects upon it.

In the discussion which follows we shall be examining the conditions under which a person may be said to *know* what he is doing, the main point being that sometimes he does and sometimes he doesn't, but that there is in any case no reason why he always should. Much of the time, in other words, we do *not* know what we are doing, and that in itself is neither unusual nor alarming.

Clarification of this issue is essential to an understanding of neurosis, for one of the most frequent strategies employed by neurotic individuals is to maintain that they are not doing what they appear to be doing, or, alternatively, that not knowing what you are doing constitutes an unusual or unsatisfactory state of affairs characteristic, for example, of illness. To complicate matters further, the fact that people *can*, in certain circumstances, know what they are doing is taken in some brands of psychotherapy to suggest that knowing what you are doing is a good thing. I shall argue that this, unless suitably qualified, is unfortunate.

Any psychotherapist with experience of neurotic patients is likely to have been impressed again and again by the extreme incongruity which often arises when a comparison is made between what a patient is doing and what he or she professes to be doing. The significance of the person's activity seems, that is, to be lost on the person himself. The ways this can take place vary, but at times the incongruity is so great that the therapist can barely resist the impression that deliberate deception is involved. For example, a woman claims that she has a 'phobia' of choking, and so is unable to eat anything solid. Her greatest fear, she says, would be occasioned by eating boiled sweets. And yet she arrives for only her second therapy session with a peppermint boiled sweet rattling cheerfully against her teeth. She does not claim to have improved, and is still as afraid as ever of choking. When asked about the sweet in her mouth she looks somewhat puzzled for a while, and then answers blandly that peppermints 'don't really count'.

Again, one can be faced with the kind of incongruity shown in the behaviour of some 'anorexic' patients, who may be resorting to the subtlest of subterfuges in hiding food or otherwise contriving not to eat it, but at the same time showing genuine terror at the prospect of approaching death from starvation. Less dramatic, perhaps, but no less puzzling, is the frequency with which patients simply fail to make connexions between their own activity and what, from their point of view, 'happens to' them. The man who is assailed by nausea every time he is due to become involved in a social engagement, and who is prepared to undergo surgery rather than consider the meaning of his predicament, even though the latter seems obvious to everybody but him; the woman who 'inexplicably' wanders off and loses her memory every time her mother and her husband fall foul of each other; the flamboyant redhead who becomes almost incoherently anxious and bemused after being sexually assaulted by three different men in the space of as many months, and yet still persists in the highly seductive behaviour which presumably led to the incidents in the first place. In its own way compulsive behaviour—rituals of washing or dressing, for example—is equally puzzling. The person 'knows' that his behaviour is 'silly', the fears on which it is based not really justified, and yet he feels compelled to persist. If he cannot simply *stop* washing his hands, must it not be because he is ill?

Our task, then, is to justify the suggestion that there is nothing fundamentally unusual or qualitatively different from normal about such incongruities as these, *except* that the neurotic is making a special kind of use of what is in fact a familiar condition of human psychology.

The classic psychological explanation of how somebody can be doing something of which he himself remains in ignorance is that offered by Freud in his concept of 'repression'. For one reason or another—usually because recognition of what he is doing would prove painful or threatening to his self-esteem—the person is protected from confrontation with the real nature of his enterprises through the operation of a defence mechanism which 'represses' its significance, i.e. renders it 'unconscious'. Freud distinguished between two types of repression: 'primal repression' and 'repression proper'. In the case of primal repression, unconscious mental contents are prevented from becoming conscious through the activity of a kind of mental 'censor', a metaphorical watchman who stands at the gates of the conscious mind with the purpose of rejecting or ejecting unacceptable ideas or impulses which seek to find their way into consciousness. Repression proper is the process by which contents of the conscious mind can be made unconscious. This is achieved by their having withdrawn from them the mental energy needed to keep them conscious.

Stated in this somewhat bald manner, there is clearly rather a simplistic mechanism about the concept of repression which leaves a number of important questions unanswered. How, for example, are the decisions to reject unconscious contents made, and how is withdrawal of mental energy achieved? What, indeed, does 'mental energy' consist of? How do unconscious mental contents exercise an influence over the person's actual activity? Unsatisfactory though Freud's answers to these questions may often seem to present-day psychologists, he does, in one particular passage,[1] elucidate the problem in a way which foreshadows a number of modern approaches, and which may considerably aid our own discussion:

We now seem to know all at once what the difference is between a conscious and an unconscious presentation. The two are not, as we supposed, different registrations of the same content in different psychical localities, nor yet different functional states of cathexis [mental energy] in the same locality; but the conscious presentation comprises the presentation of the thing plus the presentation of the word belonging to it, while the unconscious presentation is the presentation of the thing alone. . . . Now, too, we are in a position to state precisely what it is that repression denies to the rejected presentation in the transference neuroses: what it denies to the presentation is translation into words which shall remain attached to the object. A presentation which is not put into words, or a psychical act which is not hypercathected, remains thereafter in the *Ucs* [Unconscious] in a state of repression.

What Freud is saying, put simply, is that we can behave unconsciously as long as we do not attach words to what we are doing. What he fails perhaps to stress is that this is by no means only a pathological process, and that, furthermore, when we do succeed in attaching words to our activity, when we give a reflective account of what we are doing, the result is frequently for us to mislead ourselves as well as others.

Experience is prior to language. Language elaborates and reveals our experience and allows us to operate upon it, but just as it can be used positively in this way, so it can be used negatively by misidentifying the significance of our experience. This negative use of reflection is particularly evident when we seek to transform an understanding of what we are doing into a kind of *identity*.

This latter point is made particularly convincingly by Sartre in *Being and Nothingness*, where he develops his concept of 'bad faith'. What people *are*, Sartre says, lies in their pre-reflective, continuously unfolding activity, and what they *say* they are can only be a particular version of themselves which they are offering for public, or even merely their own, consumption. What I say I am is always set in a broader activity in which I am engaged, and which I cannot at the same time comment upon; the 'I' of 'I am . . .' is always beyond what it is claiming to be, standing apart from it, so to speak. Therefore, when I claim for myself some particular identity, or when I try to give some kind of total account of myself, I cannot escape misleading, and being misled—I am in 'bad faith'.

Not only, then, is it not unusual for people to do things without being able to give an account of what they are doing, but for them to succeed in doing so with any completeness is not even possible. As Harré and Secord put it:[2]

The standpoint from which one monitors one's monitoring of a perform-ance, from which one gives commentaries upon the way one is doing something and with what aim, is not itself capable of figuring in an account, given from that standpoint. The commentator himself is not capable of description as a part of the psyche. He must necessarily escape observation, since he is the observer. Thus the standpoint from which commentary is made must always be one remove from experience, and cannot have attention focused upon it.

Our activity, then, comes before our reflection upon it, and reflection can tell us only what we have done, not what we are doing. The eye that is seeing cannot see itself.

There is a tendency at least implicit in the thinking of many psychotherapists to see conscious awareness as somehow 'higher' than the unconscious mental phenomena from whose influence they seek to free their patients. However, our discussion so far suggests that this may be putting the cart before the horse. This is a point made by Hayek in an interesting paper which he calls 'The Primacy of the Abstract'.[3] In this paper, Hayek puts forward the idea that our experience may be organized by what he calls 'action patterns'.

These are to be understood as kinds of templates which cannot in themselves be given to conscious awareness, but which determine, from 'above' as it were, what we actually experience:

It is generally taken for granted that in some sense conscious experience constitutes the 'highest' level in the hierarchy of mental events, and that what is not conscious has remained 'sub-conscious' because it has not yet risen to that level. There can of course be no doubt that many neural processes through which stimuli evoke actions do not become conscious because they proceed on literally too low a level of the central nervous system. But this is no justification for assuming that all the neural events determining action to which no distinct conscious experience corresponds are in this sense sub-conscious. If my conception is correct that abstract rules of which we are not aware determine the sensory (and other) 'qualities' which we consciously experience, this would mean that of much of what happens in our mind we are not aware, not because it proceeds at too low a level but because it proceeds at too high a level. It would seem more appropriate to call such processes not 'sub-conscious' but 'super-conscious', because they govern the conscious processes without appearing in them. This would mean that what we consciously experience is only a part, or the result, of processes of which we cannot be conscious, because it is only the multiple classification by the super-structure which assigns to a particular event that determined place in a comprehensive order which makes it a conscious event.

And:

The point in all this which I find most difficult to bring out clearly is that the formation of a new abstraction seems *never* to be the outcome of a conscious process, not something at which the mind can deliberately aim, but always a discovery of something which *already* guides its operation. This is closely connected with the fact that the capacity for abstraction manifests itself already in the actions of organisms to which we surely have no reason to attribute anything like consciousness, and that our own actions certainly provide ample evidence of being governed by abstract rules of which we are not aware.

The human being's most developed activity, therefore, is always 'out in front' of what he can say about himself. As we noted in the previous chapter, we tend to think of characteristically human behaviour, in the loftiest sense of the term, as being the result of some kind of conscious deliberation. What we find, however, is that such deliberation is in truth frequently more an account we give *after* the event. Not, of course, that we cannot do things deliberately. But what we do deliberately is done in the context of projects which we cannot know beforehand, though we may discover them as we go along.

There is, then, on the face of it nothing particularly unusual in the neurotic's inability to say what he is doing, nor is there necessarily anything ominously pathological about his failure to give an accurate account of his actions. What is interesting is the *use* which it seems can be made in neurosis of the phenomena we have been considering.

In his account of bad faith, Sartre gives an excellent example of the kind of use an individual might find for it:

. . . A homosexual has an intolerable feeling of guilt, and his whole existence is determined in relation to this feeling. One will readily foresee that he is in bad faith. In fact it frequently happens that this man, while recognizing his homosexual inclination, while avowing each and every particular misdeed which he has committed, refuses with all his strength to consider himself '*a paederast*'. His case is always 'different', peculiar; there enters into it something of a game, of chance, of bad luck; the mistakes are all in the past; they are explained by a certain conception of the beautiful which women can not satisfy; we should see in them the results of a restless search, rather than the manifestations of a deeply rooted tendency, etc., etc. Here is assuredly a man in bad faith who borders on the comic since, acknowledging all the facts which are imputed to him, he refuses to draw the conclusion which they impose. . . .

The homosexual recognizes his faults, but he struggles with all his strength against the crushing view that his mistakes constitute for him *a destiny*. He does not wish to let himself be considered a thing. He has an obscure but strong feeling that an homosexual is not an homosexual as this table is a table or as this red-haired man is red-haired. It seems to him that he has escaped from each mistake as soon as he has posited it and recognized it; he even feels that the psychic duration by itself cleanses him from each misdeed, constitutes for him an undetermined future, causes him to be born anew. Is he wrong? Does he not recognize in himself the peculiar, irreducible character of human reality? His attitude includes then an undeniable comprehension of truth. But at the same time he needs this perpetual rebirth, this constant escape in order to live; he must constantly put himself beyond reach in order to avoid the terrible judgment of collectivity. Thus he plays on the word *being*. He would be right actually if he understood the phrase, 'I am not a paederast' in the sense of 'I am not what I am'. That is, if he declared to himself, 'To the extent that a pattern of conduct is defined as the conduct of a paederast and to the extent that I have adopted this conduct, I am a paederast. But to the extent that human reality can not be finally defined by patterns of conduct, I am not one.' But instead he slides surreptitiously towards a different connotation of the word 'being'. He understands 'not being' in the sense of 'not-being-in-itself'. He lays claim to 'not being a paederast' in the sense in which this table *is not* an inkwell. He is in bad faith.[4]

What seems to distinguish neurotic 'bad faith', 'repression', or self-deception from a *natural* disjunction between words and actions (what one describes oneself as doing in contrast to what one actually does) is, then, its apparent purposefulness. In the normal run of events there are actions which *cannot* be accessible to reflective awareness or which cannot easily be put into words; on the other hand, in the case of neurotic self-deception, the person seems to be involved in an attempt to *prevent* his actions being put into words— he seems to be concerned to keep the significance of certain of his actions out of his awareness although he could do otherwise.

As has been pointed out, our most fundamental strategies, or, in Sartre's terminology, projects, are, at the time we are carrying them out, unknowable by us—though they may be apparent enough to somebody else. We may, again, be engaged in activities (like riding a bicycle, for example) the mechanics of which are hard to specify (you cannot *tell* someone how to ride a bicycle) although we are aware that we are carrying them out. Nevertheless, in pursuit of our projects, we may also at times call upon a repertoire of well-practised skills the nature of which is reflectively clear to us and which we can turn on or off at will. If we put these into action unthinkingly— habitually perhaps—we are, by reflecting for a moment, easily able to 'read off' their meaning: we can see what we're up to. The striking thing about the neurotic is that he seems to be engaged in relatively low-level strategic activities of this kind, the meaning of which seems clear to us, but which he seems to experience as unspecifiable— either he cannot say what he is doing (e.g. protecting himself from social encounters by means of symptoms) or is unable to criticize his own performance (e.g. cannot see that his social manner is unusually submissive). In other words he seems to treat his own behaviour *as if* it was of the kind we might accept as unspecifiable, although to others it looks rather like the kind of practised skill which we normally expect to be available to conscious awareness. What may make us particularly suspicious is that his concern that 'something is the matter' with him betrays a certain kind of awareness, a certain ability to evaluate his performance which, however, stops short of recognizing the obvious implications. This may be what distinguishes the neurotic from the eccentric—the latter simply gets on with his unusual activities, appearing to be 'lost' in them, while the former somehow stands outside his activities, and yet is unable to criticize them in the way which 'standing outside' would seem to permit.

In a penetrating study of the problem we are considering, Fingarette[5] describes the kind of neurotic strategy we are concerned with as a failure of the individual to 'spell out' his or her engagements or activities in particular cases:

> This is the situation in which there is overriding reason *not* to spell-out some engagement, where we skilfully take account of this and systematically avoid spelling-out the engagement, and where, in turn, we refrain from spelling-out this exercise of our skill in not spelling-out. In other words, we avoid becoming explicitly conscious of our engagement, and we avoid becoming explicitly conscious that we are avoiding it.

The question which immediately arises, naturally enough, is that of *how* someone achieves an intention not to spell out their engagements (and not to spell out that they are not spelling them out). To some extent, the ground has already been prepared for such an understanding, since it was established in the previous chapter that there is nothing unusual in people having intentions of which they are not aware. What we have to indicate specifically, then, is how somebody can not be aware of severing his activity from his reflective consciousness *intentionally*.

Sartre suggests that this can be achieved on an analogy with going to sleep:

> Let us understand clearly that there is no question of a reflective, voluntary decision, but of a spontaneous determination of our being. One *puts oneself* in bad faith as one goes to sleep and one is in bad faith as one dreams. Once this mode of being has been realized, it is as difficult to get out of it as to wake oneself up; bad faith is a type of being in the world, like waking or dreaming, which by itself tends to perpetuate itself. . .[6]

It is, of course, not easy to go to sleep on purpose. Sleep, as Fingarette suggests in his book, is something that happens to one rather than something one can make happen. And yet, I think, Sartre's analogy is an instructive one, since 'going to sleep' represents a special kind of alliance between what one can control and what one cannot. We learn the conditions which are conducive to sleep, and we take advantage of them; we put ourselves in the position in which sleep is likely to overtake us when the conditions are right (i.e. we go to bed, switch the light off, shut our eyes, etc.). In the same sort of way, the neurotic strategist puts himself in the position most suitable for remaining ignorant of what he is 'up to', and then allows, as it were, nature to take its course.

If the psychotherapist consults his own experience of his patients' self-deception, he will surely find clear instances of the kind of process under discussion. Indeed, the psychotherapeutic situation is one of the few in which neurotic self-deception can be observed closely—and indeed challenged—as it takes place. If the neurotic's task is one of misrepresenting to himself the significance of his strategies (for fear of what they will reveal to him), the presence of the therapist means that he has the additional problem of maintaining self-deception in the face of a critical consciousness (that of the therapist) which is *not* in an unspoken alliance with him; not only does he have to avoid his own critical scrutiny, but he also has to develop ways of avoiding the therapist's. Here, of course, we are back with the concept of resistance which was discussed in the previous chapter.

It is not difficult for the patient to misrepresent to the therapist (and himself) activity which has taken place outside the therapeutic situation, for in this case he can make use of straightforward 'bad faith'—he can confuse what he does with what he 'means' to do, or with what he 'thinks' he is doing. His behaviour within the therapeutic situation is not so easy to disguise, because, as has been said, he is under the critical gaze of the therapist. He can achieve his aim of non-recognition of what he is doing only by *not looking* at it, or by *distracting* his own attention when asked to look, or by steadfastly looking *somewhere else*.

Most therapists will, perhaps, be familiar with the way a person can 'not look' when his attention is drawn to what he is doing: he may suddenly become vague, in an odd way defocused, his eyes may literally become slightly glazed, his attention somehow scattered and imprecise, his thinking blunt and jumbled. In my own experience this kind of defocusing is the most striking, and perhaps the most common, method of maintaining self-deception in therapy.

The distraction of the person's attention from recognition of his strategies seems often to be achieved by means of symptoms, and it is to symptoms also that the patient may look when he wishes simply to divert his gaze from the direction indicated by the therapist to a (for him) less problematic area. On the whole these seem to be somewhat lower-level tactics than that of defocusing, and they are also, perhaps, from the patient's point of view, less successful. In the case of distraction, a patient may indulge directly in some kind of symptomatic behaviour—possibly but not necessarily connected with an obsession or phobia—in order to draw his own, and if possible also the therapist's attention away from his deeper projects. In the second case he may just stubbornly insist that it is his symptomatology, and not he, which is the problem. If these methods of maintaining self-deception are less successful than 'defocusing', it is largely because they are more obvious, more easily pointed out by the therapist, and almost impossible after a time not to recognize. Indeed, those patients who drop out of psychotherapy relatively quickly often seem to do so because their heavy reliance on either or both of these methods of maintaining self-deception is beginning to be eroded, and they are left with no alternative either to recognizing what they are doing or to leaving the situation altogether. Defocusing, however, is a much more subtle tactic: precisely at the point at which it is most obvious (to the therapist) it is also most difficult to see (for the patient).

There are a number of points about this account which it is important to understand. In the first place, I do not wish to suggest that in all cases the therapist is in a position to see better than the patient what the latter is 'really' doing. He does not establish the 'real' reasons for the patient's behaviour on the basis of some kind of expert appraisal, and simply tell him of his findings. If he is struck by the contrast between the patient's avowed intentions and his actual activity, his task is to *negotiate* with him a view of his behaviour which may account more satisfactorily for the incongruities observed. Because people are not static entities, there can be no 'correct' view of what they are or final version of what they are doing. For this reason, patient and therapist have to come to an agreement about what is happening which seems a useful basis for further exploration. If he is guided by this principle of negotiation (about which more will be said in the next chapter), rather than by any notion of technical mastery of the situation, the therapist will have little cause to be worried about the 'accuracy' of his statements to the patient; the latter will determine the pace of their relationship as well as the degree to which he accepts the therapist's influence, and is unlikely to take the therapist's utterances, whether accurate or mistaken, at their face value. Therapists who get worried about whether they have said the 'right thing' frequently operate in a context in which they feel they ought to be omniscient, if not omnipotent.

A further point I wish to make is that, although much of the therapist's time may be taken up in attempting to agree with the patient an alternative view of what he is 'up to', and consequently in fostering in him an awareness which formerly he did not possess, the *ultimate* aim of therapy cannot be to make people 'aware'. Awareness of self-deceptive strategies is a means of achieving mastery over certain aspects of one's behaviour, not an end in itself. For, as we have seen, the totally conscious person is an impossibility.

It is at least arguable that psychology and psychotherapy have traditionally concentrated too one-sidedly on conscious awareness as an ideal of human nature. It may not, for example, entirely be a caricature of psychoanalysis to represent it as contrasting 'healthy', conscious behaviour with the sexually and aggressively charged impulses of our unconscious minds, and this would suggest that most of our actions which are not the product of, or immediately accessible to, our reflective awareness are likely to be, as it were, tainted with *id*. As far as it accounts for our pre-reflective activity by reference to the unconscious, psychoanalysis carries with it, therefore, inescapable moral overtones: there is something slightly deplorable—almost even depraved—about the man whose actions are not bathed in the light of consciousness.

Many of the more modern psychotherapeutic techniques also tend to carry with them an implication that 'knowing yourself' is the most important aim to which you can aspire. George Kelly's 'repertory grid technique',[7] for example, provides one way in which a person can become aware of the ways in which he is interpreting ('construing') the actions of others, and the assumptions he is making about them. Briefly, the technique depends upon the patient specifying in what way any two people known to him are alike, and different from a third. This procedure can, of course, be carried out for an indefinite number of 'triads' of the patient's acquaintances, and is aimed at revealing to him the 'personal constructs' by means of which he orders his interpersonal world. Again, Kelly suggests that a person may learn a good deal about himself by writing a sympathetic autobiographical sketch of his life up to the moment of inquiry. It is probably true that the limitations of these techniques were clear enough to Kelly himself, but the use to which they are frequently put by some of those therapists who have been influenced by his writing seems often to fail to recognize that they cannot tell the person 'what he is like'. For reasons which have already been elaborated, the person somehow slips away from the light of his own inquiry, even when he is earnestly trying not to; he is inevitably in important ways different from what he says he is.

It seems, then, that if psychotherapy is characterized as a procedure for achieving self-awareness in any complete sense, it must be doomed to failure. Much of our most intricate and rich experience, many of our most complex skills, perhaps the majority of the rules which guide our action in day-to-day life, the very process of abstraction itself, may all, it seems, be out of reach of reflection. And if we succeed in pinning down and defining an aspect of our experience, or a strategy hitherto unrecognized, in the very process of doing so we become anchored in a standpoint which is itself unanalysable—we are being guided, in the terms used by Hayek, by new action patterns, or, in Sartre's, by new projects which are inaccessible to reflection. In so far as psychotherapy is aimed at self-awareness, then, it stands in danger of becoming an exercise in bad faith, and in so far as we try, as psychotherapists, to congeal our patients into a state of being 'understood' we are, to put it dramatically, denying them the very essence of their human nature. Whatever we are, we are not what we suppose ourselves to be or declare ourselves to be, and directly we *know* what we are (rather than what we were), we have fallen into self-deception.

However, there are some conclusions we should be careful *not* to draw from these considerations. I repeat that it is not my intention to suggest that self-critical reflection is a waste of time; that people are in all circumstances incapable of acting under the guidance of reflection; that therapy should be nothing but a prolonged indulgence in raw experience and wordless action.

If, however, as was concluded in the last chapter, people are free, and if the foundation of their being is unknowable in the sense we commonly use that word, then it would seem mistaken for psychotherapy to aim at any particular kind of frozen ideal of what people should be (for example, socially, sexually or vocationally 'adequate'; able to achieve 'heightened awareness' of themselves or others; well-rounded; outgoing; being at one with their physical bodies; free of 'unrealistic' fears; able to achieve 'peak experiences' with satisfactory frequency; able to be socially assertive; and so on and on). As *ends*, these aims are unsatisfactory if for no other reason than that, having achieved them, the person is still left going somewhere, and it would be unfortunate if he was led to feel that, for the sake of his 'mental health', he should know the name of his destination.

But if psychotherapy cannot set (*final*) positive and concrete aims for its patients, it can nevertheless make its intentions clear in a somewhat more abstract manner: that is, psychotherapy can be a procedure which helps people to clarify their misconceptions about themselves, and to accept that they are free to go where their actions, projects and strategies are taking them. Neurotic self-deception seems often to rest on the misconceptions which patients have about themselves, and human nature in general (for example, that anger is not permissible, that 'nice' mothers never feel irritation or rage with their babies, and so on), and which they maintain with great tenacity. At the centre of their misconceptions, often, is the *finality* which they perceive in them—they find themselves petrified, as it were, in a form which they experience as unbearable or unacceptable. For the therapist to offer them another, if different, final state to aim at is simply to supplant one neurotic solution with another, and is equally misconceived. It is, then, not the therapist's business to peddle miniature Utopias for individuals to inhabit, but, by negotiating with the patient a new view of his predicament, to help him free himself from his immobility and send him on his way.

An important part, but only a part, of the therapeutic process of negotiation, will be for the therapist to help the patient to an awareness of some of the strategies which he is using in the service of self-deception. In this context, the kinds of techniques advocated by Kelly, and others, may play an important role. There are of course several technical procedures which rely heavily on reflective awareness and which help to clarify to the patient, before his very eyes so to speak, the nature of some of his strategies (though, once the game is up, they will be replaced by *new* strategies which will in turn *not* be available to his awareness, until again substituted by new ones, and so on). An exercise developed by Mair,[8] and based on what he calls a 'conversational model' of psychological relations, is a good example of such a procedure. In this, one person writes a character analysis of another which he is prepared to show him and discuss with him, and a further analysis which, initially at least, he is not prepared to show him, though as both parties gain confidence in the relationship they may reveal views which they were at first anxious to conceal. The insights which both parties may gain from this procedure (some of them, certainly, not easy to put into words) will be clear to anybody willing to try the experiment.

There are also, of course, many other techniques aimed at the clarification of interpersonal strategies, etc., but the point at issue here is that their value will depend on the context in which they are used: for example, is the patient supposed to discover only what the therapist thinks he should, or may he draw any conclusions he likes? Is he being moved from 'neurotic' position A to 'healthy' position B, or is he, so to speak, getting help in freeing his propeller from weeds so that he can go where he wants?

It is in fact precisely in 'freeing' people that reflective psycho-therapeutic approaches can be most useful. Too often, however, reflective procedures (like psychoanalytic interpretation, etc.) are seen as bringing about *understanding* and self-knowledge of a kind which enables the person thenceforth to carry around with him an enriched version of himself from which he can, as it were, read off suitable responses at appropriate moments; choosing, in a controlled sort of way, actions to fit his circumstances in the bright light of full consciousness. Far from freeing the person, however, this is freezing him into the mould of what he currently accepts about himself.

With these arguments in mind, I think it possible to advance an alternative view of reflection and a rather different purpose for the kind of negotiating procedure which the psychoanalysts call 'interpretation'. *The point of understanding what you are doing now is to enable you to do something else.* This is exactly the point of interpreting neurotic behaviour—by seeing what his current projects are the patient is able to undertake new ones, not simply to add to his repertoire of conscious actions, or, more negatively, to stop doing what he was doing before.

Self-consciousness tends often to disrupt or explode what it reflects upon. Whether riding a bicycle or reading a book or talking to friends, if you become self-consciously aware of what you are doing you may well cease to do it effectively. 'Understanding', then, becomes a way of exploding the person's current projects and strategies, making them historical, and leaving him free to follow new ones. Paradoxically, then, the use of techniques for promoting self-consciousness in psychotherapy should be aimed at, and have the inevitable result of, allowing the person to become unself-conscious again.

Frankl's technique (already referred to in Chapter 2) of 'paradoxical intention', for example, makes good use of this principle: patients who find themselves doing things they don't want to do (e.g. stuttering) are asked to do them *on purpose*, and, according to Frankl, frequently find themselves unable then to produce the unwanted actions. A similar approach has been used in psychotherapy with families as well as individuals by a group of American therapists[9] who suggest to patients, again paradoxically, that they carry out with conscious deliberation interpersonal strategies which up to that point they had been practising unawares.

The, perhaps often unspoken, psychotherapeutic ideal of the fully conscious person, performing his life with admirable virtuosity as, with his inner eye, he reads from the richly orchestrated score his self-knowledge has revealed, has, when one comes to think about it, something rather sickening about it. For it is impossible to act self-consciously and in good faith; the most successfully 'self-conscious' people of our time are probably confidence tricksters and television compères. Where reflection gives us control over our behaviour it does so at the expense of its spontaneity and its honesty—the latter because we cannot in truth *help* being spontaneous, and to do something self-consciously is to hide from view our spontaneity, to conceal our real, unself-conscious intention.

It is a common observation in social psychology that people may become conscious of themselves only because they can be objects of the consciousness of others: you learn about yourself through the eyes of others. Just as the other's consciousness of you turns you into an object, so your self-consciousness turns you into an object for yourself. Frequently this is a disrupting experience, a 'project-exploding' situation from which you struggle to break free to a realm of unobjectified activity. Neurotic patients frequently describe experiences (surely not entirely unfamiliar to the rest of us) which seem to centre on this kind of fear of being 'objectified' by others— so much so that a patient may feel, for example, that he cannot function properly in public places; he feels frozen with fear, his facial muscles refuse to form the expression he strives for, he is unable to eat in restaurants under the gaze of others, and so on. On the other hand, the confidence trickster, the orator, those television performers whose whole aim is *not* to appear to be performing (pundits and 'personalities') try deliberately to arrange their activity to conform to the objectification which is imposed upon them by the viewers. Their conscious manipulation of the situation means, however, that they are necessarily dishonest as far as their self-presentation is concerned; their being is concealed—unless for example, through a producer's error, they are revealed by the camera in an unguarded moment.

The phenomena of self-consciousness have fascinated psycho-logists to an extent where many have become more concerned with the deliberate manipulation of appearances than with man's capacity to act as a spontaneous agent. An analysis of 'non-verbal communication', for example, in which it is noted that a person's gestures and facial expressions may be interpreted by others as signifying something about that person, may be used to train people deliberately to emit non-verbal cues designed to convey a particular message. This, obviously, is precisely the art of the con-man—he looks and behaves like a retired British army colonel, with all that

that implies, though he is really an ex-convict in illicit pursuit of other people's money. The line between therapy and deceit is thus a very thin and delicate one. It is one thing to suggest to a person that he is conveying a certain impression of himself which conflicts with his actual intentions and so gets him into difficulties. It is quite another to suggest to him *how* to convey impressions which will conform to approved social expectations. The impression one gives, in other words, must, to be genuine, be linked to one's (ultimately) unself-conscious intention, not to certain concealed manipulative aims. Analyses such as those of Goffman[10] of the ways in which appearances influence social intercourse, penetrating though they are, stand in danger of developing if we are not careful into a psychological technology of deceit.

The aim of reflection and interpretation (negotiation) in psychotherapy, then, should be to free the individual from one project or set of strategies so that he can adopt new ones. Far from advancing an ideal of self-knowledge, we should in fact be using it as a means to an end—an end to which it is in fact paradoxically opposed. Instead, it might be (and often is) helpful to encourage patients to *trust* their non-reflective, unself-conscious activity, since the ultimate aim of psychotherapy can only be to enable the person to set off down paths he does not already know. Similarly, the therapist must at times trust himself to act unself-consciously within the therapeutic situation, and it is perhaps one of the greatest difficulties in conceptualizing and communicating about psychotherapy that so much of importance happens, when it happens, beyond the reach of reflection. Far from this being shamefully unscientific, it is inevitable that psychotherapy should have its tacit, unspecifiable aspects which can in no way be engineered before the therapeutic event, so to speak, and can only be characterized after the event, when they have become history. On the whole therapists do not yet seem to have come to terms with this satisfactorily, and beginning therapists are often ill-prepared to accept and exercise tacit skills and unrehearsed activity without feeling that they have departed disastrously from some kind of therapist's handbook, and entered regions which are reprehensibly unprofessional.

1 Freud, S. (1915). *Standard Edition of the Complete Psychological Works.* Trans. and ed. James Strachey. Vol. XIV, p. 201. London: Hogarth.

2 Harré, R. and Secord, P. F. (1972). *The Explanation of Social Behaviour.* Oxford: Blackwell.

3 Hayek, F. A. (1972). The primacy of the abstract. In A. Koestler and J. R. Smythies (eds.). *Beyond Reductionism*. London: Hutchinson.
4 Sartre, J.-P. (1969). *Being and Nothingness*. Trans. H. E. Barnes. p. 63. London: Methuen. Reprinted by permission of Philosophical Library, Inc. Copyright © 1956 by Philosophical Library, Inc.
5 Fingarette, H. (1969). *Self-Deception*. London: Routledge & Kegan **Paul**.
6 op. cit., p. 68.
7 Kelly, G. A. (1955). *The Psychology of Personal Constructs*. Vol. 1. New York: Norton.
8 Mair, J. M. M. (1970). Experimenting with individuals. *British Journal of Medical Psychology*, **43**, 245.
9 See for example P. Watzlawick, J. H. Weakland and R. Fisch. (1974). *Change*. New York: Norton, and J. Haley. (1963). *Strategies of Psychotherapy*. New York: Grune & Stratton.
10 Goffman, E. (1971). *The Presentation of Self in Everyday Life*. Harmondsworth: Penguin Books.

7

Aspects of Negotiation

Although it is often referred to as such, psychotherapy is obviously not a 'talking cure'. Apart from affording temporary feelings of relief at having 'got things off one's chest', talking on its own does not seem to be a particularly fruitful way of dealing with one's problems. Nobody solves problems simply by juggling them in his head. Psychotherapy, then, is not just an armchair debate between two (or more) people, but an active relationship which has implications reaching out beyond the therapeutic setting. The patient does more than talk: he acts and experiences.

Nevertheless, for most forms of psychotherapy, talking is what therapists and patients seem to be doing most of the time, and verbal communication provides the vehicle for much of what happens in the therapeutic situation. Unimportant in itself, talking, therefore, seems to serve some important therapeutic ends.

It would not be possible in any book on psychotherapy to provide exhaustive coverage of all the things that can happen during the course of therapy; it may be that a therapeutic result could be brought about by entirely unexpected and unique sets of circumstances which could in no way be legislated for in advance. On the other hand, some processes occur with such regularity that they seem almost inevitable. The process of negotiation—a concept already used several times in earlier chapters—is one of the most outstanding of the regular features of therapy, and constitutes one of the main reasons for talking.

Before the patient can do anything about his problems, he has to negotiate with the therapist a view of them about which both can agree; successful therapeutic work proceeds, at least in part, on the ground of experience which is shared between patient and therapist. Each has to know, in other words, what the other is talking about.

As we have already seen, it is no simple matter for a person to know what he himself is talking about, let alone someone else. Except in some very basic areas of our experience, largely confined to our relations with the physical world, it is not obvious that we share a common view to any great extent: the meanings we attach to people, ideas and relationships are largely individual, even though our vocabulary often gives them a misleading appearance of objective identity. Moreover, even when we have our own meanings clearly in sight, they are liable to shift and change with new experiences. There is, therefore, no objective 'truth' about people which can be known; there is an indeterminate number of perspectives on any person, including his own, some of which may be more stable than others, but none of which can be said to be either fundamental or permanent. What a person 'is', or is doing at any point in his development, is therefore a matter of negotiation between interested perspectives. In psychotherapy, these are the perspectives of the patient on the one hand and the therapist on the other.

There seem to me to be two main elements of negotiation: understanding, and persuasion. Clearly, if you are to find out what another person is talking about, it is important that you understand him; and if the significance of what he is saying eludes you at first, he may have to persuade you of its relevance. Again, if the therapist is to influence or encourage the patient to change, he may well find that merely understanding him is not enough—he may have to persuade him that alternative views of his predicament are possible.

On the whole the psychotherapy literature has concentrated on understanding far more than on persuasion (to conceptualize both as parts of a process of negotiation is rare in psychotherapy[1]). The way in which the therapist may be said to 'understand' his patient has undergone a fairly radical change, theoretically speaking, over the years, and we shall consider this development shortly. That persuasion has not featured greatly in psychotherapeutic thinking until relatively recently may well reflect a certain nervousness psychotherapists feel about being exposed to accusations of 'influencing' people. It was at one time common for therapists to contrast the neutral freedom of 'psychological' therapies with the distasteful manipulativeness of behavioural methods. In the former case the therapist preserved his neutral mask, scrupulously avoiding imposing his personality upon the patient, for fear of using him for his own 'pathological ends', while the behaviour therapist, it was felt, surreptitiously manipulated the stimuli which would, according to his theory, determine the appropriate responses. Either type of therapist could, in fact, feel superior about the other: the psychotherapist could accuse the behaviour therapist of making damaging use of his powers, while the latter could sneer at the former for ignoring the fact that he is a determining stimulus in the patient's environment whether he likes it or not. Both these approaches, however, make the error of characterizing human relationships as *determining*. The behaviour therapist proclaims the error boldly, and so fails to see that his patients do not *have* to follow his influence; the psychotherapist implies a mistakenly deterministic view by trying so hard to *avoid* determining his patient's reactions. The result is that he fails to make rational use of the influence which is open to him.

As we have seen, patients' actions are not determined by their therapists, and therapists are not responsible for what patients do. The therapist's attempts to persuade his patients of the cogency of his perspective, or the usefulness of a certain possible course of action, may or may not be successful, and what the patient decides to do in the end is his responsibility. Nevertheless, the degree to which the therapist is able to influence the patient may be a crucial factor in the latter's arriving at a new perspective or setting out on a new course of action. This influence is, in the last analysis, an intensely personal matter, and one which the therapist must come to terms with, however much he might prefer to hide behind the guise of professional expert, impersonally applying a mechanical technique. How effective an influence he is will depend in part upon the extent of the basis of common understanding the therapist is able to establish with his patient.

In more orthodox psychoanalytic psychotherapy, 'understanding' was, perhaps, often seen as a largely one-way affair in which the therapist could understand the patient better than the patient could understand himself, largely because the therapist had access to the mysteries of the Unconscious and the patient did not. One of the tasks of therapy in this kind of situation was, then, for the patient to come to understand himself in the same terms as those used by his therapist. 'Interpretation' was, largely, the vehicle by means of which the patient was to be persuaded of the validity of the analyst's perspective.

In many ways, of course, this follows the technical model of medicine: the doctor knows what is good for the patient, and the patient gets better when he comes to accept and act upon the doctor's view. In psychiatry, certainly, it is this model which is used to determine the 'sanity' of the patient's perspective: in traditional psychiatric diagnosis it is not *what* the patient tells his doctor which is important so much as *how* he tells it. Is he slow ('retarded'), is his speech articulate and his logic clear, does he describe things in a way which makes conventionally good sense, and so on? The actual, 'interior' significance of what the patient *means* is of no interest to the psychiatrist, who is looking simply for symptoms and signs of 'illness'. The patient will be judged 'better' when the symptoms and signs have vanished, i.e. when the form of his communications is again in line with what is conventionally acceptable. Similarly, the psychoanalyst will be listening to the patient's free associations not for their surface meaning, but for indications of unconscious pathology according with Freud's formulations. The patient's ability to accept the analyst's interpretations of what he is actually saying for what he is 'really' (unconsciously) meaning, will be an indication of his improvement. In a nutshell, understanding in this sense consists in the therapist's reinterpretation of the patient's communications into a form which fits the former's theoretical framework, and this process is achieved with the help of some kind of technical lexicon. In recent decades this kind of approach to understanding has been radically challenged, and to a large extent replaced, by its polar opposite.

In psychotherapy, the writings of such theorists as Rogers and Kelly have led to a widespread acceptance among therapists generally of a view of understanding as 'empathy'. Rogers in particular stresses the therapeutic importance of the therapist's understanding the patient *from the patient's perspective*. In order to grasp the meaning *for him* of the patient's experience, the therapist has to put himself in the patient's shoes, to try his level best to see the world from where the patient sees it. Rather than the patient having to learn the therapist's language and theoretical system, the therapist has to learn the patient's. In this, he has to attend not so much to the patient's words, as to their meaning for the patient.

As we have already noted, Rogers considers this kind of empathy to be one of the essential conditions for therapeutic change (the other two being warmth and genuineness). Kelly also makes the relativity of perspectives central to his psychology—to understand what another person is doing entails an understanding of the unique organization of his 'personal constructs', and such an under-standing can only be gleaned through painstaking inquiry with the person himself. To attempt, as psychologists often do, to explain others by 'measuring' them with questionnaires of introversion-extraversion, neuroticism, etc., is one-sidedly to impose upon them the *psychologist's* way of looking at the world. But people act on the basis of *their* conceptions, not those of the psychologist, and their actions cannot be understood in any other context.

In a rather similar vein, R. D. Laing[2] has striven to shift the attention of British psychiatrists from the formal conventionality of what patients say to the meaning *for them* of their communications. 'Psychotic symptoms', Laing suggests, may be the understandable, perhaps inevitable, result of patients' experience, rather than mere indications of disease pathology; 'psychosis' thus becomes a way of dealing with an 'unlivable situation' rather than a 'mental disease', a way which may, moreover, be *understood* by the psychiatrist who is willing carefully to investigate with the patient the significance of his experience.

The more modern view of 'empathy', particularly as expounded by Rogers, gave impetus to strategies of research into the accurate understanding of one person by another which had been a focus of interest in academic social psychology for some time. Much of this research, as pointed out in an earlier chapter, has a curiously mechanistic bias, and rests on the assumption that 'understanding others', is something like a *skill*, which some people are liable to have relatively more of than others. In the therapeutic situation, this becomes extended to the view that some therapists will be more empathetic than others, and that those who 'have it' will, following Rogers' views, be more therapeutically effective than those who do not. As we saw, there is a degree of evidence for this latter view, though it seems to depend more on how patients *see* their therapists than on an objective demonstration that some therapists 'possess' empathy while others do not.

The bias towards conceptualizing empathy as a kind of skill which people either have or do not have is probably a reflection of psychology's pervasive concern with 'traits' rather than with processes. Psychologists interested in the broad area of personality have—naturally enough, perhaps, and sometimes with fruitful results—tended to concentrate on those aspects of people's personal functioning which seem to possess considerable stability. A person is recognizable as the *same* person from one day to the next, and this depends as much on the familiarity and stability of his personal style as on the constancy of his physical appearance. Part at least of our definition of sanity rests on there being a considerable degree of predictability in personal behaviour. These relatively stable aspects of personality ('traits'), apart from their obvious intrinsic interest, have also been of particular concern because they are relatively easily measurable. What more natural in this setting, then, than to consider 'empathy' as yet another instance of a trait? (And what more inevitable than that psychological research 'findings' about empathy should reflect the assumptions which are made about it at the outset?)

In fact, research findings in this area are, as so often in psychological research, equivocal, and to provide a detailed review here would make tedious reading. In general, the stability of empathy as a trait which somebody can express at different times and in different situations seems to depend very much on the method which psychologists use to measure it, and, because psychologists rarely use the same methods in their research, results are conflicting. The evidence for a stable trait of empathy is thus not strong, though there is some work[3] which suggests that some people may be consistently more accurate than others in judging what particular people are likely to do in particular situations.

Although a general, stable trait of empathy has not been convincingly demonstrated, there have been some interesting findings concerning the *sort* of people who have been found to have a measurable degree of accurate empathy in particular research studies. The interesting point about this research[4] is that people who are better able to make accurate judgments about others tend *not* to be people who have a particular psychological theory about 'what makes people tick'. Conventional professional psychologists have in this way been found on the whole to make less good judges than have intelligent laymen, especially where the latter are people of wide-ranging—perhaps artistic—interests. Although one in the eye for the professionals, this is scarcely a surprising finding. The majority of psychological theories are—some might say necessarily—simplified models of human behaviour, appealing as a rule to a handful of singularly uncomplicated mechanistic concepts. Though they may be of some use in marshalling the 'facts' of mass behaviour, they are unlikely to deal effectively with the complexities of the individual case, and it is small wonder that a reasonably intelligent and sensitive person is likely to make better guesses about others if he relies more on the skills he has spent his life developing than on the crudely insensitive conceptual equipment of traditional psychology.

The particular emphasis of this kind of research on empathy is, then, blatantly materialistic. Empathy becomes a kind of psychological possession which, in the therapeutic situation, therapists may possess to a greater or lesser extent. Since, as we have said, therapist empathy has been shown in some research studies (though the evidence is by no means consistent) to be related to positive therapeutic outcome, it therefore becomes important for therapists who have not 'got' empathy to acquire it through training—they may, for example, be instructed in the kind of therapeutic 'responses' which are judged by impartial observers to be empathetic. In this sort of procedure, the absurdity of psychological materialism is fully exposed, and in attempting to turn empathy into a technical skill, we have lost sight of its nature as a *process* of understanding; an active experience is substituted by an appearance. Having discovered that understanding is an important ingredient of psychotherapy, the technical therapist immediately becomes preoccupied with finding out how to *appear* to be understanding, overlooking the fact that understanding is an *interpersonal process*.

However, not all psychological research in this area has been quite as crass as I have so far suggested, and some consideration of further research findings might help to take our inquiry a step further.

Some of the earlier research studies in the area of 'person perception'—a concern in the field of social psychology closely related to the concept of empathy—noted[5] that accurate judgment of one person by another is facilitated by actual similarity in personality between those involved. In other words, I find it easier to understand you if you are already like me in the first place. This finding has also received support in more recent research studies.[6]

In many ways, this observation makes good sense, focusing as it does on the process by means of which understanding is achieved through shared experience. Curiously, though, some of the psychologists carrying out the earlier studies somehow felt understanding on the basis of similarity to be cheating. Possibly because they thought that empathy should be some kind of, perhaps rather esoteric, skill, they seemed to feel that a person does not deserve to be called empathetic if he achieves accurate understanding of another simply because he is himself a rather similar person. 'Putting yourself in somebody else's shoes' should be a more effortful and clever procedure. They were also worried about the possibility that good judges of others might just be using social stereotypes which result in accurate description more or less by accident.

More recently, however, psychologists have come to the realization that there is nothing illicit about this kind of understanding,[7] and indeed it may *only* be on the basis of shared experience that understanding, or even real communication, is possible. Even so, one can understand that some uneasiness should be occasioned by such a view. For example, simply by *assuming* that everyone is like yourself you are bound to be right some of the time purely by chance, and yet this process looks more like what Freud called 'projection' than like true understanding.

What makes the difference, perhaps, between empathy and projection is that with the latter there is no readiness to compromise in situations where experience does not happen to be shared (combined, possibly, with the assumption that if people do not react like oneself, then there must be something the matter with them). What distinguishes the empathetic person, therefore, may be, in cases where he does not happen to share the experience of another, a willingness to *learn* how the other has come to see things the way he does. Empathy (if it must be treated like a trait) then becomes a willingness to find out about others rather than an ability to make accurate judgments about them from the outset. The essential point, however, is that understanding itself can only be based upon a shared 'position', however this may ultimately be achieved.

There is little doubt that recent emphasis on the importance of empathy in psychotherapy, even if it has here and there been tinged with a degree of naïve psychological materialism, has done much to minimize the violence which therapists could wreak on their patients. For the therapist simply to undercut his patient's experience and attempt to replace the conclusions it has led to with views derived from his own theoretical posture seems at best arrogant and at worst dangerous. The worst effects of such an approach can be seen most clearly in traditional psychiatric institutions in which diagnosis and the physical treatment of 'illness' are the central concerns of those involved. Psychologically, patients in such institutions are simply neglected: they are not people with problems, but objects with diseases. Nobody bothers to find out who they are; they are merely observed for the signs and symptoms they may emit or cease to emit.

And yet, again, understanding on its own is not enough. There is no obvious reason why 'being understood' should lead to great therapeutic change, although it may help someone to get a more objective view of himself and to become aware of activity of which he was formerly not aware. Understanding is, however, the necessary prerequisite for negotiation. Therapist and patient must learn each other's language if they are to be susceptible to each other's influence. Therapeutic communication consists of persuasion as well as understanding, an effort to learn as well as a sharing.

In this respect, the therapeutic situation may be likened to that of master and apprentice. The apprentice learns the master's skills, comes to see, as it were, his point of view by exposing himself to the experiences which the master has been through. The master cannot teach him directly, but knows what position he should take up in order to find out for himself. Whether therapist or patient is master or apprentice will vary according to who is trying to learn what from whom; in the process of negotiation each may have to struggle to recast those elements of his experience which are not available to the other in terms of elements which the other does possess (or at least possesses partially), or deliberately to place himself in the position of the other to find out what follows from it.

Learning, understanding and communication take place in a context of lived experience, not in any abstract cerebral sphere. Things are *known* through the bodily relations one has with them, and having an abstract idea of principles is a long way from experiencing bodily what they were derived from. If the reader doubts this assertion, let him compare the theoretical 'knowledge' of changing a wheel on a car or a washer on a tap, or making an omelette, with the actuality of doing it. Who ever learned to play the piano by reading a treatise about it? This is well recognized in the acquisition of, and communication about, manual and artistic skills, but it is often overlooked by those who, like psychotherapists, tend to spend much of their education immersed in abstract ideas. And yet most students will recall a point at which what they had learned about in books suddenly 'came alive'—and underwent a radical change of meaning—when they confronted the problems in their embodied activity.

The psychotherapist who seeks to understand his patient's problems by mentally 'searching the literature' for similar cases and drawing abstract parallels is likely to go sadly astray. If he cannot find things *within his own lived experience* which match what his patient is telling him, he must resolve either to find out by becoming an apprentice, or to acknowledge his inability to say anything particularly helpful about it. Fortunately, therapists probably do share with their patients a knowledge of the kinds of distress which the latter complain of, far more than the 'pathologizing' influence of the illness model of psychiatry encourages them to admit. Who has not been afraid of what people think about them ('social anxiety'), superstitiously cautious and ritualistic ('obsessional'), suspicious of the opinions and intentions of others ('paranoid'), sexually unresponsive ('impotent', or 'frigid'), depressed ('depressed'), excited ('manic'), and so on and on? Any therapist who prefers a technical lexicon to his own experience rejects *sharing* with his patient for attempted manipulation of him, and runs the risk of cutting him off, perhaps cruelly, from the support he needs to pursue the therapeutic exploration further. What, indeed, may *make* the therapist a master worthy of an apprentice is precisely that he does share the patient's 'pathological' features, but is able to view them in a different light or use them in a different way. In this respect, it is of interest that comparison of the personalities of psychotherapists with those of psychiatrists inclined to physical treatment methods, in most research studies, reveals a greater amount of 'neuroticism' or 'psychopathology' amongst the former group.

That understanding may arise from the bodily sharing of similar experience is a principle made wide use of in some of the techniques used by 'growth' psychologists, in particular in the 'encounter group' movement. 'Group cohesion' may be quickly established by encouraging participants to take part in certain exercises—exploring each other by means of touch, gazing into each other's eyes, etc.—or members may be told to act out physically the emotions they are talking about, and so on. Frequently members of such groups find these and related experiences illuminating and rewarding. Sometimes, on the other hand, such 'encounters' seem to be tinged with a kind of evangelistic zeal which blunts the more critical, and self-critical, faculties of those taking part. This is perhaps particularly the case where such procedures are linked to some kind of 'growth' ideal about how people should be—e.g. that it's good to express emotions, essential to be in touch with your body, desirable that everybody should be warm and loving toward everybody else. In such cases, the pressure to conform to the social standards set by the group tends to sweep the participant beyond the point at which he can assimilate the effects of these 'experiential' procedures into his personal construction of the world, and, though he may find himself in a somewhat exalted and elated state for a few days, he is likely quickly to find himself back where he started. It is certainly part of the negotiating process for me to put myself in your position to see if I find what you found there; but I must still be free *not* to find what you found, and to negotiate the discrepancy with you. If you insist that I have *got* to find what you found, because you know what's *good* for people and I don't, the essential quality of negotiation is destroyed.

Understanding, learning, sharing and communicating are perhaps the inevitable goals of our negotiating with each other, and are central not only to psychotherapy, but to almost all human activities. But it might be unfortunate if we saw them as ends in themselves: if, for example, mutuality pure and simple came to be seen as 'the' therapeutic goal, or as the ideal form of human existence. There is no doubt that understanding and communication as pervasive characteristics of society would be welcome replacements for the kind of concealed tribalism and 'club membership' which characterize most modern social intercourse, but the question remains, what would they be for? What could we do with this warm mutuality, once we had got over the novelty of basking in it? When we negotiate, we are not negotiating simply in order to share, but to share *something*.

That 'something' seems to me to be very much to do with our individuality, the furthest reaches of our inarticulate activity, the unknowable vanguard of our projects. What we may *eventually* come to recognize through negotiating and sharing its validity with others, is inevitably born in isolation, and too much 'therapeutic' emphasis on the cosiness of empathetic mutuality (an emphasis which sometimes expresses itself in group psychotherapies as an intense hostility to individual activity) threatens to cut us off from the very source of our activity. The result is what Cooper [8] calls 'a sterile, "emptied-out" form of group existence'.

If, by insisting that everything the individual does must be understood or understandable, we fail to accord validity to his individuality, we are likely to poison his creativity with despair. As has been said before, the aim of psychotherapy must be to free the person actively to pursue his projects wherever they lead him, not simply to anchor him in some kind of safe social haven where he can feel at one with his fellows. Neurotic strategies tend themselves to be immobilizing: they protect the person from the risks involved in giving himself over to pure activity. But life is a risky business, and many of those risks have to be borne in isolation. However much we may hope eventually to share our personal discoveries with others, we have to make them alone by taking risks, and if we try to protect people from the isolation of risk-taking by understanding them, we either prevent them from making discoveries in the first place, or plunge them into despair when they find themselves alone.

What this means in practice is that *trust* should take over where understanding ceases. Where my experience no longer follows yours, where we have exhausted all possibility of finding or expanding areas of our experience which overlap, I can at least support you in your isolation by trusting your experience to be valid.

The master-therapist may recognize as familiar in his own

experience many of the strategies used by the apprentice-patient, and through painstaking negotiation may encourage him to gain the personal skills necessary to deal with his problems. But it is obviously both possible and beneficial that an apprentice may develop skills and directions for his activities different from or beyond those of his master, and where this happens, he should be trusted to get on with the job without interference.

1 This has, however, been done in the field of social psychology by Harré and Secord, whose book *The Explanation of Social Behaviour* has been referred to in the previous chapter.
2 See, for example, R. D. Laing. (1960). *The Divided Self.* London: Tavistock, and (1967) *The Politics of Experience and the Bird of Paradise.* Harmondsworth: Penguin Books.
3 e.g., R. E. Fancher. (1969). Group and individual accuracy in person perception. *Journal of Consulting and Clinical Psychology*, **33**, 127. This paper contains references to Fancher's earlier work, which is also relevant.
4 See the review article by R. Taft. (1955). The ability to judge people. *Psychological Bulletin*, **52**, 1. Fancher's work is also relevant in this respect.
5 Cronbach, L. J. (1955). Processes affecting scores on 'understanding of others' and 'assumed similarity'. *Psychological Bulletin*, **52**, 177. Also: A. H. Hastorf and I. E. Bender. (1952). A caution respecting the measurement of empathic ability. *Journal of Abnormal and Social Psychology*, **47**, 574.
6 See, for example, A. A. Adinolfi. (1971). Relevance of person perception research to clinical psychology. *Journal of Consulting and Clinical Psychology*, **37**, 167. Also: E. J. Phares and K. G. Wilson. (1971). Internal-external control, interpersonal attraction, and empathy. *Psychological Reports*, **28**, 543.
7 See the paper by Adinolfi referred to above, and L. Christensen. (1974). Generality of personality assessment. *Journal of Consulting and Clinical Psychology*, **42**, 59.
8 Cooper, D. (1967). *Psychiatry and Anti-Psychiatry.* London: Tavistock.

8

The Practice of Psychotherapy

In this final chapter I shall attempt to draw together some of the observations which have been made earlier in this book, and then proceed to a consideration of their significance for the professional practice of psychotherapy.

My wish is to present a sketch of the psychotherapeutic process largely free from traditional theoretical preconceptions—a sketch, that is, which takes the personal experience of both therapist and patient seriously. The best way of doing this I can think of is to suggest how the course of therapy might run for a novice therapist faced with a new patient. In no way do I want to suggest that what follows provides a model of psychotherapy: it is intended merely as a more or less arbitrary device for organizing the phenomena which have been considered in earlier chapters.

It is quite likely that the first thing to be experienced by our beginning therapist and his new patient will be an alarming confusion. The patient, finding, as it were, his symptoms under attack, finds also that they shift, change, disappear, re-emerge subtly altered, give way to preoccupations and fears the existence of which he had not before suspected. This is not the mere mechanical operation of 'symptom substitution', but a situation which arises when the *meaning* of 'symptoms' is challenged (even if only implicitly) by the therapist's scrutiny.

The therapist, correspondingly, may find that the tools, skills and techniques which he has learned about in theory seem in some strange way to have no real application; the patient does not react as he is supposed to, his symptoms are stubbornly unresponsive, or suddenly vanish for the wrong reason, and, what's more, without the patient seeming to care or be pleased. The therapist may find himself being drawn into ways of relating to his patient which were not discussed in the textbooks and which make him feel professionally uncomfortable—answering questions which he doesn't really know the answers to, trying to meet needs he hasn't even identified, finding himself engaged in lengthy interactions the content of which he simply doesn't recognize from his theoretical training; he may discover at the end of the therapeutic session that for an hour or more he has been acting without apparent purpose or direction and has no clue about what has actually taken place. His anxieties about this state of affairs may be greatly heightened by his patient asking him what 'the point' of it all is, or observing that therapy doesn't seem to have 'done him any good' yet.

Clearly enough, what both patient and therapist need in a situation such as this is some way of organizing it. As far as the therapist is concerned, this may be achieved by the resolute, if somewhat desperate, application of a theoretical model, and, in face of all the confusion, the patient may be grateful enough to have such a model imposed upon him. If no organization at all is achieved, either patient or therapist or both may take fright, conclude that the patient cannot be helped (is for some reason 'unsuitable' for the kind of treatment being proffered) and close off the therapeutic contact.

However, if the participants, in particular the therapist, are able to accept their experience with a measure of equanimity and examine it in good faith, a third option is open to them. And that is to explore the meaning *for them* of the predicament in which they find themselves, to look for a way of drawing out of their situation an organization which in a sense it already contains, which is unique to it, and which, between them, they have given it. So we see that the confusion of the earlier stages of therapy is alarming only if it is seen as not conforming to a state of affairs which *should* exist (from the patient's standpoint, according to his expectations; from the therapist's, according to his theory). If, on the other hand, the confusion is seen as the more or less inevitable result of two strangers trying to make sense of each other's experience and intentions, it may lose much of its threatening character, and the joint attempt to investigate and elaborate the meaning of their situation for the participants may then become the central focus of therapy.

The emphasis in the first half of therapy thus becomes one of clarification and negotiation. Before therapy can proceed, patient and therapist have to co-operate in reaching for a shared understanding of the nature of their enterprise, and indeed of the nature of the patient's problems.

The ground for the negotiation is formed by the different perspectives of therapist and patient on the latter's problems. Where the patient sees symptoms or immutable personality traits (self-descriptions) which cripple him and hold him back from social activity, etc., the therapist is likely to see strategic evasions by means of which the patient actively keeps himself from feared situations. The patient will see himself as sufferer, the therapist will see him as agent. While the therapist may attempt to 'explode' the patient's projects, and thus render him free of them, the patient will manoeuvre self-deceptively to remain unaware of them. It may perhaps be helpful to indicate some of the issues around which such negotiations can centre.

A particularly frequent circumstance is one in which a person will use his symptoms in a way which prevents face-to-face confrontation with aspects of his nature which, if he were to take them seriously, would inescapably lead him to the conclusion that he was basically bad, or basically worthless. Thus, for example, a woman whose view of the world simply excludes anger or aggression as a justifiable human response, suddenly finds herself 'blacking out' in situations where (from an external observer's viewpoint) anger would be appropriate. The therapeutic task in this case may be for the therapist to negotiate with her a new way of looking at the situations in which she faints. To her there seems to be no common element in these occasions. She does not see anger as an appropriate response to them because, for her, anger is not possible; it simply does not exist as an available reaction. She thus has to become the therapist's apprentice in learning how to be angry.

Again, deep and pervasive feelings of worthlessness may lead a person to take up a stance in the world as an invalid—suffering perhaps from a whole range of debilitating physical symptoms (dizziness, nausea, stomach pains, headaches). The symptoms are of course 'real'; they are the physical expression of anxiety, but they have become detached from the *meaning* of anxiety. Because the symptoms are 'there', it is possible for the patient to use them to withdraw from the world and yet still be a *person* in it, albeit a sick person. An invalid can be loved, even admired as one coping heroically with adversity, and can thus maintain an element of self-respect. Stripped of his illness, on the other hand, such a person is brought face to face with what appears to him as his incompetence, cowardice, uselessness, inability to gain a purchase on the world in the way 'real people' seem to, yawning emptiness in his relations with those around him. In this kind of situation (of which there are many variants, not all involving an 'invalid' role) the therapeutic negotiation tends to centre round the individual's (often inordinately high) standards of personhood: he may need to learn that weakness or fear do not disqualify one from being loved, that courageous action does not necessarily entail self-destruction, that he is not identical with those aspects of himself which he hates. It is on this kind of renegotiation of personal standards that the psychotherapeutic approach of Albert Ellis (see Chapter 2) seems to concentrate most heavily.

The question of *risk* is one which seems also frequently to arise in the course of therapeutic contact, as we have already briefly noted, and may again appear in a variety of guises. This may be expressed by patients themselves in some kind of metaphor—e.g. 'it's better not to enter a race at all than to enter it and lose'. In this sort of situation symptoms—as so often, puzzling and inexplicable from the patient's point of view—arise to lay the person low just when he or she appears to be coping successfully with life, perhaps following promotion at work or the establishment of a new and apparently promising relationship. Or possibly, as much to his own surprise as to that of those around him, the person finds himself turning down opportunities or leaving situations which he has long desired or for which he has worked hard. Here again there is unlikely to be any recognition—until, that is, the process of therapeutic negotiation is well under way—that any fear of failure is involved. Having achieved some kind of success, and therefore established a degree of self-respect, etc., such a person seems to become intensely threatened by the possibility of failing in the course of further exposure to the situation. So nothing is followed through, and, though he does not see it this way, the person himself brings about the result he most fears: he aborts failure, so to speak, but in doing so abandons success. This kind of control of intolerable anxiety in risk-taking is of course frequently under discussion in the therapeutic literature.[1]

There are of course also those for whom any kind of risk is inadmissible, and who for this reason do not even get as far as any initial success. Their lives may be overshadowed by a gloomy, fatalistic pessimism which may resemble an intense, perpetual, hovering depression. No project is worth embarking upon, no pleasure worth indulging, no joy worth reaching towards; for, once achieved, it will only be snatched away, leaving behind it nothing but dust and ashes. Since love must lead to bereavement, it is better not to love, but to remain resolutely behind the battlements, warding off any advances the world may make. In a particularly sensitive and insightful paper,[2] Scott and Ashworth have shown the effects that this kind of attitude can have on those around the individual who adopts it; how, for example, parents may 'close off' their feelings for a child for fear of what may happen if they continue to involve themselves with it. Presumably 'normal' pessimism is not dissimilar in intent, and is less an expression of an appetite for gloom than an attempt at rendering the world a less (unexpectedly) painful place. For the pessimist, there can only be nice surprises.

It is presumably most often the case that the person who avoids risking a continuous engagement in the world for fear of failure also recognizes that he does not *control* the world. For if he could *make* things go his way, the likelihood of failure would be greatly diminished. Rather, he sees the world in terms of himself versus an inexorable Fate. This leads us to a consideration of those people who make use of an alternative strategy, that of attaining mastery over the world's unpredictability. Perhaps the easiest way of controlling the complexity and the confusion of the events taking place around one, and hence the anxiety associated with the probability of unexpected demands being made, is to attempt to limit in some way the spatio-temporal dimensions of one's existence. Personal moral standards again dictate, of course, that this has to be done blamelessly, and so by factors outside the individual's control. Symptoms—perhaps of a phobic nature—can be particularly useful in limiting contact with the world, and keeping the person's activities confined within a relatively manageable sphere of operations. An 'agoraphobic', for example, may *be overcome* by fear when venturing forth into the world, but does not recognize that he or she *is afraid*. Indeed, he *wants* to go out, to go to parties, etc., as he used to. It is of course precisely here that the self-deceptive strategies discussed earlier play such a major role: the person uses his symptoms to solve, without conscious dishonesty, the problem of how to run away without being a coward. (Agoraphobia may of course have many meanings; such symptoms are discussed here for illustrative purposes, and there is no intention of suggesting that this is what agoraphobia is 'really' about.)

Again, a person may simplify the world, and thus make it more controllable, by simplifying the ways in which he construes it. Thus his judgments about those around him may rest on a rigid, narrow, black-or-white moralism which enables him comfortably to categorize any event or relationship which might otherwise take him by surprise. Or, alternatively, the world may be simplified in its social structure (people who are for me versus people who are against me), or some other crude and all-embracing principle. Kelly's psychology of personal constructs is particularly helpful in understanding the structural properties of the individual's approach to the world. In this kind of situation also, of course, the patient's conception of the world has for him the quality of absolute reality, and the therapist's task may be to persuade him that alternatives are possible.

The measures discussed so far which people may take to increase their control over what happens to them are on the whole defensive, in the sense that they involve to some degree a retreat from anxiety-arousing circumstances. It is also, of course, possible to attempt to exercise control by more positive procedures, as for example is the case with magic. It is well recognized, for instance, that obsessional rituals frequently seem to involve an attempt to control by magic (in ways obviously analogous to religious rituals) the evil that may befall the patient or those he loves. Sometimes also obsessional rituals seem to be used by patients as a means of controlling themselves, or at least as a way of checking up on what havoc uncontrollable aspects of themselves might have wreaked while they, as it were, were not looking. Once again it is the premises on which their behaviour is based which may need to be the focus of therapeutic negotiation—the premise in particular that the world is unbearable if it cannot be controlled.

The 'game-playing' quality of the patient's behaviour is another feature which may well attract the therapist's attention. In this kind of situation it may begin to dawn on the therapist that much of the behaviour which his patient experiences as painful and barely supportable does in fact play a very positive part in helping him maintain a position of considerable psychological gain, and indeed, if it wasn't for the fact that he *suffered* for it, the manipulative aspect of the patient's behaviour would become blatantly obvious to all, including himself. Eric Berne describes a variety of such 'games' in his book (see Chapter 2), and it would be pointless to reiterate them here. In my own experience, one of the commonest, and most rewarding, games that can be played is that of victim, or martyr. Both involve suffering, and so can be expected to command respect and sympathy, and both entail a kind of unassailable moral superiority which necessarily blinds the onlooker to the fact that the victim, or martyr (once, that is, martyrdom has been achieved), has to *do* nothing further to earn respect or justify moral superiority. He has, at the expense it is true of some discomfort, arrived at a position from which he can never put a foot wrong. Here, as in the other situations discussed, it is likely to be the *meaning* of his behaviour which will become the centre of therapeutic interest: the patient may emphasize the painful and inescapable nature of his predicament, while the therapist may try to alert him to what it is doing *for* him.

If the course of negotiation has been successful, the patient may well by now be facing the prospect that his symptoms and behaviour have meanings of which he had been unaware, and yet for which he must bear the responsibility. Having gained some understanding of his situation, he is confronted by the alarming prospect of having to do something about it. In many ways this may be the most difficult and painful stage of psychotherapy.

The *painfulness* of change, the fact that the abandonment of symptoms is often accompanied by depression and despair, though by no means ignored in the therapeutic literature, seems often to surprise patients and alarm therapists, to the point that the former may break off therapy and the latter conclude that things must somewhere have gone awry. One of the central features of this pain, and one which does not seem to figure greatly in theoretical discussions known to the writer, seems to consist simply in the agony of having been *wrong*. Over and above the obvious disadvantages of losing the protection of neurotic, self-deceptive strategies, a person may feel very keenly indeed a sense of shame and wastefulness at having used them in the first place. 'Resistance' in psychotherapy is, as we have noted, most often seen as resistance to giving up neurotic symptoms and the protection they bring, but less often as resistance to other implications of changing away from neurotic strategy. To change your approach to a problem implies, however, that your former approach was wrong. And if the problem in question happens to involve almost everything your life has stood for, including the way you relate to the people in it, having been 'wrong' brings with it an infinity of—for you—shameful memories and wounding self-accusations of wasted time. Moreover, there is the added problem that you can no longer recognize yourself as the person you used to know, and there is a terrifying uncertainty about how the person you now have the opportunity of becoming behaves: you don't know what to do to be yourself.

What enables a patient to embark upon the course of accepting responsibility for himself depends presumably on a complex set of circumstances and seems to vary greatly from person to person. More often than not it seems that the process cannot be hurried. It may be the case during the earlier stages of negotiation in therapy that the therapist quite quickly sees regularities and significances in the patient's behaviour, which seem indeed extraordinarily obvious, but to which the patient remains blind despite repeated efforts from the therapist to point them out. And then one day, perhaps several months later, the patient may suddenly see the same thing that the therapist has been seeing all along. Furthermore, the patient's discovery is likely to have a very *personal* quality about it, and it is only after examining it for some time that he realizes the similarity between his discovery and what the therapist has been struggling to show him for weeks. It seems in this way often to be the case that, just as scientific or intellectual discoveries seem to follow a certain stage of development in the general cultural climate,[3] so individuals have to be in some sense 'ripe' for personal discoveries. It may be, as perhaps the non-directive approach of Rogerian client-centred therapy would suggest, that the activity itself of two people—patient and therapist—investigating seriously and in good faith the meaning of the former's situation and of the relationship between them leads to a natural 'ripening' of this kind on the patient's part. Or it may be that the therapist's persistent attempts to persuade his patient to view himself in a different light are accepted only slowly and grudgingly, but do eventually bear fruit. The result, in any case, is that therapist and patient suddenly find themselves sharing a view they formerly did not share, and it is these discoveries of commonality which afford some of the most rewarding moments in psychotherapy. Where before they had been engaged in a hard round of diplomatic—and occasionally more overtly confronting— negotiations, the two participants suddenly find themselves co-operating in an elaboration of experiences they share in common, and each is able to illuminate aspects of the situation which had, perhaps, existed for the other as no more than barely formulated questions. Like two strangers in a railway carriage who discover some personal circumstance in their background which they share, therapist and patient find themselves suddenly with a common foundation on which they can build successfully and productively. And, as a consequence, they may find that they are able to *reveal* things about themselves where before they felt a frustrated isolation.

Earlier in therapy, attempts at such self-revelation may have met with little success. It is fairly common, for example, for patients to ask the therapist to tell them 'what he thinks' of them, or in some way to expound his theoretical beliefs. Most frequently, efforts on his part to do so, however honestly undertaken and attentively received, are met with a curiously disappointed puzzlement, and consequently therapists may feel reluctant to make the attempt in the first place. This is often perceived by patients as a stubborn, mystifying secrecy on the therapist's part. From the latter's point of view, however, it may rather stem from a recognition that there is little point in laying his cards on the table until the time is ripe. The turning point may be reached in a variety of ways, but usually arises out of an actual experience the patient has undergone, perhaps within, but equally possibly outside the therapeutic situation. A young man who has for years resisted and obscured the realization of his own anger and hatred, and hedged himself around with obsessional rituals to protect himself against them, suddenly hurls a plate at his mother's head, misses, and smashes the window. Not only does he discover thereby that he *is* angry, but that he can express his anger without totally disastrous consequences, and *immediately* abandons his obsessional precautions against it. At his next therapeutic session he is able to discuss with his therapist a view of himself, and its implications, which this incident has (for him) brought to light, a view which his therapist has been trying to convince him of for months. Such discoveries may also be made in less dramatic ways.

In some ways, as has already been discussed in this book, the recognition that one has been using self-deceptive strategies in the past renders their future use impossible. (No doubt the same *behaviour* can be used, but as part of a repertoire of practised actions, not self-deceptively as the vanguard of one's activity.) This does not mean, however, that change is not hard work. It has already been suggested that to become responsible and to learn a new stance in the world demands courage. It may be that the discovery of a view of himself which he can *share* with his therapist is to an extent an encouraging experience for a patient, but he is nevertheless likely to find himself faced with burdens which only he can carry. Although the symptoms which formerly helped him to avoid the situations he most feared may have lost their centrality and importance quite early in therapy, he is still faced with having to tackle those situations. As was discussed in Chapter 5, it is at this stage in particular that the techniques devised by behaviour therapists may be helpful in encouraging the patient actively to face and challenge the feared situations.

A person's attempts at meeting situations which formerly he has dreaded and avoided may not always be attended by unqualified success. He may panic, or despair, or experience a renascence of his old symptoms. 'You have', as one patient said, 'to work at your problems *beyond* breaking point.' Fortunately, because the fears are exaggerated and the person usually stronger than he suspects, it is likely to be the problems which disintegrate rather than the person.

At this stage of psychotherapy it is likely that the therapist finds himself less in the role of negotiator, and more in that of accomplice and support. The understanding which by now he shares with his patient of the latter's position may enable him to clarify more quickly and acceptably than before the reasons for the occurrence of stumbling blocks to the patient's progress, and much of his time may be spent in simply aiding and abetting the patient's experimentation with his new stance in the world.

More or less about this time, however, one particular myth of psychotherapy may arise (though not necessarily so) to disturb the therapeutic peace. This is the myth of there being a recognizable end-point to therapy. It is again an expectation created by mechanistic thinking that there will come a point when either patient or therapist or both will recognize that the former is 'better'. It is not infrequent for a patient to ask his therapist, perhaps somewhat hesitantly, if he thinks he's better. Somehow, it seems, there must come a point when a patient is finalized as a competent, normal person. As far as the patient is concerned one of the reasons for feeling he needs this kind of reassurance may be that he doesn't particularly *feel* like an end-product. Indeed, although his symptoms may have disappeared, although he may be living in some respects a new life, doing things he has not done for years—or possibly has never done before—he may not feel 'better' at all. It may be necessary at this point for the therapist to negotiate with the patient a view of people as *not* 'better' or 'worse', 'normal' or 'abnormal', and the patient may realize that his earlier dread of his own incompetence and his fear of facing the world's demands were in part based on a false premise that 'normal' people do not have these problems. Even though, in other words, he has lost much of his former view of himself, he may not yet have abandoned entirely his former view of others, and may be waiting in vain to obtain the kind of idealized situation he imagines they occupy. In a rather similar way, it is often discouraging and disappointing for a therapist to find, despite—from his own point of view—vast improvements in a patient's symptoms and ability to cope with life, that the latter does not jump for joy and acknowledge with gratitude all that has been done for him.

This is, of course, only really a problem for patients and therapists who have accepted a model of human functioning which envisages an ideal product. It has already been suggested that successful psychotherapy can (in good faith) do no more than help free somebody to pursue their existence. It cannot guarantee a kind of painless end-state in which all life's obstacles are surmounted. Indeed, it is possible for psychotherapy to open a person's eyes to fear, despair, travail and grief, where formerly he did not see them. But at least, in *looking*, he can do something about them. The end of psychotherapy coincides more or less with the assumption of responsibility, and there is nothing *necessarily* marvellous about that; the rest of life has to be lived.

This rather sketchy outline of some of the things which might take place in the course of psychotherapy suggests, if nothing else, that a reliance on the therapist's part on some kind of technical expertise need play no very great role in psychotherapy. What is important, however, is his willingness to enter into a personal relationship with his patients, and to rely upon his personal experience in testing out his therapeutic hunches. The nature of his personal relationship with patients might vary widely; at times it may be one of struggle and confrontation, at others of encouragement and communion, but throughout it should be of the kind characterized by Martin Buber[4] as 'I-Thou' rather than 'I-It'. In other words, the therapist is, whether he likes it or not, likely to be immersed *in* the relationship, rather than standing apart from it in an analytic, calculated, categorizing way (Buber's distinction is one which has been found illuminating by many modern psychotherapists).

This does not mean that the therapist cannot or should not make use of his experience of therapy. On the contrary, much of what he does he will do in the light of previous experience, and his perception of what happens in any particular psychotherapeutic encounter will inevitably be shaped by his experience of earlier ones. Indeed, it is this experience more than anything else which qualifies him to be considered a professional psychotherapist. This experience is, however, personal, rooted in his own history and his own activity; it does not have to seek authority from any impersonal objectivity of the sort beloved of 'behavioural scientists'.

As has been argued before, the instrument whereby the therapist understands his patients is none other than himself. The argument for this view, in the slightly different but related context of social psychology, has been well put by Harré and Secord:[5]

We believe that a human being is a system of a different *order* of complexity from any other existing system, natural or artificial. We believe this to be evident in the fact of human self-awareness and in the characteristically human linguistic powers. Thus for the purposes of any science which deals with phenomena specifically associated with performances that depend upon these higher order capacities any model of less complexity is void. Thus, machines, computers in their present state of development, and animals, are *all* inadequate, though none are wholly useless, as sources for concepts with which to delineate a sufficiently powerful model of man, which can be of any real use 'in the scientific understanding of social phenomena. The only possible solution is to use our understanding of ourselves as the basis for the understanding of others, and our understanding of others of our species to further our understanding of ourselves.

The therapist's richest source of information about what goes on in people is what goes on in himself. To accept, elaborate, and build upon this is to be scientific, in the sense in which that term has been developed in this book.

In his understanding of others, no one has in any case the possibility of being anything but personal in his approach, and hence subjective. This is, however, the special kind of subjectivity which can be shared and developed with others, not the inflexible, dogmatic, opinionated subjectivity which is often contrasted with an 'enlightened', impersonal objectivity. Perhaps, indeed, dogmatic subjectivity fulfils a useful purpose as a defence against the crushing weight of impersonal objectivity as the latter is used as a 'scientific' cudgel, but since we have abandoned the latter, we have no need of the former. Our task, whether therapists or patients (or scientists), is to investigate and negotiate the degree to which our subjectivities overlap.

The psychotherapist who chooses to ignore his experience of himself when trying to understand his patients may end up weaving theories or building psychological models which are likely to be remarkable, to the unclouded eye, only for their banality and conspicuous lack of truth, even though they may well be accepted by that section of the intellectual (or indeed wider) community which has a vested interest in 'objectivity' and mechanism. Ultimately, this is likely to lead to a view of patients' experience and, more particularly, behaviour as intrinsically meaningless.

At the risk of labouring an example used earlier in this book, let us take once again the case of a young woman who complains of 'frigidity'. She has, she says, lost all interest in sex, and cannot bear her husband to touch her, although he is a 'good husband' and she loves him. Now there are several ways in which the professional helper might approach her problem. The 'objective' approach (probably that most frequently taken by psychiatrists and psychologists, in Britain at least) is to accept the complaint as a *datum* in this patient's situation. The problem then becomes one of *reinstating* her sexual response, either mechanically by juggling in some way with her anatomy or body chemistry, or by means of some kind of 'retraining' method using conditioning procedures. Explanations of her condition likely to be invoked will in all probability be in terms of 'the physiology of the human sexual response' or of a mechanistic behavioural psychology. When she says she 'hates to be touched', this is more likely to be understood as a description of an inappropriate sensation than as an experience carrying *meaning*, and as a consequence will be taken as an indication of (almost literally) her wires having got crossed in some way, rather than as a statement about her relationship with her husband which should be taken seriously.

If, on the other hand, the therapist looks within himself for some strand of his experience which resonates in sympathy with the patient's complaint, he may find the beginnings of an understanding which can be formed with her about what it *means*. He may, for example, *know* what it is like not to like being touched, and he may be aware of his reasons, in the past perhaps, for not having liked being touched, and he may speculate that his patient may have similar reasons of which, however, she is unaware. It is at this point that he must avoid the errors of a negative subjectivity. He must not, that is, assume that this woman's reasons for disliking being touched *must* be the same as his, and he must not consequently insist, more or less subtly, that she accept his version of the state of affairs. Instead, through the process of negotiation, he should test the correctness of his hypothesis by helping her to elaborate her own meanings and to find out where they end up; in this aspect, negotiation is very similar to scientific experiment. The importance of his own experience in this kind of situation lies in making the formation of hypotheses possible. The ensuing procedure of negotiation will determine how much therapist and patient do share in the experience of disliking being touched, but in any case may allow the latter to discover for herself what disliking being touched means to her. The reciprocity of negotiation is again well stated by Harré and Secord: [6]

When we try to persuade the person to 'see' his situation differently, to attend to other aspects of a situation than those he was considering, and so on, we are trying to change the meaning of the situation for him. We try to get him to ascribe different meanings to things and situations from those he ascribed before which influenced his past choice of mentalistic predicates. If this is true, it must be possible for our subject to counter-persuade us to see the matter his way too.

It seems obvious that the likely outcomes of the 'objective' approach on the one hand, and the 'subjective' approach on the other, will be different. In the first case, the woman in question will find herself the harbinger of a 'sexual dysfunction' which may or may not be improved by mechanical intervention, but which will enable her to persist in her relationship with her husband much as before, in the role of faulty (or repaired) machine. In the second case, the patient may arrive at a reformulation of her position, in which disliking being touched means something about her relationship with her husband—e.g. that, in some sense at least, she does *not* love him and see him as a 'good husband', and has reasons for not doing so. These reasons could of course be of widely differing kinds, ranging from her own expectations of what a husband should be (which her husband cannot live up to), to her husband's expectations of what a wife should be (which she cannot accept). Whatever the final outcome for their relationship—whether divorce or an idyllic sex life—she will at least be permitted the role of a fully functioning person.

The 'subjective' approach is, then, made possible by the therapist's determination not to depart from an understanding of the situation which is rooted in his own experience. For him, 'not liking to be touched' has a *meaning* (in personal terms) which he is not willing to abandon in favour of a *meaningless*, abstract notion of 'sexual dysfunction' which appeals to some kind of unknown physical or behavioural pathology.

Without *some* basis in common experience, understanding between therapist and patient is impossible, for each remains an enigma to the other. This does not, on the other hand, necessarily mean that one can only understand and communicate with people whose problems and experiences are identical to one's own. As suggested in the previous chapter, it may still be possible for two people to learn about each other through a reciprocal master-apprentice relationship in which each starts from the position that the other's experience is valid. Even so, some initial overlap in experience is essential, and it may well be true that the more patient and therapist share in terms of experience, the more possible it will be for them to develop a therapeutic understanding. This would perhaps seem obvious if it was not so often overlooked. It is surprising how often one will find on the therapeutic scene unmarried marital counsellors, childless child psychotherapists, and in general therapists attempting to deal with situations—for example, death and bereavement—of which they have no personal experience. In the case of such fundamental human experiences as these, theoretical knowledge is but a pale substitute for personal familiarity with them. In order to understand the significance of an individual's heart sounds, a physician must have a background of experience in listening to such sounds—a mere description in a book, in the absence of actual experience, would tell him nothing about this individual. Similarly, it is impossible for somebody who has not experienced the state of marriage, of parenthood, or the event of death, to develop the necessary standards by which to judge the experience of others in these respects. These are experiences 'the want of which', as Kant put it, 'no scholastic discipline can compensate'.

Rather than a therapist's credentials reflecting a certified training in a particular theory, or the acquisition of a set of pseudo-technical skills, the above observations seem to move us towards judging his worth by appeal to the width of (and his sensitivity to) his personal experience.

This may in many ways seem an alarming prospect. It is impossible to see how therapeutic brass plates could either honestly or succinctly give an account of their owner's breadth or depth of experience, or his qualities as a person, and in any case one imagines that in no time at all the kind of sickening shorthand description which comes to be imposed on people in this sort of context ('Great Human Being') would be institutionalized in the form of training and the award of certificates and degrees.

But if we are to take seriously the *personal* nature of psychotherapeutic activity, and if we reject the professional mystification of psychotherapy by appeal to the acquisition of certain technical skills, or indoctrination in a particular therapeutic approach, then we must at least attempt to formulate an alternative. The temptation here, as ever, is to buttress a personal stance by reinforcing it with some kind of impersonal criterion which will carry with it the authority of 'reality'—i.e. to formulate general standards to be met by psychotherapists, without regard to the fact that they are individuals. We can perhaps at least in part avoid doing this by appealing once more to the notion of social negotiation. Who is to be accounted a 'competent' psychotherapist will be a matter for negotiation, and not of objective criterion. There may be certain aspects of his activity which a psychotherapist can appeal to in order to differentiate himself from, for example, faith healers, well-meaning friends or out-and-out charlatans. He may, for instance, have a commitment to make what he does public, and to expose its intellectual foundations; he may point to the length of his experience, and convey the dedication and seriousness with which he views it and reflects upon it. He may, in other words, point to aspects of his activity which at least *provide a context for* the development of personal understanding of therapeutic issues. But in no way can he *guarantee* that he has indeed developed such understanding. No matter how great his age or experience, how long his training or the string of letters after his name, his worth and wisdom as a therapist will either emerge or evaporate anew in each individual therapeutic relationship.

This is not to say, however, that the issue of professional accreditation can safely be disregarded. Patients have a right to know whether their potential therapists have at least been exposed to the kind of experience likely to make them competent, and whether or not they are so considered by their colleagues. Unlike many other professional guilds, in which the competence of an individual member may be judged by reference to the quality of his work, psychotherapeutic organizations can unfortunately offer little in the way of reassurance to prospective consumers. This is partly because of the difficulties involved in demonstrating that psychotherapy 'works', but even more perhaps because of the theoretical dogmas which divide psychotherapists. Such divisions tend to focus therapists' attention on demonstrating suitably strong allegiance to a particular dogma in order to be admitted to this or that therapeutic club, rather than on developing a personal understanding of therapy which may be shared with others. Before this problem can be resolved, therapists of all persuasions may have to spend more time in elaborating their actual experience of psychotherapy, and less in trying to force their experience to fit preconceived notions of what will make them respectable in the eyes of the 'scientific' orthodoxy.

The fact that he can in the last analysis rely on little more than his personal resources (and accepting that psychotherapy is a fundamentally personal relationship) means that the therapist may well have to come to terms with certain limitations on his activities. For reasons which have been discussed above—reasons, that is, which have their origin in the nature and extent of his personal experience and familiarity with certain kinds of human situations and conditions—he may find that there are people he cannot help. There may, for example, be people who are wrestling with problems of which he has no conception, or whose personal development far outstrips anything he has encountered. In such cases it may well be wiser for him to recognize the hopelessness of being able to form a useful therapeutic relationship with the person concerned than to rely on technical expertise to pull him through any situation. If he is misled by some notion of professional expertise into feeling duty-bound to take on such patients for therapy, he may well find the therapeutic roles being reversed, so that he learns more from his patient than the latter from him. Of course, if he is able to acknowledge this state of affairs, then no harm may be done, and indeed the experience may prove mutually enriching for both, but it seems on the whole more likely that he will find himself becoming increasingly anxious and self-doubting, perhaps falling back on mystifying professional authority which can only impair the relationship and bewilder the patient.

This does not mean that the therapist has in some way to be morally superior to his patients, but merely that there may be some situations in which he is unlikely to be of much help to them. If, for example, a therapist is engaged in the same kind of self-deceptive strategies as his patient, it is likely that they will reinforce each other's problems rather than resolve them. Having said this, however, one has to recognize that (apart, possibly, from a feeling of happy unanimity which the participants may experience) there are no objective criteria by means of which the presence of such a state of affairs can be recognized. The main safeguard, perhaps, would be the existence of a psychotherapeutic community which acknowledges the personal nature of therapy and which affords the individual therapist opportunities for consultation, discussion, support and supervision.

In my anxiety to represent psychotherapy as a fundamentally personal undertaking, I do not wish to suggest that questions either of technique or of theoretical study are anathema, or even merely irrelevant. The psychotherapeutic literature, in all its aspects, is a rich source of ideas concerning ways in which therapeutic 'movement' may be achieved, negotiations initiated, and patients encouraged to cope with their problems. What I am concerned to stress is that such ideas and techniques can only operate flexibly in the context of a personal relationship, and carry no guarantee of success as purely mechanical ways of changing people. There is, moreover, nothing sacrosanct about them, nothing which justifies their becoming the patented property of any particular group or profession: they can be effective only as they are freely adapted to the needs of each particular therapeutic situation. It is, of course, essential for the psychotherapist to be well versed in the intellectual problems as well as the therapeutic efforts and achievements of the professional community to which he belongs, just so long as he does not attempt to turn his knowledge into a mystique and convert his profession, or a section of it, into some kind of élite magic circle.

It will certainly be feared by many that any conceptualization of psychotherapy along the lines of that offered here, if accepted, would destroy all possibility of conducting rewarding research work in this area. All possibility of making and communicating findings of lasting worth becomes lost, it might be felt, in an infinitely variable sea of individual and personal bits and pieces of experience. Orthodox methods of psychological research, it might be argued, even though they may not have advanced our understanding of psychology very far, at least contain the *possibility* of so doing, whereas to accept the formulation offered here would be to abandon all hope and to consign the entire field to the individual whims and impulses of its practitioners. I feel myself, however, that the very reverse might be the case.

It is true that acceptance of a view of psychotherapy as *personal* leads to very different kinds of research strategy from those to be found in orthodox approaches, but it may well be the case that psychological *understanding* will be greatly increased by departure from orthodoxy. We may, of course, have to sacrifice prediction, control and 'general laws' to such understanding, but, because these are in any case in principle unattainable, the loss is really no loss at all.

As a first step, we may agree with Harré and Secord[7] that:

The processes that are productive of social behaviour occur in individual people, and it is in individual people that they must be studied. It is here that the vitally important dimensions of spontaneity and idiosyncrasy occur. To achieve full scientific status, then, social psychology must make room for attempts to unravel the modes of generation of social behaviour 'within' the person. And this can be achieved only from the basis of an intensive study of particular cases, in which one may hope to discern the productive and generative 'mechanisms' at work, such as the evaluation of reasons, the making concordant of beliefs, and so on. It is precisely this kind of study that the statistical method makes impossible, since it is concerned to eliminate idiosyncratic features of people by the use of controls, and by the method of random assignment to classes. This is usually coupled with the assumption that changes produced externally and extrinsically to a person are determinative of his performance, attitudes, and so on, an assumption which effectively eliminates the dimension of spontaneity, and the vitally important capacity to consciously monitor performances, which is very characteristic of human behaviour and plays a very large role in determining the form the reactions take. It is in the detailed study of particular cases that we shall make progress towards discerning the patterns of reasons, feelings, beliefs, impulses, and so on that are responsible for the external relations and overall patterns discerned by the use of the statistical method.

It is also possible to go a step further and to suggest that, as far as psychotherapy is concerned (and many other psychological situations, come to that), the very procedure itself *is* psychological research, and its usefulness as such, as well as its communicability, will depend on a recognition of its personal nature and the consequent development of a language of common experience, and a fundamental attitude of good faith towards that experience, in which its findings can be shared and elaborated.

Psychological research then becomes a *co-operative* venture, in which both psychologist and subject (or therapist and patient) attempt to realize the scientific aim, rather than (as it has been in recent decades) a *competitive* situation in which psychologist tries to outwit subject, or trick him into revealing in an unguarded moment something about himself which can in any case be of only fleeting interest.

Indeed, orthodox research procedures often seem to be almost perversely aimed at obscuring important matters of psychological interest. This is achieved, as has been said, partly through the use of a methodology which is concerned with measurement for its own sake rather than with the phenomena which present themselves in the research worker's experience, and partly through a widespread obsession with generalities. Many psychiatric patients, for example, are able to give the interested inquirer quite fascinating insights into their (often very individual) experiences of physical treatment methods such as electro-convulsive therapy and the use of tranquillizers and anti-depressants. A patient may describe, for instance, the generally blunting effect that tranquillizers have had on his perception of the world around him—the whole of his experience becoming dulled, and not just his anxiety. (One man who of his own accord gave up his tablets had to shut his clock in a cupboard as its ticking had suddenly become unbearably loud.) Again, anti-depressants may make a person feel more cheerful, but without his knowing why: he has a kind of chemical euphoria which is unrelated to the events which happen to him, and which is thus a source of an entirely new kind of confusion. The use of questionnaires or other standardized, 'reliable' and 'valid' measures of mood or ability, averaged out across an inevitably heterogeneous population, make it extremely unlikely that, for example, a useful phenomenology of drug usage could be elaborated. A personal, co-operative exploration of a patient's experience of drugs in relation to his individual problems and difficulties might do much more to achieve a genuinely scientific understanding of the factors involved.

In some ways, then, psychotherapy, in the sense in which it has been treated here, can be taken as a model of psychological research rather than just another field of study for it. If as the result we have to do without the security and authority of an (illusory) impersonal objectivity, we may at least find ourselves with the opportunity of sharing a common basis in experience on which to build a developing understanding of our own nature.

1 See for example a useful paper on this subject by J. Steiner, M. Jarvis and J. Parrish. (1970). Risk taking and arousal regulation. *British Journal of Medical Psychology*, **43**, 333.
2 Scott, R. D. and Ashworth, P. L. (1967). 'Closure' at the first schizophrenic break-down: a family study. *British Journal of Medical Psychology*, **40**, 109.
3 Arthur Koestler, in his book *The Act of Creation* documents particularly convincingly the way in which cultural or scientific developments take place (often independently) when the time is ripe.
4 Buber, M. (1958). *I and Thou*. Edinburgh: Clark.
5 Harre, R. and Secord, P. F. (1972). *The Explanation of Social Behaviour*, p. 87. Oxford: Blackwell.
6 ibid., p. 113.
7 ibid., p. 134.

Index

Index

Page references in italics refer to names in the endnotes to chapters.